I0683383

Saving Grace

Safe Havens 1

Sandy James

Sandy James
sandyjames.com

Printed in the United States of America
First Printing: June 2013
ISBN: 978-1-940295-04-6

Acknowledgements

A big "THANKS" to my critique partners—Cheryl Brooks, Nan Reinhardt, Leanna Kay, and Mellanie Szereto—for all their help getting this book ready.

To Sandy Owen—I love working with you! Thanks for taking me on as a critique partner!

To my family—I truly appreciate all you do to support my writing. Love you all!

And to my agents—Joanna MacKenzie and Danielle Egan-Miller of Browne-Miller Literary—for letting me take this little venture into the historical side of romance.

Chapter One

San Francisco, California—April 1881

She didn't intend to kill him.

Standing outside the suite at the San Francisco Arms, Grace Riley lifted the hand she'd clenched into a tight fist. It took all of her strength to make herself knock. Her other hand dropped, stroking her wool skirt, feeling the slight bulk of the weapon hiding in a deep pocket. One caress to give her control and remind her that she was no longer the prey.

She counted the seconds and fought the dichotomy of wanting the door to be opened yet hoping Stephen Shay wasn't there. The man answered the door himself instead of sending a servant to perform the task.

They would be alone.

That nauseating thought made her want to turn and flee.

No. No running away.

She *had* to know, unable to face the nightmares of speculation any longer. Living in limbo had become unbearable—even more unbearable than being in his presence again.

Dressed in his typical black suit, Stephen folded his arms over his chest and leaned a shoulder against the door. Those obsidian eyes fixed on Grace, sending a shudder ripping through her.

"I was afraid you wouldn't come, my sweet." With a sweeping gesture, he invited her inside.

She swallowed the enormous lump of fear rising in her throat. It settled in her chest, making it hard to breathe. Reminding herself why she'd come, she made her feet move. He shut the door behind her, the sound akin to a lid closing over a tomb.

Stephen doffed his coat and laid it over the arm of the sofa before walking over to the bureau and pouring himself a drink. He raised his glass. "Would you care for one?"

She shook her head, wishing he would stop pretending he was anything but a cold-hearted bastard. She wanted the information, and then she wanted to get the hell out of there and as far away from San Francisco and Stephen Shay as she could run.

"Where is Jake Curtis?" The words were forced out between clenched teeth.

Downing the drink in one quick swallow, he grimaced as he filled his glass again. "Ah, Grace. Always in such a hurry. We should spend some time…catching up. I've missed you. How is your father? I do hope he's well."

She narrowed her eyes, the only sign she would offer that she'd even heard his words. He knew damn well that with the exception of her brother Matthew, she hadn't seen hide nor hair of her family in years, especially her good-for-nothing father. Surely Stephen's overpriced detectives had told him *that*. They'd made her life a waking nightmare, tracking her as if she were some common criminal.

A shaky breath helped her control both her temper and her fear. "Where is he?"

His smile was downright reptilian. She imagined a forked tongue darting out between his thin lips.

"Have you been in the company of cattlemen for so long you have forgotten the niceties of polite conversation?"

Grace bit back an acidic laugh.

Niceties?

What did he know about niceties?

She gritted her teeth. "Tell me where Jake Curtis is, or I shall leave. Now."

Stephen nodded at the papers scattered across the table. "What you seek is in those." He took a sip from his glass, but his eyes never left her. "May I inquire what I am to receive in return for the time and expense to find him for you? You owe me, my dear."

A scoff burst out before she could bite her lip.

Owe him? *Owe him?*

All she owed him was the same misery he'd caused her.

He took a couple of steps closer.

It took every ounce of her strength to not take a few in retreat.

"You look well, Grace. You have grown even more beautiful with age, just as I knew you would. Oh, you were a beauty when you were younger. But now there's a...wisdom about you. So many years have passed, yet it seems only yesterday. You were so sweet. So young. How long ago was it?"

Twenty years.

Twenty long years spent as far away from him and his world as she could put herself. Dear Lord, she'd been running her whole life. The urge to pull the gun from her pocket was almost irresistible as the horrible memories she'd kept at bay for so long pushed their way forward.

No. Not now.

There was no time to panic now.

Throwing back the last of the amber liquid, he set the glass down. "Why so quiet tonight, my sweet? I was hoping to make this reunion...*special*. Supper will be sent up shortly. Then we can get reacquainted."

Supper?

As if she would stay a moment longer than she absolutely had to.

Share a meal with him?

She'd sooner starve to death.

No, she was getting what she came for, then she would leave as fast as her feet could carry her.

Summoning up her courage, Grace reached for the papers.

Quick as lightning, Stephen rushed to the table as his hand shot out and grabbed her wrist. He jerked her so hard she lost her balance and stumbled against him. A low chuckle rose from his throat.

"I knew it. I knew even back then what kind of woman you are." His mouth dropped to cover hers.

Grace froze.

No. No. No.

The word echoed like the ticking of a pendulum clock. This wasn't happening. This couldn't be happening. Not again.

Never again.

She bit his lip as she brought her knee up hard, connecting with the vulnerable targets between his thighs the way her brother had taught her.

With a curse, he pushed her away. She stumbled back onto the sofa. As he took deep breaths and wiped the back of his hand across his bleeding mouth, she scrambled back to her feet and hurried to grab the papers.

His chest slammed into her back, pushing her thighs against the table. "You bitch! You'll pay for that!"

Struggling, she twisted against the strong arms that held her own against her sides. She fumbled for the gun, trying to free it from the deep folds of her skirt. He hauled her toward the big four-poster bed, her dangling feet making it impossible for her to escape. She kicked his shins as she thrashed about, trying to inflict enough pain that he would release her.

He tossed Grace on the bed. She rolled to her back and groped for the gun. Her hands shook so hard they wouldn't obey her mind.

Stephen stepped away from the bed and removed his tie and waistcoat as though he had all the time in the world. "You'll see, Grace. Things will be good between us again. I have waited far too long for this." He draped his clothes over the settee. As he unfastened his cufflinks, he came back to stand next to the bed. "You are mine. You were then. You are now. *Mine.*"

She wrenched the gun free and pointed it at his chest. "No."

He clucked his tongue and reached out to her. "Give me the gun,

Grace. You don't even know how to use it."

"Leave me alone!" Scooting across to the far side of the mattress, she struggled to keep the gun steady so she could back off the bed and grab the papers.

Stephen lunged.

Her finger clenched, squeezing the trigger.

The shot made her ears ring and her hand sting. An acrid smell filled her nostrils. The gun slipped from her hands and landed with a soft thud on the thick carpet.

He staggered back as his hand covered the left side of his chest. Dark blood oozed between his fingers, staining his dove-gray vest.

His eyes found hers. She could almost see his life ebbing away.

"You...bitch. You've...killed...me."

Her brain went numb. Somehow, she stumbled to the table, snatched the papers, and found the door. When she reached the hall, she ran. A few doors opened, and strangers gawked as she passed them. She didn't pause to explain, didn't even slow down until she gained the street.

She'd killed him—she'd really killed him. Tears sprang into her eyes as she tried to slow her pace and blend with the people walking on the crowded sidewalk. His passing from this world gave her no joy, and she feared her soul would be damned for eternity because she'd taken his life for revenge.

Focusing on why she'd come to San Francisco, Grace touched the papers she'd wrinkled and smashed into her pocket. Her life didn't matter anymore. Nothing really mattered anymore.

Except Jake.

Chapter Two

The Twin Springs Ranch outside White Pines, Montana—One week later

A person only pounded on a door in the middle of the night if there was trouble.

Adam Morgan stubbed his toe against a chair, cursed, then hurried to tug his shirt over his head. He stumbled out of the bedroom as he pulled on his pants.

The knocks grew more urgent as thunder rumbled in the distance. He flew down the stairs and grabbed the loaded shotgun he kept next to the door. A quick glance out the window told him he wouldn't need a weapon to deal with his petite visitor. He set the gun down and opened the door.

The woman had been reaching up to knock again when he jerked the door open. She pulled her fist against her chest and gasped in surprise. Big, brown eyes stared at him, but she didn't move to come inside. She simply stood on the porch, shivering from the cold spring rain that had soaked her through.

Someone needed to lead this odd little dance. "Ma'am, might I ask why you're beating on my door in the middle of the night?"

She shivered as she wrung her hands. Throwing him a furtive look, she tossed back a question of her own. "Is–is Jake C–C–Curtis here?"

Her teeth chattered so hard it took him a moment to figure out what she was asking. "Jake? You're looking for Jake? At this hour?"

She nodded. The poor woman looked like a cat someone had thrown into a lake. The rain plastered her loose hair against her cheeks and neck. Her clothes clung to her body. Another shiver wracked her. "I–I n–need to–to see Jake."

"Why?"

Jake had never been the type of person to get himself into trouble with a woman—especially since his marriage—so Adam dismissed the notion she was searching for Jake to resolve some romantic tryst. She also appeared a mite old for the twenty-year-old cowboy Adam had raised as his own son since the boy was nine.

"Is–is he here?" she asked again.

He hadn't realized how labored her breathing sounded until she rasped out her question.

Since she didn't appear to be a threat, he answered her. "He's living in White Pines now."

Why did the defeated frown on her face bother him so much? From the pain in her eyes, she might as well have taken a punch to the stomach.

With the back of a shaking hand she smoothed back some wet tendrils of hair sticking to her cheek. "Is th–that the t–town wh–where the stage st–stopped?"

He inclined his head toward the south. "'Bout three miles that direction. Did you just walk all the way here? In this storm?"

With a curt nod, she turned to leave.

Was she daft?

The woman couldn't be planning to walk three more miles back to town on muddy roads and in the pouring rain to try to find Jake in the middle of the night.

Adam had been ready to call her back to offer some dry clothes and hot food when her knees buckled. She collapsed to the ground, reminding him of a discarded ragdoll.

He hurried to her side, knelt down, and smoothed away the wet hair that had fallen on her face. His fingers were greeted with hot, wet skin. The poor woman had gone pale as milk. Without a moment of reticence, he scooped her up into his arms and carried her inside.

Kicking the door closed behind him, he called for his daughter. Water dripped from both him and his guest, pooling on the wooden floor. Waiting a few beats, he shouted again. "Victoria!" He was rewarded with the noise of movement on the second floor.

"Daddy?"

"Grab some towels and come to the guest room." He took the stairs two at a time, leaving a trail of water behind.

"Towels?" His daughter hurried toward him down the second-story hall. Her eyes widened as she gave the belt on her robe a last tug. "What on earth…?"

"Towels, princess. Please."

Adam carried his burden into the guest room, wincing as he realized he'd called Victoria by his pet name for her. A woman of twenty-one probably didn't appreciate her father using a childhood endearment. But that's what Victoria would always be regardless of her age—his little princess.

She hurried into the room and spread a couple of towels over the quilt. Adam set his burden down on the bed while his daughter lit the lamp. He crouched to take off the woman's shoes as Victoria tried to peel off the thin coat the woman wore, although thinking of it as a coat was giving the pathetic garment more credit than it was due. The shoes were so worn they almost came apart in his hands.

"Who is she?" Victoria rubbed the stranger's hair with a towel.

"Not a clue."

The woman shivered hard enough to make the bed shake.

His worry increased. Fevers could easily turn deadly. "We need to take off these wet clothes and get her dry."

"I'll get a dry nightgown and more towels." Victoria hurried out of the bedroom.

Adam reached for the buttons of the woman's tattered shirt.

Her eyes flew open, looking as wild and panicked as a cornered animal's. She sat up and slapped at his hands. Her cheeks had flushed crimson, and her breath came in wheezing gasps. "D–don't touch me. I–I won't let you touch me."

He pulled back, splaying his hands. "Whoa, ma'am. I just wanted to get you dry."

"D–don't t–touch me!"

Thankfully, his daughter strode back into the room and took charge. She dropped the bundle of dry clothing on the rocking chair and moved to the bed to lay a comforting hand on the woman's shoulder. "You're safe here. You have a fever. Let us take care of you."

Turning her frightened eyes to Victoria, the woman trembled. "Safe? Safe here?"

"Very safe here. I'm Victoria." She inclined her head at Adam. "That's Adam—my father. We'll take care of you. Let's get you out of these wet clothes."

It took her a good, long time to think it over before she nodded. Shaking fingers reached up to work the buttons of her shirt. She couldn't hold her hands still enough to do much good. Victoria brushed her hands away and took over the job.

The women needed some privacy, so Adam nodded to his daughter, stepped out of the room, and closed the door behind him.

No surprise that Daisy was already puttering around the kitchen in her thick robe. The housekeeper probably heard him bellowing at Victoria. But even if she hadn't, the plump little woman always seemed to know what was happening in the Twin Springs ranch house. He often wondered if she could see through walls.

"Land's sake," Daisy said. "Never a dull moment 'round here. I'll get some hot tea ready, then I'll see if Victoria needs any help."

Taking a seat at the kitchen table, he put an elbow against the wood, propped his head on his hand, and closed his eyes. Judging from the increasing noises of the wind and rain slapping against the house, the storm would be a raging a good long while. Thunder made the smooth floorboards vibrate beneath his bare feet.

Forty-five was too damned old for this kind of nonsense. Mystery women shouldn't come pounding on his door in the middle of the night.

Daisy patted him on the shoulder, so he made the effort to open his eyes. She held out a cup, and he accepted the offering, hoping it held some of her typically strong coffee. Murmuring his thanks, he took a few sips before putting the drink down and closing his eyes again.

His mysterious visitor wanted to find Jake. Probably a good thing the boy lived in town now so Adam could find out her motives and intentions before they got together. When she woke, he would be able to ask his questions and puzzle through what she wanted. Then he'd find out whether Jake needed any sort of protection. As far as he knew, the boy had no family. He'd been an orphan when Adam had dragged him back to the Twin Springs many years ago.

Since he wasn't going to get any answers sitting in his kitchen, he polished off the rest of his coffee and headed back up to the guest room.

The door stood ajar. Nudging it with his foot, he peeked inside. "Am I intruding?"

"You can come in, Daddy. She's sleeping." Victoria pulled the patchwork quilt a little higher and smoothed the surface with her slender hand. "She's got a high fever."

Fever.

Damn but he hated that word. Once a fever set in, things were in God's hands. The best they could do now was keep her warm and comfortable and pray she recovered.

Victoria gathered together the wet linens and the woman's ragged clothing. "Who is she?"

"Not sure. She's looking for Jake."

"Jake? Why?"

"Didn't get much time to ask." He nodded at the clothes in Victoria's arms. "That's all she came with. Didn't even have a bag with a change of clothes."

"Poor thing."

Poor thing, indeed. Alone. Destitute. Sick. What man would let any woman in his family find herself in such dire circumstances? All he could do was shake his head in frustration and disgust.

With a nod that set her waist-length braid to bouncing, Victoria glanced back at the sleeping guest. "Will you stay with her? If she wakes up, she might be frightened. I should help Daisy. We'll need to make some broth and hot tea, too."

Lightning dimly lit the bedroom and the sound of thunder rumbled in the distance as he glanced at the sleeping woman. She was so fragile. Thin. Delicate. She clearly hadn't eaten well in a long time. If her clothes were any indication, she didn't have much to call her own. "Did she tell you her name?"

"Her name's Grace, but that's all I got out of her before she fell asleep."

"Go on, princess. I'll sit with her for a spell."

"Thank you. I'll bring up something for her to eat soon." She stopped as she passed him, stood on tiptoe to kiss his cheek, and then stepped out of the room.

Another clap of thunder sounded, loud enough to make the pictures on the wall shake. The woman whimpered and mumbled a few words Adam couldn't understand. When she shivered again, he grabbed the blanket folded over the arm of the rocking chair and spread it over her sleeping form.

His mystery woman was very pretty. Slender neck. Long, brown eyelashes. He wished he could stare into those brown eyes of hers again, especially if he could see something reflected back at him other than fear, pain, and sickness.

Reaching out, he smoothed her bangs away from her forehead. Victoria had combed out the woman's hair. The chestnut locks didn't quite reach her shoulders. The women of White Pines would be outraged that she wore it so short, but the trait called to him. There was obviously nothing vain or pretentious about Grace.

Settling himself in the rocking chair, he took up the vigil. Her breathing sounded raspy, much as Victoria's had when she'd developed a fever and attacks of coughing her seventh summer. Every now and then, Grace would mumble in her sleep. He could only pick up a few words, and connecting them would be a hard puzzle to solve. A scary one at that.

Jake.

Matthew.

Stephen.

Murder.

***

"No! Don't touch me!"

Adam jumped out of the rocking chair, thinking someone had broken into his home and attacked his guest. It took a moment for his sleep-hazed thoughts to clear before he realized she was in the throes of a nightmare. It took a few more moments before his heart settled back into a normal rhythm.

Thrashing around on the bed, she dislodged the quilts that covered her.

He sat on the edge of the bed. "Wake up."

Her dream tormenter wouldn't free her, and she struck out at him, catching Adam's chin with a strong right hook.

Grabbing her wrists, he held them firm. "Wake up now. It's just a bad dream."

Her eyes flew open, but their dark beauty was dulled by the fever. "Don't let him hurt me."

"No one's going to hurt you here, Gracie." The endearment seemed to fit better than Grace as it rolled off his tongue.

She sat up so quickly she almost slammed her forehead into his. "I'm safe here?"

Nodding, he let her wrists loose so she wouldn't feel as though she was his captive. "You're safe here."

When she leaned in to put her cheek against his shoulder, he instinctively wrapped his arms around her. So thin, so delicate. So very warm. After only a few moments, her breathing slowed, although he could hear how full of congestion her lungs were with each inhale and exhale.

He didn't want to let her go. This woman needed someone to watch over her.

He appointed himself to the job.

Chapter Three

Grace opened her eyes slowly, trying to make sense of her foggy thoughts.

Sunlight streamed through the window, painting a white rocking chair in brilliant light. A soft mattress cushioned her body, something she hadn't felt in so long she honestly couldn't remember the last time. Heavy woolen blankets under a chuck wagon had served as her bed for most of her adult life.

She tried to sit up and winced. Every muscle ached. Her unfamiliar nightgown was damp, sticking to her skin. As she pushed the mound of covers aside, a sudden coughing spell racked her weak body.

When she could finally draw a breath, she grew determined to get out of bed. She tried to stand on shaky legs. Perhaps if she could get a look out the window, she could remember where she was.

Think, Grace.

Things came back in disjointed fragments. Sitting in the crowded car for the interminable train ride from San Francisco. Catching the stage and bouncing around mile after endless mile. The taste of a stale cheese sandwich—the only thing she could afford with the last of her money.

The illness had come on so rapidly with a fever so high most of her memories seemed nothing more than a cross between her wishes and her nightmares.

She'd doggedly pursued the only solid lead she'd discovered in years. A shudder ripped through her as she remembered the cost of that lead.

Dear for her.

Even dearer for Steven Shay.

The information said that Jake Curtis would be at the end of this miserable trip. She'd prayed the whole way that she would find him at long last.

Had she made it to the Twin Springs ranch? She vaguely recalled a smelly man with a tarnished star pinned on his stained vest explaining how to get there. The rain had started not long after she'd begun her trek.

After that, her memory became a blank slate.

The view that greeted her through the window didn't bring any recollections.

Beautiful, yes.

Familiar, no.

The mountains looming in the distance called to her heart. So peaceful. So serene. She could gaze upon that sight for the rest of her life and be content.

Fate had always had other things in store for her than a place to call home.

The door opened with a loud creak. She whirled around too quickly, making her head spin before another coughing spell hit. Strong hands guided her back to the bed, and then the back of a cool hand pressed against her forehead.

"You shouldn't be up, Gracie. You'll spike another fever."

Gracie?

No one had ever called her Gracie before. Hearing the nickname in that rich baritone voice felt like a caress. She stared at the source.

The man was handsome. Dark hair fanned his temples with enough gray to show his maturity. His eyes were a deep blue, and they didn't seem to miss anything. The hands that pulled the blankets over her were tanned and calloused. She'd never taken the time to notice a man's hands before.

She'd seen him, a vague figure from her feverish memory, nursing her by offering her water and broth and bathing her face with a damp cloth. "Thank you," was all she could manage.

"You're welcome. Do you remember my name?"

"I'm sorry…it's just things are kinda hazy."

"I'm Adam Morgan. You're my houseguest 'til we get you well."

His smile reached something inside her, causing a flicker of warmth she couldn't attribute to her fever. She brushed the uncomfortable feeling aside. Thirty-five wasn't the time to suddenly become interested in the opposite sex.

With the exception of her brother, Matthew, she'd had no use for men. She cooked for them and tried to be friendly, but not a single man had ever been more than another cowboy on another cattle drive. They liked her cooking more than her company, which suited her fine. Matthew kept her from being too awfully lonely.

"How are you feeling?" His comforting voice broke through her thoughts.

"Better. How long have I been sick?"

"Five days."

When Adam tried to smooth his hand across her forehead again, Grace turned her head. While she was grateful for his help, she simply didn't like to be touched.

He frowned. "You're still a mite peaked. I've been worried about you. A fever like that can steal away a body's strength."

"Fever?" No wonder she'd been in this sickbed five days. Who had seen to her personal needs? Surely Adam hadn't helped her with...*everything.*

Grace wanted to crawl into the nearest hole, pull moss over her head, and hide.

"Your face is getting awfully red, Gracie. Is your fever spiking again?"

His concerned frown confused her. She was nothing more than a stranger, why would he be worried about her? She didn't want him to care. She didn't want *any* man to care. "Where am I?"

His hand dropped away. "The Twin Springs."

The Twin Springs!

She'd made it after all.

"Where's Jake?" She tossed the covers aside and jumped to her feet.

The world spun and her body protested the quick movement. As her legs gave way, she groped for the bed.

He caught her, sweeping her up in his arms and setting stern eyes on her. "Need to stay in bed, ma'am."

She would've argued if she'd been able to fit in any words between coughs.

He sat down on the rocking chair, settling her in his lap.

"Th–this isn't proper," she scolded.

"I'm not about to let you make yourself sick again, not after all I did to get you better. We almost lost you."

If she had the strength, she might've fought against his tight hold if for no reason other than it was inappropriate. She hated being touched—hated being held even more.

It took her a moment to realize that the typical fear never came. This man could touch her, hold her close, and not terrify her. In his arms, Grace didn't feel trapped.

She felt protected. Cherished even.

Nonsense.

She'd never met him. Why, for all she knew, he could be dangerous. A debaucher. A cattle rustler. A ne'er-do-well.

More nonsense.

This home belonged to a wealthy family. Judging from his age, Adam was the patriarch of that family.

He smelled nice. An odd thought, but his clean, masculine scent wrapped around her, calming her. With a resigned sigh, she relaxed against him, simply too weak to struggle. At least that was the fib she told herself.

"Why are you looking for Jake?" He settled her more comfortably.

It took all her strength to tell this kind man her lie. "He's my brother."

He grunted softly.

Could he know she was lying? She hoped her responding shrug told him she didn't care what he thought.

"Now, it's not polite to ask a lady her age, but you're a bit older than Jake." He cleared his throat in that way men liked to do when they said something stupid. "Not that you're ready to be put out to pasture or anything."

She smiled at his embarrassment, knowing he couldn't see her. The smile quickly faded. She hated lying to him, especially after all he'd done for her. "Yes. I'm a *bit* older."

"But you're his sister?"

She couldn't speak the falsehood again, so she quit the topic. "Who took care of me when I was ill?"

"You're *still* ill."

"I'm fine." A cough bubbled to the surface at that horribly inopportune moment.

His chuckle made it hard for her to frown at him. "I can see you're fit as a fiddle."

"Did you take care of me?" Her cheeks had to be a startling red judging from the heat rising from them.

"I did mostly. Victoria helped."

He *was* a debaucher!

"You're married!" Grace struggled to get off his lap. Weak or not, she couldn't stay in that comforting embrace.

"My wife passed a few years back, Gracie."

That statement took the wind right out of her sails. How stupid was she for having judged him so harshly?

Once burned, twice shy.

Yes, he *looked* safe. And strong. And stalwart. But looks could be deceiving, and she was always one to learn her lessons well.

"How much older are you than Jake?" Adam asked.

She carefully framed her response. "Jake was born on my fifteenth birthday."

Grace waited for him to say something. Anything. The silence became unbearable.

About the time she was going to say something to end the awkwardness of sitting in his lap, he said, "I'll take you into town to see him."

She bumped her head on his chin when she sat up. For the first time, she was close enough to allow hope to swell in her broken heart. Then she remembered the recent months of fear and false leads, quickly tempering that hope. "You will?"

He nodded before standing up, resettling her in his arms and carrying her to the bed. "Time for you to rest."

"When will you take me to see Jake?"

"When you're well. Sleep now, Gracie."

***

Grace flicked her hand across the surface of the water, watching the ripples fan out. She breathed in the rose scent, hardly believing where she was.

A bathtub. In a real bathroom. The Morgans had to be wealthy to afford water piped right inside their home.

She'd actually squealed when she saw the tub, a new fixture in the home according to Victoria. When she'd told Grace she could have a bath if her fever stayed at bay, she'd never mentioned a real bathtub.

Assuming she'd have a quick scrub in a wooden barrel, she'd squealed when Victoria led her to the bathroom. The beautiful tub—glazed white with legs shaped like animal claws—made her believe she'd died and gone to heaven.

Still much too weak to do everything for herself, she let Victoria help her undress and get into her bath. The water smelled of roses as did the petite pink soap her hostess handed to her.

Although the cowboys she worked around often teased her unmercifully, Grace enjoyed being clean, choosing to wash up every evening if given the chance while they continued to reek of cattle manure, dirt, and sweat. After suffering from illness for so long, she wanted nothing more than to scrub every inch of skin and every tress of her hair clean.

Those tasks completed, she sank deeper into the water, content to remain submerged until her skin pruned. The opening of the door made her sink deeper in the tub.

"It's me," Victoria called in her typically cheery voice. "I brought a fresh nightgown and robe for you. Are you ready to get out yet?"

"I'd stay all day if I could."

"I know exactly how you feel. That's my favorite place to be when I need some time alone to think. Since we put it in a few months ago, I've been known to hide out up here just to get away from the menfolk. I'd let you stay longer, but you shouldn't catch a chill now that you're getting your strength back." She dropped a towel on the floor next to the tub and held another out. "Time to get out."

Grace accepted Victoria's much-needed help drying and dressing. She felt as weak as a newborn filly, and only her stubborn pride kept her on her feet.

"I'll clean up in here." Victoria grabbed the wet towels and nodded at the door. "Get back in bed, and I'll come help you comb and braid your hair in a few minutes."

Grace nodded and walked out of the bathroom with her pride firmly in place. Once she reached the hallway, she sagged against the wall, unsure she could make the rest of the journey back to the bedroom—her home for the last week. Putting one foot in front of the other and leaning heavily against the wall, she worked her way toward her bed.

A clucking tongue made her look up. Adam stood in the hall, hands on his hips, frowning at her.

Her face flushed hot.

He moved to her side, wrapped a strong arm around her waist, and hauled her up against his side. "You've got no business moving around on your own."

"I'm fine." She didn't have to glance up to know he'd be rolling his eyes.

"I can see that." That warm voice held enough humor to force a smile from her.

He walked her to the bed, pulled back the clean covers, and settled her on the mattress. "Swing your feet up there, and we'll get you warm again."

Victoria came in to fuss over Grace's hair, but Adam stayed. His eyes drilled holes through Grace.

"I'm sure you have better things to do than watch over me." She smoothed trembling hands over the quilt.

"I might. But I'd rather be here."

"Why?"

"'Cause the time has come to answer a few questions about you and Jake."

Oh, bother.

She'd put this conversation off as long as she could. Now she'd have to keep lying to the man about her true ties to Jake.

That didn't sit well, making her stomach knot. He'd been so kind, and she surely would have died if he hadn't taken her in and nursed her back to health.

She gave him a feigned shrug of indifference with a silent prayer he'd let the whole matter drop. "What is there to know?"

"If you'll both excuse me." Victoria smiled at Grace and then at her father. "I'll leave you two to talk."

Much to Grace's relief, as Victoria walked out the door, Daisy came right in. The tray of food she carried would give her the perfect excuse to stall.

"Daisy, it's so good to see you," she said. "Thank you so much.

I'm starving."

If the food was the worst thing she'd ever tasted, she'd still eat every last bite of it. And she'd eat it so slowly that Adam would have to give up and leave. How many times had someone told her she could try the patience of a saint? She planned to use that stubbornness now to avoid an inquisition.

"I want to see you eat every bite on this tray." Daisy helped her sit up enough to put the tray over her legs. "Nice hot soup. Some buttered bread. Cold milk. Is there anything else I can get for you?"

Privacy.

"No, thank you. This is perfect. Thank you for going to so much trouble."

"No trouble at all. You just holler if I can get you anythin' else." Daisy's chubby cheeks had the most adorable dimple, and everything she'd said and done while Grace was sick only made her more endearing.

How would she ever repay these people for their kindness?

"I hate to impose, but I'd love another book to read." She nodded at the leather-bound tome sitting on the dresser. "I finished that one. Any story would be wonderful."

Daisy picked up the book. "You're the only person I've ever known who reads as much as the Morgans. I'll fetch you another and bring it up after I finish my baking." She shut the door as she left the bedroom.

The soup was delicious. Despite her growling stomach—which was probably loud enough for Adam to hear—she took her time eating. If she could drag the meal out long enough, perhaps her host would give up and leave her in peace.

Instead, he settled himself in the rocking chair and watched her the way a hawk considers its prey.

No wonder.

She was a stranger. She might have slept in his home and eaten his food, but she'd shared nothing about her life except half-truths. Lying tasted bitter on her tongue, especially since she somehow knew he suspected she was lying. Yet there was no way to tell him about what had happened so long ago.

The shame would be more than she could bear.

When she finally put the spoon down, he asked his first question. "Why are you searching for Jake?"

Holding up a finger to stall him, she picked up the bread and took a bite, chewing far beyond what was necessary. Yes, it was childish. Adam had to see right through her ruse.

His chuckle told her the game was up. "You're gonna have to talk to me sometime. Might as well be now. Putting things off will only make it more difficult."

She heaved a resigned sigh and offered what she could to keep him from growing even more curious. "I'm searching for Jake because I'm worried about him."

"Explain."

The snort slipped. "How long do you have? I assure you, the tale's long."

His smile was so warm that a bolt from the blue hit her, making her wish she could tell him *everything*. She couldn't, although something about Adam Morgan made the weight she'd carried for so long seem a little bit lighter.

"Just start at the beginning," he coaxed. "If we run past supper, I'll have Daisy bring up another tray."

One, long deep breath and she began. "When Jake was born, there was no way Matthew and I could care for him properly."

"Matthew?"

"My brother—my *other* brother. We were both so young when our momma died." Grace swallowed hard. The memories might be old, but the wounds remained raw. "The nuns said they knew a couple who wanted a family but couldn't have a child of their own. They'd been married such a long time. They had a nice farm. I knew Jake would be happy with them, that they'd love him."

That was supposed to be the way the story went.

And they all lived happily ever after...

Real life never had happy endings.

He arched an eyebrow. "Nuns?"

"At the convent. They took us in. Jake was born there."

"What about your mother?"

"Mama died." That *was* the truth, even if the way she'd stated it was meant to dissuade further questions she couldn't answer frankly.

Adam sat there, rocking in the chair and staring at her with piercing blue eyes. The man probably knew how handsome he was and how his stare could send shivers racing across a woman's skin. "Why now?"

"Now?" Blinking a couple of times, she needed a moment to figure out what he was asking. "Oh, *now*. I heard news that his adoptive parents had been murdered. I was terrified for him. I had to find him."

He ran his fingers over his light growth of whiskers on his strong chin. "That happened over ten years ago."

"I've been out of touch."

"No one's *that* out of touch. Jake's parents were murdered when he was eight."

"I've been running chuck wagons for long drives for a very long time. Years and years. I–I didn't find out until a few months ago. I've been searching for him ever since."

And every single lead had been a blind alley. Only her absolute panic had forced her to go to Stephen for help. She had to know for sure her son was alive, that he was safe and sound.

"After his family died, he got himself shipped to an orphanage," Adam said. "He became friends with Ty Bishop there. They ran away together. Lived on the streets in Denver for a few months. I took them in when Jake tried to pick my pocket to get money to buy food so they could stop eating out of garbage cans."

Adam watched Grace closely. He'd deliberately been blunt. Downright cruel. She might claim to be blood kin, but he needed to know exactly how much this woman cared about Jake.

Judging from the pain in her eyes, she cared. A lot. Now, he needed to know the *real* reason Jake's sister was finally trying to find him. There was clearly more to the story than his houseguest was willing to divulge.

"I–I didn't know." Tears filled her eyes. "He ate...I didn't..." She bowed her head and breathed a shuddering sigh.

He felt lower than a snake's belly when she choked out the first sob. The rocking chair kept moving when he jumped to his feet. Setting the tray aside, he took her hands in his. They were ice cold. She tried to pull them back. He won the tug of war.

"I'm sorry, Gracie. I shouldn't have—"

"I left him." The words squeaked out.

"You had good reason."

"He ate garbage. I'll never forgive my—"

"Stop it. Right now." His tone was harsher than he'd intended, but it served a purpose. She stopped rambling and stared up at him. "You didn't know."

Grace shook her head as she jerked her hands back and buried her face in her palms, crying hard enough she started coughing again.

As if he'd let that nonsense go on. "Stop it, Gracie."

He pulled her hands away and eased her toward him. She didn't resist his embrace, but she felt as stiff as a freshly cut pine board. Her tears soaked his shirt.

Between her sobs and coughs, she kept blaming herself for Jake having to live on the street.

Adam wasn't about to let her make herself sick all over again. "It's over, darlin'. It was a long time ago. I brought him back here. Ty, too. And they've been living a good life. Jake has a wife now."

That got her attention. Her mutterings came to an abrupt halt as she stared at him with enormous red-rimmed eyes. "Wife? He has a *wife*?"

At least she'd stopped crying. "Yes, ma'am. Married up with Emily Spencer last year. They're expecting their firstborn in a few months."

"A *baby*?"

He answered her hesitant smile with one of his own. "A baby. You're gonna be an aunt."

She was awfully pretty when she smiled, even if her eyes were swollen and she still hiccoughed from crying. "I should go."

"Go?"

"To White Pines. I've abused your hospitality long enough."

A shake of his head was his response to such a ridiculous statement. "You're not going anywhere. Least not 'til you're feeling better. Then I'll take you to White Pines myself."

Chapter Four

Victoria pushed a clothespin over the corner of the last sheet, relieved that the wash was finally done. Arching her body, she groaned at the stiffness in the small of her back. A good day's work, but she was paying the price. The sounds of approaching hoofbeats pulled her gaze to the long tree-lined road.

The horse and rider moved as one. Confident. Strong. Imposing. Tufts of dirt flew from churning hooves. As the duo came closer, she drew in her breath and held it. The stallion had perfect conformation. Her father would be pea green with envy over that fine an animal. So focused on the horse, it took a moment before she considered the man.

Her breath rushed out in a gasp.

God, he's handsome.

A girlish notion of her Prince Charming riding up on a stallion to beg for her hand and take her away to his palace resurrected, burning like hot coals in her chest. With a shake of her head, she shoved the useless fantasy back into hibernation, never wanting to feel that kind of painful longing again.

She was what she was and had given up wishing to be something more. Twenty-one and single in a territory where men vastly outnumbered women. That spoke volumes. Nor could a cowboy riding a Paint ever be Prince Charming.

He came right up to where she stood in the grass, surrounded by sweet-smelling laundry that billowed in the breeze. His grin washed over her like warm sunshine.

She'd been wrong. *Handsome* didn't do the man justice. Surely there was another word—a better word—that could describe this cowboy. He scattered her thoughts so thoroughly none came to mind.

Sun-bleached hair jutted out from under his weathered hat. Strong forearms stretched from the rolled-up sleeves, and his broad chest filled out the shirt in a way that made her mouth go dry. Warm brown eyes twinkled from a tan face. He had the most delectable cleft in his chin and a dimple on his right cheek.

"Afternoon, missus." He tipped the brim of his weathered hat. "I'm hoping this is the Twin Springs ranch. I'm Matthew Riley."

He offered his hand to her and then quickly withdrew it to remove his worn leather glove. Reaching out again, he gave Victoria the most charming smile. A flush heated her cheeks when she clasped his calloused fingers and palm. His firm handshake rocked her arm all the way to her shoulder.

"I'm not a missus. I'm Victoria Morgan. *Miss* Victoria Morgan.

And yes, this is the Twin Springs." Despite wanting to make a good first impression, she couldn't help but frown when she realized what was happening. "You best get that ill-mannered animal out of my clean sheets right quick."

His horse had managed to knock over some of the big branches propping up the sagging clotheslines. The wash she'd just finished hanging dangled mere inches above the ground. The stallion pawed at the sheets it had already dragged down. The more Matthew tried to control the contrary animal, the more clean linens fell in the grass and dirt. The irritation wasn't enough to sweep away her fascination with the man, but it did prompt a frustrated stomp of her foot.

"You're ruining my wash! Do something!"

He dismounted and tugged at the clothes that had wrapped around his horse's chest and legs. Peeling layers of wet sheets, he dropped them to the ground. Picking up a lacy camisole, he stared at it for a moment until he sheepishly held it out to her.

She shoved it into the deep pocket of her skirt, wondering if her own face turned as crimson as his.

When he'd finally freed the animal from the cloth cocoon, he grinned at her as if he'd just slain a dragon, doing little to curb her irritation as he handed her a soiled shirt. "There. All better now."

"*Better?*"

Clenching her jaw so hard she was amazed she didn't crack a tooth, she bit back a sarcastic retort. Gathering up as many items as she could, she took a couple of deep breaths in an effort to control her temper, hoping the exercise wasn't in vain.

"I'm searching for my sister." He mirrored her frown as Victoria continued gathering up her wash. "She was heading out this way." He picked up a stray washing cloth from under a hoof and tossed it atop the pile of wet laundry in her arms. "Have you seen her? She's tall with brown hair she wears kinda short. 'Lot taller than you. Probably stopped by nine, maybe ten days back. Might even be as much as two weeks."

Could he be more insufferably rude? He didn't offer an apology, nor did he even try to soothe her feelings over the mess. Most of the laundry would have to be rewashed, and some of the items had ripped and would need mending. How could anyone be raised with such a lack of manners?

"Well, aren't you a regular gentleman," she muttered, more to herself than him.

His lips thinned to a grim line as he looked around the last of the laundry that still littered the ground. Then understanding dawned on his face. "You're mad about the wash? Some clothes got a little dirty.

Nothing to get all huffy about." He shook his head with such a patronizing grin, she was tempted to throw something heavy at his head. "Was my sister here?"

"If your sister is Grace, then she's here. She's been mighty sick—"

Before Victoria could even finish her explanation, Matthew grabbed her roughly by the upper arms and scowled down at her.

Heavens, but he was tall. Smelled nice too—like fresh-cut hay and leather. Her wet laundry sank back to the ground.

"Sick? How sick? What's wrong with her? Where is she?"

All she could do was gape at him as he gave her one firm shake. Even though he was so handsome she couldn't seem to get a logical thought to find its way from her brain to her mouth, she couldn't abide by the man's offensive manners.

"Answer me, damn it!"

She shot back her own scowl. As if she'd ever let a cowboy intimidate her. "There's no need to curse, Mr. Riley. I would appreciate it if you'd take your hands off me."

He released his grasp as if her skin had burst into flames.

"Thank you. Now, I'll take you to Grace. There's no need to be fretting. She's much better now. Go put that rude horse of yours in the barn so we can go inside."

With a heavy sigh, she gathered the soiled linens back into her arms to rewash.

She waited a few moments for him to tie up his horse, then she led him to the back door. At the top of the steps leading to the kitchen door, she stopped and glared at him, intent on waiting as long as it took for him to realize what she wanted. It hadn't taken too awfully long for her to train Jake and Ty in the use of proper manners. Surely *this* cowboy wouldn't be any different. As though dealing with a stubborn colt, Matthew simply needed a firm hand.

The man was obtuse. His gaze shifted between her and the door a couple of times before he grabbed the handle and jerked it open.

Daisy fussed over something cooking on the stove. She glanced over her shoulder and gasped. Putting down her wooden spoon and wiping her hands on her apron, she came over to try to help Victoria with her burden.

"God's hooks, Victoria." She smoothed back some stray brown hairs that had escaped her tight bun. "What happened to the laundry?"

"An impolite horse with an equally rude rider tore it down and stomped all over it." She dropped the rest of the wet, dirty burden on the table. "This is Matthew Riley." Victoria nodded at Daisy. "That's our housekeeper, Daisy." She folded her arms over her chest. "He's come to see Grace—just as soon as he takes off his hat, his gun, and his muddy boots."

Matthew had no idea why he put up with Victoria's impertinence, even less of a notion why he immediately snatched his hat from his head and toed off his boots. Dismayed at his own hasty compliance, he refused to give on her third request. No one was coming between him and his Colt.

"Your gun, too, Mr. Riley. You can hang it and your hat on those hooks." She nodded at the row of wooden pegs mounted on the wall next to the door.

"I'm not taking off my gun."

Laughter bubbled in his chest when her face hardened into a scowl. No woman could intimidate him—especially one as tiny and feminine as this one. She was so small she'd blow around like a tumbleweed if a stiff wind came her way.

"If you don't leave that gun down here," she warned, "then you're not going upstairs to see Grace."

He could stand here and argue with her, but something told him that would be wasted time and breath. She might not be the least bit intimidating, but she was clearly as stubborn as a mule. With a resigned sigh, he unbuckled his gun belt, hung it from one of the pegs, and turned back to her.

"Anything else, your majesty?" He gave her a condescending bow.

Those hazel eyes of hers turned darker, warning of an approaching storm. "There's no need for sarcasm, Mr. Riley. This is *my* home. I'm allowed to set my own rules."

"Take me to Grace."

A rude reply, but he'd never felt quite as off balance as he found himself when facing Victoria Morgan. Dismissing the unsettling feeling, he followed her through the kitchen to a living area as large as any he'd ever seen. The library off the living area made envy shoot through him.

A simple glance, yet he'd never seen so many books, all of them sitting in neat rows along more shelves than he could count. Grace had sacrificed so much over the years, giving up buying things for herself to make sure they constantly had something new to read. A few shelves of the Morgan library held more books than he'd ever have the pleasure to read in his lifetime.

Victoria's voice pierced his thoughts. She stood a few steps up the staircase, her hand resting on the railing. "That's the library. Grace is upstairs."

He hadn't realized he'd taken several steps toward the treasure trove of books. "Sorry."

Her spontaneous smile stole his breath away. "It's my favorite room too. I love to read. Grace sure has enjoyed our books since she's been here. Why, I'd guess she goes through at least two stories a day."

Before he could reply, she went up the stairs. The sway of her hips set her long, dark braid brushing against her narrow waist—a waist that obviously didn't require a corset. He followed, mesmerized by everything about her. Slender fingers gripping the railing. Narrow feet mounting each step. The gentle swish of her skirts with each movement.

A shake of his head brought back his sanity. Perhaps being in the company of roughneck cowboys and having an older sister as the only female in his life had left him ripe to appreciate any woman who threw him a pretty smile. He tried to think about Grace and the fury he still felt over her sneaking away in the dead of night like some thief and not even telling him why. That anger kept him grounded, steeling him for the confrontation to come.

Victoria knocked on a door with the back of her knuckles. "Grace?" She eased into the bedroom. "Are you awake?"

When he saw his sister sitting in the bed, reading a book, and leaning back against a mound of pillows, relief rushed through him. Pushing his way inside, he practically shoved Victoria out of the way.

The book slipped from Grace's hand and tumbled to the floor.

"Grace! My God, I thought I'd *never* find you." Anger swelled in his chest, moving aside the relief that she was safe. "What in the hell were you thinking? I thought Shay had—"

"Matthew!"

"Thank God, Shay didn't—"

"Not here. Not now." Her frantic eyes shifted to Victoria as she clutched at the edges of her quilt.

He glared at his sister and then at Victoria. "Can we have some privacy?"

Victoria's slender hands stroked the braid she'd pulled over her shoulder. Her smile seemed as cold as ice. "Why, Mr. Riley, you're quite welcome. I was happy to bring you up to see Grace, and it was a pleasure to have done so much for her since she fell ill."

How was he supposed to respond to that? "You're a bossy bundle of fluff, aren't you?"

Fire flashed through those eyes, so hot, he wondered if they'd shifted red for a moment. "You're insufferable." She glanced to Grace. "How do you tolerate him?"

"We get along fine," he replied to the ridiculous question.

Her indignant sigh lasted several seconds. "Call if you need me, Grace."

"Thank you, Victoria."

The door closed softly behind her.

"Matthew, why are you being so rude?"

He shrugged. Something about that tiny women got under his skin, irritating him as bad as a prickly rash. He focused that agitation on his sister. "What the hell were you doing?"

"I had to leave."

"Why?"

"I was trying to find Jake." She gave him a lopsided smile that did nothing to soothe his anger.

"Jake?" No wonder she'd run. That was a wound his sister carried that might never heal. "I thought his trail went cold and we'd given up on finding him."

Her expression changed in a heartbeat as the smile vanished. "I've never given up. *Never*."

"I still don't understand why you'd sneak off like that. You could've told me. We could've searched together."

She bowed her head as her teeth tugged on her bottom lip. "I couldn't tell you. I–I asked for some help."

Matthew was getting damned sick and tired of the story falling out in bits and pieces. "Help? What in the devil are you talking about?"

She wrung her hands in her lap. "I had to know. I had to. I couldn't live with... I needed help to find Jake." She trembled. "I went to Stephen Shay."

"*What?* Are you loco? After everything he's put you through, why in the hell would you go to that snake? Jesus Christ, Grace. What happened to that smart brain of yours?"

Her hands clenched into tight fists. "I needed to find Jake. I *had* to find him."

"So you'd sell your soul to the devil?" He wanted to hit something. "After all these years of running, after all we've done to keep him off your trail, how could you?" His words had become a roar.

"I had to." A fit of coughs seized her before she could say anything more. "I–I needed to–to know he was safe." More coughs, punctuated by a whimper. "His parents were murdered."

His jaw dropped. "Murdered? How?"

She was so lost in her illness, she couldn't answer him. Her whole body shook, and he put his hand on her shoulder and rubbed, not sure what to do to help her.

"I'm sorry. I didn't mean to shout."

All the years of hell they'd been through drowned his concern for Jake. Grace said his adoptive *parents* were dead, not the *boy*. But Matthew's whole life had been spent protecting Grace from Stephen

Shay, and she'd up and gone to him for help?

He couldn't stop scolding her. "Shay? Shit, Grace, you really went to *Shay*?"

"Oh, Matthew. I shot him. He tried to— And I wouldn't— The gun just went off and—" The words tripped over each other, and he could barely understand them. "I–I…killed him. They're going to hang me." Another coughing spasm wracked her slender body.

No wonder she was so upset. Before he could even form a coherent thought about what to say to Grace's frightening confession, the door flew open, slamming against the wall.

A man stood in the frame, hands on his hips as he took in the scene. His eyes narrowed, then he moved to the bed, grabbed Matthew's bicep and jerked him to his feet before sitting down in his place. He held his arms open to Grace, and Matthew gaped in shock when she fell into his embrace and leaned against his shoulder while the man rubbed her back and soothed her in low tones.

"Shh. I'm here. It's okay now, Gracie."

Why wasn't she shoving him away? Hell's fire, the last time one of the cowboys had tried to hug her, he'd nearly choked on his balls when she kneed him in the groin. Instead of fighting, she seemed to melt into this man's arms.

It took several minutes for her to settle down and her coughing to subside. When she finally lay back against the pillows, her eyes were red.

The man pulled the quilt higher up on her chest, gave her hand a friendly pat, and stood up. Then he turned to face Matthew.

The fury in his eyes almost made Matthew take a step back. "You. Outside. Now."

He was so startled by the command in his host's tone, he did as he was ordered.

After the man softly closed the door, he launched his anger. "Do you have any idea how sick she's been? We almost lost her."

Matthew felt lower than dirt. "I didn't know."

"You do now. I take it you're Matthew."

"Yes, sir." He held his hand out. "Matthew Riley."

"Grace was worried you'd come. I'm Adam Morgan." His handshake was as firm as his voice.

Morgan.

That explained the vixen Victoria. How could she have been concerned with something as silly as some downed sheets? She'd probably been spoiled her whole life by her rich rancher daddy. No wonder she was so damned bossy.

Finding some of the manners his sister had tried to instill in him, he nodded at the bedroom door. "You have my gratitude for taking care of Grace. We'll repay you."

Adam waved a hand in dismissal. "Not necessary."

"I'll be finding a place to stay nearby so I can take my sister off your hands."

"She's not going anywhere. Least not 'til she's well enough to travel."

Not about to be indebted to the man, Matthew insisted, "I can get her settled in a boarding house. There's a small town near here, right?"

A stubborn shake of Adam's head was the reply. "She'll stay *here*. Now, I've got some questions. Come to the kitchen, and we'll grab a cup of coffee."

***

Sitting across from Grace's brother, Adam tried to measure the man's character. He had to brush aside his initial anger that Matthew had upset her so much. At least her coughing had settled down.

After pouring two cups of coffee, he sat at the kitchen table opposite Matthew. He slid a mug to the cowboy as Daisy excused herself and left through the back door.

"I assume you came here looking for Grace."

Matthew nodded. "We were supposed to be signing on for another long drive, but when I went to fetch her, she'd up and disappeared. She left all her things behind. The only clue I had was a silly note telling me not to follow. As though I'd let her go off all alone in the world with—" He cleared his throat.

"You and your sister have a nasty habit of never finishing sentences."

Matthew shrugged, his face becoming a mask that was impossible to read.

"How'd you find her out here in the middle of nowhere?"

The topic perked the young man up. "Wasn't easy, but I've got a knack for tracking people. Years of practice. Gotta admit she made it tough. Had to choose between two possible stagecoach routes." He grinned. "I got lucky and found her on my first choice."

Since the words were flowing freely again, Adam did some fishing. "How long have you been herding cattle?"

"Going on twenty years. We've been squirreling some money away hoping for a spread of our own someday." Matthew's gaze drifted around the kitchen. "Nothing like this, mind you. But a place we could call our own. A home."

"You're a cowboy and Grace runs the chuckwagon?"

"Yes, sir. She could make a feast out of boot leather. Cowboys never go hungry when she's cooking. The woman has a God-given gift."

At least Adam was finally getting something in the way of personal information about her. "If you don't mind my asking, why isn't she married? Pretty filly like that, there oughta be a hundred single men in line trying to court her."

"Grace doesn't... She wouldn't..." Matthew worked through the thought, several emotions clearly displayed in his eyes. Anger. Fear. Pity. "Grace doesn't want to marry. Ever."

"Doesn't want to marry?" The Riley siblings were a riddle with no easy solution.

Matthew shifted his cup in his palms. "I'll be taking her off your hands now. You've no idea how grateful I am that you helped her. I'm mighty obliged."

"Where you heading from here?"

"No plans yet. I need to talk to Grace. Probably another long drive if we can find one. You know, I still can't rightly figure out why she came to Montana."

So she was keeping secrets from *both* of them. She clearly hadn't told Matthew she'd found Jake. Adam wrestled with his best course of action.

He wasn't ready to let Grace go. A sobering thought, but he already felt a commitment to her—a need to shelter and protect her. She was a wounded bird needing gentle care and time to heal. The poor woman still cried out in her dreams every night.

He'd developed a habit of sleeping in the rocking chair as he soothed her through the demons haunting her sleep. Some nights she was so terrified that he had to hold her in a bear hug to help her through the worst of them.

He'd spent her days of convalescence at her side, playing chess or cards. Sometimes he read to her from the books she loved so much. The bond between them was already growing, and the notion of losing her was enough to set his stomach to churning.

He had to keep Grace close. "How'd you like to work for me 'til you both get your plans ironed out?"

Tendering the offer was easy because Adam needed the help. He'd decided when Jake left he was going to bring in this one last herd. Then he would enjoy never dealing with another cow again. Unless he was eating it. He'd already spent too many years of his life looking up the backside of a steer.

Besides, he was only forty-five. He could do something else he'd enjoy now. Perhaps breed horses.

Until the last herd was gone, he'd taken over Jake's duties of tending the steers. Since Grace's arrival, he'd spent so much time with her that Victoria had picked up the slack, helping Ty as often as she could. His daughter had better things to do than work with cattle, and he felt guilty for expecting so much from her. She should be finding a husband, settling down, and raising a family.

Jake's help was missed, and from the stories Grace had told Adam, Matthew knew his way around livestock. The bonus of the whole situation was that if he kept her brother close at hand, Adam could continue to keep watch over her and try to help solve some of her problems.

Hell if he hadn't already made up his mind. He'd known from the moment he'd scooped her feverish body into his arms.

Grace was going to belong to him.

Now he just needed to convince her.

Matthew seemed to consider the offer for a moment. "I'll stay on if Grace will. You know, she's a great cook."

"So I've been told. Think she'd work the chuckwagon on my drive?" Victoria usually handled the cooking, but it was far from her favorite task. Offering the job to Grace could be the solution to more than one dilemma.

"I'm sure of it," Matthew replied with a nod.

"Then I'll be speaking to her about it later." Standing up, Adam offered the man his hand again. "Glad to have you on board. Victoria will show you around."

"I appreciate the job, Mr. Morgan."

"Adam will do."

"Adam it is."

Grabbing his hat from where it had rested on a hook, Adam settled it on his head and left through the kitchen door.

Victoria was approaching with an armload of cut flowers. Stopping her before she entered, he explained the jobs he was offering to Matthew and Grace. She nodded and carried her burden inside.

Matthew frowned when Victoria piled the blooms on the large wooden table. The smell of sunshine and the flowers followed her in.

"Daddy says you're staying on for a while. We can take a ride so I can show you around the ranch. Then we'll get you set up in the bunkhouse. This laundry will wait 'til later."

Daisy walked through the door just as Victoria placed the last of the clothes on the table. "Don't go frettin'. I'll fold 'em up before I get supper started."

"Thank you, Daisy. Matthew's staying on to help with the last drive. He'll bunk with Ty." She turned to Matthew. "I'll be back in a minute." Then she left the kitchen humming a tune.

Not knowing what to do while he waited, he sat back down at the table.

"You're Grace's brother." Daisy folded a shirt with practiced ease.

"Yes, ma'am. I'd like to thank you for taking such good care of her while she's been sick."

She shook her head as she reached for another shirt. "Been Mr. Morgan takin' care of her. He won't let nobody do much for Miss Grace."

He knit his brow. "He's been taking care of her? She doesn't usually cotton to strangers—especially men."

With a chuckle, she moved to the stove to stir something that smelled mighty tasty—almost as good as food Grace cooked. "She surely cottons to Mr. Morgan. They spend most of the day together."

He still couldn't believe what he'd heard.

Let a man tend her?

Not Grace.

He spent a few minutes trying to get used to the notion, wondering if whatever was producing the mouth-watering smell would be supper and if he would be invited to attend now that he worked on the Twin Springs.

Victoria's happy hum floated into the kitchen.

As she strolled into the room, Matthew's mouth fell open in surprise. The woman was wearing denim pants and sporting a cowboy hat. Giving her a long head-to-toe appraisal, he had to admit that the outfit looked great on her slim figure. The denim was tight enough to reveal the beautiful curves of her hips, and it dawned on him that the temperature in the kitchen had grown decidedly warmer.

Damn it all if she didn't look mighty fetching in that getup, even if she was just playing at what he did to earn his way in the world.

"Is there a particular reason you keep staring at me? I'm not exactly homely enough to gawk at." She straightened her hat.

Homely?

He'd seldom seen a woman as attractive as Victoria Morgan. Her dark brown hair suited her pretty heart-shaped face. He couldn't quite tell if her eyes were truly hazel or more green because they tended to take on a different hue depending on whether she was in the sunlight or not. He possessed not a single clue as to what could possibly make this woman think she was anything short of beautiful.

"I didn't mean to stare. I'm just not used to seeing a lady in pants."

Her eyes flashed a bit of spark that he found oddly enticing considering how little liking they had for each other when they'd met.

"I see no reason why I should have to be uncomfortable when I ride. Have you ever ridden astraddle a horse in a skirt, Mr. Riley? Not exactly the easiest thing to do."

"Most ladies have the courtesy to wear a split-skirt, Miss Morgan. Let's a man know she's a lady."

The fire in the woman's eyes could start a forest burning. "I see no reason to be a hypocrite who wears pants and calls them a skirt."

She walked out the kitchen door and practically slammed it in his face.

This one had a temper. She needed a firm hand, like a fine unbroken filly. He followed her as she went to the barn where his horse was still tethered.

He was shocked no ranch worker came along to help get her horse ready for a ride. She probably had more than one—horses, not stablehands. The scent of roses followed her and drew him along as if he was a hungry fish teased by wiggling bait. He shook his head to break whatever spell she was weaving with the swing of her long braid above that gorgeous backside.

To see her go inside a stall, croon at a gorgeous black mare, and slip a halter over her head came as a shock. Sure, the woman had been hanging out wash, but she was the rancher's daughter. Even though he'd only had a short look around, Twin Springs seemed prosperous. Almost lush. Victoria obviously didn't *need* to work.

"Need a hand?" He plucked a stalk of fresh-smelling hay and let it rest in the corner of his mouth. Nasty habit, but it was better than smoking those God-awful cigarettes some of the other cowboys favored.

"No, thank you." She threw a saddle blanket over the mare's back. "This is Cleo. I raised her from a newborn." She nodded at Matthew's Paint. "He have a name?"

"Sin."

"Why Sin?"

"'Cause he keeps me too busy to commit one."

Her laughter was melodic. Delicate hands smoothed the blanket flat and then ran affectionately up the mare's neck and down her muzzle. When Victoria grunted as she hefted the saddle onto the horse, a grin lifted Matthew's lips.

Damn, but the woman was tiny.

She had the mare ready in no time. Before he could offer any help, she swung up onto the saddle, tossed him a saucy smile, and kicked her horse into a trot.

If this was a race, the woman was cheating.

He grabbed his stallion's reins, threw himself onto the animal's back, and followed.

"And there," she said, continuing a story he'd obviously missed the beginning of, "is where we head out to the open range." She turned to smirk at him. "I'd take you there, but I imagine you've already seen enough cattle to last you a lifetime."

God, but she was pretty, near to taking his breath away. "Never worked a ranch before."

"Then welcome to Twin Springs."

Chapter Five

Grace stood at the stove, stirring something in one of the pots scattered across the surface.

Adam hung his hat up and frowned. "You shouldn't be out of bed."

"Nonsense. I'm feeling much better. I'm stiff from not moving."

"Then maybe we'll take a short walk after supper. Stretch those legs of yours."

"I'd enjoy that. I'm really tired of being stuck inside." After tapping the wooden spoon against the rim of the pot, she set it aside. "Victoria told me Daisy left."

"On the morning stage. She went to be with her sister when she gives birth to her sixth."

"Oh, my. Six?"

He nodded.

"I figured I could at least make you a nice supper. I owe you so much." A glance down at her clothes fixed a frown on her face. "I shouldn't be wearing your wife's clothes."

He turned her own word back on her. "Nonsense. They'd only be gathering dust and moths. It's nice to see them put to good use."

She nodded, but a frown remained as she turned back to the stove.

Whatever Grace was cooking smelled delicious. Daisy might be a good cook, but something inside him warmed at the idea of his Grace making a meal for him. "Daisy'll be away for a couple of months. Before she left, she even hinted that she might stay there permanently."

"Misses her family, I reckon." A glance down at her messy hands caused a gasp. She quickly smoothed her palms down her apron then considered her faint reflection in the window. "I must be a sight. There's more food on me than in the pots." Picking up the corner of the white apron, she wiped at smudges of flour on her chin. She didn't get them all.

Adam crossed to her. Turning her to face him, he put a finger under her chin and lifted until she glanced up.

She seemed hesitant to make eye contact, looking this way and that until she finally took a breath and let their gazes meet.

He could drown in those soulful brown eyes. Rubbing the flour away with his thumb, he watched a blush creep over her cheeks. The dark circles were still under her eyes, but they receded more each day. Her lips were the prettiest shade of pink.

He needed to kiss her or he'd lose his mind. Approaching with the same caution he'd use with a wild doe that had caught a dangerous scent, he leaned in. Slowly. Steadily. Waiting for any sign that she would run.

Grace tilted her head and stared at him with the most curious expression.

This woman didn't realize his intentions. Had she never been properly kissed? She didn't seem to understand what he wanted of her.

"Gracie?"

She hummed in reply, her gaze still searching his.

"I want to kiss you."

Could her eyes open any wider? "You do?"

"Yes, darlin'. I do."

The look of fright took him by surprise. No, this woman might've been kissed, but she'd never been kissed with affection. From what he'd gleaned from her nightmares, she'd suffered much at the hands of some man. *Stephen* was the name that haunted her.

Her trembling told Adam she needed to have control—that this needed to be a dance where, for once, he didn't lead. Grace would set the tempo.

"But I won't kiss you unless I have your permission."

"You won't?"

"No, darlin'. I won't. Unless you want me to."

Her head bowed. "I do." Her voice quavered as her cheeks flushed darker.

She was afraid, yet she would conquer that fear to be honest with him. She pleased him more than she could ever know.

With a gentle lift of her chin, he leaned in. He was past ready to learn her taste, having fantasized about her kiss, her touch, imagining what sparks would fly between them when they finally came together.

His wounded bird would fly one day.

Thank God, he had one virtue—patience.

Before he could press his lips to hers, the door jerked open, shattering the tender moment.

Grace let out a small squeal and hurried back to the stove. She picked up the spoon and attacked whatever was in the closest pot.

Victoria came inside, muttering to herself. "Insufferable. Arrogant. Why I never—" Her words came to an abrupt halt when she looked up. Her frown changed to a knowing smile. "My apologies. I interrupted."

"No," Grace called over her shoulder. "You didn't."

"Yes," Adam said, grinning at his daughter. "You did. Gracie and I were about to share a—"

Whirling around, Grace dropped the spoon. "Adam!"

He chuckled, as did his daughter. "It's fine, princess. Looks as if it's about time to call Matthew and Ty in for dinner."

Victoria's grin sank into a fierce frown. "Don't even mention his name to me."

"Ty?" he teased. His daughter had made her feelings about Matthew Riley as plain as the stars in the big Montana sky on a cloudless night.

"No. *Him.*"

An accusing finger pointed at the cowboy as he strolled in the door, passing the row of pegs where he should've hung his hat and gun. Matthew sat down at the table, dropped his hat on the bench, and threw Victoria a crooked smile.

"Matthew." Grace dragged out his name like a mother scolding a naughty son. "You need to hang up your hat."

"My hat?" He glanced down at the bench. "Why, I'll be. I forgot again, didn't I?" A quick toss landed it perfectly on one peg. "How 'bout that?" He winked at Victoria whose cheeks flamed in response.

"And?" Victoria tapped her foot against the wooden floor.

"And *what*, Miss Morgan?"

"Your gun, Mr. Riley."

"As I've told you a million times. Nothing comes between me and my Colt."

A frustrated stomp replaced her tapping. "You're insufferable."

"And you're bossy."

It took all the self-control Adam had not to laugh. The couple had been at odds from the moment Matthew had been hired on at Twin Springs. In a matter of days, the friction grew as Victoria laid down the law while Matthew broke each and every one of her rules.

They were matched in every way. Stubborn. Smart. Hardworking. And the heat between them could keep the whole town of White Pines warm the whole winter through.

He should sit them down for a long talk. They were smitten, yet each seemed unable to express their true feelings. That frustrated attraction chafed them both.

Talking to them would be futile. They wouldn't listen to him. When he'd been that young, he'd never appreciated sage advice, either. Besides, Adam had enough problems in his own love life. Victoria and Matthew would have to stumble through until they figured things out for themselves. If their little tortured dance went on too long, he'd try to straighten them out.

"Victoria?" Grace asked. "Could you please call Ty in for supper? Everything's ready."

Ty came strolling through the door as Victoria opened it. "Looks as if I won't have to."

The cowboy hung up his hat and gun before sitting at the bench next to Matthew.

Victoria favored Matthew with smirk.

He frowned in response.

Adam shook his head and chuckled, grateful that he wasn't a young pup anymore. Too much nonsense, fuss, and bother.

Helping Grace put the rest of the food on the table, he held the chair for her to sit. Taking his own place at the head of the table, he bowed his head, expecting the others to follow his lead. A quick prayer was ended by a round of *amens*.

Ty grabbed the first bowl, sniffing before shoveling a good half of the mashed potatoes onto his plate. "Smells mighty good, even if it ain't Daisy's taters."

Grace let the pleasure of the praise sink in. Would she ever tire of hearing compliments on her cooking? Not that the roughneck cowboys she traveled with were very forthcoming with praise. Loud belches sounded just as good to her ears. Appreciation was, after all, appreciation.

"Thank you, Ty."

She took the bowl, spooned out a small portion of the potatoes on her own plate, and then passed the bowl to Victoria.

As everyone ate, Grace worked up some courage. Not that she'd ever been remotely brave, nor was there any reason for her to fear Adam Morgan. But she did. She feared him in a way she'd never feared any other man.

In the time she'd been recuperating from her fever, she'd learned a lot about him, and she liked everything she discovered. He was kind, patient, and so very tender when he took care of her. Each time he touched her, her heart leapt and a knot of need formed in her gut. He frightened her almost more than she could bear—because for the first time in her life, Grace was attracted to a man.

Not just any man.

The perfect man.

A man who would never approve of the way she lived. A man who would despise her if he learned about her past. A man who could break down all the protective barriers she'd constructed around her battered heart.

The time had come to run away again.

"I've decided to go to White Pines tomorrow," she announced. "I need to meet Jake and find a place to stay for a few days."

Adam slammed his fork down hard enough the dishes on the long table rattled. His calm, measured words contrasted his fierce frown. "I'll take you into town to meet Jake when—"

Matthew interrupted, his fist hitting the table and jostling the dishes that had just settled. "Jake? Jake's here? That's why you came to

Montana? Jesus Christ, Grace. You said you were searching again, but why didn't you tell me he was *here?*"

"Because I knew how you'd react." She focused back on Adam. "I'd like to find a place to stay in White Pines."

He shook his stubborn head. "There's no reason for you to stay in town. You can stay on the ranch as long as you want, Gracie. Besides, you're going on my long drive. We won't be ready to head out for at least another week."

"I can't stay here, Adam." The hand she used to pick up an empty bowl shook. "I can't go on that drive with you. I need to see Jake, then I need to go. I *have* to go."

"Bullshit."

She gasped. In all the time she'd been in his company, she'd never heard Adam curse beyond an infrequent *damn* or *hell*, even though she'd seen frustration clearly written on his face. "But I have to go to—"

"Victoria?" Adam spoke to his daughter, all but ignoring Grace's words. "Would you mind cleaning up the dishes? Gracie, it's time for you and me to take that walk." He stood, grabbed her hand, and hurried her out the door before she could even protest. At least he had the common sense to grab her shawl from one of the pegs on their way out.

She stumbled after him until he reached the tree-lined road that led from the ranch.

He stopped long enough to drape her shawl around her shoulders. Taking her hand back in his, he led the way in a more leisurely pace.

"Sorry, darlin'. Don't want you coughing again." His grip on her hand was tight.

She should pull away. Yet they had so little time left together, and she so loved the warmth that swept over her whenever they touched.

They'd reached the end of the long path where it met the main road to White Pines before Grace found the courage to speak. She needed Adam to understand even though she couldn't understand herself. She'd only known him a short time, but she felt roots already digging deep, trying to keep her grounded to this place.

To him.

She needed to run before the roots plunged too deep for her to ever pull back up.

As they stopped walking, she turned to face him. In the moonlight, his frown didn't seem so intimidating.

"It's time for me to go, Adam. I need to see Jake, then I need to be moving on."

God, how she wanted to pretend this hadn't all been make-believe. Living on a beautiful ranch. Reading to her heart's content. Spending time with a man who seemed to enjoy her company as much as she enjoyed his. A man she could learn to love.

But none of this was real.

It could never be real.

She'd murdered a man, and her past would surely catch up with her. Nor could the rest of her ghosts stay in the closet forever, no matter how hard she tried to keep them jammed deep inside. Despite what she felt for him, she couldn't let him know what she truly was. A disgraced woman. A person who'd left a helpless baby behind. A murderess.

How could she ever bear the scorn in his eyes if he found out all she'd done?

Grace shook her head, banishing her dreams. "It's time for me to leave."

"Why?" His hands encased hers, giving them a gentle squeeze as his warmth seeped into her veins. "Why do you want to leave me?"

The words wouldn't come.

He leaned closer, those wise eyes of his holding her captive. "Don't you understand what I feel for you?"

She gave her head a curt shake.

"I want you."

Her breath caught.

"I'm going to kiss you now."

Every nerve in her body tingled. Never had she thought she would respond physically the way she did to something as simple as Adam's frank confession. He hadn't even kissed her, yet the butterflies in her stomach were already beating their wings in a frantic flurry. Her heart pounded hard enough she was sure he could hear it.

He waited, his mouth inches from hers as his gaze searched hers. Knowing he meant what he'd promised back in the kitchen—that he would only touch her with her permission—made her feel powerful after years of utter helplessness.

"Yes," she whispered. "Yes, you can ki—"

Strong arms wrapped around her as firm lips touched hers. A simple kiss before he pulled back. She pressed her palms against his cheeks. His evening whiskers tickled her palms.

"More, Adam."

A warm chuckle still fell from his lips as he kissed her again. The pressure built as he slanted his mouth over hers. Warmth blazed a path from her face, down her neck, and through her belly. It became an inferno when it reached the juncture of her thighs. She wanted to drown in the new sensation, to enjoy being lovingly touched by a man.

His thumb pushed against her jaw, drawing it down. Grace wasn't sure what he wanted until she opened her lips and his tongue slid past them to stroke hers.

The feeling was so fresh, so foreign, she almost pulled back. But the more he caressed her tongue with his, the more she wanted him never to stop.

By the time he ended the kiss, her lips felt hot and swollen. Both she and Adam panted for air, deep and hard. At least she wasn't the only one affected by the kiss.

"I don't want you to go, Gracie."

I don't want to go.

Hard as it was, she bit back the words.

He tugged her tighter against him, and she laid her cheek against his shoulder, tucking her face against his neck. His scent comforted her. She'd missed so much in her thirty-five years. Never knowing the warmth of a man's loving embrace. Never feeling the thrill of a real kiss.

How much more could Adam teach her? Could he make the melody he'd begun in her body become a virtuoso? Could he help her forget the horrifying memories and replace them with joyous ones?

He gave her a squeeze. "I don't want you to go."

"I know."

"Then stay. Please stay."

"And do what? Be your housekeeper? People will talk, Adam."

"Let them. I don't give a damn about gossip."

Neither did she—especially among people she'd never see again. But he had to live here, and she wouldn't be the one to drag his reputation through the mud. Small towns were unforgiving. Even if anyone knew she was at Twin Springs, her illness would be explanation enough as to why she'd been on the ranch so long. Now that she'd recovered, the gossip would start in earnest.

"Are you cold, darlin'?"

"No."

"Then why are you trembling?"

She couldn't answer him.

"We should be heading back."

The moonlight filtered through the branches of the pines. Such a beautiful night in such a beautiful place. The crunch of the dirt and gravel beneath their feet added to the melody of the crickets who'd come out to sing in the cool night air.

Adam interrupted their song. "I'll take you to White Pines tomorrow. You can see Jake."

"And?"

"And we'll figure out what to do next. *Together.*"

***

Matthew waited on the porch steps, watching the couple make their way back to the house.

Adam touched a kiss to Grace's forehead, nodded at Matthew in greeting, and excused himself to tend to some chores in the barn.

"That man has feelings for you, Grace."

A sigh slipped from her lips. "I know."

"You have feelings for him. I can tell."

She frowned. "I know that, too."

"What are you going to do about it?"

"What do you *want* me to do, Matthew? Marry him? Settle down?"

"Why not? You deserve a little happiness."

Her hand flipped in dismissal. "You *know* why not. There are *bushels* of why not. You think I want Adam to find out about Jake or watch them hang me?"

"Grace…"

"I'll go into town. I'll find Jake and see with my own eyes that he's okay. Then we can head out to find another cattle drive."

"So you'll do what you do best?"

"Which is?"

"Run away."

Victoria came out the back door and glanced from sister to brother. "It seems my timing's very poor today. I didn't mean to interrupt."

"It's fine," Grace replied. "I fear I overdid a little. I should get some rest."

Matthew had a hard time not unleashing his anger at his sister. She'd never done anything as foolhardy as going to Stephen Shay to find Jake. Shay's obsession with her had tainted her whole life. *Both* their lives. He was damn sick and tired of running.

That bastard was dead, and she was safe here. She had a protector, someone whose feelings obviously ran deep. Why would she throw all that away? Why would she give up this chance—their first real chance—to settle down?

He didn't wish to speculate whether his newfound notions of putting down roots had anything to do with the pretty brunette who seemed to enjoy vexing him on a daily basis.

"You wouldn't want to get sick again," he said to Grace. "You'd waste precious time to make your escape."

She went inside without another word.

"Escape?" Victoria asked.

Damn, but he wished he'd kept his mouth shut. "Just a jest between brother and sister."

She walked down the steps, heading toward the laundry that was still hanging on the line.

He jumped to his feet and followed. "Let me help."

"No, thank you." A teasing smile came his way. "You're a little too hard on my linens."

He had to laugh at that, his mood changing from annoyed to happy in a heartbeat just being around Victoria. He plucked a clothespin from the end of the sheet she tugged from the line. Together, they stretched it and folded it into a neat bundle. Their hands brushed as he surrendered the sheet to her care. Eyes locked for a moment that extended an eternity.

She glanced away. "Thank you, Mr. Riley."

"Matthew. Call me Matthew."

He had a hard time reading her expression. Irritation had always been so plain in those hazel eyes, but this new emotion was much softer, much more mysterious.

"Matthew."

The whisper of her voice raised gooseflesh on his skin.

Something forced him to reach out to touch her braid. He rubbed her thick hair between this thumb and finger, marveling at how soft it was. Then he realized what he was doing and dropped it.

"Thanks again for helping fold the sheet." Victoria strode away as Matthew trailed behind.

Her voice followed her through the door. "You best be taking that hat off if you're going inside my house."

With a chuckle, he pretended not to hear and strode through the door with his hat securely on his head.

Chapter Six

Grace approached the Four Aces with her heart lodged firmly in her throat.

Adam had wanted to accompany her inside, but she insisted on going to Jake alone. One wrong word and Adam would know she'd been lying.

His opinion probably shouldn't matter so much, but it did. More than she wanted to admit—even to herself. Besides, he had business in town, and she didn't want to keep him from that convenient distraction. He'd be by to fetch her in an hour or so, ready to take her back to Twin Springs, where she feared she didn't belong.

Being honest with herself, she didn't want him there when she found the elusive Jake Curtis. Who knew what would happen when she finally saw him?

Sweet merciful Lord, how many times had she pictured her first meeting with her son?

A fantasy of their perfect introduction had formed over the years. She would calmly explain her story—the tale of being his sister that she chose rather than spilling the whole humiliating truth. No, she could never tell him *everything*. Jake would give it a quick think. Then he'd open up his welcoming arms and accept her into his life without a moment of hesitation.

A wonderful, happy family reunion.

That fantasy comforted her through the agonizing years of thinking about her child.

Child?

Jake was twenty—had turned twenty the day she reached thirty-five. Their shared birthday had always been a secret bond, a cosmic strand that stretched between time and space to connect them. They were family. Surely he'd accept a new person into his life, especially one who shared his blood.

Now that the ominous moment had arrived, Grace was terrified of both the fantasy and the reality. Could she bear it if Jake greeted her with scorn?

What would he think if he knew the things she'd done? If he knew why she'd given him up? If he knew she'd killed his father?

Taking a steadying breath to regain control over her wayward thoughts, she gave one of the batwing doors a push and peered inside the saloon.

The place was dim, the only light streaming in through the distorted glass of the front window, leaving odd patterns of sunshine on the sawdust-covered floor.

"Hello? Anyone there?" Her words echoed through the cavernous room.

"Damnation!" The feminine voice drifted in from just off the main room. "Double damnation!"

Her heart hammering in her chest and terrifying memories assaulting her from every direction, Grace hiked up her skirts and ran to the kitchen. She skidded to a stop when she saw the blonde. Thank God, she appeared to be safe.

The girl couldn't be older than eighteen. Long curls cascaded in a riot around her shoulders. She was slapping lumpy icing on a cake that leaned precariously like the famous tower in Pisa.

Grace closed her eyes, trying to control her trembling and forcing her recollections aside. When she opened her eyes again, the girl was still focused on her task, unaware of the intrusion.

"Are you all right?" Grace asked.

Her words surprised the girl. When she jumped, the knife she'd been using pushed the cake the rest of the way over. It toppled to become a mass of crumbled pastry and pink icing.

"Oh no! I killed the cake."

Grace found a smile. "Oh, my. It appears you did."

The blonde turned to face her, revealing a well-rounded belly. "That was for Daddy's birthday, and I ruined it." Tears sprang into her eyes, then she let out a small sob.

"Please don't cry." Hurrying to the girl, Grace took her into her arms, feeling terrible for having destroyed her hard work. She had to put this to right. "I can help you fix it."

A couple of sniffles later, the blonde nodded. "I sure can't. Cooking is impossible." A delicate hiccough bubbled up. "God, I hate crying. Seems as if I've been doing nothing but weeping for seven months. Having a baby isn't easy." She eased away. "Who are you?"

"I'm Grace Riley. I'm looking for Jake Curtis. Have you seen him?"

"First thing every morning. I'm married to the rascal."

"Married? To Jake? But you're so...*young*." Grace's gaze dropped to that rounded belly.

Sweet merciful Lord.

She was going to be a grandmother. Her heart skipped so hard she got lightheaded.

The blonde smiled as all traces of her sadness fled her face. She gave her middle a pat. "Old enough to have this little one."

It took all Grace's restraint not to reach out and lay a hand on the girl's stomach, knowing that child was a part of Jake. Of her. "You barely look old enough to be a mother."

"I turned eighteen last March. More than old enough." Her hand caressed her unborn child. "Jake and I are gonna be a mama and papa in a couple of months. Daddy says that's a good thing, that havin' this baby settled us both down." She nodded toward the other room. "This here's my daddy's saloon. Jake helps him run it. Daddy says Jake'll be a great businessman once he learns some tricks of the trade." She tilted her head, fixing bright blue eyes on Grace for a long moment. "How do you know my Jake?"

"I'm his sister." The lie spilled from her lips. Nodding at the mess that was supposed to be a cake, Grace tried to take her mind off the falsehood that always tasted so bitter when she spit it out. "I can help you with that."

"Truly?"

"Cooking's what I do best."

"It's what I do *worst*. But I was asking if you're truly his sister."

A decisive nod punctuated the fib. "I'm truly his sister."

The girl reached out a hand with bits of icing clinging to her fingers.

Grace shook it anyway.

"I'm Emily."

"Please to make your acquaintance, Emily."

Needing the familiarity of preparing food, she moved around the kitchen, gathering the supplies to bake a new cake because Emily's appeared beyond redemption. When Emily groaned and rubbed her belly, Grace pulled out a barstool for her.

Emily gave her a grateful smile as she sat. "Baby's getting to be mighty active of late. And very big. Like his papa. Jake told me he didn't have any kin. If you're his sister, why isn't your name Curtis?"

Grace stopped short and turned to gaze at Emily. How much of his past had Jake shared with his wife? She sure didn't want to say anything he might not want his wife to know. Then again, they were married. Emily probably knew more about him than Grace ever would.

"What do you know about Jake's childhood?"

"He lived with Adam Morgan from the time he was a little boy. Before that, he lived out on a farm 'til his mama and papa were killed. He never mentioned a sister. Were you sent to the Denver orphanage too? He hates talking about that."

Tears stung Grace's eyes, the guilt an impossibly heavy weight on her heart. If only she'd known. If only she had tried harder to find him.

If only...

She squared her shoulders and her resolve. The past was the past. She couldn't change it. All she could do was hope for better things in

Jake's future.

"No, I wasn't. He was only a couple of hours old last time I saw him. I'm not a Curtis 'cause that's the name of the family who raised him. I'm his blood kin. I kept our father's name. I was too young to look after him, and I started hiring out on cattle drives as soon as I knew he was with his new parents. There wasn't much else I could do to earn a living, and spending his childhood on a chuckwagon wouldn't have been a life for him."

Emily twirled one of her long curls around a finger. "Why didn't you both stay with your mama?"

"My mother died." The grief still felt like ice encasing her heart. Grace grabbed an apron, wrapping it around her waist and thinking of it as a piece of shining armor to protect her from all the bad memories and lies.

Piling the cake ingredients next to a ceramic bowl, she added them one by one, hardly even thinking as she measured, poured, and stirred. Cooking was therapeutic, and her emotions were running so hot and heavy she had to keep her hands occupied. In short order, she shoved two round pans full of batter into the oven.

The women chatted as Grace cleaned the kitchen, absorbing every story about Jake that Emily seemed happy to share. The tales acted as a balm on her wounded heart.

"You know, he looks like you," Emily said. "Your eyes. Your nose, too. You look like family." Jumping off the barstool, she went to Grace and gave her a hug, which took her entirely by surprise. "Jake always wanted a family. He told me the baby and I were his family, but I could tell he was sad. Now you're here."

Jake always wanted a family.

Grace's blinked against threatening tears. "His brother's here too," she barely squeaked out.

"Brother? Jake has a brother, too?"

"Matthew." The name was nothing but a whisper.

"What did I say? I didn't mean to make you cry." Emily's lip quivered for a moment, and then she began to weep.

Grace pulled Emily back into her arms. "I–it's not your fault. I'm just happy to finally find Jake. I've been searching for so, so long. Will he be home soon?"

Emily nodded against her shoulder.

Jake. After all the long years, she'd finally be face-to-face with him.

Grace glanced up to see a short, round man waddling into the kitchen, pressing the ends of his handlebar moustache between his fingertips. He stopped and stared at the two women.

"Who died?" he asked.

"Daddy!" Emily squealed, pulling herself away from Grace. "This is Jake's sister. He has a sister. And a brother."

The man rubbed the moustache again, seeming to consider Grace for several moments. The wisdom in his eyes caused a moment of fear before she reminded herself that no one could see into her soul.

"Jake's lived at Twin Springs long as I can remember," the man commented. "Don't recollect any mention of kin."

"He doesn't know about me. I mean, about *us*." Thoughts were pinwheels spinning as she tried to find a way to explain everything to the man's satisfaction. "Matthew and I are related through Jake's birth mother."

"You're his sister?"

She nodded.

His expression softened, and he extended his hand. "I'm William Spencer. Folks 'round here call me Will." His laughter was as infectious as his daughter's. As if his train of thought came to an abrupt halt, he sniffed. "What exactly is that heavenly smell? Sure cain't be Emily's cooking." His wink at his daughter marked the teasing as affection.

Using the ends of her apron, Grace lifted the cake pans from the stove to see how the batter was doing. "A birthday cake. For you, Will."

"Well, let me grab the good whiskey, and we'll go into the saloon and celebrate."

***

Grace's laughter brought a smile to Adam's face.

He'd kept his distance, giving her room and waiting for her to decide how to approach Jake. The boy had a kind heart, but he'd suffered so much after losing his parents. Knowing there had been a sister out there all along might not have set well. Jake had been known to get riled from time to time, and Adam didn't want Grace to be on the receiving end of his temper.

Heading to the Four Aces to be sure things were going well, he'd been waylaid by the odious town marshal. The man gossiped more than any of the town's old busybodies, and he'd kept Adam standing there talking about nothing of importance long enough to make him worry about what was happening to Grace.

After extracting himself from the ridiculous conversation, Adam hurried back to the saloon. Grace's melodious laughter ended his worries and drew him like a siren's song. Pushing open the swinging doors, he smiled when he saw the happy little group.

Emily and Will sat at one of the round tables, talking away while Grace smoothed white icing over a two-tiered cake, wielding the butter knife much like a conductor waving a baton at a grand concert. She smiled, seemingly content to listen to the chatter around her. When Will stuck a finger into the bowl of icing, she gave him a playful swat.

Jake was nowhere to be seen. If only he could be as accepting of Grace as Will and Emily obviously were.

Adam knew better. Jake held tight to the resentment of his childhood. This road wouldn't be easy for her to travel.

"Looks as though I'm in time for dessert." He threw her a smile as he doffed his hat.

She glanced up from the cake, her eyes sparkling.

God, he loved the way her face lit up when she was happy, shining as bright as summer sunshine.

"Adam Morgan." Will gave the table a hard slap with his palm. "Well, well, well. You're a sight for sore eyes. Ain't seen you in at least a pair of weeks."

"Been busy, Will. Had a mighty sick woman on my hands."

He winked at Grace, whose cheeks flushed in response.

Will's gaze shifted from Adam to Grace and back again. "You mean our Grace? She's been sick?"

"She's been staying with you?" Emily asked.

"Yep. Had a wicked fever I nursed her through."

Their curiosity was palpable as they looked at each other and then at Grace.

"How'd she end up at the ranch?" Will asked.

"Stumbled onto my spread, searching for Jake. Couldn't bring her into town 'til I got her back on her feet."

Will's knowing eyes—used often to size up people—focused hard on Grace.

She seemed oblivious as she finished icing the cake.

"Been staying out at the Twin Springs, has she?" He twirled the ends of his moustache. "Folks gonna talk."

Her head snapped up. "I don't give a rap what anyone says. I'm here to see Jake, then I'm moving on. Now if you'll all excuse me, I have some dishes to wash." She picked up the empty bowl and marched into the kitchen, head held high.

"Em?" Will asked. "Can I have a moment alone with Adam?"

Hoisting herself out of the chair, Emily accepted her father's helping hand. "I'll keep her busy for a few minutes."

She shuffled after Grace into the kitchen.

"What's the real story with this woman, Adam?" Will asked the moment Emily was out of earshot. "Hate to think she's here to stir up trouble for my son-in-law."

"Grace won't cause you any grief. She's exactly what she says she is. She's been tracking Jake for a long time. I think she carries a burden of guilt for having left him at the orphanage when their mama died."

"That's what she told you?" Will's teasing tone wasn't a surprise. "Opened up like that, did she?"

"Never that plainly."

"Then how do you know she's what she says she is—that she and this Matthew are Jake's kin?"

"She almost died trying to find him. By the time she made it to the ranch, she was burning with fever."

Trying to convince his friend that Grace was genuine came easy. Yes, there was more for her to share. Much more. But her concern for Jake appeared sincere.

"What harm can it do to tell the boy he's got a couple of relatives? Let him decide what he wants to do about it."

Grace swallowed her anger that she and Adam were targets of gossip. She came back into the saloon, carrying forks and plates as Emily followed in her wake. The men stopped talking midsentence. She wasn't sure what *that* meant but figured Will was trying to ferret out her motives. Adam would set the man straight and convince him she had nothing in mind but meeting Jake.

She trusted Adam.

That revelation came as a shock—enough of a surprise she got a little dizzy.

With the exception of Matthew, she'd never trusted *anyone* before. Especially men. Trust got a person hurt. Not even family could be totally depended upon to do the right thing. Her father had taught her that lesson well. Matthew was the only exception.

But she trusted Adam.

And that frightened the hell out of her.

"Who wants cake?" She tried to keep her inward alarm from tainting her tone.

If she hadn't set the plates down, she would've dropped them when she saw the silhouette of a man standing between the swinging doors, holding them open as he took in the scene.

Jake.

He looked so much like Matthew at that age he took her breath away. She was elated to see none of Stephen in his face.

"Finally," she whispered.

"Jake!" Emily lumbered over to his side.

He wrapped a protective arm around her shoulder.

She leaned her head against his chest. "You won't believe who's here to see you, sugar."

The couple strode into the bar, and he pulled out a chair for his wife. She took a seat and smiled up at him.

Then she turned her face to smile at Grace. "This is your sister, Grace Riley. You have a sister. Isn't that wonderful?"

He whirled to face her, a fierce scowl fixed on his hard mouth. "Sister? What do you mean *sister?*"

Judging from his reaction, finding out he had a relative was unwelcome. Not that she blamed him, especially after all Adam had told her about Jake's childhood.

His frown deepened as he narrowed his eyes at her. "Don't know what kind of cruel game you're playing, lady, but I ain't got a sister."

"Easy there, son," Adam said. "Give her a chance to explain."

"I ain't got a sister," he insisted, turning that glare on Adam. "I don't know who the hell she be. Don't rightly care. But she ain't my *sister.*"

Grace swallowed her hurt at her unrealistic hope he'd accept her without a struggle and bravely stepped toward him. Her palms were moist as she clenched her hands into fists.

There was nothing to do but face this head on, despite her fears. "I *am* your sister, Jake. Our brother Matthew is here too. We came to find you."

The glower he shot at her wounded like a knife in the belly. "If you're family, where were you when they took me to that damned orphanage in Denver?"

She shook her head, feeling the sharp sting of guilt she knew would never leave. "I didn't know about what happened to your adopted parents. I didn't know about the orphanage, either. If I had, I would've come for you. I lost track of you after the Curtis family adopted you. I–I didn't think you'd want to know about me—that you'd be happier with your new family."

His face flushed red. "If Adam hadn't taken me in, I'd still be living on the streets, stealing to survive. You ever eat garbage, lady?"

"I'm so sorry, Jake. I truly am." She wiped away a stray tear with the back of her hand. God help her, she wanted to run to Adam and beg him to make this right.

No one can ever make this right.

"Please, please forgive me," she begged. "I just want to get to know you. Please, Jake. I'm your sister."

"Lady, you spill that lie one more time, and woman or not, I'm gonna knock your teeth out."

Adam stepped between them. He put a steadying hand on her

shoulder, and she drew strength from the comforting gesture. "Calm down, Jake. Hear the lady out."

"Heard all I intend to." He stomped across the bar, sawdust jumping with each heavy step until he reached the staircase. "Emily? You coming?"

"I'll be up shortly, sugar."

A few moments later, the slamming of a door echoed from the second story.

Emily spoke first, giving Grace a hesitant smile. "He doesn't mean it, Grace. You were such a surprise, and this is just…hard on him."

Afraid she'd burst into tears if a single word escaped her lips, Grace simply nodded.

"It'll take some time for him to accept this," Adam added, squeezing her shoulder. "He'll come 'round."

Her broken heart told her otherwise.

"I reckon I've got a good solution to all of our problems," Will declared with a sly grin.

Pulling out a chair for Grace, Adam helped her take a seat. Having known Will for going on twenty years, he was well aware of the mischief the man liked to make. While most of his plots and plans usually turned out well in the end, they'd been known to cause some worry for more than a few people. From that grin, Adam just might be the one who found himself inconvenienced.

He sat down next to her and covered one of the hands she'd pressed to the table with his own. "Since this solution of yours obviously involves us, care to enlighten everyone?"

"Jake needs time to get used to the notion of having a sister. If she's staying out at your ranch, he won't get a chance to know her."

Adam sure didn't appreciate the direction this conversation was heading. "Drop the other boot, Will. You're cooking up a scheme."

"Grace should stay here for a spell. Give her a chance to get to know her brother."

"It'll stop any gossip about her staying out at the Twin Springs, her being healthy now and all," Emily added with a smile, clearly warming to her father's plan. "There's an empty bedroom on the second floor. Grace can bed down there."

"No," Adam replied, not even giving the plan any real consideration. He squeezed her small hand tightly before realizing he might be hurting her. But damn, he didn't like this idea. Not one bit. "Grace is coming home with me. We've got a cattle drive coming soon."

"I appreciate the offer, Will," Grace said. "But I can't take your charity." She glanced to Adam. "I can't take *your* charity, either. You don't need me on that drive." A shuddering sigh escaped her lips as she dragged her hand from under his and dropped it in her lap. "I reckon it's best if Matthew and I head out now. We could still catch up with a long drive we heard about if we leave tomorrow."

"You're not leaving, Gracie." Adam's tone was strained. "Not after you've come so far. Give the boy some time. He'll come 'round."

"Never said I'd be givin' you charity," Will added. "Nope. No free rides at the Four Aces." A huge grin made his gold tooth twinkle in the light. "What exactly can you do, Grace?"

"She can cook," Emily said with an enthusiastic nod. "And with the baby coming, I won't be able to anymore."

"Damn fine blessing that is," her father replied. "Give you room and board if you'll stay and cook, Grace. Maybe give Emily a hand getting things ready for the baby and helpin' her after my grandbaby's born."

"Absolutely not." Adam had no intention of allowing Grace to stay at the Four Aces. While he liked and trusted Will, he couldn't shake the feeling that he needed to protect this woman, even from the hostility of her own brother. Once the customers started pouring into the bar and got even a glimpse of her, she'd have ten offers of marriage within a heartbeat.

Hell no, she wasn't staying in town. Not without him.

"Adam," Grace said in that calm voice he'd heard her use whenever she was trying to bend Matthew to her will, "you've been so kind, but—"

"You're not staying here, Gracie."

"Don't you see? I *need* to do this. It isn't fair for me to take and take and never give. I can work for Will. I can earn my way in the world. I've been taking care of myself since I was fifteen. Besides, in a few weeks, I'll be gone."

He scrubbed his hand across the back of his neck. There were no logical reasons he could throw at her to force her to stay at Twin Springs. Yet he simply couldn't find it in himself to agree with her decision.

This woman was a riddle that he was committed to solving. He enjoyed her company, and the longer he spent with her, the more he saw that she needed him.

Even more, he was beginning to think that he needed her as well. "We'll talk about this at supper."

"Adam..."

"After supper. We'll talk then. Now, it's time to head home."

Chapter Seven

Grace handed the plate to Matthew without taking a biscuit.

Her appetite was gone, and anything she ate would be a lump in her nervous stomach that churned more each time she remembered Jake's angry expression, the hateful tone of his voice. Not that she blamed him. God only knew how he'd react if he ever learned the whole truth.

"He shouldn't have shouted at you." Matthew passed the plate of remaining biscuits back to Grace—a silent scolding for her not eating much. "You did right by that boy. You gave him a family instead of a childhood spent in the back of a wagon with nothing but roughneck cowboys to teach him about life."

"He didn't really shout," she said. "He was just…upset. I can't imagine what's going through his mind, finding out he's got kin after all this time."

Adam took the plate from her, dropped a biscuit on his own, and passed the dwindling supply to Ty. "Shock or not, he was rude. I don't want you staying there. You shouldn't have to face that anger every morning 'til he accepts the truth. You've gotta give him some time."

Matthew furrowed his brow. "Staying? What do you mean *staying?*"

From the time he'd been a child, they'd always been together. He'd sacrificed so much to help her, spending years working cattle drives to keep her away from Stephen Shay as that devil stalked her as though he were a lawman searching for a criminal with a hefty bounty on his head. He deserved a life of his own, and being at Twin Springs, he might have finally found that life—especially if the feelings between him and Victoria could be nurtured until they fully bloomed.

Just another reason to be moving on.

Her mind was set. "I've been offered a job as a cook, and I intend to take it."

"Where? At that–that saloon?" Matthew asked. "You're not working in a saloon, Grace. It's not proper."

"Oh, spare me." She rolled her eyes as she grasped his meaning. "I've worked alone with men my whole life. I've got no reputation to protect."

He still frowned. "Why can't you stay at the ranch? I can keep an eye on you here."

Adam grunted and nodded.

Now wasn't the time to remind Matthew that the reason he needed to look out for her had died. "Because I can't keep imposing on Adam and Victoria."

"You're not imposing, Grace," Victoria said, taking the last biscuit.

Adam grunted again.

He was good and mad, and she knew she should be trying to soothe him. He'd been so kind. The man saved her life, but that wasn't reason enough to stay on at Twin Springs. She would ruin his good name among the townsfolk, and she didn't want the law showing up on his doorstep to arrest her for murder.

Every night she prayed to God for forgiveness for all she'd done, and every night she became more certain she was destined to be alone as penance for her sins.

Her already shaky composure vanished like a frightened wren. She would've pushed her plate away and fled upstairs to sob into her pillow but resorted to moving food around with her fork. Hopefully nobody noticed she was on the verge of tears at the notion of Adam ever knowing what she'd done. She belonged in jail not on a beautiful ranch with a man so wonderful that thinking about him made her heart ache.

"What's wrong?" Adam asked.

Grace hated how easily he could read her. No wonder he took all the matches in the kitty whenever they played cards. "I'm fine."

"You don't look fine."

She shrugged and swallowed hard. "Despite your kind offer, I *am* imposing. I'm going to White Pines tomorrow. I can't keep accepting your charity."

"I'm not offering charity. You can earn your keep just as easily at the Twin Springs as you can at the Four Aces. Daisy's gone. I need a cook and housekeeper."

"You've got Victoria to cook for you until Daisy gets back."

"Daisy might not come back, and what about the cattle drive?"

"She'll come back. She loves you and Victoria. And we both know you don't need me on that drive."

Matthew busied himself with shoveling food into his mouth, but he watched them both, hardly blinking.

Victoria shot him the same scowl she used every time they ate to point out that his table manners were less than impeccable.

Grace had tried hard to teach him to eat more refined, but when a body grew up fighting a bunch of hungry cowboys to get enough to fill his belly, manners weren't all that important.

With a shake of her head, Victoria turned her attention back to Grace. "I can't cook as well as you do. I'd miss your company, too. Please stay."

"Oh, Victoria. I thank you for that, but I need to go. I wish I could explain it so you'd understand. I have to move on."

Adam stood up and carried his empty plate to the sink. He dropped it hard enough it shattered.

His show of temper should've made her uneasy. Every time cowboys got too unruly, she retreated to the chuckwagon to wait out the storm, hoping none of them ended up beaten up enough to need her to stitch up a wound.

Yet that urge to run for safety wasn't there.

He gawked at her barely touched plate of food. "Since it appears you're done eating, we're going for a walk."

Uncharacteristically sarcastic, he indicated the door with a flourish of his hand. Then he grabbed her shawl from one of the pegs and held it open, waiting for her to join him.

Avoiding him wouldn't help, and a walk would give them some privacy. Her heart was heavy as she thought of all the things that might have been between them. If only she was somebody else. If only they'd met in another place or another time. If only she hadn't done all she'd done.

It didn't matter if she wanted to stay. She wouldn't bring shame to Adam's doorstep. No, there was no other choice for her than to run as soon as she had enough money.

As Matthew said, that was what she did best.

For the first time in her life, the notion of leaving made her heart as fragile as glass. She'd always been willing to go on another cattle drive or hire on another chuckwagon. Disappearing came easy. She'd met and fed almost every cowboy in the West.

Yet not once did the notion of leaving anyone cause her pain.

As much as she hurt at the mere thought of walking away from Adam, actually doing so might kill her. He was a part of her now, buried deep in her heart, and losing him would be akin to having one of her limbs ripped from her body.

Grace let Adam wrap the shawl around her shoulders and lead the way out of the house. As they walked down the long road, she didn't resist when he took her hand in his, instead wanting the warmth and comfort he provided to seep into her veins.

They strolled along, quiet and contemplative until they reached the road to White Pines—the place they'd shared the incredible kiss that had replayed in her mind a million times. Hard as it was to acknowledge, Grace wanted him. Simply remembering his words— remembering that he wanted her as well—was almost enough to make her change her mind and stay on the ranch.

And do what?

Pass a few weeks together as if the rest of the world didn't exist?

Become his lover?

Sweet merciful Lord, *that* was tempting. Even her fear of the physical act of mating couldn't keep Adam out of her thoughts. Every time he touched her, he burned a little more of that fear away until nothing was left but the gnawing emptiness inside her that only he could fill.

But they could never be. She couldn't take Adam as a lover. She couldn't hide out on the ranch, wishing the rest of the world would simply disappear.

She couldn't make this real.

At the end of the road, he turned her to face him, just as he had the night before. "I don't want you to leave."

His familiar words made fresh tears sting her eyes. "Please don't make this harder than it is."

"Damn right, I'm gonna make it hard. I plan to make it impossible. I don't—"

Grace placed her fingertips gently against his lips. "Please listen for a second." She shyly pulled her fingers back. "I've decided something, and I want you to hear it."

Adam took her hand in his again.

"I have to stay in town, but I'm not leaving right away. I'm going to stay here. In White Pines. At least 'til things are right between Jake and I."

The smile on his face told her he still didn't understand. She had to set him straight, no matter how much it hurt.

"I'm living at the Four Aces, Adam. I won't bring gossip down on your good name."

"Grace..."

"We both know what will happen if I stay."

"What exactly will happen? What has you so afraid?"

"I'll let you take me to your bed."

He looked properly shocked—an appropriate reaction because so was she.

While the notion had been perpetually in her thoughts, she never imagined she'd have the courage to say it aloud. She found that when she was with him, all the walls she'd constructed around her mind—and her heart—fell away, crumbling to dust. All she wanted was for him to teach her that when a man and woman came together, it could be an act of affection rather than violence.

"Say something," she blurted out, unable to bear the stilted silence a moment longer.

He grinned, his teeth gleaming white in the moonlight. "Thank you. That's probably the nicest thing anybody's ever said to me."

A laugh bubbled out of her.

God, how Adam loved to hear her laughter. His smile quickly faded. She wanted to leave him. Now that he'd found someone he could love, she was ready to walk away.

But why?

And how could he force her to stay?

Force her.

That was the problem. He was forcing his wants on a woman who'd clearly been hurt before. While he still hadn't sorted the whole story out, relying mostly on nightmarish mutterings and tidbits of information that both Grace and Matthew dropped when their guards were down, he saw the bigger picture. Someone had forced her to run her whole life. That man had hurt her, both in body and in mind. No wonder she had a hard time opening up.

Adam couldn't *force* her to stay. While his feelings for Grace were deeper and stronger than their short time together should have cultivated, they were there nonetheless. And those feelings told him she would someday belong to him.

Now, she needed to come to the same conclusion on her own.

Taking her to the Four Aces and leaving her there would be agony. He couldn't protect her. He couldn't shelter her so none of the bad things that had happened would repeat. He couldn't keep other men away from her.

It was time to draw on some of that eternal patience everyone claimed he possessed. He was going to have to let Grace go to one day bring her back. "You win, darlin'."

"I win?"

"I'll take you to town tomorrow. You can stay at the Four Aces and get to know Jake. For now. But I'll give you fair warning."

She cocked her head. "Fair warning?"

"One day soon, I'm bringing you back home with me." He tugged her into her arms. "For good." His mouth covered hers.

She tasted sweet, and he didn't have to coax her this time when he deepened the kiss. She opened her lips with a gentle nudge, and damn if her tongue wasn't every bit as wild as his.

His heartbeat echoed in his head, loud and steady. Despite his best intentions, he couldn't help but press his palms against her backside, the one he'd admired far too often. As her arms slipped around his neck, he pulled her hips hard against his, letting her feel his arousal.

For a brief moment, she stiffened. His tongue stroked across hers, letting her know this was good. This wasn't a man forcing his will on a woman. This was something they shared because they belonged to each other. Whatever happened between them was right, and he'd never hurt her or let anyone else hurt her, either.

He drew her closer, and she melted against him. His lips left hers as he nuzzled his face against her slender neck. She smelled like vanilla and her skin was impossibly soft. He kissed his way to her ear, where he traced the delicate edges with his tongue. She shuddered and moved her hips restlessly against his erection.

If he didn't slow down, this interlude was going to get out of hand. One more hard kiss and he eased away, putting a bit of space between their bodies. She shivered, so he reached out to rearrange her disheveled shawl.

Her gaze dropped to the ground, and even in the dim light of the moon, he could see the flush on her cheeks. "You make me forget myself."

Since she wasn't watching him, he let a satisfied grin cross his lips. "Oh, darlin', you make me forget myself too."

The corners of her lips twitched into a hesitant grin, and her eyes rose to meet his. "You'll take me to town tomorrow?"

He gave her a thick sigh and a curt nod.

Taking her hand into his, he was pleased that she fell into step beside him.

Back at the ranch house, Matthew was waiting for them, frowning like a disapproving chaperone as he sat on a porch step and chewed on a piece of hay.

Adam opened the door for her, gave her one quick kiss, and let her go inside. He shut the door, ready to go check the livestock in the barn.

Even from a distance, Matthew had seen their heated embrace, although he'd quickly glanced away to give them some privacy. While he wanted Grace to be happy, he felt that as her brother, he needed to know Adam's intentions. "She's fragile."

Adam stopped and turned back with an incredulous stare. "Fragile? You referring to Grace? The same woman who handles dozens of rowdy cowboys on every long drive?"

"I know she's mighty stubborn and a bit sassy, but deep down, she's as delicate as a china doll. I'd hate for anyone to hurt her."

"You're saying this to me because...?"

"Because for the first time in her life, she cares for a man. That means you could hurt her more than anyone else ever did."

A quick nod came in reply before Adam went to the barn, leaving Matthew to his thoughts.

Those thoughts were abruptly interrupted as Victoria came marching from the back of the bunkhouse.

She tried to skirt around him to go up the stairs, but he jumped to his feet, spit out the hay, and put himself in her path. "Howdy."

"Good evening."

His tongue felt too thick to move. He had to say something because she reached for the door again and he wasn't about to lose her now that she was so close. "How–how you doin'?"

"I'm very well, thank you. I need to talk to Grace. If you'll excuse me..."

He moved with her when she stepped to one side. "It's a right pretty night."

She took a quick step back. "It–it is?"

The catch in her voice filled him with confidence, telling him that she was affected by his presence. "Yes, ma'am. Would be a pity to go inside and not enjoy it."

"It would?"

"Don't suppose you'd care for taking a walk?" He inclined his head to the road Adam and Grace had recently traveled.

Victoria was such a mystery. Not that he'd been around women enough to have even a small understanding of how their minds worked. He had no idea what thoughts were flying through that busy brain of hers, but her expression kept changing. When those emotions settled, she stared back at him with a bit of apprehension in her eyes.

"Come on, Victoria." He extended his elbow. "Walk with me. I promise not to bite."

A quick smile warmed him. "O–okay. I'll walk with you. For a spell." She strode toward the road, avoiding his offered arm and acting as though she wanted to get to the end of the road as fast as her legs could carry her.

He dropped his elbow and matched her stride for stride. "Why are we in such a hurry?"

She slowed her steps until their frantic march turned into an easy stroll.

The farther they moved away from the house, the more he relaxed. His world was now the gentle chirps of crickets, the light of the moon streaming through the trees, and the sway of her slender hips. Holding his breath, he reached out to hold her hand.

Her response was to glance down and smile. That beautiful grin made his heart skip a quick beat.

When the road to the ranch house met the road to town, Matthew stopped, turning her to face him. He reached out to take her other hand.

Everything about her branded on his brain. Long, slender fingers that were perfect entwined with his. Dark hair that shimmered in the moonlight. Skin as white as alabaster. She smelled of roses.

She shyly stared at the ground, so timid compared to her normal feisty personality. Her teeth tugged on her bottom lip. He almost said something to get her riled up to see that spark of life he loved so much.

Victoria glanced up at him. "Shouldn't we head back now?"

He shook his head, unable to get even a single word out. He stared at her mouth, totally lost in the thought of how she would taste and trying to build up the courage to find out. Before he could make a move, she shocked the hell out of him by rising to tiptoes and pressing a quick kiss to his lips. Then she dropped her gaze.

"Please pardon me," she whispered. "I–I don't know what came over me."

"Maybe it's the moonlight. Tends to make a person a bit loco from time to time." Had he not been holding her hands in his, he would have given himself a good sound slap for being an imbecile.

"'Swear not by the moon, the inconstant moon.'"

The familiar words were said so softly, he almost missed them. "You've read *Romeo and Juliet*?"

Her eyes flew wide as she searched his face. "You've heard of Shakespeare?"

He probably should have been offended. While he might have spent most of his life on the back of a horse, he wasn't ignorant. A frown bowed his mouth.

"I–I didn't mean—"

"It's fine, Victoria. I know you didn't intend insult."

"I truly didn't. I'd do anything to make it right."

"Anything?"

She nodded and smiled.

"Kiss me again."

"I–I couldn't."

It was hard not to grin at her embarrassment, but women tended to take offense to teasing. They had overly tender feelings that were easily bruised.

"Then may I kiss you?" he asked.

"Oh, yes," she replied, sounding a bit breathless.

Trying not to feel awkward, he slipped his arms around her waist. She felt so right pressed up against him, although she had to stand on tiptoe again to reach his face.

Such a tiny woman...

Her sweet breath brushed his chin as he lowered his head to meet her halfway. Suddenly, he was drowning in the feel of her, the flowery scent of her skin intoxicating him akin to strong whiskey.

His mouth covered hers, and not for some chaste kiss like the one she'd given him. Matthew let Victoria feel the desire that had been eating away at him from the moment he'd laid eyes on her.

Her response came swiftly and passionately as she wrapped her arms around his neck and thoroughly kissed him back.

He growled and deepened the incredible kiss by teasing her lips until she parted them, then he slipped his tongue into her warm mouth, capturing her surprised gasp. This woman had never been properly kissed before. He wasn't about to let her walk away without learning how a real kiss could make her burn.

She moaned, mimicking the slide of his tongue over hers. He couldn't get enough of her, lifting her clean off her feet. Her hands trembled as she laced her fingers through his hair, knocking his hat from his head.

"Oh, Matthew," she purred before kissing across his cheek to his ear. "I do like the way you kiss."

The warm breath from her whispered words sent fire racing straight to his groin.

Never in his life had he thought about anything pertaining to his future beyond him and Grace owning a small ranch of their own. As he cradled Victoria's small, soft body against his, the future was *all* he could think about.

Victoria standing at the door of a small cabin, smiling as he returned from his chores. Victoria lying naked on a bed, arms open in invitation. Victoria with a gently rounding belly as she carried his child.

The images brought about sobering reality that hit him with the intensity of a bucket of ice water. He'd forgotten who she was— an innocent. He'd forgotten what she was—the only daughter of a wealthy ranch owner. And he'd forgotten that he was nothing but a dirt-poor cowboy who was reaching far too high.

He let go of her.

Victoria stumbled back a couple of steps. The confusion in her eyes pierced his heart, but he only bent over to grab his hat and put it back on.

"Matthew? What—"

"We need to get back."

"But—"

"*Now*, Victoria." This time, he didn't even offer her his arm.

Her lip quivered as she clenched her hands at her sides.

He'd hurt her.

"Victoria..." He reached for her arm. "Just listen."

She slapped his hand away. "Don't touch me! Don't you *ever* touch me again!" She hiked up her skirts and sprinted for the ranch house.

When he followed, she picked up the pace.

Damn, but she was a fast little vixen. He wanted to catch her, to apologize, to set her straight, but she was already mounting the stairs before he could reach her.

She hurried inside, slamming the door behind her.

He stopped, trying to catch his breath. He was a fool, the humiliation made worse when Adam came out of the barn.

"Trouble?" he asked as he walked over. "She looked a mite upset."

"We had a disagreement. That's all."

Shifting his gaze from the door to Matthew and back again, Adam frowned. "Looks to be more than a *disagreement*."

Matthew shrugged, wishing the awkward conversation would end. "She's fragile."

Déjà vu. "Are we talking about the same woman who chased Ty around the yard with a broom for forgetting to take off his muddy boots?"

"Victoria's mighty stubborn and a bit sassy, but deep down, she's as delicate as a china doll. I'd hate to see someone hurt her."

He hated having his own words turned back on him, even if Adam was right. "I'd hate for someone to hurt her too."

"Are your intentions honorable?"

Honorable?

What was honorable about wanting to marry a woman when he couldn't afford the kind of life to which she was accustomed? All he had to give was his word.

"I'll leave her be, Adam. I won't hurt her again."

Chapter Eight

"You sure you want to stay?" Adam asked for what seemed like the thousandth time since Grace had told him she was moving to the Four Aces.

Holding tight to her patience, she reassured him again. "It'll be fine. I need to spend time with Jake. And I–I need to take care of myself."

Her tone sounded frightened, even to her own ears. She had to do this, so she'd just have to put some starch in her spine and face Jake and his hostility, hoping someday he'd forgive her. At least for what she'd share about the past.

What right did she have to expect his forgiveness? God knew she'd never forgiven herself.

The rest of the late afternoon ride passed in almost unbearable quiet. Victoria sat next to Grace, which forced her to push closer to Adam, making her thigh brush his with each bump. Matthew rode his stallion, setting his pace to match the speed of the wagon. Four people traveled in close enough proximity they could have enjoyed a pleasant conversation. Instead, nothing passed between them except furtive glances.

Every so often, she caught Victoria looking over to Matthew. Just as often, she saw him staring at her. Something had clearly happened between them, but it wasn't her place to ask. A person who'd made as many mistakes as she had shouldn't hand out advice.

Adam stared at the road ahead almost as if he was purposefully trying to avoid her. Was he so angry he couldn't even force himself to speak?

He wasn't the kind of man to play games. No, he obviously had something important on his mind.

Was he worried about her? Was that why he repeatedly asked whether she really meant to stay with Will? Or was he pleased to be rid of her?

Adam wouldn't lie to her. Nor could he hide his feelings when he'd kissed her. There was something important happening between them, and now she needed to decide exactly how far she would let that road take her.

She sighed in relief when the town came into view.

He looked at her, a frown fixed on his handsome face. "You're really staying?"

Grace wanted to appease him, to put her hands against his cheeks and kiss him long and deep and tell him all she felt.

But she couldn't. "Yes, I'm really staying."

The wagon ground to a stop in front of the saloon. After he climbed down, Adam lifted her out of the wagon. Although she was on her feet, he left his hands on her waist.

"I'll be fine, Adam."

His lips thinned to a grim line. "I don't like this, Gracie. There's no one to look after you here."

Matthew nodded as he reached into the back of the wagon to lift out the small trunk, ignoring Victoria who was clearly waiting for him to help her out of the wagon. "I don't like this, either, Grace."

She shot her brother a frown, both for his bad manners and his words. "There's no threat here." *Not anymore.* Her gaze settled on the trunk Adam had given her. "I shouldn't take those clothes. They belonged to your wife. Surely, Victoria will want to—"

His lips brushed an interrupting kiss on her cheek. "We've had this argument already. I won. Remember?"

She chuckled as he turned her loose and went to help his daughter out of the wagon. "I remember. Thank you for being so generous."

Will pulled the front swinging doors open as she reached them. "My new cook is finally here! Had to choke down Emily's lunch, and—" He glanced over his shoulder. "—I sure as hell don't wanna choke down her supper, too."

Matthew followed her into the saloon. "Where do you want Grace's trunk?"

"Up the stairs, second door," Will replied as Adam and Victoria came into the saloon.

"I think I'll go up and get settled in." Grace headed toward her new home.

"I'll give you a hand." Victoria followed her to the staircase.

Adam watched Grace mount the steps. She turned back to glance at him. Everything in him wanted to go to her, throw her over his shoulder like a sack of grain, and carry her right back to the wagon.

Instead, he sighed and nodded.

She nodded back before she retreated down the hallway.

He turned to Will. "I need you to watch over her. I don't like leaving her here."

"I'll be keepin' an eye on her." Will shifted his gaze from Adam to the empty stairway and back again. Stroking his handlebar moustache, he gave him a smile. "You got intentions for that filly?"

"I've got *lots* of intentions. She just doesn't accept all of 'em yet."

"You'll do right by her, Adam?"

"Why the sudden concern?"

"Being she's Jake's sister, I'm kin. I've a need to watch over her well-being."

Matthew came stomping down the upstairs hallway, turned back and shouted, "Yes, your majesty!" A door slammed as he marched down the stairs. As he passed Adam and Will, he grumbled, "That woman will be the death of me."

"'But love is blind, and lovers cannot see,'" Adam quoted after Matthew walked by.

Will arched a brow. "That be Jake's brother?"

"Yep. Matthew Riley."

"He's taken with Victoria?"

"Oh, yeah. And she's every bit as taken with him."

"Weddin'?"

Adam shrugged. "Both are a bit stubborn, so it might take them some time to figure things out." His gaze moved to the stairs when Grace descended. "Might take Grace some time to figure things out too. I'm keepin' you to your promise to watch out for her."

"Yes, siree, Adam. I'll make sure there's ain't no trouble from the customers."

Will's words made Adam's gut twist into a painful knot. Leaving Grace here was going to mean every unattached male in the territory would be coming to get an eyeful of the new woman. "Keep her out of the saloon when you've got customers—just like you do Emily."

"Sounding a bit possessive, ain't you?"

"*Very* possessive." He reached out to take Grace's hand when she came to stand beside him. "You all settled in, darlin'?"

"All settled in. I should go start supper." There was a touch of fear in her brown eyes. "Are–are you leaving now?"

"Not yet. I've got some business in town."

Will slapped Adam's back. "Stay to supper?"

"I do believe I will."

***

Jake and Emily hadn't come to eat when Grace served dinner to Will, Adam, Victoria, and Matthew. Not that Adam was surprised. The stubborn streak in Jake ran a mile wide, but the crestfallen look on Grace's face had set Adam's anger building. The least the boy could do was listen to Grace's side of the story.

As he helped her with the dishes, she kept her thoughts to herself. He wanted to ask her what was flying through that far too clever brain of hers, but she seemed content to pass the short time they had left together in quiet. How he would ever be able to get in that wagon and drive away remained a mystery.

He caught Jake's voice out in the saloon. "Grace, will you excuse me a moment?"

"You're leaving? You're heading home now?" Her eyes were wide.

He kissed her forehead. "Not yet, darlin'. Just need to talk to someone for a minute. How 'bout we take one last walk after that?"

"I'd like that." She nodded at the sink. "I'll meet you out front when this chore's done."

Adam went to find Jake. The boy was pouring whiskey and talking to two cowboys. The saloon had grown crowded while they ate, souring his mood.

Jake glanced up, locked gazes with Adam, and nodded. A few moments later, he joined him at the end of the bar.

"Jake, I'm wanting a word with you."

"Sir?"

"We need to talk about Grace."

Jake's mouth fell into a fierce frown. "She's gonna stay in the room next to Em and me. Can't say I'm liking *that* much. Can't you take her back to the Twin Springs?"

"You need to give her a chance."

"Don't wanna."

This wasn't going to be easy, not that Adam had expected Jake to welcome Grace with open arms. "Keep an open mind, son. Think about this from her point of view. She was only fifteen when you were born."

"On her birthday."

"Who told you that?"

"Matthew. Came to talk to me after you and Grace left yesterday. Wanted to 'set me straight,' so he said. Can't blame him for what happened, though. He was only a little boy when she tossed me away like some runt puppy."

"She tried to do right by you, Jake."

The young man sighed. "I guess it was my fault our mama died. Left her and Matthew alone as much as it did me. Still... Couldn't she have raised me? She didn't send Matthew away."

"He was old enough to sit a horse and help on cattle drives."

"Why'd she have to up and give me away?"

"How could she have kept you? She didn't have any money. Had to hire herself to cattle drives to earn enough to eat. Might've been different if she were your mother. She might've seen the responsibility differently. But she was a girl with two younger brothers to look after. She did what she thought was best. Was she supposed to care for a newborn while she slung chow for hungry cowboys and watched after Matthew?"

Jake dropped his gaze to the bar he rubbed with a towel as if trying to remove some spill that wasn't there. "No, I 'spose not. But——"

"You're a smart young man. You know she doesn't deserve your hate. She didn't murder your parents. There's no way she could have predicted that. She gave you a family she hoped would make you happy and provide you a home."

After a few moments of turning it over in his mind, Jake shrugged. "Emily likes her. She needs a woman to be close at hand, 'specially with the little one on the way. Grace seems...kind."

It was more of a concession than Adam had expected, considering all Jake had gone through. "You'll give her a chance?"

"I'll try."

"You'll help Will keep an eye on her?"

That got his attention as Jake lifted his gaze to Adam's. "She in some kind of trouble? Don't want no trouble around Em and the baby."

"No trouble. She has nightmares. Someone hurt her bad. Still haunts her."

A lopsided grin lit Jake's face. "Has nightmares, does she? You're sharing a bed with her then? Aren't you both a mite...*old* for that?"

Adam chuckled, despite himself. "No, son. I haven't had that particular pleasure yet, nor would I brag about it if I had. I've slept in a rocking chair in her room. And as for my overly *advanced* age, I can still whoop your sorry behind if I have to. I'd keep that in mind if you're thinking about giving Grace any grief."

"I'll keep an eye out for her, and I'll tell Em about her nightmares so she can go to her if she hears something during the night."

"That's my boy." After cuffing Jake on the shoulder, Adam went to Grace, who now stood at the entrance to the kitchen.

She leaned a shoulder against the door where she must have been watching Adam speak to Jake.

The noise level in the saloon had dropped despite the growing number of customers. Every man gaped solely at Grace. Some with dropped jaws. Some with admiration. Some with pure lust.

His mood darkened in a heartbeat.

He crooked his finger.

She smiled and hurried to his side.

With a scowl directed at every other male in the Four Aces, he took her hand and dragged her out to the boardwalk.

It wasn't until she stumbled after him that he realized he was walking too fast. "Sorry, darlin'."

The sun had set, and the night air grew chilly. When she shivered, he wrapped an arm around her shoulder.

Their walk was slow, their silence uneasy. He had so much he wanted to say to her, especially now that he'd made up his mind. He'd already known his intentions, but talking to Jake and hearing the possessiveness in his own voice sealed her fate.

Grace belonged to him now.

He just had to find the appropriate way to tell her so.

Had she been any other woman, he would've ordered her to come back to the ranch with him. Then he would drag her back to town the next day to stand in front of Reverend David and recite their vows. Of course, he'd make love to her tonight so she'd have no good reason to turn him down. Sneaky, yes. But a foolproof plan.

He couldn't do that to Grace, not after all she'd survived.

When they reached the alley by the general store, Adam tugged her into the dark so they could have some privacy. As he folded her into his embrace, he sighed in contentment.

This was where she belonged—in his arms.

At that moment, he didn't give a damn whether bad memories shadowed her. He didn't care that she was still keeping something from him. And he didn't know how he could ever leave her at that saloon. All alone.

Grace was grateful to Adam for finding them a secluded moment. She ran her palms up his arms until they rested on his shoulders. She pressed her cheek to his chest and sighed. All she wanted was to stay in his embrace. When he kissed the top of her head, tears threatened at the sweetness of the gesture. How easy it would have been to go back to the ranch with him—*too* easy.

She had to keep reminding herself that this wasn't real. Her sins had ensured it.

"Last chance, Gracie."

"Hmm?"

"To come back with me tonight."

"You know I can't."

His exhale hung in the air. "I'm gonna wear ruts in the road between White Pines and the Twin Springs."

"No, you won't. You've got too much to do to worry about me. Aren't you leaving on the cattle drive next week?"

"Those plans might change."

"Change? I don't understand. Why would they change?"

"I'm not sure my being gone that long is a good idea. Might need to stay a little closer to town."

"Please don't do that for me."

"Don't you understand?" His finger coaxed her chin up until she was gazing into his handsome blue eyes. "From the moment you knocked on my door, everything I've done and everything I will do is for you."

He kissed her before she even knew his intent. A damned exciting kiss it was too, making every nerve in her body tingle from the roots of her hair to the tips of her toes.

Grace pressed herself against him, drawing from his strength and hoping it would become her own when she watched him drive away.

As Adam's tongue glided across hers, she mewled her approval. The way he made her body sing, she could hold nothing back. She couldn't get close enough to him, wanting to drown in the emotion only this man had inspired.

Love.

She loved him, and damn if that thought didn't make her tremble.

Love wasn't supposed to happen to her. The past should have assured that. The mistakes she made, the choices she regretted, the murder she'd committed all with the same intention—to keep Jake safe.

Love wasn't for people like her.

She loved him anyway.

He kissed her, tenderly and long, caressing her back. When he finally pulled back, he gave her a hard stare. "You're staying put. Promise me."

Promise him *what?* That she'd stay in White Pines forever? Or just for the few days she'd granted herself to get to know her son?

Grace glanced away, afraid he'd see the answer in her eyes.

"Look at me."

After a deep breath, she obeyed.

"You're staying where I put you. Promise me."

"Adam, I–I can't. You don't know about me, about my past."

"I don't give a damn about your past. All I care about is your future. Promise me, Grace, or so help me…"

Grace.

That was one of the few times he'd called her *Grace* instead of *Gracie.* He was good and angry.

"So help you what?" she asked. "How can you expect me to stay when you don't know anything about—"

"I told you, I don't *care* what you think you've done that's so horrible you need to run away from me. Promise me or I'll carry you right back to my wagon and hold you under lock and key until you do."

If only he knew the truth, he wouldn't be saying such things to her.

He sighed and his voice softened. "I love you, Gracie."

The world stopped spinning. The moon fell from the sky. The stars all burned out.

To her, hearing those words from Adam was every bit as much a miracle. "You–you can't. You don't even know me." A tear spilled over her lashes. "You don't mean it."

He grabbed her shoulders and had to stop himself from giving her a sound shake. Instead, he growled deep in his chest. "Listen to me. I love you."

A choked sob rose from her chest. "But I don't *want* you to love me!"

"Why?"

"You deserve a good woman, Adam. Someone people could look up to. I'm just a–a–"

"A what?"

She buried her face against his chest.

"One day, you'll learn to trust me," he whispered in her ear. "I'm still waiting for my promise."

She wiped away some stray tears with the backs of her hands. "Fine. I promise. For now. If you knew all there was to know about me, you wouldn't care if I left or not. You'd probably put me on the next stage passing through White Pines."

Adam's frustration finally got the better of him. He grabbed her hand and dragged her back to the Four Aces as she hurried along beside him. He shoved the swinging doors open and pulled her through, taking her toward the stairs.

The loud male voices followed them through their trek across the saloon.

"Ain't you a pretty little filly! You new to White Pines?"

"Hey, gorgeous. You married?"

"I've got a claim that's bound to strike gold. Why don't we have a drink? We can plan the weddin'."

Adam tried to scowl at each man. Single women coming to Montana were few and far between, especially pretty ones like Grace. If any of those men found out how well she could cook...

He couldn't make it to the staircase fast enough.

She dropped his hand and tried to climb the stairs.

He caught her elbow and hauled her back into his arms. There, in front of everyone, he kissed her. Ignoring the whistles and cat calls, he let every man there know that he'd staked a claim on Grace Riley. He let *her* know as well. He didn't end the kiss until he felt her surrender and sag against him.

"You're staying put," he said. "I love you. I can't lose you. Please promise me you'll stay. I won't leave 'til you give me your word."

She laid a trembling hand against his cheek. "Oh, Adam. Don't you realize? I love you too. I shouldn't, but I do."

Gathering her skirts in her hand, she hurried up the stairs. The saloon had grown quiet enough, the door closing on her room echoed with the force of a cannon blast.

***

Matthew was coming out of the kitchen when he saw Adam grab Grace and kiss her. Right in front of everyone in the saloon.

Emily stepped around him on one side, and Victoria gawked from the other.

"Did you know about them?" Emily asked.

"Not for a fact," Victoria replied. "But I sure hoped."

"I knew." Matthew smiled, crossing his arms over his chest. "I knew from the first moment I saw them together."

Victoria stepped around him to stare at him face-to-face. She gave him a stern frown he found incredibly attractive.

Damn, but the woman had grit.

"Why would he kiss her right here in front of everyone?" she asked. "It's not decent."

Matthew snorted a laugh at her. "So prim and proper, aren't you?"

Her responding glare could have burned his skin.

The cat calls started again, this time directed at Victoria.

Matthew gave the stink eye to as many men as he could. When one grew brave enough to walk right up to her and run his shaky fingers over her braid, Matthew pushed her behind his back and grabbed the stupid cowboy by the vest.

Giving the man a sound shake that knocked the hat from his head, Matthew growled deep in his chest. "Keep your filthy hands to yourself or I'll hit you so hard when you wake up, you'll need a shave."

When he drew one hand back—ready to throw a jealous punch—cool fingers covered his fist.

"Don't," Victoria murmured.

He glanced back at her. "But he touched you."

"I'll survive. Don't get yourself thrown in jail. Not for me."

"He touched you."

Her other hand covered his fist. "Please, Matthew. *Please* just let him go."

Releasing the cowboy's vest and giving him a shove, Matthew said between clenched teeth, "Touch her again, and you'll regret it."

The offender scrambled to pick up his hat and scurry out of the bar.

Matthew leveled a hard stare at the rest of the crowd. "Anyone else want to touch what doesn't belong to him?"

It was quiet enough cricket song could be heard drifting in the night air.

"I can't believe you'd humiliate me like this! I'll never forgive you, Matthew Riley!" Victoria turned and marched across the saloon, heading for the front doors. She shoved them open hard enough that they continued to swing in her wake.

All he could do was gape at her. He'd defended her, damn it! She should be grateful not scolding him.

Adam came to stand at his side. "You sure seem to have a way with my daughter."

"Women. I swear to the Lord above I'll never understand a single one of them."

Adam cuffed his shoulder. "Good to learn that early, boy. Save you lots of aggravation later on. C'mon. We need to head back to the ranch."

Chapter Nine

"Have a seat—both of you." Adam waited for Victoria and Matthew to sit down.

He had a million things on his mind, mostly about what needed to be done so he wouldn't have to leave Grace in White Pines for too long.

Too long?

One night already seemed to last forever.

God help him, he loved her. There was no way he was leaving on that long drive now if there was chance she would bolt the moment he was gone. She wouldn't run from him—at least that was what his heart wanted to believe. There was something nipping at her heels that never let the woman breathe fresh air or enjoy a moment of true peace.

Correction—*someone* nipping at her heels. And that someone was named Stephen.

Grace might wish to run from her past, but Adam had every intention of looking it square in the eye. Then he'd release her from its wicked hold over her life.

"I'm not heading out on this cattle drive," he announced.

Two sets of stunned eyes stared back at him.

Victoria cocked her head. "I don't understand, Daddy."

A knock drew Adam's attention. Ty stood in the doorway. "You wanted to see me?"

"Come on in, son. I was just explaining that I'm gonna let you deliver the cattle to Denver. I'm sitting out this last trip."

"Why?" Victoria asked. "You always go on the drives with us."

"I thought Grace and I were going with you," Matthew added. "That's why I stayed on here at the ranch."

Adam swallowed a chuckle. If Matthew believed a cattle drive was only thing tying him to Montana, he was deluding himself. "Let's just say I've had a change of heart. I want to stay closer to town."

"Because of Grace." Matthew set his jaw. "I don't think she'll leave. Not now."

"I don't, either, but I need to keep an eye on things. Anything you can tell me that might help me understand what she's so afraid of?"

Matthew's shoulders rose in a shrug. "There's not much to tell. Besides, it's her place to share anything she wants you to know."

Adam sighed, although he respected Matthew holding tightly to Grace's secrets. Nothing worthwhile ever came easy. The puzzle that was Grace Riley had a surplus of pieces, and the solution sure wouldn't be simple.

"Then I'll just have to wait 'til she's ready to confide in me." He turned his attention to Ty. "Can you leave with the cattle in a couple of days, or do you need a little more time?"

Ty rubbed his hand over his chin, deep in thought. "Two days oughta work. I'll be needing to hire on two more for the drive."

"I'll go," Matthew offered.

"No," Adam replied. "I've got another job for you."

"I'll go," Victoria chimed in. "If there's only three of us, I won't have to cook everything."

Adam shook his head. "Got another job for you, too, princess. Ty?"

"Sir?"

"Do what needs done to get the cattle to market."

"Would it be all right with you if I stay on in Denver for a few weeks?" Ty asked. "Got a letter from my sister. She's wantin' me to visit."

"Which sister?" Adam asked.

"Bess. Number six. I think she feels bad that she wasn't able to keep our pa from dumping me at that orphanage. She and her husband said they wanted me to stay to get to know my nieces and nephews next time I got near Denver."

"Go," Adam replied. "Get rid of those blasted steers and go see your family."

With a nod, Ty ducked out of the office.

"If Ty's making the cattle drive, what am I supposed to do for you?" Matthew asked.

"I need those mares we talked about getting. You're gonna go pick out half a dozen or so good ones and bring 'em back. That way we'll be able to breed more horses come spring."

"Would be easier with Ty's help, but I can always grab some cowboy from town."

"No need. It's a two-man job. Victoria's going with you."

The room was as quiet as an ancient mausoleum. Victoria and Matthew stared open-mouthed at Adam before slowly turning to face each other.

"I–I couldn't. Daddy, surely you don't mean— With *him*?"

Her words forced the indignant mask to drop from Matthew's face as he narrowed his eyes. "I don't work with *women*. Why, I'd have to spend all my time coddling her. She'd never be able to keep up with the pace I'd set."

Her spine straightened and her chin lifted. "I assure you, *Mr. Riley*, that I can hold my own. I'd gather you'd be hard pressed to keep up with me." Her eyes met her father's. "When do you want me to leave?"

"Me?" Matthew shot her a frown. "You think you could round up half a dozen mares all on your own?"

She answered him with a curt nod. The moment he started laughing, her eyes shot enough heat that had it been real fire, it would have burned him to nothing but a charred carcass. "I don't need your help. Six mares are easy."

"I changed my mind, Adam." Matthew crossed his arms over his chest. "I don't need help. I definitely don't need *her* help. I'll bring those mares in myself, and I'll pick some damned good breeding stock, too."

She wagged her finger at him. "I don't need your help. I'll leave first thing in the morning, and I'll get much better horses than *you* could ever find."

Adam shook his head. Would they ever figure out the friction bubbling to the surface hid deeper feelings? A damn shame too because they suited each other in every way.

She was a special kind of woman who needed a special kind of man. Someone who wouldn't bend to her strong will. Someone who could match her passion for life. Someone who wouldn't be intimidated by her clever wit.

He let their squabbling go on for a few minutes until it petered out. Drumming his fingers on the top of his mahogany desk, he said, "Are you two finished? 'Cause I have a word or two to say in the matter."

"Sorry, Adam." Matthew turned to give Victoria as much of his back as he could.

"Sorry, Daddy." Victoria scooted to the edge of the settee. Nothing but stubbornness kept her from slipping off the edge.

"You're *both* going to get those mares. Victoria, you've got a great eye, but bringing in six or more won't be easy, especially for one person." She opened her mouth as if to protest, but he held up his hand. "No argument."

She sighed before nodding.

"Matthew, I expect you to help pick the best, and taking Victoria with you gives you a second pair of eyes, a pair that knows good horseflesh."

He glanced over his shoulder at her before giving a brusque nod.

"Good. It's settled. You can leave in the morning."

Without another word, they both rose and left the office, giving Adam a chance to think about the plans he needed to make to bring Grace back to Twin Springs.

Back home where she belonged.

Chapter Ten

Seeing Grace eased the tightness in Adam's chest.

"Adam!" She smiled and moved the frying pan away from the flame rising from the burner. After giving her hair a quick swipe, she smoothed her palms down her white apron. "I didn't expect you this early."

He strode across the kitchen, took her into his arms, and kissed her soundly, savoring how she always melted into his embrace.

After a kiss that was too short to please him, she put a little distance between them as her cheeks reddened. "You always make me forget myself." She turned her attention back to the stove. "Have you eaten breakfast?"

"No, ma'am." He'd been in too much of a hurry to see her. Pulling the stool back from the work table, he sat down.

"Well, then…" She flipped some delicious smelling bacon. "I'll set another place."

He was content to watch her puttering around the kitchen, and it was easy to see how much pleasure she got from cooking.

She stepped away from the stove long enough to grab a mug and fill it with coffee. Handing it to him, she smiled and blushed a little deeper red. "I–I'm glad to see you."

As she turned to move away from him, he grabbed her hand and dragged her back to his side. "I'm glad to see you too, Gracie." He kissed the back of her hand.

Her smile lit up the whole kitchen, and she lightly ran her fingers up his arm and over his shoulder as she walked away. "I'll make you a nice breakfast."

Jake came shuffling in, his clothes shabbily donned and his hair still bed-ruffled. One suspender dangled from his pants, and only half his shirt was tucked in.

Adam had seen the boy in that state just about every morning he lived at Twin Springs. Working late hours in the Four Aces couldn't be easy.

"Mornin'," Jake mumbled, not really directing the greeting at either Adam or Grace. He plopped down on the empty stool next to Adam.

Grace poured Jake some coffee and set the mug in front of him. He nodded but didn't thank her.

Crossing his arms over his chest, Adam leaned back, unsure whether he should scold the boy for his lack of manners.

She beat him to the punch. "You're quite welcome, Jake. I hope you enjoy the coffee."

Jake's eyes followed her as he sipped the coffee, but one taste coupled with her sassy response forced a smile to his lips.

Scooping food onto two plates, she set them in front of the men. Adam said a quick prayer, and she went back to work by the stove as he and Jake dove into their meals.

The first forkful of scrambled eggs made Jake's eyes fly wide. He glanced to Adam who snickered and ate some more of his own food.

Emily must have been as bad a cook as Jake and Will often complained.

Grace, who'd been watching them both over her shoulder, smiled at Adam.

He returned her grin with a wink.

Shuffling steps announced another person entering the kitchen. "Somethin' sure smells wonderful." Will plopped down on the third stool, eyeing the almost empty plates. "Can I please git me some of them vittles, Grace? My, oh my, they smell tasty."

She was already handing him a cup of coffee. "That's what I'm here for."

"I've been thinking," Adam said as Grace piled food on Will's plate, "that we could probably get Reverend David to perform our wedding in a couple of days."

She stopped moving, gripping the plate with white knuckles. "Wedding? You think there's going to be a *wedding*?"

"Of course. That's what two people in love are supposed to do. I figured you wouldn't want to wait too long. I'd like to see it done soon so I can take you back to the ranch."

"Married? Y–you can't be serious."

The quiver in her voice helped him keep his temper. He didn't want her afraid of him, but they belonged together. The faster she got that straight in her mind, the easier things would be.

"I'm dead serious. We're gonna be married. Soon."

"I'm not marrying you, Adam." She finished assembling Will's breakfast and carried it to the table. "I'm not marrying anyone. *Ever*." She dropped the plate so hard, a couple of bacon strips and some toasted bread bounced onto the table.

Will quickly picked up the food and placed it back on his plate. He grabbed up his fork and shoveled food into his mouth as he watched the couple with amusement in his eyes.

Adam almost asked Jake and Will to give him and Grace some privacy before he realized he might be better off with allies. And perhaps witnesses. "Yes, you are, darlin'. You're marrying me just as a soon as I can make the arrangements."

"Married? I think not."

"I think so."

Grace attacked the dirty pots and pans she'd dropped into the sink, hating the troubling thoughts crowding her mind.

Married?

Had the man lost his mind? She was a murderess, not that he knew that.

But married? "I–I can't. I–I'll be leaving town soon."

A hand on her arm spun her around. The water and suds clinging to her hands flew to leave a trail of wet spots across Adam's shirt.

"You're not going anywhere, Grace." The harshness of his tone eased. "You can't leave. You belong here—with me."

Sweet Lord, how she wished that were true. She wanted to belong somewhere. She wanted a home she could call her own.

She wanted Adam Morgan almost more than living.

"I can't." Her voice was a mere whisper.

His finger lifted her chin.

She resisted, placing her wet palms against his chest.

He won the battle. As his mouth descended toward hers, she broke away from his embrace, hurrying to the opposite side of the table to put an obstacle between them.

"Oh, no, you don't, Adam Morgan! If you kiss me, I'll forget myself again."

Chortles came from Will and Jake. Until the sound reached her, she'd forgotten that she and Adam weren't alone. Where was a deep hole she could crawl into?

"Grace Riley, I have had about enough of this nonsense." Adam's voice was so stern, she winced. "You love me, don't you?" He took a couple of deep breaths. "You do. You told me so. You can't take it back now."

"I don't *want* to take it back." She dropped her gaze to the floor. "You know I love you."

"You *are* going to marry me."

"I can't talk about this now." She inclined her head at Will and Jake.

"You can, and you will." He started to move around the table, closing in on her.

She squealed and darted to the other side.

Blue eyes bored holes right through her, probably seeing more than she wished they would. "What are you so afraid of?"

She wanted to shout her answer. *You! I'm afraid of you! If I let you in, I'll die when you find out what I am and leave me!*

All she could do was shake her head.

"I'll protect you. I won't let the nightmares come true."

Her head snapped up. "Nightmares?"

"You had one every night at the ranch."

"Adam! What will Jake and Will think, you being in my room at night?"

Their audience seemed to be taking the whole scene in as if they were attending an engrossing play.

Her face couldn't possibly get any hotter—even her ears felt on fire.

Adam ignored her protest. "I know who you're afraid of. His name's Stephen, and I won't let him hurt you again."

Grace's heart slammed so hard in her chest, she couldn't catch a breath. He knew. If Adam had listened to her nightmarish jabbering, he knew at least some of her secrets. He probably knew about Stephen Shay.

Did he know she'd murdered the man?

No.

If he did, he'd *never* be talking about a marriage. If he knew the truth about Jake, wouldn't he be running the opposite way rather than proposing?

Merciful God, how much would he hate her if he discovered what she'd done? Yet he knew enough to understand some of her past.

And he still wanted her anyway.

Sweet Lord, he really *did* love her.

She stopped running away—for good—and moved closer to him. "You know about Stephen?"

"Not as much as I want to or as much as I need to so I can keep you safe." He stopped before he reached her and opened his arms wide. "I love you and I want us to be married, Gracie. Neither of us is perfect. We both come with a past. But together, we can leave the past behind and make a new future."

"Married?" she whispered.

"Married." He nodded, the sincerity of his feelings and his conviction in his eyes.

She ran into his arms so fast she stumbled.

Adam folded his arms around her and kissed her soundly.

"Oh, for the love of..." Will shoved his stool back and stood up. He threw a frown at Jake. "I finally get a decent meal and Adam Morgan's gonna steal away my cook."

***

Matthew dropped his saddle bag next to his bedroll.

Victoria turned the rabbit he'd caught, flipping the long stick holding it over the fire so that both sides cooked.

He should say something, make small talk or thank her for skinning the rabbit. The ride out had been quiet, but he was used to hours of boredom doing nothing more than looking up the south end of steers. Some cowboys enjoyed singing. Some liked to chat. He'd always preferred the solitude of his thoughts.

Victoria had helped him find seven mares that would please Adam. They were now grazing or bedding down in the clearing. Sin and Victoria's mare were getting some much needed rest as well.

Victoria started the fire as he hunted their dinner. With the exception of shouted orders as they captured the horses, silence prevailed—as it did now that they'd set up camp for the night.

He cleared his throat and nodded at the rabbit. "Smells good."

Her only response was a nervous smile as she flipped the skewer again.

Fishing around in his saddlebag, he found his book. Settling down on his saddle blanket, he opened it to the dog-eared page and started reading his favorite sonnet for what was probably his thousandth time.

She cocked her head. "What are you reading?"

He didn't want to tell her, so he just grunted. He should have thought about her curiosity before he chose which book to bring with him. Old habits died hard, and he seldom went anywhere without something to read. His embarrassment made the quiet seem more welcome than before, and why in the devil he even cared about what the woman thought was beyond him.

"Why won't you tell me? It doesn't look like a dime novel or anything." She drew up on her knees as if to stand up, probably to see for herself.

"It's Shakespeare," he blurted out. "Just some Shakespeare."

The smile on her face washed over him. "I *love* Shakespeare."

Launching into a story from his past, he tried to divert her attention. "Grace and I read his work all the time. Hell, we wore the spines out of some of the books. We'd play a game some days on the trail. We could only quote Shakespeare all day—none of our own words."

"Oh, my. That had to have been a challenge."

"Yes, ma'am. But neither of us wanted to be left without a reply. Sure didn't want to lose the game. Drove the other cowboys plum loco 'cause they had no idea what we were talking about."

"Which story did you bring? I'm partial to *Romeo and Juliet*, but Daddy taught me to appreciate *Hamlet* and *Julius Caesar*, too. You could read aloud to me."

He wished he'd brought a book of plays instead of sonnets. What would she think of him to know he was moved by words of poetry? Heaven knew he'd bloodied several noses over the teasing he'd received from uneducated cowboys who'd been amused by his tastes in reading material.

Victoria got to her feet. "Is it *Midsummer's Night Dream? Twelfth Night?* I like both of them. Maybe I could read it too? We could take turns reading the parts."

Matthew stopped her hesitant steps with an outstretched palm. "It's not any of his plays."

"Then what are you—"

"Sonnets! I'm reading Shakespeare's sonnets! Are you satisfied now?"

With a frown, she sank back down next to the fire and turned the rabbit hard enough he was surprised it didn't flip right off the skewer.

What kind of ogre was he to yell at a beautiful woman because he was embarrassed to admit he loved Shakespearean sonnets? "I'm sorry. I didn't mean to snap at you."

She narrowed her eyes and set her lips into a tight line.

"I'm sorry, Victoria."

The silence was deafening.

"Would you like... I mean, I could...read some of them to you."

"You would do that? For me?"

He nodded, hating how easily her moods could sway him.

He would have to keep his guard up around her or he'd find himself nothing better than some little lapdog, jumping at her beck and call. Grace had always told him the day would come when he'd meet a woman special enough to turn his life upside down. He'd always laughed in response.

Until the day his horse tore down Victoria Morgan's laundry.

Reading gave him something to do while she finished cooking their supper—something other than trying to make conversation with a woman who made him so tongue-tied he felt like an imbecile.

Sinking into the text, he read his favorite of the Bard's sonnets, the thirteenth.

O! that you were your self; but, love you are
No longer yours, than you your self here live:
Against this coming end you should prepare,
And your sweet semblance to some other give:
So should that beauty which you hold in lease
Find no determination; then you were
Yourself again, after yourself's decease,
When your sweet issue your sweet form should bear.

Who lets so fair a house fail to decay,
Which husbandry in honour might uphold,
Against the storm gusts of winter's day
And barren rage of death's eternal cold?
O! none but unthrifts. Dear my love, you know,
You had a father: let your son say so.

Too late, Matthew realized his error. This sonnet, above all the others, kept Victoria firmly in his thoughts. While he wasn't an old man—only twenty-seven on his last birthday—he often felt as though life was passing him by.

He had no home. No wife. No son. There was no one waiting for him at the end of each long drive. There was no family looking forward to his return. And as the Bard advised, time was short. Soon, he'd be past the age to marry and start a family of his own.

Oh, he'd made plans. None that he'd followed through on. He and Grace squirreled away money whenever they got paid, hoping to one day own a spread of their own. Then they could stop running and settle down.

But it was nothing more than a dream.

Stephen Shay's strange and dangerous obsession with Grace made sure those plans never came to fruition. At the end of almost every drive, the bastard was there, sitting like a king in his fancy Pullman car and trying to get to her. Too many times, Matthew had to grab their pay and sneak his sister out of town as if she were some common criminal.

Stephen Shay was dead now—his soul finally in hell where it belonged. For the first time in his life, all Matthew wanted might be within his reach.

He stared at Victoria. She sniffled a little, as though holding back tears. Before he could say anything, she pulled the cooked rabbit from the fire, used her pocketknife to cut off a leg that she dropped on her own plate, then handed the skewer to Matthew.

They ate in awkward silence until she dropped her rabbit leg and jumped to her feet. "I–I'll be back."

He watched her head into the small grove of trees, wondering if her desire to weep came from the same melancholy he felt after reading that damned sonnet. The woman had a tender heart. Yes, she was more stubborn than should be allowed, but she also had one of the sharpest wits of anyone he'd ever known—including Grace, whose intelligence constantly flustered cowboys who thought women were the weaker and less clever sex.

Everything about Victoria appealed to him. Those eyes that could change from hazel to green. That hair that he wanted to unbraid, spread over her shoulders, and watch spill down her back. That body that he'd fantasized touching, running his fingers and his palms over every hill and valley. Just thinking about her made him hard.

She was taking an awfully long time. Maybe she'd wept for a spell and was now attending to some personal needs. Still, she shouldn't be away so long. His mind went wild, imagining the dangers that could befall a woman alone in the woods. Snakes. Wildlife. Just plain getting lost.

He got to his feet. "Victoria?"

Only crickets answered his call.

Scolding himself for being a nervous ninny, he took off after her, following the clear path she'd left. "Victoria? Where are you?"

She stood in a clearing, standing in a shaft of moonlight that painted her dark hair blue. Her back was to him, her arms wrapped around herself in a hug. All he could do was stare until he saw how her shoulders shook.

If she was sobbing that hard, it wasn't because of Shakespeare.

Striding over as fast as his legs could move, Matthew shouted, "What in the hell happened?"

Victoria jumped and whirled around to face him. Tears glistened on her cheeks, gleaming like ice in the moonlight. She tried to wipe them away with her sleeve. "What the devil? You scared the life outta— What exactly do you think you're doing?"

He knelt next to her and ran his hand down her legs, still surprised that the woman had the gall to wear pants. They made it difficult for him to find out what had been making her cry. "Was it a snake? Where'd he bite you? Or did you twist your ankle?"

Her hands kept pushing his away as he worked his way up her body, and she swatted at him each time he touched her. "I'm fine. Leave me be. Stop."

By the time he'd risen to his full height, panic had him fully in its grasp. He turned her by grabbing her hips until he was staring at her backside. "Did you fall on your—" He put both palms on her behind.

"Stop it!" Victoria turned around and took a step back. "Stop touching me! What made you think I was hurt?"

"You were crying."

She gaped at him.

When she didn't make any move to explain, Matthew ran his hands over her arms, checking for broken bones. "Did you fall or something?"

Victoria jerked her arms away. "I told you, I'm fine. I just needed some privacy."

"Your *privacy* was taking an awfully long time. Why, when I take a piss, I'm not gone more than—"

"Matthew!"

Damn it, but he constantly forgot there were different rules on what a man could say to women. How was he supposed to remember when he seldom spent time in their company? Grace would box his ears if she'd heard. "Sorry." The contriteness fled as he remembered why he'd come after her. "You made me worry."

Victoria stared at him, wondering if he realized how frightened and angry he looked when he'd burst through the trees to find her—like an enraged, charging bull. She'd indulged herself in some much needed tears to try to wash away the hurt she'd felt when he'd read that blasted sonnet, but he'd interrupted.

He couldn't possibly know that the Bard's thirteenth was a knife through her heart, rending her soul with words about family and future. All she'd ever known was that she wanted children of her own. A home. A man to care for. A man who cared for her. She wanted what her parents enjoyed in the years they'd shared.

Yet here she was, a single woman in a territory full of men who outnumbered her nine to one, and she still remained alone. Oh, there had been plenty of proposals, mostly from miners or cowboys who couldn't honestly be considered husband material. They were after her money or simply wanted her because she was a woman, not because she was the *right* woman. Few men were brave enough to face her father, and he protected her like a treasure.

Twenty-one—an old maid with no real prospect for ever being anything else. And now that her father was making plans for a new life with Grace, Victoria would not only be an old maid, she would be the old maid in the way.

The spinster daughter her father would have to care for the rest of her life.

The tears threatened again, so she turned her back, not wanting Matthew to see them. God, how she hated showing him any weakness. The man was smug enough. To let him know he'd gotten to her, that he'd wounded her heart?

He spun her to face him so fast he made her dizzy. "What's wrong?"

She shook her head and tried to cover her face with her hands.

He grabbed her wrists. "Why are you crying again?"

Her throat hurt with the need to scream at him that *he* was the reason she was crying. He was everything she wanted and could never have. "Why do you even care? You hate me, remember?"

"Hate you? Where in the hell did you get that ridiculous notion?"

Weeping or not, she lifted her face to his and gawked at him. "You told me so."

"I never—"

"*Yes*, you did." She jerked her wrists free, pulled her hat off her head, and threw it to the ground. "You hate my hat."

"For Christ's sake, I don't hate your hat."

Her trembling hands ran down her thighs. "You hate my pants, too."

"I don't hate them. Just think women should wear women's clothes and do women's work. You need to stop pretending to be something you're not."

Victoria gasped, her sadness quickly giving way to anger. Matthew Riley knew exactly what to say to set her off with the intensity of a stick of dynamite. "Women's work? Pretending to be..." Drawing in a breath between clenched teeth, she hoped to find some calm. It eluded her. "Are you saying I wasn't helpful in picking out those mares?"

A hand waved in dismissal. "No. That's not what I meant. You did a great job. Doubt too many women could do half as good as you did."

She gave her eyes an exaggerated roll. "Careful. That bordered on a compliment. You sure wouldn't want someone to hear you praise me. He might think you didn't hate me."

Matthew took a stride forward, set his hands against his hips, and glared down at her. "I already told you. I don't hate you."

His nearness set her heart to pounding, making her want to take a step back in retreat. She stood her ground, refusing to give him that kind of power over her. "Doesn't matter. All I want is for you treat me like any other cowboy."

"Impossible."

"Why? Why is that so impossible?"

"Because I never wanted to do this to any other cowboy."

Before she understood his intentions, he drew her into his embrace and covered her mouth with his.

This wasn't at all the chaste kiss Kenny Barlow had given her after the harvest dance. It wasn't the kind of kiss Ty stole when he had the crush on her back when she was seventeen. This was a possessive kiss that she'd never thought to receive from a man who made her weak in the knees just to look at.

And, heavens above, how he could kiss. She opened her lips to his probing tongue, rubbing hers against his in a caress that sent lightning racing through her body.

Her arms raised of their own accord, slipping around his neck as she wantonly pressed herself against him, wanting to get closer and closer, wanting to be swallowed by his heat. He growled, his hands sliding down her back until his palms rested against her backside. When he pulled her against him, the hard proof of his desire was there for her to feel.

He dragged his mouth away and buried his lips against her throat. She arched against him, drowning in all the sensations he sent ripping through her. Her blood was hotter than a branding iron. A moan slipped from her lips.

"You're so soft," he whispered against her ear before he ran his tongue around the edges. "Do you know how much I want you? How hard it's been to see you every day and not be able to touch you?"

As if she could possibly form a coherent response to such enticing questions. Her heart beat wildly and her breath came in ragged gasps. She should stop him. She should push him away. A good girl would. The magic he worked on her body sure didn't make her feel like a good girl.

A hand rose to cover her breast. The newness of the contact made her tense.

Everything came tumbling back to Matthew the moment Victoria stiffened against him. Her body went as rigid as a board.

What in the hell was he doing? She wasn't the type of woman to give herself to a man for the sheer sake of sharing some passion. She wasn't a widow or a working girl. She was the wealthy daughter of the owner of one of the largest ranches in Montana, and Matthew was trying to tumble her in the grass.

A virgin to boot.

He jerked away from her, giving a small push away. "I–I'm sorry."

The confusion on her face almost broke his heart. She'd felt it too—the passion that flared between them so hot and sweet. Her features hardened until her mouth twisted into a fierce scowl.

"How dare you?" she whispered, though the words hit as harsh as a shout.

She had a right to her anger. Hell, he'd been pawing her. He hung his head in shame.

"Why?"

"Why what?" he asked.

"Why don't you want me?"

At that moment, he decided that he would never understand how the woman's mind worked. "You think I don't want you?"

She blinked a few times before nodding.

"Sweet Lord, Victoria... I don't know how to explain it to you."

All the softness he'd seen as he'd kissed and caressed her vanished. She squared her shoulders and marched past him, heading back to the camp.

He grabbed her upper arm. "Wait."

Her eyes closed.

"Let me explain. It's not what you think."

She jerked her arm away, opened her eyes, and glared at him. "Don't ever touch me again."

"Victoria, please—"

"*Ever.*" Breaking into a run, she left him alone in the clearing to mentally kick himself for his stupidity.

Not want her?

Matthew had never wanted another woman half as badly as he wanted Victoria Morgan. The images from their walk returned—the images of what the two of them could build, of how they could make a family.

Not want her?

Hell, yes, he wanted her. And damned if he didn't realize that there were some tender emotions hiding in all that desire—feelings he'd never acknowledged before, probably because he'd never felt them for another woman.

Not want her?

He loved her.

He loved her enough to leave her be.

Chapter Eleven

"We've got to ford here." Matthew stared at the river, wishing he could come up with a better solution. "After those rains last week, it's still high. Best place we've found. If we go any farther south, we'll have to camp another night."

That was the last thing in the world he wanted to do. After the awkward ending to their evening, he wasn't sure he could handle being alone with Victoria without making a horse's ass out of himself again. As it was, he hadn't caught a wink of sleep. Through the long night, he'd stared at her slim figure as she slept, wishing and wanting things that could never be.

She thought the whole situation over for a moment as if he'd asked her opinion. He was the one who had the experience at moving animals. She should listen to him and do exactly what he told her to.

Victoria finally nodded, raising his temper. "As good a place as any. You cross. I'll start sending them after you."

Hearing his sister's scolding voice in his head, he bit back a sarcastic reply. He returned her nod and forded the river.

Six of the seven mares made it across before a duck hiding in the reeds panicked. With a loud quack and the frenzied rustle of wings, the mallard took flight, spooking the last horse. The mare squealed and ran, but she headed up the river bank instead of across the water.

"Damn it!" The best of the breeding stock was running away.

About to tell Victoria to come on across so he could ride out to try to chase the horse down, he swallowed the words when she jerked her horse around and galloped out in pursuit.

"Victoria! Get your ass back here!"

Her response was drowned out by the sound of the river rushing on by as if things hadn't just gone to hell.

Having no choice, he herded the rest of the mares and stopped them in a clearing near the river bank. His heart pounded a rough rhythm as he waited for her to return. Pictures of the horrible things that could be happening played over and over in his mind. As he tried to calm his thoughts, he scanned the banks of the river, wondering if he should simply ride out to catch her. Minutes seemed to pass as hours.

Then something floated down the middle of the tumbling river.

Victoria's hat.

"Damn it!"

Reining his horse around, he dug his heels into the animal's sides, riding hard to try to save her.

"Damn it!"

Shouting the same curse over and over, he leaned forward, urging his stallion on. He scanned each log, each piece of debris floating along with the river, fearing Victoria would be clinging to one of them.

From the distance, he saw her—on the correct side of the swollen river—still on her horse and leading the runaway mare with a lasso. Both woman and horses looked utterly undisturbed by their ordeal.

He, on the other hand, felt as if someone had given him a sound beating.

"Damn it, Victoria! I was worried sick. You shouldn't have gone after that damned mare!"

She rode like a queen, back as straight as an arrow. "Nonsense." Her voice held an air of condescension that fired Matthew's temper even hotter. "She's the best of the pack. I didn't want to lose her."

He slapped his hat against his thigh. "What were you thinking? You could've broken your fool neck."

"Chasing a mare for a country mile? Doubt it. Why'd you leave the rest of the horses?"

"Your hat floated by."

"Did you grab it?"

All he could do for a moment was blink at her audacity. "Are you daft, woman?"

She shook her head as she paraded right past him, leading the now docile runaway. "The least you could've done was caught it."

Sin reacted to the nearness of the strange mare, snorting and rearing. Matthew dropped his hat and tried to rein in the stubborn animal. The horse backed up until his rear legs sank in the soft, wet dirt. Before he knew what was happening, Matthew found himself flipping off the end of the saddle and onto his back, sliding down the steep bank of the river. He hit the water with an enormous splash.

Her laughter rose above the sound of the river.

He sat in the shallows and spit out the water that had rushed into his mouth as though he was some stone cherub in a fancy fountain.

Victoria dismounted, still laughing hard enough she finally leaned against her horse. "You should see... You're covered in..." She turned to face her horse's neck, gripping the animal's mane and laughing hard enough her whole body shook.

Dredging his way back up the slippery slope, he thought of how she'd demanded he treat her like any other cowboy.

If that's what the lady wants, that's what the lady is damn well gonna get.

As he neared the summit, he grabbed the waistband of her pants and jerked.

Victoria sprawled on her backside in the mud and slid down the same bank he'd just crawled up. She squealed all the way down.

He stood on the edge, looked down at her, and laughed. Then he picked up his soaked hat and slapped it on his head.

Sitting in the shallow of the river, she spit out water. "How *could* you?"

"You laughed at me."

She smacked the water on either side of her. "That's why you did *this* to me?"

He grinned. "Told me to treat you like any other cowboy, didn't you?"

A dark eyebrow rose in question.

"Had a cowboy laughed at me, that's exactly what I would've done to him." He held out a hand. "Let me help you up."

She crept back up the steep bank, almost reaching the summit before her foot slipped and she found herself face first in the mud. Sputtering, she tried to wipe away the thick layer of dirt covering her face.

"Look at you. A pig in a mudhole." He reached for her again. "Enough fooling around. Give me your hand."

Through the mud caked on her face, she frowned. "Fine. Here's my hand."

He clasped her outstretched fingers, but before he could haul her the rest of the way up the bank, her frown changed to a sly smile. She gave him a good yank, sending them both tumbling back down the muddy slope.

As they landed at the bottom, Matthew found Victoria sprawled next to him, still chuckling.

The urge to shout made his throat burn until her happiness slowly infected him. The humor of the situation washed over him the same way as the water.

He wrapped his arms around her, rolling her to straddle him. "Dirty trick."

Her smile could charm the anger out of a raging buffalo. "*Very* dirty."

He smoothed some of the mud away from her cheeks. First one, then the other, letting his fingertips caress her skin. "You're a mess."

She mimicked his touch, her cool fingers rubbing the mud from his face. "So are you."

He couldn't stop himself from kissing her. The moan from deep in her throat when he thrust his tongue into her mouth told him she liked it.

Had the water not been so damned cold, he would have been content to ravage that sweet mouth for the rest of the day. When she pulled away, her teeth started to chatter, and their connection was lost. He began to fear that was all there would ever be between them—tender moments stolen, enjoyed, and rapidly gone.

But never forgotten.

They awkwardly rose, crawled back up the slope, and rounded up their horses. As she mounted, she threw him a saucy smirk. "You really should have grabbed my hat. It was my favorite."

The woman had grit.

The sun was now low on the horizon. "We lost too much time," he said. "Probably have to camp again for the night."

She sighed. "I figured. Can't be driving those mares in the dark." She flicked some mud from her hand. "I've gotta get this stuff off me anyway. Sweet Lord, I must look a mess."

Mud bath or not, she was still beautiful. Her clothes were plastered to her body, revealing such luscious curves it took all his control not to ride up next to her and drag her from her saddle onto his lap. Then he'd kiss her again just to get her riled up.

God, how he loved her sass.

"You look fine." A dollop of mud fell from his chin. "I think we better find a nice lake to clean up in."

"I know just the place." She clucked at her mare, took off toward the meadow at a canter, and prodded the waiting horses into motion.

***

"Potatoes?" Grace asked over her shoulder.

"Please." Adam pulled out a stool and sat down next to Will at the kitchen table.

Since Grace had come to the Four Aces, Adam took all his meals there. The ranch was quiet and lonely since she'd left.

Besides, the tension between her and Jake remained taut enough to worry him. By riding into town, he could keep an eye on them both.

Will sniffed the wonderful scents and grinned. Then he turned to Adam and tossed him a fierce frown. "Sure we can't postpone that wedding of yours? Just a year or two?"

Grace smiled as she set the plate full of food in front of him.

He smiled back. "Sorry, friend. Just don't see that happening. I want to get her home."

"Home." Her whisper was as reverent as a person seeing a cathedral for the first time.

"Home. With your husband."

She squeezed his shoulder. His hand covered hers and gave it a pat. A wistful look crossed her face before she bowed her head and returned to the stove.

Emily and Jake came into the kitchen, and he pulled out a chair for his wife.

"Everything smells wonderful, Grace," Emily said, lowering her burdened body onto the chair.

"I'll get you both a plate ready." Grace grabbed two empty dishes from the stack next to the stove.

Jake frowned at her, and Adam wasn't sure exactly what was flying through the young man's mind. As she set their dinners in front of the couple, Jake's scowl grew fiercer.

"Thank you." Emily smiled up at Grace.

Jake remained silent.

A lesson in manners was past due.

Adam arched an eyebrow at his adopted son. "You got something to say to Grace for that fine meal?"

Jake just grunted.

Emily slapped his upper arm. "She's your sister. Be polite."

"She ain't my sister!" He jumped up and pushed his chair back hard enough it toppled over. "Why you people insist—"

"Stop it!" Grace slammed her own plate down on the table where she was about to take a seat next to Adam. "Let him be. You can't make him accept me." She turned and tried to step away, but Adam grabbed her wrist.

"Wait." He leveled a hard stare at Jake. "I think it's past time to put all our cards on the table."

"I don't want to put—"

"I don't particularly *care* what you want right now." Adam wrapped an arm around his fiancée's shoulder. "The tension in here is thicker than molasses, and it's hurting Grace."

"I tried to make peace with her," Jake said.

"Bullshit," Will replied. "You've avoided the woman at every turn. She didn't kill your parents, boy."

"I know that!" he snapped back.

Will smacked his palm on the table. "Then why ain't you even *talked* to her?"

"I can't!" His breaths came so hard, his nostrils flared with each exhale. He was finally losing the control he'd held for so long. The words tumbled from him in a shout. "Ever since I met her, I can't stop rememberin'. Every time I see her, I see what happened to them. I see them, lyin' there on the grass. Dead!"

"Oh, Jake." Emily laid a hand on his arm. "It's past time to let go of that grief. Grace would've come for you if she'd known. Right, Grace?"

Grace had been twisting her hands in her lap until Adam placed his hand over hers. A tear slipped down her cheek as she nodded.

The frown stayed fixed on Jake's face. "But—"

A loud whack echoed through the kitchen when Will swatted the back of Jake's head. "You've got a mighty thick skull, boy. Grace never did you no harm. She wanted you to have a family. Hell, she was only fifteen, nothing but a damn kid herself. It ain't as if she was your mama. She didn't know about mothering, so she got you a mother. You should be grateful."

"I know that." Jake rubbed his head and scowled at his father-in-law.

"Then you need to forgive her," Adam said.

A whisper rose from Grace. "He needs to forgive *himself* first."

The woman was sharp—sharper than all the rest of them. Adam had never considered Jake blaming himself for his adoptive parents' deaths. But Grace knew—probably because she'd faced loss herself when her mother died and when she'd had to leave Jake behind.

Adam squeezed her fingers. "You're right, darlin'." He turned back to Jake. "You were a little boy. You couldn't have stopped those bandits—"

"I hid! I hid in the barn like a damned coward!"

Grace was the one who went to Jake. She stopped in front of him and clenched her hands together. "You are *not* a coward. You did what your parents asked, didn't you? They told you to hide so you'd be safe. You were being a good son."

"I wasn't a good son." He hung his head. "I could've—"

"Could've what? Died along with them?" She answered her own question with a shake of her head. "You can't keep torturing yourself over what could've been. You did what you were supposed to do— what your parents wanted you to do. It's time you learned that." She glanced over her shoulder to Emily. "If you hadn't obeyed your parents, Emily would never have known your love, and the child you'll share would never have been created." Her gaze returned to Jake. "Every child is a gift from God. He meant for you to live." She reached for him with a trembling hand. "I know you'll probably never be able to accept me, but you have to forgive yourself and let the guilt and bitterness go. For your wife. For your baby."

Emily hoisted herself off the stool with her father's help. When she lumbered over to Jake, she took his hand and placed it on her rounded belly. "*This* is why you're here. Our baby. Would you want our baby to die trying to save us? *This* is what your parents wanted for you. They wanted you to live."

Jake's hand caressed his unborn child. He released a shuddering sigh and glanced over to Grace. "I'm sorry."

"So am I," she replied.

"I never gave you chance to explain."

"You had every right to hate—"

"I don't hate you, Grace."

Wiping away a tear with the back of her hand, she started to walk back toward the table. Jake snaked a hand around her upper arm to drag her to a halt. "Wait." He took Grace's hand and placed it on Emily's belly. "Your nephew's kicking."

Adam watched her closely. Grace understood Jake's need to forgive himself so well because she'd never forgiven herself for leaving him behind.

Her hand continued to tremble until her eyes suddenly flew wide.

"She kicked," Grace said, her voice quivering.

"*He*," Jake corrected.

She just smiled.

The healing had finally begun—for both of them.

Chapter Twelve

Victoria knelt next to the stream, trying to pick the clumps of mud out of her hair. The task was next to impossible because her hair was so long and thick. For the first time, she was tempted to simply grab a pair of shears and lop it off as short as Grace's.

Unbuttoning her shirt, she pulled it off. Flakes of dried mud floated around her like a dirty snowfall. The shirt was probably past saving, but she tried to wash it anyway. Marks she could live with, and it still might be useful to wear when she mucked out stalls. The horses never offered their opinion of her clothes.

Even when I wear pants.

She scrubbed the shirt with her cake of soap, beat it against a rock, and then rinsed it best she could. No doubt about it. There would be stains that would serve as nothing more than a constant reminder of Matthew Riley.

She sighed, thinking the man was as stubborn as those stains and that he was probably going to be as permanently set in her mind as those marks were on her shirt. After wringing out the water, she hung the shirt over a tree branch to dry and returned to the stream.

Kneeling down again, she dunked her hair in the water and tried to work the soap through the tresses. There would probably still be some dirt clinging, but maybe she could run her comb through the wet hair and pull more clumps out that way.

God, how she wished she was back at the ranch and could soak in her beloved bathtub.

Closing her eyes against the harsh suds, Victoria worked her hands through the strands, plucking more bits of dirt out of her hair and wishing she'd taken the time to braid it when she'd awakened that morning.

As if she could have predicted the mud bath he was going to give her.

She giggled. Yes, she was a mess, but she'd gladly pay the price again. For the first time since she'd met Matthew, she'd seen the real man. He had a sense of humor. He had spontaneity. He could be charming. Grace had told her that he was a diamond in the rough—not that she'd been seeking advice on how to win the man.

Who exactly was she trying to fool? She'd already opened her heart to the blasted cowboy, probably from the first moment she saw him in the distance when he stole her breath away—right before his horse had muddied her clean laundry.

What is it with that man and dirt?

Strong hands were suddenly in her hair, smoothing the soap over the long tresses. She didn't startle. Somehow, she knew he would come to her. She only wished she knew why.

Desire?

Affection?

Or simple lust?

There were no words between them. His fingers threaded through her hair, drawing out scraps of mud. He helped her dunk her head again then retreated to crouch a little farther away.

Touching her had been a mistake, but Matthew hadn't been able to stop himself. Seeing her now, he wasn't sure how he could ever walk away. Her shoulders were bare, the straps to her camisole having slipped down her upper arms. In the moonlight, her skin looked as smooth as porcelain.

Victoria finished rinsing her hair and then flipped her head back, making her wet hair arc high over her head to slap against her back. As she turned to face him, her taut, pink nipples strained against the nearly transparent damp fabric.

His cock hardened in response.

He reached out for her before he could talk himself out of doing something so insane.

With a tug, he pulled her to him, lying back against the moss as she sprawled out on top of him. She mumbled what he figured was an apology, but he couldn't even process what she'd said. He stopped her words by cupping her neck and dragging her down into a heated kiss.

She tasted sweet, and when his tongue swept into her mouth, she responded with equal passion. Again and again, he plundered her, wanting her surrender, his tongue moving in and out, mimicking the act he so desperately desired.

There was no stopping this time.

His head swam and his ears buzzed. Overwhelmed by her taste, her scent, the feel of her breasts against his chest, he could hardly catch a breath. The kiss turned carnal, and he wanted to drown in it—to let all the feelings she sent ripping through him take control. Her hunger fed his own.

"Don't leave me," she whispered.

"Never. I'll never leave you."

She broke away from the kiss and unbuttoned his shirt with trembling fingers, each button taking much longer to give up the fight than he could stand.

She must think I'm made of iron.

Otherwise she wouldn't have teased him with her maddeningly slow pace. The woman was everything beautiful and desirable, from her silky hair to her pretty little toes.

Grabbing her knees, he sat up until her legs straddled his hips. He captured her mouth again for another tongue-dueling kiss. His hand moved between them and slipped up her wet camisole until he covered one of her breasts with his palm. Her hardened nipple branded his skin.

He moved his hands to her waist and lifted her until his mouth could reach her breast. Through the thin, wet material covering it, he drew her nipple into his mouth.

"Oh, God." She cradled Matthew's head against her breast, arching into him and splaying her fingers through his hair.

As he smiled and shifted his attention to her other breast, his fingers slipped up between them to tug at the ribbons holding her camisole together. They gave little resistance, and he pulled his lips away long enough to part the garment, reaching in and cupping each of her breasts in his hands.

She tightened her legs around his hips as he slowly rose to his knees, holding her hard against him before he laid her back on the moss. He settled himself between her thighs.

"I want to be inside you." He rocked against her.

A tear spilled from the corner of her eye.

He kissed it away. "What's wrong?"

Instead of giving him words, she led him back into a heated kiss.

Matthew ended the intoxicating kiss, crouched back and stared down at her. The woman was a work of art. The face of an angel. Full breasts. A slim waist. He reached for the front of her pants.

Her hands covered his. "I need... I should...."

Leaning in, he kissed her, hard and quick. "What is it?"

Her gaze shifted as if she was afraid to look him in the eye. "I've never been with a man. I want you to be my first."

Sobering sanity came back with a flood of alarm. He'd expected that she was a virgin, but hearing it spill from her lips reminded him of all it could cost her if he took her as his lover.

What in the hell had he been thinking?

Victoria deserved so much more than a dirt poor cowboy for a mate. He was about to rob her of the most important gift she would give a husband.

Pushing himself away, he scrambled to his feet to find her camisole. He picked it up and held it out to her as he grabbed his own discarded shirt.

"Matthew? I–I don't–I don't understand." She was on her feet, facing him with her armed crossed as trembling hands covered her breasts.

"Get dressed." The order came out much harsher than he'd meant, but he was having a hard time regaining any kind of self-control. He had to get away from her. Quickly.

She clutched her camisole to her chest. "I–I don't understand. You said you wanted—"

"Get dressed. *Now*. Before I do something I'll regret."

"Something you'll—" The hurt he'd seen in her eyes was slowly replaced with rage.

He turned his back and donned his shirt, taking a few deep breaths and trying to still the staccato rhythm of his heart. When he finally found the strength to turn back around, he was greeted by a stinging slap across his cheek.

He deserved far worse.

"I'm not some *toy* you can play with and then discard. I thought you cared for me."

"I do!"

She took a hesitant step back. "Then why?"

Because if I make love to you, I'll never let you go.

She would never understand that this was for her own good. He'd have to push her away with a lie. "Because I don't want to get married with a shotgun aimed at my back."

Her gasp echoed through the clearing. "I hate you, Matthew Riley."

A myriad of apologies tried to force their way through his lips. He kept his jaw clenched shut, reminding himself he was doing this for her, that she would regret giving him her chastity when he had nothing to offer in return.

Chapter Thirteen

Adam closed the stall gate and spun at the sound of a familiar sharp whistle.

Victoria and Matthew were back and perhaps had sorted through some of the tension and finally acknowledged their attraction.

Latching the gate, he went out to greet them.

He was probably a bad father to allow his unmarried daughter to head out on the trail alone with a man, especially since they'd been gone a few nights. Victoria had always played by her own rules. No one in his family had ever given a care about being anything other than who they were—gossip be damned.

His daughter had been raised to ride like a boy and work like a boy, even if she was a pretty girl. She'd been every bit as rambunctious as Jake and Ty, and the three of them found themselves in a peck of trouble from time to time. She might be beautiful and smart, but there was nothing fragile about her. There'd been no need to coddle or chaperone her. In fact, making her strong in a land that could break the weak seemed more important than turning her into a prissy, prim girl who couldn't take care of herself.

Adam had been dirt poor when he and Clara married and came to Montana with nothing more than a grant for several acres and their hopes and dreams. By the time Victoria came along, they'd hewn out a two-room cabin, living modestly when he discovered how much money could be made in the cattle business. They'd invested their profits in more animals, knowing if the gamble paid off their family wouldn't have to struggle anymore. As much as they'd wanted more children, the Lord had never seen fit to bless them with another.

Victoria worked alongside her parents, never complaining and always rising to any challenge. Yet now that he was wealthier than he'd ever dreamed, his daughter was paying a high price. The many men who gave her attention saw her as a means to a fortune rather than the woman she was. They weren't worthy of her, and she'd always been smart enough to turn them away.

She was lonely, and he didn't know how to fix things for her. An answer to his prayers—the right man—had ridden into her life.

A shame that the younger generation couldn't see things with the wisdom of age. Matthew and Victoria were perfectly matched, and the sparks flew as though metal struck flint every time they were together. After they'd had a few days of privacy—working side by side as Adam and Clara had early in their relationship—perhaps they'd seen through their stubborn pride and discovered how much they belonged together.

Matthew was a gentleman, and if he'd taken Victoria to his bed, he would marry her.

"Daddy!" Victoria herded the last of the new horses into the largest corral. "What do you think of the stock?"

Adam looked them over and nodded. "Mighty fine, princess."

Matthew had tied his stallion to the hitching post and was closing the gate to the corral. "They'll give you some fine colts and fillies, especially if you cross them with that big black stallion of yours."

"Might just pair a few of them with yours," Adam replied. "Sin's a nice looking animal. Might throw some good stock—maybe with Victoria's Cleo."

No other words were spoken, and the silence sure didn't bode well. He shifted his gaze from Victoria to Matthew and saw the strain.

Things hadn't gone as well on the trail as he'd hoped.

She dismounted and led her mare toward the barn. Every step she took, a few flakes of dried mud would fall from her pants, and there were rips and stains on her shirt.

"What in the hell happened to you?" he asked. "You're toting enough dirt on you to start a garden."

She gave him a lopsided smile. "Had a little problem fording a river."

Matthew scowled at Victoria. "Wouldn't have had a problem if *someone* could follow orders."

"You don't get to order me around, Matthew Riley. I'm *your* boss."

"Boss? *Boss?*" He narrowed his eyes. "*Adam's* my boss. All you are is a pain in my ass."

Yep. Things definitely hadn't gone well.

Sad to say, it appeared as if the relationship was even worse than the sorry state it had been in before the couple left.

Adam gave his neck a frustrated rub and diverted the topic. "Thought you'd both like to know that Grace accepted my proposal. We're to be married in two days."

"Oh, Daddy! How wonderful!" Victoria gave her father a quick kiss on the cheek before leading her mare into the barn.

Matthew's eyes followed her.

Adam had to clear his throat twice to get the cowboy's attention. "Hope you don't mind my being part of your family."

Jerking off his glove, Matthew extended his hand. "Mighty pleased for you both. Gotta admit, I never thought Grace would take a husband. Glad to see you changed her mind."

Adam shook his hand. "Well...let's just say it wasn't easy, but I think she sees the wisdom of it now." He leveled a hard stare. "Is there anything I should know before I bring her back here? We're mighty isolated, and I'd hate to find out too late that Grace has some problems that could follow her to my front door."

The man thought the question over for long enough to raise Adam's concern. "No," Matthew finally answered. "I'm pretty sure the only problem Grace had is dead and gone."

"Nice to know." A nod at the barn. "What exactly happened out there? She's spittin' mad at you. Don't need to go load my shotgun, do I?"

Matthew's lips thinned into a hard line. "No, sir. No shotgun. Hell, she probably wouldn't have me even if you pointed it at *her*."

"Sounds bad."

"It was."

"I'm heading into town to see Grace. Care to join me and fill me in on the details?"

With a chuckle, Matthew brushed the dried mud from his thighs. "I think I need a swim in the lake first. Why don't you head on into town and I'll join you later?"

***

Victoria sank deeper into the tub, leaning her head back against a rolled up towel and closing her eyes. A contented sigh fell from her lips. There was nothing she enjoyed more than a soak in her tub.

Would she ever be clean again? As she scrubbed herself from head to toe, she found mud behind her ears, underneath her fingernails, and even between her toes. Now that her skin and hair were clean, she indulged herself in a good, long soak—and a good, long sulk.

Her father was taking Grace as a wife.

About time he moved on with his life.

Victoria missed her mother, sometimes enough to bring tears, but her father needed Grace in his life. She'd feared he'd die of his grief after her mother passed.

It was easy to see Grace held his heart in the palms of her slender hands from the moment she'd collapsed on the doorstep. Thank the good Lord, she hadn't led Adam on a merry chase to win her. Grace obviously loved him as much as he loved her.

A frown bowed Victoria's lips. When Grace came to live at Twin Springs, things would change. While Daisy often needed a hand in the kitchen and with chores, Grace handled things with no trouble at all. Daisy had already wired a message that she was staying with her sister for quite a while to help care for her brood of nieces and nephews. When Grace came back to the ranch, Victoria would be as necessary as a fifth wagon wheel.

Lord above, how she hated thinking that she'd be in the way. Newlyweds—even older ones—didn't need someone constantly underfoot. They would probably try to include her in things they'd rather do alone, which would add to her burden of guilt.

Not only would she be entirely in the way, but Matthew would be leaving. What need did a ranch have for a cowboy with only a dozen or so horses and no cattle? Ty would stay on because he was like a son to her father. Adam had already deeded him a parcel of land he could use to build a home when he was ready to take a wife. Ty still fit in here.

Only Victoria was in the way.

Matthew would head out of a small town like White Pines just as soon as his sister was married and settled. When he rode out for some new cattle drive, he'd be dragging Victoria's battered heart with him and probably never even know it.

Why couldn't he want her? Yes, his body lusted after her, but only because she'd been a warm and willing woman. Why couldn't he want her as his own? As a wife and companion? As a mother to his children?

Probably because he loved his life exactly the way it was.

"Settling a cowboy down is like trying to hold a tornado with a lasso," her father always said.

Matthew didn't want her. He'd pushed her away like a leper. That wound to her pride still stung. When he left, she'd stay behind, mourning what could have been the rest of her life.

If only she had someplace else to go. Perhaps her father would let her travel back East, someplace like New York City. Maybe she would get on a big ship and sail to England. As if those bustling locales would make her heartache disappear... She was fairly certain her father wouldn't let her leave with no real purpose for the trek.

New York wasn't for her. Neither was England. And the ranch would be Grace's home after the marriage.

Victoria didn't truly belong anywhere now.

I want to run away!

Bad idea. Her father would simply chase her down. No, if she was going to escape, she needed a damned good reason.

She'd keep her eyes and ears open for the right opportunity. A teaching position in another town. A rich family who needed a governess. Anything that would save her from living a lonely life in White Pines.

***

Matthew dove below the surface, rinsing the rest of the soap from his body and hair. Took a lot of scrubbing to get the mud off.

Was Victoria having the same problem as she sat in her fancy bathtub? Naked.

Despite the chill of the water, his cock swelled just thinking of how beautiful she was—of how close he'd come to possessing her.

No more of that.

His thoughts betrayed him at every turn. Try as he might, he simply couldn't banish Victoria from his mind.

How easy it would have been to take her there by the water. She'd been willing. He'd been drowning in his desire for her. His pride wouldn't allow it. He couldn't live with himself if they had to use her money to live, and he sure couldn't support her in the lifestyle she was accustomed to.

Until he had something more to offer her—a home and enough money to keep food on the table—he didn't deserve her. Taking her virginity would have robbed her of the chance to make a good marriage.

His blood boiled when he pictured her with another man. There was no way he could stay in town to watch her marry, have children, and find happiness with someone else.

As soon as Grace and Adam tied the knot, it would be time to go. There were more long drives to work, and perhaps he'd take half the money he and Grace had saved and search for a spot somewhere he could own. If that time came, he would come back for Victoria—as if a woman that beautiful and that wealthy would be able to keep men at bay long enough to wait for some miracle that might never happen. It seemed unbelievable that she hadn't already been claimed.

Hauling himself out of the lake, Matthew rubbed his body dry, dropped the towel, and jerked on his clean clothes. As soon as he could get Sin saddled, he would head into White Pines to see Grace at the Four Aces.

And while he was there, he could use a good, stiff drink or two.

Chapter Fourteen

Jake was tending bar when Matthew walked through the front doors. He waved, so Matthew headed that direction, leaned against the bar, and dropped his hat on the surface.

"What's your poison?" Jake asked.

"Beer."

Matthew sat back nursing his drink and watching Jake.

The guy had a relaxed way of dealing with the patrons, and they obviously appreciated his wit and good nature. The family resemblance was there, especially when he smiled. He had Grace's eyes and mouth.

After Matthew finished his drink, Jake offered a refill. Instead of walking away to tend other customers, he stared at the stairs leading to the upstairs bedrooms. "What's Grace's story?"

"Story?"

"She's...different. Kinda timid. Why ain't she got a husband already? What with her looks and all. Figured men would be sniffing after her skirts from the time she was first becoming a woman."

He wasn't sure exactly what Jake was asking and how much Grace really wanted people to know. Honesty was the best policy. "She didn't want a husband."

Jake let out a chuckle. "If I was a woman, can't say I'd want one, neither. She's nice looking, though. And the way she cooks? Hard to believe someone didn't grab her up anyway. You thinkin' of staying on here after she and Adam get hitched?"

"Haven't decided yet."

Jake took the curt response in stride and went back to waiting on other customers.

What exactly was Matthew supposed to do when Grace and Adam wed? With the changes Adam had made at the ranch, he wouldn't be needed any longer—especially when it was obvious that Ty would stay on. If Adam expanded his horse breeding plans, there might someday be a call for two ranch hands, but as things stood, the place only needed one. He wasn't about to let Adam keep him on the payroll just because of Grace. His pride wouldn't allow it.

After Matthew drained his beer, Jake looked down the bar and raised an eyebrow.

Matthew gestured for a refill.

Draining that glass in short order, he thought about Victoria and generally felt sorry for himself. After he left the ranch, he wouldn't be seeing her again unless he traveled back to Montana to visit Grace. He didn't anticipate making that kind of trek often. His sister was going to be a married woman, and she didn't need her bachelor brother constantly underfoot. He'd probably go back to the life he knew best— being a cowboy.

Any return trip he made to Twin Springs to visit was sure to include Victoria. Perhaps Victoria's beau. Or worse, a husband. Children that belonged to another man, a man who would have the right to put his hands on her whenever he wanted.

Matthew gulped the remainder of his beer, slammed the mug on the counter ,and gestured to Jake.

"More beer?"

"No. Whiskey."

***

The knock on Grace's bedroom door came as a surprise. Adam had left hours ago.

"Grace? You in there?"

Jake.

"Coming!" She threw open the door.

"Um…" His gaze shifted from her to the stairs and back again. "I wasn't sure if I should bother you, but…" He shrugged. "Didn't rightly know who else to ask."

"Ask? About what?"

"Your brother… I mean, *our* brother."

She'd assumed Matthew had returned to the ranch with Adam. "Matthew? I don't understand."

"He seems intent upon drinking the bar dry."

All she could do was blink a few times as his words registered on her mind. "Matthew doesn't drink."

"He does tonight."

She stood there, speechless in shock.

When their long drives were over, most of the cowboys would blow a good portion of their pay at the closest bar and brothel, but Matthew had never followed their example. If the siblings had been lucky enough to avoid Steven Shay's attempts to find her, he usually bought a new book, a new shirt and pants, and saved the rest of his earnings. He'd been known to bed down with a welcoming widow or two, but drink?

If he was trying to tie one on, no doubt it involved Victoria. Grace needed to go to him, but she didn't relish the catcalls and stares she'd get from the other customers.

Yet Matthew needed her, and Jake wanted her help. "Right behind you."

"Thanks, Grace."

She followed him down the stairs, quickly finding her brother in the crowd. A bottle of cheap whiskey sat on the bar next to his weathered hat.

Ignoring the crude remarks that followed her like a shadow, she reached his side and picked up the half-empty bottle. "Did you drink *all* of this?"

He downed a shot of whiskey, took the bottle from her, and splashed more liquid on the counter than in his glass.

Jake reached over and retrieved the bottle.

Matthew turned to Grace and shot her a smile. "Well, well. How ish my lovely shister this fine evening?"

Grace looked him square in the eye. "You're drunk."

"Not yet, but 'men at some time are the masters of their fate.'"

"You're quoting Shakespeare? *Now?* What's wrong with you?"

Matthew scowled. "'She's beautiful, and therefore to be wooed; she is a woman, therefore to be won.'"

"I am *not* in the mood to play our old game. Tell me...are you drinking because of Victoria?"

He pondered that one for a moment. "'But love is blind, and lovers cannot see what petty follies they themselves commit.'" He pointed at his empty glass.

Jake shook his head in response.

An appeal to Will got the same reply.

"'Though those that are betrayed, do feel the treason sharply...'"

She narrowed her eyes. "'It will come to pass, that every braggart shall be found an ass.'"

Turning to his sister, he simply said, "Touché." Looking down at Jake, he made one more plea. "What'sh a guy gotta do to get a drink 'round here?"

Jake shook his head again and tossed her an entreating look.

"Go home, Matthew," she ordered. "You're embarrassing yourself."

"Fine. I'll go. Sheems my bushiness isn't wanted here."

Grace bit her tongue to keep from scolding him like an overprotective mother. He grabbed his hat and put it on his head, albeit in a crooked fashion. Heading toward the front door, he had some difficulty finding a straight path to reach it.

Jake walked back to her with a frown on his face. "You want me to follow him?"

She sighed. "No. He'll just get mad. Sin will get him home."

"Who's Sin?"

"His stallion. I'll go make sure he gets headed in the right direction." At the entrance she pushed open the swinging doors and watched the spectacle that was her drunken brother.

It took him a few tries to get on his huge horse, but at least he was facing the stallion's ears and not its rump when he was done hauling his way into the saddle. She should've taken Jake up on his offer, but when Sin headed in the right direction without any assistance from his rider, relief washed over her.

At least the horse seemed to know the way home.

Grace returned to the bar and stopped to talk to Jake. "I'm sorry you had to see that. Matthew's never done anything like that before. He's a good man. He's not a drunk. Our father was a drunk, and Matthew wouldn't—"

"Our father drank?"

She hadn't meant to stir up questions. Since avoiding the topic now wasn't an option, she spoke as if they shared a father. "Yes. He drank and gambled. He wasn't...a good man. I haven't seen him since before you were born, and I don't care to see him ever again. Not even sure he's still among the living."

He gave her a brusque nod. "Adam thinks well of Matthew, so I reckon I'll let this one pass. Man's entitled to blow off steam now and then. What's eatin' him?"

"I'm not entirely sure, but I think it's got something to do with Victoria."

"Reckoned." Jake went back to work.

Grace made her way quickly back across the saloon, ducking the grabby customers to reach the safety of the stairs. She thanked God that she was going to be heading back to the ranch soon.

It appeared that she might be needed there.

***

Once he was back in the barn, Matthew dropped most of the animal's tack on the ground instead of taking his usual care. He simply couldn't find the will to work. Somehow, he managed to get Sin into a stall, but the horse had to take most of the credit for the endeavor.

Instead of going to the bunkhouse, he found himself standing at the back of the house, staring up at Victoria's bedroom window.

What did she look like when she slept in a bed instead of on the cold, hard ground? Did that gorgeous mane of dark hair spread over her pillow? Was her nightgown as transparent as her wet camisole?

Closing his eyes, he imagined covering her small frame with his own body as he slowly sank inside her welcoming warmth. Damn, but just the thought of her made him hard as a rock.

Why couldn't the whiskey drown her out of his mind? What kind of spell had this woman cast?

Memories assaulted him with everything about her—her scent, her face, her laugh. He'd never be able to escape his own mind.

Watching her window, he wished she would magically appear. Then a notion hit him.

He bent over, picked up a pebble and tossed it at her window. When there was no immediate response, he repeated the action. Several times.

The window finally opened.

Victoria pushed her head outside to find out why it sounded like a hail storm when the night sky was clear enough to see stars. Seeing Matthew grinning up at her, she had no idea what to think. "What in heaven's name are you doing?"

He put his hand over his heart. "'But soft! What light through yonder window breaks? It is the east, and Juliet is the sun. Arise, fair sun, and kill the envious moon who is already sick and pale with grief that thou her maid art far more fair than she.'"

She could only gape at him, her heart hammering as she wondered if the man had lost his wits. When he took a couple of stuttering steps closer to the house, she realized he'd been drinking. "Go to bed."

"'She speaks: O, speak again, bright angel! For thou are as glorious to this night, being o'er my head as is a winged messenger of heaven...'"

The man's drunk, she warned herself. The words he chose made her ache to hear more affectionate quotes, even if he was too deep in his cups to know what he was saying. He might not truly mean any of it, but she needed to hear him anyway.

Before she could think too hard on why she was doing something so foolish, she gave him what he wanted. "'What man art thou that thus bescreen'd in night so stumblest on my counsel?'"

His grin was wide enough to reveal the sparkle of moonlight on his white teeth.

He took a quick, stumbling step before he spoke again. "'By a name I know not how to tell thee who I am; my name, dear saint, is hateful to myself, because it is an enemy to thee; Had I it written, I would tear the word.'"

With a shake of her head, she laughed. "You really should go to bed."

Matthew put both of his hands over his heart and grimaced as if wounded at her words. "'O, wilt thou leave me so unsatisfied?' Come down, Victoria. Come down to me, my fair Juliet. Come meet your Romeo."

"I shouldn't."

"But I love you!"

A gasp escaped, loud enough it had to echo off the distant mountains. "You *love* me?" Tears welled up in her eyes when she heard the words she feared she'd never hear from a man—especially the one she loved with all her heart.

He didn't mean it. He *couldn't* mean it.

She glared at him, angry that the alcohol was making him speak of love when he couldn't possibly have those kinds of feelings for her. "Don't you say that to me! Don't you *dare* say that to me!"

He dropped to one knee and placed his right palm over his heart. "Victoria Morgan, I love you! Come down to me and let me show you how much!"

***

Having been awakened by the pebbles that missed Victoria's window and hit his own, Adam had been patiently taking in the whole exchange from his bedroom.

Matthew was clearly sotted, and Adam hoped for a moment that the cowboy didn't find himself in that state often. It wasn't as if he showed an inclination toward being a drunk, so he decided to give him the benefit of the doubt.

He was more concerned at his daughter's response to Matthew's enthusiastic pleas, especially when the admission of love spilled from his lips. Sensing that this situation was getting entirely out of hand, Adam would have to bring the curtain down on this impromptu Shakespearean performance before either of them did something they might regret in the morning.

Yes, there was love between them, but coming together because of a drunken confession wasn't a good way to start any relationship.

He slipped on his pants, hurried downstairs, and went out the kitchen door to give the inebriated cowboy a proper escort to the bunkhouse.

When he caught up with Matthew, he put his hand on the younger man's shoulder. "Come on, Romeo. It's time for bed."

Matthew grinned like a simpleton and waved at Victoria.

"Goodnight, Juliet," Adam called up to his daughter. She started to stutter a protest, but he held up a hand. "We'll talk about this tomorrow morning. Go to bed."

She nodded and slowly shut her window.

Matthew let Adam push him toward the bunkhouse, but then suddenly stopped and turned back to glare. "'Et tu,' Adam?"

"'The course of true love never did run smooth.' Now go to bed, son."

***

Matthew woke up to a painfully loud beat throbbing in his head. He raised his hand to shield his bleary, watery eyes from the far too bright light streaming through the window.

A shuffling noise from the adjacent room drifted into the sleeping quarters. He groaned and tried to pull his blanket over his head, but he wasn't even under the covers. He'd slept on top of his bedding, still dressed in the same clothes he'd worn the day before, right down to his dirty boots.

Searching his fuzzy mind, he remembered talking to Jake at the Four Aces. Then the rest of his memories of the night just...stopped.

Had he seen Grace?

Maybe.

Maybe not.

His head seemed destined to explode. He facetiously thought about searching for his gun simply to end his misery. Rolling to his side, he hid his face under his pillow. His mouth felt as though some small, furry animal had crawled inside and died.

The door to the room opened and closed with a bang.

"You miserable son of a bitch, if you don't—" When he opened his eyes, Adam was standing there. Matthew immediately shut up.

"Miserable son of a bitch, huh? No witty Shakespeare quotes this beautiful morning?"

"Shakespeare? What the hell are you talking about?" Matthew tried to search his hazy memory, but the effort hurt his head too much.

"Get up. We need to brand the new horses today. It's hours past dawn."

He'd forgotten about the branding.

How in the hell could he possibly brand horses when all he wanted to do was die?

"You want to tell me what you intended last night?" Adam asked.

"Intended?" Matthew cringed—the sound of his own voice reverberating through his skull.

Adam tried not to get too angry, but it had been his daughter being wooed by this erstwhile Romeo. "Don't remember, do you?"

If Matthew forgot what had passed between him and Victoria, then she was bound to get hurt. She had seemed very pleased with last night's little balcony scene.

"Any of it coming back, Romeo?"

"For Christ's sake, keep your voice down."

Adam folded his arms over his chest. "You put on quite a performance last night."

"Performance? Adam, I'm *dying* here. Please stop. I can't brand right now. If I get anywhere near that smell, I swear I'll–I'll—" Hand over his mouth, Matthew ran out the back door.

Adam headed back to the kitchen to talk to Victoria, wanting to smooth some of the rough edges before she saw Matthew.

After hanging up his hat, he said, "Morning, princess."

"Good morning, Daddy." She hummed as she cooked.

Damn. His daughter thought that she and Matthew had finally found some common ground upon which they could build a future.

"Matthew coming in for breakfast?" she asked.

"Doubt it." What could he say to her? "He's feeling mighty poorly this morning."

She flipped the eggs in the skillet. "I reckoned. He was drunker than a skunk last night. I'd be surprised if he remembers anything at all. I'll have to take him some strong coffee and toasted bread later."

"You're not upset he might not recall the little...show he gave you? You heard what he said, that he loved—"

"Stop!" She took a deep breath. "Just stop. I know he didn't mean it."

"Victoria...You said—"

She wouldn't let him finish. "I know what *I* said. I know what *he* said. But it really doesn't change anything, does it? Drunk or sober, we don't suit. It was flattering, but that's all. You want some eggs before you head out?"

"Thank you, princess. If I don't say so often enough, you're mighty special."

"Thank you, Daddy. You are too." As an afterthought she added, "Please don't tell Matthew what he did or–or what he said. He'd be horribly embarrassed, and I wouldn't want that." She went back to humming as she finished breakfast.

Then he heard the quote uttered so quietly that she probably figured he wouldn't hear. "'He jests at scars, that never felt a wound.'"

His daughter really was in love with Matthew Riley

But would the stupid cowboy realize how she felt—how they both felt—before it was too late?

Chapter Fifteen

Grace smoothed the dollop of white icing over the middle layer of her wedding cake.

Her wedding cake. What a strange notion.

She'd never thought the day would come that she'd agree to become the property of some man—especially after living through years of being Stephen Shay's obsession. Although she'd eluded him, there had been times she'd felt as though her life was more under his control than her own.

She'd never wanted to belong to some man.

Adam Morgan wasn't just some man.

Her heart was near to bursting with love for him, and how that had happened so quickly and so completely still remained a mystery. It was as if all the walls she'd carefully built to shield herself had fallen like the ones that had once surrounded Jericho.

Oh, yes, she loved him. More than was probably prudent.

What would he think of her if he knew the truth, the *whole* truth she'd hidden for so long?

The terror Stephen ignited in her had died with the man, but another fear remained, every bit as frightening as what Shay might have done if he'd captured her. Would someone come looking for her one day to make her answer for her crime? Would they haul her back to San Francisco for a trial? Or would they bring a noose and string her up in the nearest tree? She shuddered and told herself she wasn't a murderess. He'd been attacking her. Surely it would be seen as self-defense.

Who was she trying to fool? The Shays were a powerful, vengeful family full of politicians and businessmen. No one witnessed the attack. No one would *ever* take her word, not if the Shays had other opinions on what happened. If they found out she'd killed Stephen, the Shays would make sure she hanged.

Why hadn't someone come after her already? She'd been in White Pines for almost a month. Shouldn't the Pinkerton detectives the Shays always hired have already found her trail? Matthew had followed it easy enough. Shouldn't the San Francisco police be hunting her down?

Maybe no one was looking for her. Maybe no one connected her with Stephen's death. Maybe she didn't truly have a death sentence hanging over her life.

Maybe she could finally be free!

Two strong arms wrapped around her waist, pulling her back against a muscular body she'd grown to recognize. Lips brushed her ear before teeth gently tugged on the lobe, sending a shiver of delight over her.

How quickly she'd learned to love the feel of Adam close to her—to enjoy the wonderful sensations only he could inspire. His lips touched her neck, kissing the sensitive skin and pulling a contented sigh from her.

"Oh, Gracie. I want you so bad."

His words made delicious heat pool between her thighs. She'd never played little love games before, and she wasn't sure what to do to let him know she felt the same.

Putting down the knife, she swiped a finger across it to pick up some icing. She turned in his arms and held up the finger. "Would you like a taste?"

He smiled, took her hand, and lifted it to his lips. Then he slowly licked the icing from her finger. "Delicious."

Before she knew his intention, he wrapped his arms around her and kissed her.

The sugary sweetness still clung to his lips. Just as Grace gained the courage to deepen the kiss, he pulled back.

She groaned her displeasure at the abrupt ending to what had promised to be a wonderful kiss. "Adam? What's wrong?"

"Not a thing."

She lifted herself on tiptoes to try and kiss him again.

He touched his lips to her forehead instead. "Tomorrow, darlin'. If I kiss you again tonight, I'm going to carry you up to your room and make love to you right now."

Adam loved how Grace blushed red at his honesty. Ever so slowly, he'd been trying to overcome her resistance, stoking the fire he felt within her whenever she allowed her guard to drop. A kiss. A touch. A caress. And gradually, she'd responded.

Now she kissed him back with as much passion as he felt for. Damn, but it was getting harder and harder to leave her at the Four Aces every night.

Tomorrow, he wouldn't have to.

Her eyes rose to meet his. "I–I want you to."

Now he'd done it. He'd gone and trapped himself with his own words because he wasn't sure if she meant *to* or *too*, and he sure as hell didn't want to guess wrong. Turned out, he didn't have to guess at all.

She took his hand and led him to the stairs.

He shuffled along behind her, not entirely sure what he should do. His body was hard and aching, screaming at him to scoop her up in his arms and carry her to her room. Respect told him to wait those last few hours to make her his wife first. He planted his feet and dragged her to a stop.

She turned and tilted her head. "Y–you don't want to...come upstairs?"

Adam called himself an idiot as he shook his head. His gut told him this was some kind of test. Grace might mean to follow through when she took him to her bed, but something told him now wasn't the time to go.

"I thought if men wanted to...do...*that*...they couldn't stop themselves. Even if the woman...didn't want to."

That statement filled in the last puzzle piece. He finally understood all she been unable to tell him.

He kissed her forehead again. "Any man who doesn't respect a woman telling him no is a rapist."

Her gaze dropped to the floor. "Some men don't respect a woman's no."

He prayed for the proper amount of patience to help her through this—and for a way to hide the rage flowing through him at what had happened to her. Should he ever meet the monster who hurt Grace, Adam would put an end to his crimes. Permanently.

While he wanted to make love to her, he would only do so when she was ready—no matter how long it took.

He put a finger under her chin and lifted. "*I* would. I'd respect a women's no."

"Always?"

He nodded.

"I–I need to tell you something, Adam. If we're going to be married, you need to know."

"What do I need to know?"

She tried to drop her chin again, but he gripped it to keep her where she was. Her teeth tugged at her bottom lip and she wrung her hands.

"You can tell me anything, darlin'. I'll still love you."

"No matter what?"

"No matter what."

"I–I'm not a–a virgin." Her face flamed a brighter red, and she tried to avert her gaze again.

He leaned in to brush his lips over hers. "I've got something to tell you." He gave her a lazy grin. "Neither am I."

Grace's eyes were as big as saucers until his words sank in. Then the laughter bubbled out of her, loud and sweet. Such a joyful sound— it settled on his heart, reminding him just how much happiness she'd brought back into his life.

She threw herself against him, wrapped her arms around his waist, and squeezed him tight. "I do love you, Adam."

"I love you too, Gracie."

***

Storm clouds darkened the sky as thunder rumbled in the distance.

Grace adjusted her hair as she looked in the mirror, praying the weather wouldn't portend her marriage.

She couldn't think like that. Marrying Adam was the right thing to do.

So long as her past wouldn't catch up with her.

The dress was lovely, the pale pink suiting her brown hair and eyes. Pretty pearl buttons held the bodice together. Lace bordered her wrists and the neckline. She'd left her hair down, and it brushed her shoulders as she moved, longer now than it had been since she was fifteen. The monthly ritual of cutting it no longer comforted her, even though Adam told her he loved her exactly as she was—short hair and all.

"Grace." Victoria laid a gentle hand on her arm. "It's time."

Emily handed her a small bouquet of daisies.

Grace gave her a smile. "Thank you for all your help with the dress. It was very sweet of you to do so much of the sewing."

"It's only fair," Emily replied. "You did so much of the cooking. Besides, we're sisters now." She tried for a hug, but her belly got in the way. "God's tears, I'm as big as an elephant."

Lightly touching Emily's rounded stomach, Grace smiled. "You're no such thing. You're beautiful. Absolutely *glowing*."

A soft knock sounded on the door before Matthew opened it. "You ready, Grace?"

She nodded, trying to push aside her fears that no matter how much she loved Adam this happiness couldn't last.

No!

Today was her wedding day. She wouldn't let anything spoil her joy.

She straightened her spine and squared her shoulders. "I'm ready."

Her brother's reflection grinned. "Damn, Grace. You sure clean up nice."

Victoria whirled to face him. "Was that supposed to be a compliment? What a horrible thing to say."

"It *was* a compliment. Grace thought so." He glanced back to Grace. "Didn't you?"

Emily shook her head and stepped between Victoria and Matthew. "Grace is getting married today. You two aren't dragging her into your fight. For this one day, can't you two put aside your quarrels and be polite?"

Victoria bowed her head. "I'm sorry."

Matthew scuffed the toe of his shoe against the floorboards. "Me, too." He sighed then held a hand out to Victoria. "Truce?"

Her hand hesitantly lifted to touch his. She swallowed hard and nodded.

"You look mighty pretty, Victoria." His voice was scratchy—as if he'd just swallowed something rough. He hurriedly turned to Emily. "You're pretty too."

"I'm about as pretty as a buffalo and almost the same size." Emily glanced to Grace. "The bride is truly beautiful."

"Thank you," Grace said, her voice barely a whisper. "We should be going."

She led the way out of the bedroom as Emily followed.

As Victoria picked up her bouquet and headed toward the door, Matthew reached out to grab her wrist. "Wait. Please."

God, he wanted to hold her. He wanted to tell her how beautiful that green dress was on her, how it made her dark hair shine and brought out the color of her eyes. He wanted to beg her to accept him, poor though he was. He wanted to claim her as his own.

Instead, he lifted her hand to his lips and brushed a kiss over her knuckles. "You're beautiful."

A blush spread over her cheeks. "Grace is beautiful."

"She is." He kissed her hand again. "But *you* are the most beautiful woman I've ever seen."

She pulled her hand back. "Thank you."

"I need to tell you something. I'm leaving in a couple of days."

"Leaving?"

"Grace doesn't need me here anymore. Now that the cattle are gone, neither does Adam. I–I need to go."

She clutched at his hand. "Why? *Why* do you have to go? Why *now?*"

How could he explain to her how hard it was to see her every day and not be able to touch her?

He squeezed her hand then dropped his own to his side. "Look, I haven't told Grace yet. I don't want to upset her on her wedding day."

Were those tears in her eyes?

Of course they were—she obviously had feelings for him. Her kisses had been so hot, so passionate. While that realization made him happier than he thought possible, it didn't change a damned thing. He didn't have anything to offer her, and he couldn't confess all he felt. No, this way was better. A clean break for both of them.

So why did it feel as if someone had buried a knife in his heart?

Victoria's hands trembled as she let her fingertips run over the petals of one of the daisies in her bouquet. "She'll be heartbroken."

"I'll tell her soon."

"I'll be—" A quick shake of her head before she glanced to the door. "Everyone's waiting. We should go."

Matthew sighed before nodding. Then he followed Victoria out the door.

***

The rain began to fall in torrents only moments after the wedding party arrived at the church, the sound of hail accompanying the wail of the rushing wind.

Grace turned to her brother. "A bad sign?"

"Nonsense. It's just a storm. No more, no less." He held his arm out and nodded toward the altar. "Adam's waiting for you."

"He's a good man." She settled her hand in the crook of his elbow.

"I know he'll be good to you, or else I wouldn't be lettin' you go." He cleared his throat. "Grace, I–I hope I did right by you all these years—that I kept you safe."

"How could you think otherwise?"

"It's hard, you know."

"Hard?"

"To let another man look after you now. But I know Adam loves you."

Leaning in, she kissed her brother's cheek. "I know I probably never said it enough, but thank you. You kept me safe—but more than that, you've been my best friend."

She tried to wipe away a tear that slid down her cheek, but Matthew held tight to the hand she'd given him and her other hand was full of daisies.

Her brother reached over to smooth away her tear with his free hand. "No crying. You're doing the right thing."

"Happy tears," she replied.

Reverend David gestured to them. Emily and Victoria had already headed down the aisle and were waiting for her. Adam stood to the right, dressed in a dark suit and appearing handsome enough to stop her heart. Jake was his best man.

Just seeing them together made her heart sing. Without even knowing it, Adam had saved her when he'd accepted Jake as his own and brought him back to Twin Springs to raise. Now, Adam would save her again by making her his wife.

Wife.

She was really going to be Adam Morgan's wife.

Matthew gave her a gentle nudge with his shoulder, and she threw him a grateful smile. Then she let him escort her to the altar.

Such a quick ceremony—it flew by before Grace could catch her breath. She recited all the usual vows, not even flinching when she promised to obey him all the days of her life.

Adam made his own promises as well, to love, honor and protect her, giving a little extra emphasis to that last vow. When Reverend David had pronounced them man and wife, Adam kissed her with enough passion that she sagged against him, forgetting for a moment that they were in a church.

The wedding party was supposed to head back to the Four Aces for a nice meal and some cake. By the time he led her to the door, the rain had thankfully stopped. The road, however, was a muddy mess from the cloudburst.

Grace fussed for a moment, afraid her wedding dress would be ruined if she tried to walk across the ruts and puddles to get to the Four Aces. About to lift her skirts and hope for the best, she was suddenly picked up in Adam's arms.

"You can't carry me all the way to the saloon."

His kiss kept her from uttering another protest. "You're light as a feather, darlin'."

Victoria's heart was full as she watched her father carrying Grace across the muddy street. Seeing them together reminded her that there was still love in the world. A squeal next to her made her whip her head around to see Jake sweep Emily into his arms.

"Jake Curtis! You put me down. I'm heavier than a horse."

He didn't answer, only kissed his wife's cheek and sprinted out onto the street, jumping puddles when they were in his path. Their laughter trailed behind them.

Standing by the front door, Victoria let melancholy wash over her. She'd never felt so alone. With a resigned sigh, she fisted her hands in her long skirt and lifted, hoping the mud would wash out.

As she took that first step, she found herself lifted into Matthew's strong arms.

"Put me down," she insisted. "This isn't proper."

As if propriety had anything to do with why she wished he would set her back on her feet. She couldn't bear being in his arms, being surrounded by his heat, by his scent. It all served to remind her just what she was going to lose. And, dear God, how could she watch him ride out of her life?

He grinned and shook his head. "Can't let you get that gorgeous dress all dirty, especially when you seem bent on bathing in mud so often."

She squirmed in his arms. "Put me down."

Stopping in the middle of the street, he stood over a large mud puddle. "Put you down? Do you mean it? How about *here?*" He held her away from his body and feigned dropping her.

She clung to him. "No! Don't you *dare* drop me!"

Cradling her against him, he asked, "Are you sure?"

She nodded against his neck, feeling like a drunk who'd been handed a bottle of whiskey. Everything about him filled her senses. Her lips brushed over his skin, sending a shudder ripping through him. That reaction brought a smile and encouraged her to do it again before she grew braver and traced the line of his jaw with the tip of her tongue.

He groaned deep in his throat and turned his face until their noses touched. "Why did you do that?"

"Because I wanted to."

"God, Victoria. Don't you know what that does to me?"

"It makes you want to run away."

"What?"

"It does! Every time we've kissed, you've pushed me away."

"I can't talk about this now." With a heavy sigh, he headed toward the Four Aces.

Her sigh echoed his as he set her back on her feet when they reached the saloon's front doors.

As she turned to head inside, he reached for her hand and pulled her back. "It's not you. It was *never* you."

"Then what is it?"

"I can't...you deserve... Ah, hell." He tugged her into his arms, planting his lips on hers. A long, loving kiss that left her wanting more.

Finding some courage, she lightly brushed his lips with her tongue. He growled and opened them for her. Lord, how she loved to kiss him like that.

He eased away first. "I wish... I wish..." He never finished the thought and withdrew from their embrace. "We need to go inside."

She clenched her hands into fists, wanting to pound them against his chest to make him tell her all that he was hiding. With as much wounded pride as she could muster, she gathered her skirts in her hands and hurried into the Four Aces.

***

"That was a lovely supper, Grace." Will patted his belly. "But now I've got a hankering for some of that cake. Been starin' at it since yesterday." He leaned in and winked. "Only took a couple swipes of icing when you weren't lookin'."

"We were just about to cut it." Grace glanced over at Adam and blushed at his intense stare, one so full of desire it rose around him like an aura.

The meal she'd spent all day cooking tasted like ashes because she'd allowed her anxiety over the wedding night to take hold.

Her whole body grew hot whenever she imagined what would happen between her and her new husband when they got back to the Twin Springs. God help her, she couldn't decide if she was excited or terrified.

So many bad memories threatened to swallow her. Several times since he told her she would marry him, she'd purposefully ignored those frightening recollections. Now that they were actually man and wife, the memories flared back to life each time he threw her a knowing smile.

She tried to hide her fear.

His lips dropped to a frown as he marched across the room. "What's wrong?"

Grace unstacked the cake plates. "Nothing. Nothing's wrong."

"Gracie..." The back of his knuckles stroked her cheek, and she closed her eyes to savor his touch. "You can tell me anything."

She opened her eyes and fussed over cutting the cake as her cheeks warmed. "I–I was thinking about...our wedding night." The last three words were nothing but a breathless whisper.

How could she tell Adam about her apprehensions? How could she possibly let him know the shame she'd suffered? It had taken every ounce of her strength to confess she wasn't a virgin. Only knowing that a couple needed honesty for a marriage to succeed helped her gain the nerve. That courage vanished whenever she considered telling him the whole story. But if she didn't, how could she explain her fears?

His hand caressed her cheek. "I'm thinking about it too. I won't hurt you, darlin'."

Grace breathed a shuddering sigh, trying to hold back tears. "I know. I'm just...worried."

Tugging her into his arms, he kissed her, long and lovingly until her worries melted and she relaxed against him.

He smiled down at her. "Trust me?"

"You know I do."

"Then stop worrying and enjoy your wedding cake." His lips brushed hers again.

Will rolled his eyes. "Oh, for the love of... Adam, would you quit pawing your wife long enough for us to get somethin' to eat?"

Adam chuckled, probably at the furious flush on her face.

She cut a piece of cake to hand to Will as the rest of the wedding party gathered around to get a slice. After she served everyone, she cut a piece and handed it to Adam.

He crooked his finger at her.

She took a step closer.

Pinching off a small piece he held it up to her lips.

Grace smiled, opened her mouth and let Adam feed her. He handed her back the plate, and she fed him a piece of cake. As she pulled her hand away from his mouth, he captured her wrist and gave her icing covered fingers a kiss.

"Best cake I ever ate." Will set his empty plate down on the table. Grace reached to pick it up, but he shook his head. "Not this time, Grace. We'll take care of the cleaning."

Victoria and Matthew each grabbed empty plates and carried them to the kitchen.

"Thank you," she whispered before turning to meet Adam's gaze. "I suppose it's time to go home."

"Are you ready?"

She nodded, knowing somehow everything would work out fine—because he loved her.

As he reached for her hand, the front doors of the saloon slammed open.

"Bar's closed, Henry," Will told the young man whose eyes were darting around. "You're a mite young to be lookin' for a drink."

"Got a telegram," the boy insisted, holding up a crumpled envelope.

"Well, then give it over." Will held out his hand.

"Ain't for you. Gotta give it to who it's addressed to."

"You're trying my patience, boy."

Adam stepped up and extended his hand. "It's gotta be for me."

"For you?" Grace asked. "Who would send you a telegram?"

"Probably Ty—letting me know he got the cattle sold." He gestured to Henry. "Let me have it."

The boy took a step back. "It ain't for you, neither."

"Then who's it for, boy?" Will asked.

"Miss Victoria."

Chapter Sixteen

"Where's Miss Victoria? This here telegram's for her," Henry insisted.

Adam reached for the message again.

Henry jerked it behind his back. "Cain't give it to you. I keep tellin' ya—it's for Miss Victoria."

"For me?" Victoria asked as she came out of the kitchen. "A telegram for me?"

Matthew stepped up to her side and tossed a scowl at Henry. "Who's it from?"

"Cain't tell you that. It's for *Miss Victoria*." Henry hurried to her, handing over the wrinkled envelope. Then he held out his dirty hand.

"For the love of..." Will dug around his pocket and set a coin on the boy's palm. "Now git."

Victoria opened the envelope and read the message. She had no idea who would be sending her a telegram because it was far too soon to have news of a job from any of the letters she'd sent requesting information. Unexpected telegrams never held good news.

ty bishop injured stop in hospital stop asks for you stop come to denver stop

It was signed *good samaritan.*

She passed it to her father. "Ty's been hurt. He's in a hospital in Denver."

Grace leaned in to wrap an arm around Adam's waist and watch as he read the message. "Ty's hurt? How?"

"Doesn't say," Adam replied. He glanced down at her and frowned.

"You'll want to go to him."

He nodded, but his frown didn't ease. "I hate to leave you, Gracie, but something's not right. I need to see what I can do to help Ty."

Victoria snatched the telegram back.

This was exactly what she'd been hoping for—a chance to escape. She'd written so many letters to answer advertisements for nannies and governesses, but the right opportunity had literally fallen into her hands. The air of mystery as to the sender made this trip an adventure.

In Denver, she might be able to find a job and make a new life for herself. It would hurt to leave her father and the ranch behind, but she couldn't wait around until she no longer belonged at Twin Springs. Her heart would break. Going to Denver would also put some much needed miles between her and Matthew.

She could leave *him* before he left *her.*

"He wants me, not you," she insisted. "You and Grace are newly married. You need some time alone, not for you to go running off to Denver."

"You want to go to Denver for our honeymoon?" Adam asked his new wife.

Before she could answer, Victoria tried putting some important points out there for the couple to think about. "No matter what you decide, I have every intention of going to Ty. Who would tend the horses if you go too, Daddy—especially if Grace goes with you? Someone has to stay at the ranch."

"Maybe Grace can—"

"There are too many animals for her to handle all alone." Victoria knew Matthew wouldn't speak up to offer his help. He already had one foot out the door.

Adam tried again. "Matthew could—"

"He's leaving. Soon. Probably in a week or so." Merciful Lord, it hurt to just to say the words. There was no way she'd stay behind and watch him ride away, not when she had the perfect reason to skip town first.

Grace gaped at her brother. "You're leaving?"

"We'll talk about it later," he replied.

Victoria pressed harder. "You'll need to watch the ranch, Daddy."

"Maybe Jake could—"

"Jake can't. He needs to be here to work for Will and to keep an eye on Emily. She's expecting, after all. Only a few more weeks until the little one arrives, and who knows how long Ty will need help before he can come home." She begged with her eyes for him to understand. "Please, Daddy. I want to do this. I *need* to do this."

Matthew held his hand out and nodded to the message.

She frowned before sighing and handing it to him. "It isn't from Ty," she said, knowing he would probably overreact.

He flicked his fingers against the paper. "The only name is *good samaritan*. You don't even know for a fact that Ty's been hurt. Why, anyone could have sent this!" He handed the telegram back to Adam. "You can't let her go by herself."

She put her hands on her hips. "Ty needs me."

"You're not going there alone." He turned and folded his arms over his chest.

"Why does it even matter to you?"

His jaw clenched. "Damn it, Victoria. I'm not letting you go to Denver alone."

"You don't have any say!" She whirled to grab the telegram from her father. "I'm going, and you can't stop me." The vow was punctuated with a decisive nod.

Grace cleared her throat, drawing everyone's attention. "Perhaps there's a compromise."

"What do you suggest?" Adam asked.

"You should stay here to care for the horses. Victoria should go to Denver to check on Ty."

Victoria scoffed at Matthew. "See? Even Grace thinks I need to go."

"I'm not finished." Grace glanced to her brother. "Matthew can go with Victoria on the stage until she can catch the train in Butte. Then he can be sure she's safely on the train to Denver."

"I'll go all the way to Denver," Matthew insisted. "That way I can make sure she gets settled and find out who sent the message."

Grace moved to his side and laid a hand on his arm. "You'll have to come back to help on the ranch. A day or two is fine because I can help, but with Ty gone, Adam will need you back here." She turned to Victoria. "Let him take you to Butte. Then you can go on to Denver. We'll wire ahead to make sure you have a place to stay so we won't worry."

Victoria hadn't wanted a tag-along, hoping for a clean break, and she sure didn't want to be stuck in a stagecoach with Matthew for hours on end.

He shook his head. "I'm going to Denver."

"Butte," she blurted out. "I'll let you take me to *Butte*. Then you come back to help at the ranch until Ty's well enough to come home." Her heart leapt at the thought Matthew would be staying until she remembered how thoroughly he'd rejected her.

No, she was the one who wouldn't be coming back. There was a new life waiting for her in Colorado. And why in the hell did that make her stomach hurt so much?

She'd made up her mind. This was for the best. She went to her father. "I'm going to go to the ranch, packing a trunk, and coming back here tonight. I can sleep in Grace's old room before I can catch the morning stage."

Her father shifted that knowing gaze of his from Victoria to Matthew and back again. While Matthew couldn't talk her out of this trip, all it would take was one word from Adam to stop her escape.

"Please, Daddy. *Please*."

He thought it over a good long while before he finally nodded. "But Matthew takes you to Butte."

"All the way to Denver, Victoria," the stubborn cowboy scolded.

"We'll see."

***

Adam held Grace's hand as they waved farewell to Victoria and Matthew.

The sun had set a few hours before, and the evening chill was setting in. He put an arm around her shoulder and tucked her closer to his side.

The wagon made the turn to the main road and was soon out of sight.

He turned to his new wife, stroked the back of his knuckles across her cheek, and smiled. "We're finally alone."

"So it would seem," she replied, a quiver in her voice.

"Oh, Gracie…" He tugged her into his arms. "I don't want you to be afraid of me. We don't have to—"

A kiss silenced him. She stood on tiptoes, pushed her arms around his neck, and pressed her mouth to his. Her tongue teased his lips until he opened them to her, then she deepened the kiss.

Her fear didn't seem to be an obstacle, but he had to take this slow. While he loved that she deliberately tempted him, she was still fragile.

After she eased away, Grace rested her cheek against his shoulder.

Adam rubbed his chin against her temple, eliciting her sigh in response.

"You confuse me," she whispered.

"Confuse you?"

"I'm afraid, yet I still want to–to let you take me to your bed."

Her honesty brought a smile to his lips. "Don't be afraid, darlin'. I'd never hurt you."

"I don't know if I can do what you want me to do."

"I've got no expectations. Let's just…see what happens."

"I'll disappoint you."

"You could *never* disappoint me."

Before she could protest, he swept her into his arms and kissed her soundly.

Her arms encircled his neck as she kissed him back every bit as thoroughly.

He carried her into the house and up the stairs to his bedroom— *their* bedroom. Deliberately ignoring the lantern, he figured the mood would be better set by the dim moonlight spilling through the window. After he set her back on her feet, he took off his jacket and draped it over the chair. Then he pulled her into his arms and kissed her again, trying to let her feel his desire without overwhelming her.

Praying for patience, he thanked the Lord that with age came control. Had he been younger, he probably would have been tempted to give in to the demanding needs of his body. He was already hard, aching. He wanted her. Desperately. But he wouldn't force Grace to do anything she wasn't ready for. If that meant they didn't come together tonight, he would try again tomorrow. And the next day. However long it took. He would show her that making love was something they could share rather than something she should fear.

She tensed against him when he slid his hand up her side, caressing her waist before palming a full breast through the soft material of her bodice. The tension only lasted a moment before she arched into his touch. Her slender hands found the buttons of his shirt.

Oh, how he loved her. He kissed her again just to show her how much.

Clothes were suddenly in the way, and they tugged and pulled at his shirt and her dress, stealing heated kisses. He wasn't able to get her arms out of her tight sleeves and growled with aggravation.

With a frustrated groan of her own, Grace stepped back, jerked her arms out of the dress, and shoved it to her waist and over her hips. It fell to the floor. Her teeth tugged on her bottom lip as she untied her petticoats and let them puddle around her feet.

Kneeling down, Adam helped her slip off her shoes. Trying to hold her gaze, he slowly peeled down her stockings. While he'd hoped to show her there was no hurry—no frantic need to rush her—he was also torturing himself. Undressing her was tantalizing—erotic and maddening. Her skin was silk, and touching her thighs and her calves became sweet torture.

He stood, pleased that she now wore nothing but her thin camisole and pantalets. Aside from her furiously blushing face, she didn't appear to be anything other than curious.

"Your turn?" she asked, her eyes sweeping him from head to toe.

With an enormous smile, he met her challenge. She'd managed to pull down his suspenders, so he yanked off his shirt and cast it aside. He kicked off his shoes and socks. Unsure of whether to take off his pants, he watched her for any sign that she didn't wish to continue. But how in the hell was he supposed to stop if she said *no* now? His body was screaming to claim her. Yet he'd find the self-discipline if he had to.

For his Grace.

With a shy glance, she moved closer. Her trembling hands reached for the ribbons on her camisole. He stepped forward to help her, giving each of the baby blue bows a tug until they gave. As the last of them were untied, the camisole parted, revealing two full, perfect breasts.

He closed his eyes and prayed again for patience.

Grace loved him even more for all the consideration he showed for her fears. His shuddering sigh told her of his hard-fought battle. He'd promised not to rush her—not to hurt her.

Adam always kept his promises.

The uncertainty vanished. All she felt was love to the depths of her soul for this man—this kind, loving, and eternally patient man.

The fire inside her he'd kindled from their first kiss—the one that flared with each stroke of his hands on her body— demanded attention. So why wasn't he touching her now as she longed for him to?

Because he was worried about her fear. He promised not to force her. She needed to give him permission.

Grace took his hand and placed it over her right breast. "I want you, Adam." Then she reached behind his neck and urged him back into a tongue-dueling kiss.

Adam slid his hands over her breasts to her shoulders where he helped her shrug out of her camisole.

She eased back and gave him a nervous smile as she untied the knot. When it opened, she reached for his hands, put them on her hips, and waited.

He tugged the garment over her hips and let it fall to the floor.

Her hands fumbled with the waistband of his pants. She was awkward. He gave her some assistance. The pants were quickly kicked aside, and he waited for her reaction.

She rolled her eyes to focus on the ceiling, afraid to get a glimpse of Adam's body. If she saw him aroused, she was afraid she'd turn and run out of the bedroom. The only other time she'd seen a man in that state, he'd used his body as a weapon. Yet Adam approached her with reverence rather than violence. His tenderness made her feel cherished.

He kissed the top of her head when she hurried into his arms and rested her cheek against his bare shoulder. "It's all right, Gracie."

She released a trembling sigh. "I'm being silly. It's just...you're so–so...strong."

"I won't hurt you, darlin'. I won't do anything you're not ready to do."

Telling herself she was being a ninny—that she was a grown woman and shouldn't be afraid of a man simply because he was aroused—she stepped out of his embrace and let her gaze find his. Ever so slowly, she lowered her eyes to look at his body. A broad chest covered with a patch of dark brown hair. A muscular stomach. An intimidating erection.

She took that important step forward to press her body against his and then brushed a kiss on his mouth. "Take me to bed, husband."

"Anything my lady wants." He lifted her into his arms and set her on the sheets.

Adam covered her body with his. Taking his time, he kissed her, letting his tongue stroke the roof of her mouth, coaxing her tongue to follow into his mouth. He acted as if they had all the time in the world.

Her hands fluttered over his shoulders to caress his back, trying to encourage him. His lips moved to her neck, which she tilted with a happy mewl. Everything he did felt wonderful—from the way his kisses spread heat through her body to how his growls let her know she was pleasing him.

When he shifted those kisses to her breasts, she let out a surprised cry at the way the action sent a jolt straight to her core. She wanted more—*needed* more. She arched up, offering herself to him.

He drew a nipple into his mouth, making heat shoot to her core. His love burned away whatever fear had lingered, branding her with passion. As he nudged her thighs apart with his knee, she spread her legs for him.

Adam moved between her thighs, and as he shifted his attention to her other breast a type of madness seized her. Everything inside her cried out for completion.

He moved back up until he was staring into her eyes. His had darkened with desire. "I want to be inside you, Gracie."

She knew what he was asking, knew that he was waiting for her permission. Her body was ready to welcome him. "Make me your wife, Adam."

His hand slipped between them, robbing Grace of her ability to think. After he stroked her, plunging a finger deep inside her body, he mumbled something about how wet and warm she was. She honestly didn't care. As his thumb found a sensitive spot, she thought she'd die if he didn't come to her. He teased and fondled until her nerves tingled and every muscle tightened. She planted her heels against the mattress and rocked her hips up.

When he pulled his hand away, she groaned in disappointment. Then he settled himself between her thighs again, his erection pushing against her entrance.

Grace tensed.

"It's all right, love. I won't hurt you."

Forcing herself to relax, she gripped his shoulders and buried her face against his neck.

He surged inside her.

She gasped in surprise. There was no pain, only a wonderful fullness. He fit her perfectly.

Adam stilled. "Am I hurting you?"

Hurting?

God, no.

But she was so lost in bliss she couldn't speak. She rocked her hips up to take him more deeply, telling him without words what she wanted. His hips replied in kind.

The rhythm he set beckoned her, making everything inside her burn. She couldn't get enough of him, begging him with whimpers to help her reach the mysterious pinnacle. "Adam. I–I can't."

His lips brushed against her ear. "Come with me, Gracie. Just let go and feel how much I love you."

And she did, finding that by letting go and trusting her new husband, she gained fulfillment. Waves of impossible pleasure rushed over her as her body clenched around him, her thighs squeezing his hips as her heartbeat roared in her ears.

Adam breathed hoarsely before he pushed into her one last time, groaning as his whole body shuddered.

He stayed inside her a long time as she idly stroked her fingers across his shoulders and down his spine, marveling at what they'd just shared. Even her toes tingled. When he rolled to his side, she followed, snuggling up against him. She couldn't find the words to tell him all she felt, so she settled for what was in her heart.

"I love you, Adam."

"I love you too, darlin'."

Chapter Seventeen

Denver's Union Station was more crowded than Victoria expected. She'd visited the city as a child, but it had changed more than she thought possible. The noise and confusion bordered on overwhelming.

According to the conductor, her trunk should've been easy to find, but every time she asked for some help to locate baggage, she got different directions.

Closing her eyes for a moment, she tried to find some calm. The whole trip—her grand adventure—had turned into nothing but a nightmare.

The worst leg had been the stagecoach ride to Butte. The swaying of the wagon coupled with the multitude of ruts and holes in the barely-there road made her head ache and her stomach pitch.

Matthew had sat across from her, nagging at her like a meddlesome old woman about going so far away on her own. He threatened more times than she could count to get on the train with her.

She simply kept reminding him that Adam and Grace were counting on him, but he continued to cajole her into letting him come along. By the time she'd purchased her train ticket, Matthew had almost slipped into begging.

Leaving him behind on that platform had been harder than she'd feared. Unless he came back to visit his sister or Jake, it was probably the last time she would ever see him. God, she couldn't seem to get that thought out of her head as he stood there staring holes through her. Her heart was as brittle as broken glass when she'd held her hand out to him to wish him farewell. Putting on the façade of friendship, she'd swallowed the tears that threatened to fall each time she thought about him moving on with his life.

He'd taken her hand, given it a rough shake, told her to be careful, and walked away as though she'd meant nothing at all to him. Most of the train trip she'd spent stewing and hurting over his callous dismissal.

Victoria choked down her lingering melancholy and focused on this new path for her life. Her father had wired ahead to the Alvord House for a room. All she needed to do was find her trunk, get it sent ahead to the hotel, and then she could hurry to the hospital to see to Ty's needs. Once she was sure he was receiving the proper care, she could focus on searching for a job as a governess or a teacher.

There had to be something she could do to feel useful again.

"Miss Morgan?"

Her eyes flew wide at the baritone voice. She gasped, placing a gloved hand over her pounding heart.

Standing in front of her was a man dressed in a black silk suit and carrying a walking cane with a silver wolf's head for a handle. "Pardon me being so forward, but aren't you Miss Victoria Morgan?"

"Yes, I'm Miss Morgan. Please don't think me rude, but...do I know you?"

He doffed his top hat and bowed before setting it back on his head. "Not yet, but I hope to have that pleasure. I'm here on Ty Bishop's behalf."

His eyes raked her from head to toe, making her feel more than a bit uneasy at this strange man making such a blatant appraisal of her.

"I must say, Ty did not do you justice. You're much prettier than he described. Quite beautiful, actually."

The same type of empty compliments from the men in White Pines hadn't turned her head. She dismissed this one the same way. "How do you know Ty?"

"We had a chance encounter late one evening. I stumbled across him as he was set upon by thieves."

"You're the Good Samaritan?"

Victoria had a hard time not staring. He wasn't handsome—not in the same rugged way that made her sigh each time she saw Matthew— but he was pleasant enough. He reminded her a little of Jake in size and in the shape of his round face, but this man had raven hair and eyes so dark they were more black than brown. His clothing was obviously expensive, and he bore an air of arrogance common to the wealthy. His smile didn't seem genuine, but she'd just met the man, so she tried not to be judgmental.

"Guilty as charged," he replied. "I routed the ruffians and escorted Ty to my doctor's home. Since he was injured so severely, Doctor Adams felt it best to have him relocated to the hospital. Ty received your telegram and asked me to meet you here so I could escort you to see him."

"How is he?"

"Improved. His broken arm has been set, but his ribs are still causing him pain. Fractured as well, no doubt. The bruises on his face may take a while to fade."

"Oh, my heavens. Poor Ty." She took in the man's expensive gold watch when he pulled it from his vest to check the time. "How was it you were there when he was robbed?"

Shouldn't the thieves have been more interested in a wealthy man than a poor cowboy?

The man offered his arm. "I'll explain on the way to the hospital. May my man see to your baggage?" When she didn't move to put her hand on his arm, he dropped it, a quick and rather angry frown crossing his thin lips. He nodded at a short man standing a few steps away. "Trey?"

The man practically jumped to reach them. He bowed to her then turned to the Good Samaritan. "Sir?"

"See to Miss Morgan's bags."

Those dark eyes turned back to her, and she felt a cold chill run the length of her spine.

"Might I suggest the Alvord House? It's one of the nicer places to stay in Denver." His gaze wandered the crowded station before returning to her. "Not that this town offers much in…amenities. I much prefer San Francisco. That is the city I call home."

Victoria shook off the air of unease that seemed to encase her, attributing it to her weariness and the anxiety at being alone in a big city after seldom leaving her home. "I–I already have a room at the Alvord."

"Splendid news. Why don't you give Trey your claim ticket? He'll make sure your things are sent ahead."

Surely letting a man who'd been so good to Ty in his time of need help her find her way to the hospital and hotel would be fine.

The shorter man held out his hand, and she pressed her claim ticket onto his palm. "Thank you, Trey, is it?"

"Yes, ma'am. Trey Sullivan."

"Move along now," the Good Samaritan said with a dismissive flip of his hand. "Miss Morgan and I will be taking my carriage." He offered his arm again. "Shall we go, my sweet?"

"I don't even know your name."

Not suspicious by nature, she couldn't help but feel that leaving in a carriage with a man she hadn't even truly met would be foolish. Perhaps after proper introductions, her nervousness would ease. The man had come to Ty's rescue. That alone spoke volumes about his character, so she swallowed her apprehension.

He swept his hat from his head and bowed again. "Stephen Shay at your service." He grinned as if that name should have held some importance to her. "Stephen *Shay*," he repeated, adding quite a bit of emphasis to his last name.

"I'm sorry, but…I don't recognize the name at all. Are you a friend of my father?"

Obsidian eyes stared at her, narrowing enough to raise her apprehension again. "I assumed *everyone* in the country knew of the Shay family. We are quite influential. Although someplace as backward as your home might not know of our reach."

His conceit almost forced a sarcastic reply, but she bit it back. "I would like to go see Ty now—if your offer of a carriage ride is still good."

"I'll take you to see him." This time he offered his arm and Victoria set her hand on the crook of his elbow. He patted it with a gloved hand. "Let us be off."

***

Stephen tugged at the fingers of his grey glove until he was able to jerk it off. Repeating the actions with his other glove, he yanked his hand free and dropped both gloves on the bureau next to his hat and cane. The bottle of scotch he'd requested sat next to a couple of glasses. He flipped the stopper off the crystal decanter and poured himself a large splash of the strong drink. Only alcohol seemed to ease the constant ache in his shoulder that remained after the bullet had been removed.

Throwing the amber liquid back with one swallow, he slammed the glass back down on the bureau and poured himself more. This time, he carried the glass over to the window. He sipped his scotch as he pulled back the heavy drape and watched the people moving about the crowded gardens. Couples strolled arm in arm around the maze of flowers and shrubs as the women twirled their parasols and threw flirtatious smiles at their escorts.

They all made him want to empty his stomach. None of them understood the demanding and driving love that had held him hostage for so many years. He clenched his jaw, grinding his teeth in frustration.

Victoria Morgan hadn't been at all what he expected. His detectives had described her physical attributes well, but they obviously didn't do enough research into her personality. Good money wasted on a report that called her timid and alluded to the fact she was undesirable since she remained unmarried at the ripe old age of twenty-one.

Given his handsome looks, obvious wealth, and family reputation bending her to his will should have been an easy task. After meeting her and escorting her to the hospital, he'd quickly learned there was *nothing* timid about the woman.

She'd ordered the nurses around, demanded the doctor's valuable time to discuss Ty Bishop's case, and taken charge of deciding the course of his treatment. While Stephen had been impressed with her almost military efficiency, he frowned at the memory. She wouldn't be nearly as pliable as he'd hoped, and his careful plans might be in jeopardy.

No!

No turning back. Not now.

Grace was finally in his grasp. He wasn't going to let some officious spinster stand in his way. He'd have to turn on some of that famed Shay charm and get her to invite him back to that little one-horse town in the middle of nowhere. He would definitely take Grace by surprise and be too deeply involved with her life for her to run away again. Then he'd simply wait for the chance to make his move.

The older brother might be a problem. The detective had reported that the man was planning to leave town. How fortunate. For once, Matthew Riley wouldn't be there to help Grace escape. The report said the younger brother—Jake Curtis—wanted nothing to do with her.

A knock at the door drew Stephen away from the window. "Come in." He downed his scotch and headed back to the bureau for a refill.

"Mr. Shay?" Trey opened the door and stuck his head inside. "You alone?"

Stephen snorted a derisive laugh. "I told you to come in. Had I been...occupied...I wouldn't have tendered such an invitation." He gestured to the settee.

Trey hurried in and took a seat. "The Morgan woman's all settled. She's four doors down, so you can keep an eye on her. Had to slip some money to the man at the front desk, but it was as close as he could put her."

"Fine, fine. Did you receive any messages from Red Maple?"

"White Pines, sir. And, yes, I got a telegram. Riley's back in town. Your detective's gonna wire us the moment he leaves. How long before the Bishop guy can travel?"

"Just a couple of weeks. Hopefully, Matthew Riley will be out of our hair by then. Have you seen to the...loose ends?"

"Yes, sir." Trey frowned and stared at the hands he was wringing in his lap. "There's been a–a small..um...*change* in the situation. Miss Riley has...she's n–not..." His voice trailed off to silence.

"Out with it."

"She's not alone."

"Of course not. You just told me her brother had returned."

His hands twisted and turned as if he was wrapping something around each of his fists. "It's not her brother. She's gone and gotten m–m–m..."

Stephen missed whatever word Trey mumbled. His patience had come to an end hours ago, and his shoulder throbbed. He threw the glass at the wall. It shattered, showering Trey with glass and alcohol.

"Tell me!"

"Miss Riley got married."

"*She what?*"

"Got m–married. To that rancher."

Not possible. Not his Grace. She would *never* take another man to her bed, not after what they'd shared. All the pieces were finally falling into place, and she'd gone and spoiled everything.

Again.

Stephen pushed aside the anger that swelled inside him. She might have been foolish enough to try to find another champion, but it didn't really matter in the end. Grace knew who she belonged to. When he finally found himself face to face with her, she would see the rightness of leaving with him—of finally coming back where she belonged.

Picking up another glass, he poured himself more scotch. Sipping the drink, he returned to the window to watch the ridiculous people and their childish infatuations. Only *he* understood true love—the type of love that had given him the patience to pursue Grace for so very long.

"It doesn't mean anything," he said over his shoulder. "They're playing house. That's all. When I come for her, she shall know the right thing to do."

"If you don't mind my asking, Mr. Shay, what are you planning to do with the rancher?"

"He will be…dealt with when necessary." He turned to level a hard stare at Trey. "Had you done your job in San Francisco, I wouldn't have had to go to these extremes."

"I'm sorry she got away, but—"

"Sorry she got away? The woman shot me!"

"Then why do you want her?"

"Because she belongs to me."

Through the years, Stephen had paid a substantial sum in his efforts to find Grace. Sometimes he was able to get close, but then she would find a way to slip through his fingers. His Grace was as elusive as a ghost. He'd never known a person who could manage to disappear so easily and so completely, and just when he despaired over her vanishing yet again, her handwritten message arrived, asking to meet him. He'd rejoiced that she'd finally stopped playing coy and had accepted her destiny.

That day, he'd found her standing next to the largest of the fountains at Woodward's Gardens. He'd hoped after all the time that had passed she'd at last come to her senses and realized where she belonged.

She told him some befuddled story about a long lost younger brother whom she desperately needed to locate, and she made it clear that she was only turning to Stephen because he had the deep pockets needed to help find the boy. His detectives had never uncovered the brother's existence before she'd come to him, but when given some pertinent information from Grace, they tracked Jake Curtis down in short order.

At first, Stephen had been infuriated at the request. She seemed to think that he *owed* her in some way, and it amused him that she saw their past in such a distorted fashion. Of course, he'd quickly promised to help her. If he was able to ascertain the boy's location, perhaps he could use that information as leverage.

Leverage meant everything in negotiations.

When he called Grace to his room to share the information his detectives had gathered, she hadn't shown her appreciation at all. In fact, when he'd wanted to renew their relationship, she'd up and shot him.

The injury hadn't changed his notion that she was still his property, but he would make sure she never attempted anything so foolish again. *Ever.* No, when the time was right, she would be properly punished. For everything.

When she fled San Francisco, Grace hadn't taken the usual care to hide her tracks and had left a distinct path for his detectives to follow. They traced her to some little hamlet in Montana called Red Maple. Or was it White Pines? Some quaint and ridiculous tiny town. Stephen was fed information almost daily as to her activities. They'd obviously failed to tell him one very important fact.

Grace was now a married woman.

As if something as trivial as a marriage mattered. Problems like that rancher were easily solved.

Yes, Stephen would show Grace that she would *always* belong to him, and his plan had started with the attack on Ty Bishop.

How easily the man had been fooled. He'd been so grateful for Stephen to "interrupt" the beating, he'd never once questioned why someone had come to his rescue. Now the next part of his plan was slowly shaping up. Victoria *would* bend to his will, and through her, he could finally get to Grace.

Stephen turned back to Trey. "Make the arrangements for the trip back. I'll be escorting the beautiful Miss Morgan and the unfortunate Mr. Bishop back to Montana as soon as he's ready to travel."

Chapter Eighteen

Grace leaned against Adam's shoulder and fought a losing battle to keep her eyes open. The sway of the wagon lulled her like the rocking of a cradle. Made sense, considering she felt as safe as an infant in the care of a loving family. Being married to Adam had given her so much she'd missed in life.

Security.

Comfort.

Love.

Of course her brother loved her, yet she'd always felt something was missing in her life. She'd made no friends, put down no roots, and spent most of her life in fear, looking over her shoulder. Now that she was Adam's wife, she reveled in the contentment. She had someone who cared for her in a way no other person ever had.

Adam filled her days with companionship as they cared for the horses and worked around the ranch. Matthew stayed on, promising to wait until Ty came home. There were times the men would be gone, but not for more than a few hours at a time. She never fretted at being alone, knowing for the first time in her life that Stephen wasn't hunting her.

Adam filled her nights with passion she'd never known existed. He was such a patient and giving lover, turning all her fears aside as he made her pleasure as important as his own. Sharing herself with her husband had awakened something inside Grace—some part of her she'd buried long ago. He could stir her desire with something as simple as a touch, even a heated glance. The prim, scared spinster had turned into a wanton.

But only for Adam Morgan.

Guilt suddenly settled on her, a heavy weight making her heart feel as if it dropped to the floor of the wagon. What did she give him in return?

The threat of the marshal showing up at the Twin Springs any day with a warrant for her arrest.

Since she'd spoken her vows, she'd been consumed with telling Adam about what she'd done to Stephen Shay. Several times, she'd tried to find a way to explain, hoping against hope he would understand and that he'd forgive her for not being the woman he deserved. Yet each time, her fears overwhelmed her before she could get the words out.

If she told him about shooting Stephen, every other secret she'd guarded her whole life would be dragged into the light of day. She couldn't bear losing her husband now—not when he'd become as important as the air she breathed.

The creaking wheel crossed a deep rut, sending her bouncing, not only jarring her out of her reverie but forcing a sudden wave of nausea. Before she could even ask Adam to stop the wagon, she hung her head over the side and lost her breakfast.

"Gracie?" He pulled hard on the reins, forcing the horses to slow and then stop. He held back her hair and rubbed her back. "Something you ate?"

"I think the milk tasted—" The thought of any food—especially the milk she couldn't seem to get enough of at breakfast—stirred up her queasy stomach. She leaned over the side again and hoped the sickness would quickly pass.

"You better now?"

She gave him a curt nod.

He reached inside the pocket of his vest and handed her one of the handkerchiefs she'd embroidered for him. "Remind me to throw out the rest of the milk when we get back. Do you want me to take you home? Victoria wouldn't mind waiting—"

"No. Please. I–I'm fine now." She wiped her mouth with her trembling hand, gave him a faint smile, and hoped she'd convinced him she was well. The horrible groaning sound her stomach made probably told him otherwise. "I know how anxious you are to see Victoria and Ty. So am I. If you take me back, they'll wonder where you are. Really, I'm fine, Adam."

"Are you sure?" He pressed the back of his hand against her forehead. "You don't feel feverish."

She tried to divert the topic. Her fears over her past being discovered had caused the nausea. That and the horrible road. "Very sure. I want to meet Ty's savior. How mysterious we don't even know his name."

"Then we'll just be surprised together. Not as though a person can be newsy on a telegram. Too pricey." He patted her knee. "Lean against me and rest. I'll get you back home as soon as we pick up the three of them. Are you sure you want this stranger as a houseguest?"

"After all he did to help Ty? Of course, I do."

White Pines came into view just as she was drifting off to sleep. With a weary sigh, she straightened up, smoothed her hands over her skirt and hair, and tried to look presentable.

Adam stopped the wagon close to the general store, threw the brake, and crawled out. "Stay here, darlin'. I'll be right back."

Emily was moving slowly down the boardwalk.

Grace waved, hoping to get her attention.

A grin spread over Emily's face. She waved back and walked toward the wagon.

Grace started to climb down until Adam came hurrying back, carrying a glass of water. "You wait 'til I can help you." He set the water on the wagon and lifted her down. Then he handed her the glass. "Thought you'd like to rinse your mouth out. Get rid of the sour taste."

"Thank you." After taking a drink, she swished the cool water around her mouth and realized there was no ladylike way to spit it back out.

Her husband's warm chuckle filled the air. "No one's watching, Gracie."

Her cheeks heated with a blush before she walked to the end of the wagon and spit out the water.

Emily giggled. "Need a spittoon?"

"Just rinsing my mouth out." She took a few sips of the water before handing it back to her husband. "Thank you."

With a nod, he ducked back inside the store.

Placing a hand on Grace's arm, Emily gave her a nervous smile. "I–I was wantin' to talk to you."

"Is something wrong?"

"No, no. Nothing like that. I–I wanted to ask a favor—a big favor."

"Anything for you, Emily. After all, we're sisters now."

"I want you there when I have the baby."

Grace's stomach roiled in protest, and she swallowed hard to force the bile back down. "Oh, Emily. I can't...I couldn't possibly..."

She'd never seen a birth before, only experiencing it through the pain of childbirth. Her memories were sketchy at best. How could she possibly take on the responsibility of bringing her grandchild into the world? What if things went wrong? What if there were complications? Surely the emotions that would rip through her at such a monumental event would give away her secret—she could never hope to control herself when she saw that baby.

Emily tightened her grip on Grace's arm. "Please, Grace. I'm so afraid." A tear spilled from the corner of her eye. "The doctor's so mean. He scolds me all the time when I tell him I'm frightened. He says pain is a woman's lot in life."

"I can't deliver a baby, Emily." Grace wrung her hands so hard they hurt. God, she wished she could explain her true fears. "Surely there's someone else, a friend...like Victoria...or–or—"

"Victoria's not back yet."

"She'll be back on today's stagecoach."

"Please, Grace. *Please*." Emily's bottom lip quivered for a moment before she burst into tears.

So did Grace.

With a sob, she tugged Emily into her arms. "I'm sorry. Please don't cry. I'll help. I will. I'll be there."

After a few shuddering breaths, Emily scrubbed away her tears with the heels of her hands. "You'll really be there? You promise?"

Grace nodded, but sympathy hadn't made her common sense vanish. "I want the doctor there for the delivery. I'll hold your hand and wipe your brow and make sure the doctor doesn't say stupid manly things."

Emily sniffled and gave her a weak smile. "Thank you. I knew you'd be there for me. You're family."

With the back of her hands, Grace wiped the tears from her own cheeks. "We can ask Victoria, too."

"Why are you both crying?" Adam asked.

Grace jumped. "You scared me!"

"Why are you two crying?" he demanded.

"I'm pregnant and big as an ox," Emily replied. "I cry all the time." She turned to Grace and kissed her cheek. "I'll talk to you later. Thank you."

"You're welcome."

Adam frowned, but Grace shook her head. "Later."

Slipping his pocket watch from his vest, he checked the time before tucking it back in his pocket. "Why don't you sit down for a spell?"

He led her to the front of the store and inclined his head to the bench that was often occupied by a couple of the town's biggest gossips.

She'd been their main target since she'd come to town. Heavens, she was glad those old men were both busy doing other things today.

"Rest," he said. "The stage is running late."

Still feeling drowsy, she accommodated him. When her head bobbed a few times, he chuckled, came to stand next to the bench, and pushed her to lean against his side. The heat of the sun and her husband's warmth lulled her to sleep.

***

Adam reached out to stroke Grace's hair. Her face appeared a bit flushed, and he considered waking her to take her to the Four Aces and get her out of the sun. The noise of the stagecoach approaching changed his mind.

Thank God, Victoria was finally coming home.

She'd only sent a couple of messages, both of which seemed a tad too cryptic for his taste. The first told him that Ty was going to be fine despite the beating he'd taken, but it also said that Victoria was thinking of staying on in Denver. No reason why. No mention of what she planned to do there.

The second message was even shorter, saying only that Victoria would return with Ty and the Good Samaritan.

Adam needed to sit that girl down and have a nice, long talk about being so mysterious with her worried father and about whatever nonsense she'd gotten into her head about leaving White Pines.

He'd probably drag Matthew into the conversation. The boy had moped around the ranch from the moment he returned from Butte. Sure, he got the work done, but his perpetual gloom spoke volumes as to how much he missed Victoria.

It was past time for those two foolish kids to get their heads on straight, put each other out their miseries, and get married.

In a swirl of dust, the stage ground to a halt.

Adam gave his sleeping wife a gentle nudge. "Gracie. Wake up, darlin'. Victoria's home."

Grace blinked a couple of times before shielding her eyes from the sun. "She's here?" Her voice was husky with sleep.

"She's here."

He stepped forward to help his daughter from the stage.

A tall, dark-haired man exited first, turning back to offer a gloved hand to the next passenger.

Victoria took the man's hand and let him assist her as she crawled out the small door. Her gaze found her father's. "Daddy!"

"Welcome home, princess."

She hurried into Adam's waiting arms.

He hugged her tightly while the stranger helped Ty out of the stagecoach. The boy appeared to be fine, the only indication of his lingering injuries being the sling holding his splinted arm against his chest.

Adam clapped Ty on his good shoulder. "Welcome back, son."

"Glad to be back, sir."

The stranger turned to face Adam just as Grace stood and smoothed her hands down her skirt. She looked up with a smile that suddenly changed into a gasp. The color drained from her face as she swayed, unsteady on her feet. "No..."

The word was a mere whisper but registered enough fear to force Adam to hurry back to her. He caught his wife as she sank into a faint.

Scooping her up into his arms, he called to his daughter. "I'm taking her to the Four Aces."

"We're right behind you." She reached for the satchel the

stagecoach driver was handing down to her.

Using his shoulder to push open the swinging doors, Adam strode into the empty saloon. "Jake? Emily? Will?"

Emily came waddling out of the kitchen, her father and Jake right behind her. "Grace!" She hurried as fast as a woman ready to deliver could to reach them. "Good heavens. What in the devil happened?" She started ordering them around as if they'd all enlisted in her own private army. "Daddy, go grab a towel from the kitchen and soak it in cold water. Jake, run upstairs and grab a blanket and pillow from our room. Adam, you lay her on a table."

Adam waited until Jake ran back down the stairs and spread a blanket over the large table. Then he laid Grace down, took the cool rag from Will, and gently stroked his wife's face. Jake and Will kept trying to peer over his shoulder.

"Back up, everyone. Give her some air," Adam said.

"What happened?" Will asked.

"She fainted."

"Why would she faint?" Jake asked. "Not really that warm today. Why, she's not even wearing a corset."

Adam shrugged although he was rapidly putting together everything else that had been happening in the past week or so.

Grace had been bothered more than once by the early summer heat. A couple of times, she'd skipped breakfast, claiming her stomach felt queasy. Plus there hadn't been more than a night or two since they'd been married that they hadn't made love because there'd been no interruptions.

Oh, yes, he knew what had probably thrown her into a faint, and his chest puffed up with masculine pride.

Did she even suspect?

Grace sat up with a start, the fear of her nightmare still making her heart race in a rough rhythm. Stephen had found her, had come to her in the only place she'd ever felt safe.

She needed Adam to wrap his strong arms around her and make the horrible dream disappear. It took a moment before the fog in her mind lifted.

She wasn't home in her bed.

Had it been a nightmare? Or had Stephen Shay truly found her?

Panic shot through her, and she groped around for Adam's hand.

"Gracie," her husband said in a soothing tone. "Breathe, darlin'. I don't want you to faint again."

Her eyes darted around, searching for Stephen.

Where was Matthew? Matthew would help her escape. Matthew always helped her run when she needed to get away.

No, Grace. No escape.

Her pounding heart echoed in her ears as she fought for breath, wanting to surrender back to the blessed darkness.

A thought rose through the terror. Stephen wasn't dead. She wouldn't burn in hellfire for all eternity. Yet no matter how hard she looked to confirm his appearance, he was nowhere to be found.

Thank God, it had been a dream after all—nothing more than a nightmare sprung from a nap during the heat of the day. She placed a hand against her chest, hoping the cadence of her heart would slow and she could catch her breath again.

"Adam?" She let her gaze wander again, searching for the devil one last time, before it settled back on her husband's face as blessed relief washed over her. "What happened?"

"You fainted."

"Fainted?"

He nodded.

"I've *never* fainted. I must've fallen asleep. That's all."

"Sorry, but you fainted this time, darlin'." He turned to Jake. "Could you please go get her some water?"

"I'll go," Emily offered before lumbering back toward the kitchen.

Victoria and Ty came walking through the front door.

"Grace? Are you all right now?" she asked.

"I–I'm fine."

Grace's thoughts were still fuzzy. Victoria was back, but how could that be if she'd only dreamed the stage arrived?

It was too hard to take in because she was reeling from the notion that she'd actually fainted. Her whole adult life, she'd been through unbearable heat, devastating droughts, and cattle drives that seemed to go on forever and a day, but she'd never fainted. Not once. Only weak women fainted, and she'd never been weak.

"Why in heaven's name would I faint?" she asked, more to herself than to Adam.

Her husband picked up her hand and gave it a squeeze. "The heat?" His arrogant— downright cheeky—grin was enough to make her furrow her brow at him.

How odd that he was so happy she'd swooned. "The heat's never bothered me before."

"It has the last few weeks."

He had her there. The early summer made her feel horribly uncomfortable. But why would that cause her to faint?

"How's your stomach?" he asked, still grinning at her.

The queasiness remained, but she had no idea why he'd bring it up now. "Why would you want to know about my—"

The understanding hit her like a slap to her face, changing her words to a lump in her throat.

No. It couldn't be.

Not at her age.

Not at Adam's age.

Certainly not so quickly.

Her eyes found her husband's.

He nodded.

She shook her head.

Then Stephen Shay walked through the swinging doors, followed by a shorter man in a gray suit.

Her hands flew to her throat. Suddenly, there wasn't enough air.

It wasn't a dream!

She needed to run, to get as far away as she could. Where was Matthew? Her heartbeat echoed in her ears, drowning out all other sounds as her gaze darted about, seeking her brother.

He wasn't near, couldn't keep her safe again. She started to pant, the unreasoning fear consuming her.

"Don't go fainting on me again." Adam stroked her cheek with the cool cloth. "I'm right here, Gracie."

Her hand reached up to cover his. "Adam." Her husband would protect her. He promised to protect her. He would slay the dragon.

No. She had to run. *Now.*

"All the color drained from your face again." Victoria patted Grace's leg. "You might want to lie back down."

All Grace could think of was escape. "I want to go home." She clutched at her husband's shirt, fisting the material in her hands. "Take me home. Now. Please, Adam. *Please* take me home."

"Stephen, come meet my family." Victoria motioned the man over to her side. "This is my father, Adam Morgan, and his wife, Grace."

Stephen's smile was still reptilian and held the power to send ice water pouring through Grace's veins.

"Charmed," he said, his voice smug. "Victoria has told me so much about you both." His white teeth flashed. "I didn't realize I had already met Victoria's stepmother."

Grace struggled to get off the table so she could flee.

Adam put restraining hands on her shoulders. "Not so fast. I need to know you're not going to faint again. Your face is as white as a sheet."

How could she explain everything? How could she tell him about her connection to Stephen?

Adam would despise her. She couldn't lose him. Not when she loved him so very much.

Hysteria threatened to consume her. "I want to go home! Please take me home! *Please!*"

Emily came back from the kitchen, carrying a glass of water. "Here, Grace. Drink this."

Grace accepted the glass with a murmured thanks and shaky hands. Forcing herself to take a few sips, she struggled to mask the terror.

Sweet Lord, she couldn't face the bastard now, not here in front of her husband, in front of all her friends. She'd lose Adam. She'd lose everything.

The front doors swung open again, and Matthew came strutting in. "Victoria! Heard you were back."

Stephen turned around, and Matthew's eyes flew wide before his face flushed red. "You son of a bitch!"

With an angry snarl, he rushed Stephen, fisted the black jacket in one hand and repeatedly drove his other fist into Stephen's face. Stephen's knees buckled, and Matthew followed him to the floor, still beating him.

Jake reacted first, grabbing a hold of Matthew's arm to try to stop the rain of blows.

Victoria stayed at Grace's side, clutching for her hand. "Stop this!"

"Matthew, stop! Please!" Grace shouted.

Dear God, this was all her fault.

Adam stood, intending to separate the men and find out just what in the hell was going on when the man who'd followed Stephen into the saloon pulled a gun. He shifted it in his hand and hit Matthew's head with the butt of the weapon. Both Victoria and Grace screamed. Matthew's eyes rolled back before he collapsed on top of Stephen.

With a disgusted grunt, Stephen pushed Matthew off onto the sawdust-covered floor and crawled several feet away.

"Matthew!" Victoria hurried to him, dropped to the floor, and rolled him until she cradled his head in her lap. She smoothed her hands over his cheek. "Wake up, Matthew. Please wake up."

Adam crouched next to them and ran his hand over Matthew's skull. "Doesn't appear anything's broken, but he's got a nice goose egg that'll probably give him a hell of a headache. Just out cold for now."

Standing, he frowned at Stephen, who was being assisted to his feet by the man who'd followed him.

Stephen grabbed a handkerchief from his breast pocket and dabbed at his split lip before holding it to his bleeding nose. "I want that man arrested. Trey, go get the marshal."

Stephen's man scurried out of the saloon.

The moment Adam had heard Stephen Shay's name, warning flags soared. It was no coincidence that Grace's nightmares were haunted by a "Stephen" and one had followed Victoria home—where Grace lived.

He leveled a hard stare at Stephen, ready for some answers. "Why would Matthew attack you?"

"I have no idea. I hardly remember the man," Stephen replied.

"When did you meet Grace and Matthew?"

"Many, many years ago in San Francisco. I was a...friend of their father." Stephen pointed an accusing finger at Matthew again. "Tie that man up."

"No!" Victoria squealed. "Leave him alone. Can't you see he's hurt?"

Just when Adam thought things couldn't get any further out of hand, a glass shattered. Whirling around, he saw Grace's trembling hand and the glass she'd been drinking from laying in shards on the floor. "Gracie?"

Her quivering finger pointed to Emily, who now stood in the kitchen doorway, a small puddle of water at her feet. "I think the baby's coming."

Chapter Nineteen

Grace's head was still spinning at Stephen's arrival, but she scooted toward the edge of the table. Her fear for Emily and her grandchild outweighed her fear of Stephen.

Adam hurried to help her down. "You all right?"

She wasn't sure she'd ever be all right again.

Pushing all other concerns aside, she focused on the one thing that couldn't wait. "I need to help Emily. You need to see to Matthew."

Jake hurried to his wife, picked her up in his arms, and mounted the stairs. "Send for the doc!" They disappeared into the shadows up the hallway.

The marshal came hurrying into the saloon.

Will was right behind, red-faced and out of breath.

"What in the hell happened here?" the marshal asked, putting his hands on his beefy hips.

Stephen wiped some more blood off his face and nodded to Matthew. "That man attacked me."

Without even asking anyone else to corroborate, the marshal turned to Will. "Well, then... Gotta take him in. Help me drag him down to the jail. I'll lock that hoodlum up good and tight 'til the judge comes back 'round." He reached down to grab Matthew's limp arm.

"You're not taking him anywhere!" Victoria smacked the marshal's hand away and leaned forward to cover Matthew.

Adam's gaze kept shifting between Matthew and Stephen. "I need to know why Matthew hit him," he whispered to Grace. "Can you trust me?"

Now wasn't the time to spill her story, but she had to protect Matthew. "I–I do trust you, but I can't explain it. N–not right now."

"Grace..."

She clutched for her husband's hand, begging with her eyes for his understanding. "Please, Adam. I have to go to Emily."

A frown bowed his lips. "They'll take Matthew to jail unless you speak up."

After everything Matthew had done for her, she couldn't let them throw him in a cell. "No. Please don't take him to jail."

"Of course, it could give him some time to cool off," Adam added.

"Grace!" Jake shouted from the upstairs.

Although she didn't like the idea of Matthew spending even a moment in a cell, she nodded. If the whole sordid tale was going to come out, she needed Matthew at her side, calm and collected rather than confronting Stephen again. His reaction to seeing their tormentor wasn't at all surprising, but that blind anger wouldn't help either of them.

Her life was falling to pieces and there wasn't a thing she could do to stop it. "I'll slip away when I can to talk to you and Matthew." She inclined her head to her brother. "Please go with him. Make sure he's safe, that Victoria's safe. Then send someone for the doctor."

Adam took a few long moments thinking it over before he nodded.

"Grace!" Jake shouted again.

Her husband gently nudged her toward the stairs. "Go upstairs, Gracie. I won't leave until you do."

Grace crossed to the stairs and hurried up them. She ducked aside to hide in the shadows and wait until Adam left. She had to discover why Stephen was there and why he'd sunk his talons into Victoria.

Adam helped Will get Matthew up, and they braced him between them. The marshal, Ty, and a distressed Victoria followed them out the front doors.

Swallowing her fear, Grace stepped out of the shadows.

As if knowing she waited for him, Stephen turned to stare up at her. "We need to talk, my sweet."

It took every ounce of courage she had to walk down even one step. Each footfall was the pounding of another nail in her coffin. The moment she reached the floor, his hand shot out, grabbing her upper arm and squeezing until tears formed in her eyes.

She refused to flinch, knowing it would only give him pleasure.

Between gritted teeth, she said, "Let me go or I'll scream."

"Scream and I'll have you arrested."

She tried to jerk her arm away.

He tightened his grip. Yanking some folded papers out of his pocket, he waved them in her face. "This is an arrest warrant. I hand this to that ridiculous marshal and you'll be sharing a jail cell with your brother."

Had it only been her own fate at stake, she would have gladly surrendered to the marshal, hoping Adam would one day understand why she'd shot Stephen. With God's grace, perhaps her husband would even forgive her for the mistakes she'd made in the past.

But it wasn't just her now.

There was a baby to think of—and sweet Lord, she was still having a hard time swallowing that. Simply knowing she carried a part of Adam with her gave her strength as she faced her tormentor. "Why did you come here?"

His smile was as cold as harsh winter wind when he tucked the papers safely back into his pocket. "Why, to continue courting Victoria of course. The moment I met her, it was...love at first sight."

"There's no way I'll let her have anything to do with the likes of you."

"No?" He glanced back over his shoulder. "Then I suppose I need to have a long talk with your...husband. Perhaps he'd like to know all about the...*virtuous* woman he married."

He might as well have sunk a blade into her heart. All she could do was shake her head.

"So you haven't told him...everything, have you? Does he know anything about our past...relationship, about the kind of woman you really are?"

She hated the way he drew out pauses when he spoke, giving certain words special emphasis—words he knew hurt people.

She wanted to turn and rake her fingernails down his face. "I've done nothing wrong."

"Ah, so somehow you've convinced yourself that your shamefully wanton nature isn't what you and I both know it is. You threw yourself at me. You seduced me."

"*Seduced?*" The word came out in an indignant shriek.

"You can lie to yourself, Grace, but you could never lie to me."

The man had lost his mind. She refused to argue the past with him, knowing he'd never understand what kind of monster he really was. "Why did you tell Victoria you barely knew Matthew?"

"I don't wish for her to know about our past...involvement. She's a fresh start for me. A breath of fresh air. After chasing a woman I was lovesick for, I finally found a woman I can...respect."

Grace pulled in a ragged breath, wishing God would mercifully strike her dead. If Adam learned all about her past, if he knew about Stephen...

Yet how could she protect Victoria if she had to keep up Stephen's charade? Thoughts spun out of control as she tried to figure the whole cursed situation through.

Her suspicions worked overtime. "You rescued Ty. How *convenient* that he's Adam's son."

"Simple serendipity, my sweet. By stumbling across that robbery and thwarting those ruffians, my good deed was rewarded by the Fates giving me a woman more deserving of my...attentions. An honorable woman."

Jake's voice bellowed from the second floor. "Grace! Emily needs you!"

"Decide, my sweet. Do you play along that we're nothing more than casual acquaintances and let me court Victoria? Or do I head over to the jail and have a long talk with Adam Morgan while I hand my papers to the marshal?"

"Matthew won't go along—"

"If he wants to protect you, he'll do exactly what you tell him to do." Stephen finally released her arm, but he grabbed her by the shoulders and gave her a shake that rattled her teeth. "Decide. Decide now, or so help me—"

"Fine. Get your filthy hands off me."

His victorious smile almost pushed her over the edge. How she wished that Derringer still rested in her pocket. Even if it meant she'd roast in hell, this time she wouldn't miss his black heart.

"You'll talk to your brother?" he asked.

She nodded and tried to pull away from him. His grip tightened and he leaned in to whisper in her ear. "She's not you, Grace, but she's just as sweet, every bit as untouched as you were. Tell me, does your...husband please you as I did? Is what you share half as warm as what we shared?"

It took every ounce of her willpower not to spit in his face. She gritted her teeth and swallowed the bile rising in the back of her throat. "Let me go."

With one of his bone-chilling chuckles, he released her.

Grace grabbed her skirts and hurried up the stairs.

Chapter Twenty

Adam knocked softly on the bedroom door. After a few moments, Grace answered. Wanting a moment of privacy, he reached out to gently grasp her hand and urge her into the hallway.

She tossed a reassuring smile back at Emily. "I'll be right back." She pulled the door closed.

He stroked her shoulders. At least she was only a little pale now, but her wan complexion couldn't overshadow the determination in her eyes. "How are things going in there?"

"Slow but steady. How's Matthew?"

"He's awake, but he won't say a word about what happened 'til he talks to you. I'd like to find some time to talk to you too." An incline of his head at the door. "But I know now's not that time. How's she holding up?"

"Emily's a trooper. Is the doctor coming soon?"

He was afraid she'd ask that. "Doc's been...delayed."

Grace's face blanched even more. "Delayed? How long?"

"Um...he's going to be a bit...late."

A blatant lie.

Doc King's message said he wasn't coming for a good long time.

Adam didn't want his wife to panic. "Listen, Gracie. There's been an accident. Jed Moore broke his leg and might have some bleeding in his belly. Doc needs to stay with him. He'll try to get here when he can."

If he can...

Grace's frantic eyes searched his before her mouth sank into a frown. "He's not coming, is he?"

At that moment, he realized he'd never be able to lie to his pretty little wife. "No, darlin'. He's not. Said any woman would know what to do." He reached for her hand. Her fingers were ice cold. "I could send for the reverend's wife. Maybe Mary or one of the ladies from church who've already had babies would know how to help."

"Emily wants me."

"But you've never had a baby." He brushed a kiss on her cheek when she frowned again and glanced away. "Yet."

The frown changed to a weak smile as her gaze returned to his. "We're having a baby, Adam."

"I know, darlin', and I couldn't be happier." He nodded at Emily's room again. "We're asking an awful lot of you to bring Emily's baby into the world when you've never even seen a birth before."

Grace looked at the floor, clenched his hands, and shuddered. Then he saw the steel in her spine. Straightening her shoulders, she raised her eyes to his. "I'll be fine." A quick glance back. "So will Emily. Is Victoria coming? Emily's asking for her."

"She will, but first she wanted to be sure Matthew woke up. Then she's getting Stephen settled in at the boarding house. I don't want him anywhere near the ranch."

Adam caught her whispered, "Thank God."

"We need to talk. I know that man frightens you, and I'm pretty sure I know why. And with the way Matthew laid into him... I know there's something bad going on, more than the fact you've both met him before. Can't you tell me—"

She pressed trembling fingertips to his lips. "After. We'll talk *after*. There's too much to do right now. Emily and Jake need me, and I need to slip out to see Matthew. I'll wait 'til Victoria can sit with Emily."

"Then you're in luck, 'cause here she is." Victoria hurried down the hallway. "Matthew's asking for you."

Grace opened the door and called softly, "Emily? Would you mind if I go to see Matthew? Victoria's here to sit with you."

"No," Emily replied. "Go on, Grace. Just please don't be gone long."

"I won't. I promise."

Victoria skirted around them to go into the bedroom. He closed the door as his daughter took a seat next to the bed.

"I'll walk you over." Adam led Grace down the hall, stopping at the top of the stairs where it was still dark and private. He turned her so he could pull her into his embrace. Her whole body shuddered as she tucked her face into the crook of his neck. "It's okay, Gracie. Let it out."

Her words tumbled out slowly. "What if Emily has trouble? I won't know what to do."

Patiently waiting as she spent her fears, he held his wife close. "Everything will be fine."

She eased back. "I'm sorry."

"Nonsense."

"I'm a coward."

He hated her defeated tone. With his knuckles under her chin, he lifted to make her look at him. "Don't ever let me hear you say that again."

"But I'm so frightened—"

"Being frightened doesn't make you a coward. We're asking a lot of you, and you're rising to the challenge. Have you ever delivered a child before?"

"Heavens, no. You knew that."

"Yet here you are, helping Emily."

Grace shrugged. "She's family. I can't let her go through this alone."

"I know you're frightened by Stephen..."

Her gaze dropped to his chest.

"But you're still here. You haven't run away. I know you probably wanted to jump on the closest horse and ride as far away from the man as you can. You've been doing that for a long time, haven't you, darlin'?"

"Please...n–not now. I can't talk about him now."

Adam brushed a kiss over her mouth. "Not now—but soon. Don't be afraid. You know I'll protect you. I'll *always* protect you."

Her eyes searched his, and for the life of him he wished he knew what thoughts were flying through that busy head of hers. He was fairly sure of at least some of what happened between her and Stephen Shay in the past.

Why in the hell that bastard had ended up in White Pines with Victoria remained a mystery, although Adam had his suspicions. He'd listen to Victoria's story and then he'd talk to Ty.

Yet another part of this puzzle he'd have to work on.

At least Victoria hadn't argued that Stephen should be a guest at the Twin Springs, so Adam hadn't found himself having to refuse her. No way he'd let that man anywhere near Grace again. At least Victoria didn't seem to feel any affection for Stephen. When she'd gone to Matthew after the fight, she'd let everyone know where her loyalties lay.

Damn, but Victoria and Matthew really needed to get things sorted out between them.

After a quivering sigh, Grace said, "I trust that you'll protect me. Let's go to Matthew."

***

Grace thought she'd brought her tumultuous emotions back under control. Then she walked into the jail.

Seeing her brother locked up in a cell was almost her undoing.

Adam had led her into the marshal's office. They found the marshal passed out at his desk, reeking of alcohol.

Her husband excused himself and hurried out to find the other members of the town council, saying they had some important business that needed attention.

Matthew sat on his stark bunk, frowning at the snoring marshal.

His gaze found hers. "Did you know he locked himself in the cell a couple of hours ago? How he managed that, I'll never know."

"You should've used the opportunity to escape," she teased before realizing just how ridiculous she sounded. "I'm so sorry."

He came to stand by the bars, gripping them with his calloused hands. "Why are *you* sorry? You didn't invite that snake. He always slithers out from under his rock. I thought he was dead."

Tears stung her eyes. "So did I."

"What exactly happened in San Francisco? All you said was you'd shot him."

Her brother seemed calm enough now, but if she told him the whole story... Too ashamed to confess, she gave her head a shake.

"Grace, so help me..."

"It doesn't matter now. I was wrong. He's not dead."

"Adam will take care of you."

"I know, but...Stephen's not here for me. Not this time."

"What's that supposed to mean—not here for you? He's always hunting you."

God help her, she felt as if she was betraying her own brother. "He's here...to court Victoria."

"No!" He shook the bars hard enough the whole structure rattled. "That bastard can't have her!"

She hurried to the bars and placed her hands over his where he gripped the metal with whitened knuckles. "I'll try to protect her."

"How? By telling her what he did to you? You'd do that to save Victoria, wouldn't you?"

Closing her eyes, she released a shuddering sigh. "I can't."

Matthew jerked his hands away. *"Can't? Or won't?* Adam would understand."

"I know that," Grace snapped back.

"Well then, why can't—"

A sob bubbled out, breaking off his words. "I can't. Stephen will have me arrested. He's carrying an arrest warrant with him."

His derisive snort was louder than the marshal's snoring. "For what?"

"Attempted murder."

His gaze settled on the drunken marshal. "Then why didn't he have that idiot arrest you?"

"He told me if I don't tell Victoria about...our history...he wouldn't have me thrown in jail. All I have to do is keep quiet."

"He raped you."

She gave her head a quick shake. "It was my fault."

"Grace... No. You didn't do anything wrong. You have to tell what he did to you."

Sniffing hard, she shook her head again. "I can't go to jail."

His eyes turned so hard, so accusing, she wanted to turn and run. "So you'll let him get his filthy hands on Victoria? Then I'll tell her myself."

If she started crying, she would never stop. She didn't let a single tear fall. "You can't. It doesn't matter who tells, Stephen would have me arrested. I can't go to jail, Matthew."

"You're a coward," he scolded. Giving the bars another shake, he turned his back on her. "Adam would hire a lawyer. He'd get you out in a heartbeat."

"I shot a Shay. No lawyer would be able to help me and you know it."

"Adam would—"

"You don't understand. I can't go to jail."

"You wouldn't be there too long and—"

"I'm pregnant."

Whirling around to face her, Matthew stared at her with big eyes until his gaze softened. "Oh, Grace…"

She leaned her forehead against the cold bars and closed her eyes. She'd cost her brother too much already. If she did nothing else, she would set him free—even if it meant going to jail.

"Just as soon as Emily has the baby I'm going to tell Adam and Victoria about Stephen. Then I'll surrender myself to the marshal. Surely Adam will be able to post some kind of bond. I won't let Stephen hurt Victoria—even if I have to stand up in court and shame myself by telling everyone the truth."

Warm hands wrapped around hers. "Don't."

She glanced up at her brother. "I have to."

He shook his head. "I won't let you do it." He splayed his fingers through his hair. "I'll warn Victoria, I–I'll try to get her to listen without telling her everything. I'll talk to Adam. He's smart. Even if I don't tell him…*everything*, he'll understand. Hell, he probably already knows most of the story."

Her heart clenched at what she feared was coming next. "And then?"

"As soon as they let me out of this goddamn cage, I'm leaving."

"No! Please–*please* don't leave me!"

Matthew reached between the bars to stroke her cheek. "You don't need me anymore."

"You're my brother. I love you." Her words fell to a whisper. "We've always been together. Always."

"It's time for your husband to take care of you. I can't stay here.

Not now. I can't watch Victoria—" His head bowed, he took a deep breath. "Go on now. Go back to Emily. How is she?"

"It's still early. Her pains aren't too difficult yet, and they're still well apart." A hard swallow. "The doctor isn't coming, Matthew. I'm going to have to deliver the baby."

"Oh, Lord. Can you do that?"

"Of course, she can." Adam's confident voice boomed through the jail, causing Grace to jump in surprise.

He strode across the way, pausing only to frown at the snoring marshal, and put himself behind her.

Strong hands gripped her shoulders. "Grace can do anything she puts her mind to."

Matthew smiled although his heart was close to breaking. His whole life—from the time he and Grace had left their home at the tender ages of eight and fourteen—they'd relied on each other. To let her safety and happiness pass to another man was a hard swallow.

Adam Morgan was a good man. He would do right by Grace.

"You're right," Matthew said. He gave her hands one more squeeze before letting his own drop away. "She can do anything. Promise me one thing, Adam?"

He quirked a brow.

"Never, *never* let Stephen Shay near her again."

"We need to have a serious talk 'bout that and 'bout something else. I'll be back shortly to get you out of here."

"What about the charges?"

"They've been dropped," Adam replied. "Victoria convinced that jaycock to let the whole situation go." He glanced back at the marshal. "Once you're free, Will and I need to have a serious discussion with you."

Victoria hurried into the office. "Grace, Emily's asking for you."

Grace leaned against her husband as if drawing strength from him before she squared her shoulders. "I need to go."

"Let me walk you back," he said. "As long as that man's still around, you're not going anywhere alone.'"

He took her hand in his and led her out of the marshal's office.

Matthew could only stare at Victoria.

She stared right back at him, those hazel eyes searching for something.

"Thank you," he finally said.

"For what?"

"For getting the charges dropped."

Her reply was a curt nod. "Do you want to tell me why you attacked him?"

"I'll leave the telling to Grace. Just one warning, Victoria—don't trust him. Don't *ever* trust him."

"I don't." She waved him off when he tried to speak again. "He's nothing but a friend. He came to Ty's rescue, but I... There's just something about him. Makes me...uneasy."

"Good. Trust that instinct."

Cautiously approaching the bars, she nibbled on her lower lip. "I–I was wondering if you were still planning on leaving."

With a frown, he nodded.

"There's nothing that could make you stay? I don't want you to...I mean...Grace is staying. Don't you want to be with...*her?*"

I want to be with you.

He held his silence.

"She'll be sad if you go."

"She has your father."

"I'll be—" Victoria turned around and wrapped her arms around her waist, taking several long breaths. "I wasn't coming back, you know."

"Pardon?"

"I was gonna stay in Denver. I'm going back there again—just as soon as I can. I only came here to see Ty home safely. I'm going back after I help Emily. I promised her I'd stay for a few days."

"Why would you go back to Denver?"

"I'm going to be a governess. There's a family who invited me to stay with them—to teach their children. I can't stay here. Daddy and Grace don't need me anymore."

"They love you."

I love you.

"I won't stay and be the object of pity." When he tried to correct her, she cut him off with a slash of her hand. "Don't waste your breath arguing with me. They love me. I know that. But I'm nothing but a burden."

"You're talking nonsense."

"Am I? What's there for me in White Pines?" She didn't even give him a chance to reply. "Nothing. There's *nothing* here for me. I have to go. I have to make a life for myself. Besides, you're—"

"I'm what?"

"Leaving."

The office door opened, and Adam and Will came inside.

Adam grabbed the keys from the desk and went to the cell. He opened the door and with a grin set Matthew free.

The marshal didn't stir through the entire process.

Victoria hurried to the door. "I should go. Grace will be needing me." She ducked outside before Matthew could find the courage to go to her.

"Head on back to the ranch," Adam said. "Ty could probably use some help. I'm staying here 'til I can take Grace home."

"Don't let her out of your sight," Matthew cautioned again. He picked up his hat off the marshal's desk and snorted. "He's drunk again."

"Appears so."

"Then he won't be of any help if Grace needs him. Hell, he wouldn't be any help even if he *was* sober."

"Don't you worry," Adam replied. "I'll take care of Grace. Stephen Shay won't get within a mile of her."

Matthew put on his hat. "I wish I could say the same about Victoria." He leveled a hard stare. "Has she told you her plans? That's she's heading back to Denver?"

With a sigh, Adam rubbed the back of his neck. "I was afraid of that. I need to sit her down for a long talk. Is it because of Shay?"

"No. She took a job as a governess. Wants to leave you and Grace to have some privacy on the ranch. She's silly enough to think she'll be in your way."

"We'll just have to set her straight then, won't we?" Giving Matthew's back a friendly push, Adam inclined his head to the door. "Go on back to the ranch. When you get a chance, bring the mare back here and leave her in the livery so Victoria can come back home when she's ready."

Matthew nodded and followed Adam and Will outside. Being in a cell had been an uncomfortable experience, but a cost he would gladly pay to keep Stephen Shay the hell away from Grace. That Stephen showed an interest in Victoria came as a surprise. Not that Victoria wasn't one of the most beautiful women in the territory, but Stephen had doggedly stalked Grace for so many years, his sudden change of heart seemed...wrong. Out of character.

And damned suspicious.

Just as he was about to say his farewells to Adam and Will so he could go fetch Sin, Matthew spotted Stephen. The snake was standing on the boardwalk, talking to his lackey.

Without a word to his companions, Matthew bunched up his shoulders, put his head down, and charged, intent upon finishing what he'd started earlier.

"Matthew, wait!" Adam called after him.

Matthew gave him no heed.

Stephen turned to face him when his little weasel of an assistant pointed his direction.

Matthew kept marching—despite the fact Stephen was now wielding his silver-topped cane like a sword.

With a swipe of his left arm, Matthew knocked the cane away as his right hand shot out to grab Stephen by the throat. He had the man pinned to the outside wall of the general store before the bastard could draw another breath. Balling his left hand into a fist, he prepared to break Stephen's jaw.

Adam shoved Stephen's man aside and had a hold of Matthew's arm before he could throw a punch. "He's not worth it, son."

Will—breathless from the jaunt across the road—nodded. "Don't want to go back in that cell now, do you, boy?"

Everything inside Matthew ached to beat Stephen into a bloody pulp. When he thought about all that man had cost his sister... Hatred drowned out any common sense. "You don't know what he did to Grace."

"Got a damned good idea," Adam replied.

Matthew glanced back at him, surprised in the wealth of emotion he heard in those five words.

"Still doesn't make you judge and jury," Adam added. "Trust me on this. Let him go. Justice has a way of working itself out."

Stephen was gasping for air and clutching at Matthew's arm.

The urge to inflict pain on him was overwhelming. "Give me one reason not to break his sorry neck."

"Because he's not worth a good man like you getting himself into trouble."

Matthew's head whipped around to Victoria's voice.

She strode over and placed her hand on Matthew's stiff arm. "Let him go. Please."

"Did he touch you?" He turned back to glare at Stephen, hoping the man could see the hatred in his eyes—hoping the man would one day feel the same fear he'd put into Grace. "Did you lay even one goddamn finger on her?"

"He never touched me. Not once. Please, Matthew. Let him go."

With a grunt, he dropped Stephen who collapsed on the boardwalk, gasping for air. "I... will...have...you...arrested."

"Arrested?" Will laughed. "Fer what?"

"Assault," Stephen's assistant answered as he tried to help Stephen to his feet. "I'm heading right to the marshal's office."

"Ain't got no witnesses." Will let his gaze fall on everyone in the small crowd surrounding them. "Nope. Not a single witnesses."

Several townsfolk shook their heads and walked on.

"B'sides," he continued, "the marshal's passed out drunk. Not gonna get much help there." He leveled a lethal stare at Stephen.

"Never gonna get much help from *anyone* in White Pines."

"You'll pay for this," Stephen rasped, still struggling to get enough air.

Matthew scoffed. "Why don't you pack up your things and get the hell out of town?"

Stephen straightened his coat, reached down to grab his cane, and narrowed his dark eyes at Victoria. "After all I've done to help Ty Bishop, you'd turn on me too?"

"About that," Adam interjected. "Were there any witnesses to Ty's robbery?"

"*I* was the witness," Stephen insisted. "*I* routed those thieves before they could kill him."

Adam swept his vest aside and set his hands on his hips. "I'm planning to have a nice long talk with Ty and with the authorities in Denver. I'm gonna solve that mystery if it's the last thing I do."

His haughty visage back in place, Stephen sneered at them all. "Then it would seem my welcome in this...fair town has worn thin. I will be leaving as soon as I can make arrangements. You ungrateful buffoons can all go to hell." He turned to his assistant. "You take care of all the...arrangements. Then you find me."

Matthew watched them walk away, the need to pound the man into the mud still choking him. His hands were fisted at his sides, and he'd clenched his jaw so tight, he feared he'd cracked a few teeth. He didn't trust Stephen to leave, and his mind warred over whether to offer protection to Grace or to Victoria.

Victoria soothed him with a simple touch. Her fingers wrapped around his right fist and gently pried his fingers open. After a deep breath, he took her hand in his.

Adam glanced at Will. "I think a quick town council meeting's in order." His gaze shifted to the marshal's office. "Yep. I definitely think a meeting's in order."

"It's over, Daddy," she whispered.

Adam only smiled in reply.

Victoria's touch calmed Matthew enough for him remember the rest of the day's events.

"Emily needs you," he said. "Let me take you back to the Four Aces."

She didn't pull her hand away as they walked together toward the saloon.

***

A common boarding house.

For the love of all that was holy, he'd been reduced to spending the night in a goddamn boarding house.

Stephen relentlessly paced the room, wondering how everything had gone wrong so quickly. The plans had all been carefully made—every piece of the puzzle falling into place so easily.

Ty's assault went off without a hitch, and the man never suspected the whole thing had been a set up.

Victoria had accepted him with only a token resistance, even traveling to this backwater town with him as her escort—just as he'd hoped.

Grace had even been properly surprised to know that she hadn't ended his life back in San Francisco.

Then why was he not staying at that godforsaken ranch, finishing his plans to spirit Grace out of Montana?

Matthew Riley.

The man had vexed Stephen from the time he'd begun to pursue Grace. Always helping get her out of town before Stephen could get his hands on her. Always managing to move her out of his grasp.

Just like today.

This time, Matthew Riley wouldn't walk away unpunished.

"I *will* have Grace. She will be mine again."

A knock on the door ended his pacing. "Come in."

Skittering into the room like a frightened rodent, Trey hurried to stand in front of Stephen.

Despite the desire to reach out and strangle the life out of his minion, Stephen sighed in resignation. "What did you find out?"

"Not gonna be easy. The ranch is pretty isolated, but snatching her up might be a problem."

"Why? She's here. She's not running away."

Trey stared at his shoes. "That rancher ain't gonna let her go easy. Might have to kill him. There's also the brother—he's not likely to let Grace outta his sight. Not after all these years."

Stephen fought the fury racing through him. The beating had left him bruised and sore, and holding a mask of indifference had become next to impossible.

He wanted Matthew Riley broken and bleeding.

Then he wanted him *dead.*

"I'll be leaving on the morning stage, but I won't go far. You, however, will be staying."

"Stayin'?" Trey asked. "If you're leavin', why on earth would I be stayin'?"

Stephen fixed his gaze on Trey. "It's time to get the brother out of the picture."

Chapter Twenty-One

"Push, Emily." Grace watched as a patch of dark hair began to emerge. "That's it. Push!"

Victoria held Emily's hand as the mother-to-be grunted and bore down hard enough her whole body shook with the effort.

"You're almost there," Grace coaxed, trying to keep the panic flowing through her out of her voice. "One more push should do the trick."

She still found it hard to believe that she was helping bring her granddaughter into the world. Funny, but she'd had a feeling right from the beginning that this baby would be a girl. She'd pictured the child in her mind a million times, blending her long ago memories of Jake's face with Emily's features.

The night had been long for poor Emily. Grace's terror had subsided as she realized she was a comfort to her. The fear of something going wrong remained, but she swallowed it and showed Emily only confidence.

The last few hours, the pains had come more and more swiftly until Grace had tears in her eyes each time she saw Emily's features contort, signaling the beginning of another pain. Offering silent prayers for Emily and her grandchild helped her focus and keep her head.

The first orange streaks of sunrise had just appeared when the baby decided she'd waited long enough. The pains came—one right on top of another.

All Grace could do was give Emily as much encouragement as possible and pray she'd soon hold the little one in her arms. "You can do this, honey. Your baby's almost here. One good push."

And what a push it was. Emily gritted her teeth, pulled her knees up, and bore down until her face flushed beet red.

The baby's head and shoulders came sliding out so fast, Grace had to work frantically to catch the tiny girl. Grabbing a cloth, she wiped away the mucous covering the baby's face, especially around the mouth and nostrils.

"Breathe," she whispered. "C'mon, sweet baby. Breathe for me."

The infant squirmed, opened her mouth, and let out a wail that made all three women weep and laugh at the same time.

Thank you, God, for this precious little life.

"Is he okay?" Emily tried to push herself up by her elbows to see. "Ten fingers? Ten toes?"

"*She,*" Grace replied with a smile as she finished cleaning up the squalling infant, "is perfect and very, very beautiful. Chubby and pink and absolutely furious, but beautiful nonetheless."

After tying off and cutting the cord, she wrapped the baby in the blanket Victoria held out for her. Victoria helped Emily lay back so Grace could place Emily's daughter in her arms.

"She's so small." Victoria ran trembling fingers over the baby's blanketed head.

"That's the way they come." Grace let a chuckle to hide the fear that still thrummed through her. So many things could've gone wrong—so many things still could. And, dear God, she offered continual thanks that she was really seeing her granddaughter with her own eyes.

"Hi, baby," Emily cooed, gently touching a fingertip to her daughter's face. "I'm your mama."

The infant opened her eyes as if searching for the voice she'd just heard.

Much as she wanted to simply stare at her new granddaughter, Grace went about helping get Emily through the afterbirth, cleaned up, and ready to see her husband, who still waited right outside the door. His footsteps pacing the length of the hall and back hadn't stopped the whole night through. Every now and then when Emily groaned or cursed after a strong labor pain, he would shout a shaky apology through the door.

Jake had only come into the room once, thinking to help his wife by holding her hand or wiping her brow with a cool cloth. After only two strong pains, the color had drained from his face. Emily told him to leave because she didn't want him swooning on her. He hadn't even tried to argue and had, in fact, fled the room as if the devil himself was on his heels.

As Emily set the infant to her breast, Victoria took her leave. The instant the door was opened, Jake hurried into the room.

"I heard crying. How's my son?"

Emily, tired though she was, gave him a smile. "Your *daughter* is wonderful."

"Daughter? I–I have a *daughter?*" He looked so wobbly, a slight breeze might've blow him over.

"Steady there, Jake." Grace laid a hand on his arm.

He turned his gaze to her. His smile was so genuine, so loving, it brought fresh tears to her eyes. "Thank you, Grace." He leaned in to kiss her cheek.

Her hand covered the spot his lips had touched.

"I'm sorry," he whispered.

"Sorry?"

"That I was so cruel to you when you got here. I'm ashamed of myself. For God's sake, you're my sister."

She swallowed hard. "You forgive me? You really forgive me?"

Wrapping his arms around her, he hugged the breath right out of her lungs. Then he turned her loose and hurried to his wife's side

Adam stood in the doorway. His welcoming smile almost reduced Grace to nothing but a blubbering mess.

Dear Lord, she was exhausted. And numb. Too much had happened too quickly, and all she wanted to do was go back to Twin Springs and sleep in her own bed with Adam's arms wrapped around her. Then, maybe she could finally think of some solution to all her problems. The weight of the past and her lies were unbearable.

He opened his arms to her.

She surrendered to his embrace and snuggled tight against him. "Take me home, husband."

"Gladly, wife."

***

Adam didn't press Grace to talk.

She'd dozed on and off as they made the trip home, barely able to keep her eyes open long enough to greet Matthew as he'd passed them on his way to take Victoria's mare to town.

Grace had done him proud. He was sure that spine of hers was made of the strongest steel. She'd been through so much in the last twenty-four hours. Realizing she was pregnant. The appearance of Stephen Shay. And she'd had to deliver a baby when she'd never even been a mother herself.

Or so she says....

He had another theory that might've seemed far-fetched when it had first formed.

Not anymore.

Now wasn't the time to force the issue. Grace would open up when she was ready—not a moment before.

Her head bobbed. He wrapped an arm around her shoulders and pulled her against him. A sleepy sigh fell from her lips as she pressed up closer.

So many questions ran through his head, but he wouldn't put them to her. Not now. There would be time aplenty after she had some rest.

Somehow, someway they'd get this whole mess sorted out.

Victoria was safe, staying on in Grace's old room at the Four Aces to help Emily with the new baby. Matthew was staying on as well, sleeping on a cot in the back room of the saloon. He'd vowed to keep an eye on Victoria to make sure Stephen Shay wasn't causing her any trouble. Knowing things between Matthew and Victoria were shaky at best, Adam had been afraid to ask him to watch over her. Thankfully, Matthew had come up with the plan on his own.

Not much of a surprise.

No one had seen hide or hair of Stephen after he'd left with his beady-eyed assistant, but there was little hope he'd leave them in peace for too long. Something told Adam that Stephen wasn't there for Victoria—she was only a means to an end.

He feared that *end* was his wife.

She might hate it, but he wasn't going to let Grace go too far without being glued to her side.

Pulling back the reins, he brought the wagon to a stop when they reached the ranch. "Gracie." He gave her a little nudge. "Go inside, darlin'. I'll put the horses away and join you. We could both use some sleep."

"I should make you some breakfast," she mumbled, still more asleep than awake.

"You'll do no such thing. Go to bed. I'll come and catch some sleep with you as soon as I get the horses unhitched."

Adam crawled out of the wagon and then lifted his wife to the ground. One quick hug before he turned her toward the back door and gave her a gentle push between her shoulder blades to get her moving.

By the time he made it up to their bedroom, he'd expected to find her snuggled under the blankets, sound asleep. Instead, she knelt in the middle of bed, wearing nothing but the beauty God graced her with.

His body responded hard and fast. "Grace... You're exhausted."

She opened her arms to him. "I need you."

As if he'd make her ask twice...

He tugged off his shoes and socks, pulled off his shirt fast enough a couple of buttons popped off, and removed his pants.

Grace crawled to the edge of the bed, and in a matter of moments his naked body was against hers. Her kiss was downright desperate. Deep and furious, her tongue rubbed over his as he growled low in his throat.

She pressed her breasts against his chest. "Make love to me."

Adam answered her with another deep kiss as he lifted her to lay her down on the bed. Covering her body with his, he parted her thighs with his knee so he could settle himself against her. She replied by wrapping her legs around his hips and squeezing.

He tried to go slow—to take his time so he could coax her response—but she dragged her nails across his shoulders and murmured that she wanted him inside her and that she wanted it *now*.

"Patience," he whispered in her ear.

His lips moved to her neck as she tilted her head to bare more of it to him. Her toes rubbed against his legs as she mewled her pleasure. He kissed along her collarbone to the valley between her breasts, teasing her with what he knew she wanted. Her hands moved to his head, fingers sliding through his hair as she gently guided him toward her breast. With a smug smile, he kissed her pink nipple, teasing and taunting with his tongue.

"Please, Adam."

He rewarded her by tugging on that taut nipple with his teeth before drawing it into his mouth.

Grace arched up against him. When his hands were on her body, he could let everything bad fall away. His world was reduced to the feel of her skin, the warmth of her lips, and the love they shared.

His kisses moved lower. Down her stomach—where he stopped to press his lips to her skin to kiss his unborn child—to the juncture of her thighs. When he nudged her thighs, she opened her legs wider. Then he kissed the very core of her, finding her sensitive nub and stabbing his tongue in and out of her tight channel.

"Come to me," she begged, tugging on his hair.

He wouldn't obey. Instead he kept up his tender assault on her senses. Only when her release tore through her did he raise himself up to surge inside her body.

Adam held her hips tight as he drove into her again and again. His name spilled from her lips in a breathless whisper and knowing she'd found fulfillment again, he claimed his own.

He never wanted their connection to end, pushing into his wife in lesser strokes and holding her against him. She felt so wonderful—so tight and so hot—if he stayed inside her too much longer, he'd get hard again. She needed her rest, not her husband pawing at her.

He broke their intimate link and rolled to his side, dragging her up against his body. With a kiss on the top of her head, he said, "Sleep now, darlin'."

When she didn't reply, he nudged her chin up so he could see her face.

His wife was sound asleep.

***

Adam woke to Grace's frantic screams. She thrashed against the covers, fighting some nightmare foe.

He held her close. "Wake up, Gracie. It's just a bad dream."

Her eyes few open, full of fear—like a cornered animal. As her gaze found his, the panic slowly ebbed and her breathing eased so she was no longer panting for each breath.

"Safe now?" she asked, her voice ragged.

"You're safe now."

Her whole body relaxed. After only a few moments, she drifted back to sleep.

It was no coincidence that her nightmares returned when Stephen Shay popped up in White Pines.

Chapter Twenty-Two

Grace slept until the early hours of the afternoon. Feeling a bit sinful for being so slovenly, she reminded herself that she'd been up the entire night helping Emily and the baby.

Reality hit her hard. Stephen had found her.

Her first instinct was to plan an escape. Running had always been what she'd done best.

The fear only lasted a few moments. A good look around the bedroom told her that her running days had ended the day she married Adam Morgan—because for the first time, she had a reason to stay put.

More than one reason...

As she rested her palm against her stomach, she closed her eyes and thanked her Maker for sending her not only a guardian angel but another child to love.

Dressing quickly, she hurried down to the kitchen.

Adam welcomed her with a warm smile.

She smiled back—until she remembered that he would want answers about Stephen Shay.

He didn't say a word as she gathered a few things to eat, even pulled out the chair for her. As she picked at her food, he took the seat next to her, sipped some coffee, and stared at her with those wise blue eyes.

Nausea roiled through her. She pushed the plate away, knowing morning sickness wasn't the only thing plaguing her. The food tasted wonderful, but her stomach was so tied up in nervous knots, she couldn't force herself to eat.

"You ready to talk now?" he asked.

"I'd rather not."

"I'd rather so."

"Can we please go into town first and see how Emily and the baby are doing?"

Grace's first thoughts upon waking had been if either of them had needed her during this night. Was her granddaughter nursing well? Was Emily getting enough rest to help her recover from the delivery? Did Victoria need any assistance in caring for them?

So much could still put both mother and child in danger...

She was turning into a nervous ninny. Would she be that paranoid raising her own baby? She'd probably worry about every sneeze, every cough.

She hadn't realized she was wringing her hands until Adam's touch stopped her.

"Gracie, what's got you so worried?"

"Emily. And the baby. What if—"

"Stop. Just stop. We'll go into White Pines. Seeing they're both fine will put your mind at ease."

A smile started to form on her lips until the next words fell from his mouth.

"We need to talk about Stephen Shay."

She started wringing her hands again. "I–I don't want to talk about him. You told me he left town. Can't we put it behind us?"

Taking her hands into his, he stroked her palms with his thumbs. "Sometimes if you face what scares you, it's not so scary anymore."

"I can't."

Stephen Shay wasn't scary—he was *terrifying*.

"I'll protect you, Grace."

Her husband's tone was harsh, probably harsher than he'd ever used with her before. Not that she didn't deserve it. She'd done nothing but divert his attention anytime he asked about her connection to Stephen. Adam was too smart by half, and she had no doubt he'd figured out most of what Stephen had done to her.

But he couldn't possibly know Jake was her son.

"I know," she replied. "I'm sorry, Adam." She heaved a weary sigh. "Can we please go see Emily and the baby first? When we get back, we'll talk. I promise."

"As soon as we get back, you'll tell me everything."

A command rather than a question.

Grace nodded, her stomach leaping into her throat at the notion of laying all her secrets bare for her husband to see.

But Adam loved her. He would understand. If not understand, maybe at least *forgive*.

"Everything," she promised. "I'll tell you everything."

They were on the road to town less than thirty minutes later. A couple of the bigger bumps made the bile rise in the back of her throat. She kept her thoughts and her nausea to herself, not wanting to be a burden.

"Sorry, darlin'. You still feeling poorly?"

The man was too perceptive. "Just a little."

"It'll pass in a few months."

She sighed. "I know."

"You know?" His head tilted, a smug grin on his lips. "Hard to believe you've been around a lot of womenfolk on all those long drives. How did you learn about morning sickness?"

Don't panic.

"Emily told me." Grace feigned indifference with a flip of her hand. "She... um... mentioned most women get queasy for the first couple of months."

She hated when he just continued to stare at her, so she turned the topic. "How do you feel about being a father again?"

At least the question pulled a true smile from his handsome face. "Can't lie and say it wasn't a surprise. At my age, I sure hadn't expected to be welcoming a new baby. Figured Victoria might make me a grandpa in a few years, 'specially after she met Matthew."

"I wish they'd stop and think about what they could share."

Matthew deserved some happiness, and Victoria Morgan made him happy, no matter how hard her brother tried to hide his feelings.

Adam gave Grace's hand a squeeze. "How do you feel about being a mother, Mrs. Morgan?"

With the appearance of Stephen Shay and the birth of Emily and Jake's baby, she'd barely had time to think. "I'm going to be a mother. Oh, Adam... We're having a child."

A baby.

Adam's baby.

A miracle, that.

She could raise her child, watch him change and grow into being a man. This baby might be a salve to ease the heartache over the things she'd missed in Jake's life. She could nurse this child at her own breast. She could tuck him in at night. She could rock him to sleep.

Oh, yes, this child is a miracle.

Adam's laugh was warm, reaching deep down and squeezing her heart. He lifted a gentle hand over to wipe away a tear slipping down her cheek. "You're going to be a mother. A damned good one, I'm sure."

Dear Lord, she loved him. How could she survive if she ever lost him?

She clasped his hand against her face and closed her eyes. "I love you, Adam."

"I love you too, darlin'."

They pulled up in front of the Four Aces, and he helped her down from the wagon. Her gaze searched everywhere for Stephen, and she literally breathed a sigh of relief. For now, he'd truly left White Pines. Perhaps knowing she'd married had ended his unholy fascination with her, and Victoria didn't need a man hounding her.

Maybe this time, he'd stay away for good.

God, please let it be so.

Adam led her into the saloon, holding the door open for her.

Will's smiling face greeted them. "Good to see ya. Here to check on the new mama?"

"Of course," Grace replied. "Did she have a good night?"

"Slept like the dead when she weren't nursin' the little one. Jake's been pacing the floor all night. Think he's afraid to put the child down. One peep, and he sets to fussing over her."

"She's gonna be almost as spoiled as Emily was," Adam added.

"Pert near already is." Will gave them enormous grin.

"Is Victoria still here?" Adam scanned the room. "Haven't seen her this morning."

"Headed out to the livery not too long ago," Will replied. "Must've just missed her. She was going to the ranch. Said Emily was doin' fine. Promised to be back after she got some sleep and a bath. Said somethin' about a good, long soak."

"She sure loves that bathtub. Well worth its price."

Jake came striding down the upstairs hall and stopped at the top of the stairs. "Will y'all keep it down? The baby's sleeping."

The infant's wails reached downstairs.

The glare Jake threw them was hotter than a bonfire. "Now look what you gone and did!" His stomps echoed behind him as he whirled to leave.

"Yep," Will said. "That's one spoiled li'l girl."

Adam pressed his hand to the small of Grace's back. "Let's go see if we can help."

The infant's squalls had petered out by the time she knocked softly on the partially open door. "May we come in?"

"Grace! You're back," Emily called. "Come in. Come in."

The new mother was radiant, sitting up in bed and watching Jake fuss over the baby.

"Have you had something to eat?" Grace asked.

"Daddy made me some eggs." She nibbled on her lower lip. "They weren't very good."

"Well, then. I'll just go down to the kitchen and whip you up something special. What do you have a taste for?"

"Anything," she replied, then lowered her voice. "So long as Daddy doesn't cook it."

"I'll see what's in the pantry."

Grace moved to Jake's side to see the baby.

Her pink face seemed serene as she stared back, and Grace felt a pinch in her heart. This was her granddaughter—a part of her.

She said something to keep from blubbering. "Hard to tell who she'll look like. Babies change so fast. Her eyes may be dark blue now, but they might soon be as brown as Jake's."

Funny, but the smile Adam threw her seemed a bit too perceptive. "You're right, darlin'. Victoria's were dark blue too—except hers lightened instead of darkened."

Jake passed the baby to Grace's waiting arms.

The little girl smelled so sweet, it brought fresh tears to Grace's eyes. "Hi, honey. Remember me?"

"That's your Aunt Grace." Jake smoothed his big, calloused hands ever so softly over the dark curls crowning the infant's head.

Adam came to stand behind Grace, looking over her shoulder at the baby. "Mighty fine job, Emily. What are you gonna call her?"

"Elizabeth Ann," Emily replied. "Daddy and Jake have called her Beth so many times, I guess that's what everyone will know her as."

Grace pressed a kiss to Beth's forehead. "It doesn't matter what you're called, does it, sweetheart. You're just too beautiful for words."

Adam's hand was suddenly on her shoulder. He gave her an affectionate squeeze. "Soon, you'll be holding one of your own in your arms."

"Grace!" Emily exclaimed. "You're gonna have a baby?"

Grace's face grew warm as she nodded.

Jake slapped Adam on the back so hard he bumped into Grace. "Why you old son-of-a-gun. I thought you'd be too old to—"

"If you want to keep your teeth," Adam warned, "you best guard the next words coming out of your mouth, son."

When Jake laughed, he sounded like Matthew.

Satisfaction swept through Grace. Jake was a happy man, and she thanked God for that blessing, knowing after all he'd been through he'd survived and come out whole.

"I almost forgot." Jake walked over to the bureau and pulled out a drawer. "I've got something for Beth." He rooted around. "Here it is."

Striding back over to them, he said, "This is all I have left from my mama. My *real* mama. You probably recognize it, don't you, Grace?" He reached out to pin a small gold heart on the soft blanket. "It belonged to our mama, after all."

The air in the room evaporated. Her heart pounded so hard, she was surprised it didn't simply explode. "Take her."

Her words were so breathless, she was grateful Jake could even understand them. He scooped Beth back into his arms. "Are you gonna be sick?"

Sick? No, not sick.

Much, much worse.

She was going to die.

The world was closing in on her, and all Grace could think of was escape. She turned and tried to grope her way to the door, her breath coming in pants. There wasn't enough air.

Not enough air!

The heart. The damned heart.

How could she have forgotten? Her fingers clutched the door frame.

Have to go. Have to run.

The heart! The memories!

Adam grabbed her by the shoulders and turned her to face him. The color had drained from her face, and she wheezed as hard as she had when she'd been ill. He'd never seen someone so frightened.

"Don't go fainting on me again." He pried her hand away from the doorframe and gently chafed the inside of her wrist. "C'mon, Gracie. Don't faint."

"I have to go! I can't...I–I have to go!" She jerked her hand out of his grasp and hurried out the door.

He caught her at the landing, where she teetered on the edge of the top step. Had he not clutched her hand, she would have tumbled right down the stairs.

When he tried to pull her into his arms, she fought and twisted like a cornered wildcat. "Let me go! I have to go!"

"Stop! Stop it, Grace!" His wife fought so hard, he was afraid he'd hurt her just by trying to keep her still. If he let her go, she'd surely run.

But where would she go?

"Shh..." He held her fast. "Shush, darlin'. Let me help you."

She went limp in his arms. Until she started to choke out sobs, he'd thought she'd swooned. The sounds were heartrending.

Adam picked his wife up and carried her to her old room. Sitting down on the bed, he set her on his lap and cradled her against him as she cried. "Shh. It's gonna be okay. I'm here. I'll protect you. Can you tell me what's wrong?"

She shook her head then buried her face in his shoulder. "I need to go. Please let me go."

He rocked her like a frightened child. "I won't *ever* let you go. I love you."

"You wouldn't. Not if you knew. You'd hate me."

"I could never hate you." He kissed the top of her head. "What frightened you? Can you tell me? It can't be Stephen—"

The name alone set her to struggling again.

"Shh. I'm here."

It took a few moments for her to finally settle down. The sobs slowly ebbed until she sagged against him.

"I wanted to die," she whispered. "I begged to die."

"Oh, darlin'. Nothing could be bad enough you should've wanted to die."

"I did." A shuddering sigh escaped.

"Tell me. If you can find the courage to tell me, maybe you can let the fear go. You can tell me anything, Gracie. Anything."

"I was barely fourteen..."

Chapter Twenty-Three

San Francisco, 1860

It was three months past her fourteenth birthday.

Grace held up one of the ribbons Mama had given her and admired the color in the mirror. To have a present at all was such a treat, but to have hair ribbons seemed almost as good as her birthdays when she'd been younger—back when they still had the house and enough to eat.

She chose the pink ribbon, loving how beautiful it looked with her brown hair.

Mousey brown, Papa always called it.

But Mama told her how pretty it was, how everyone loved to see the light shine over it, bringing out the bits of red that showed Mama had passed some of her Irish blood to her daughter.

Grace's hair had never been cut. Mama helped her comb and braid it every day and told her how her long hair made her special. Not many girls had a braid that hung to her waist.

Just holding the ribbon made her feel closer to Mama. Her birthday had been Mama's last good day—the last time she'd been able to sit up and spend some time with her children.

Matthew had snuggled up to Mama's side, but he was only seven. Grace was a grown-up fourteen. She couldn't cuddle against Mama as if she were a baby anymore—no matter how desperately she wanted to wrap herself around her mother. She had to be strong for Mama and for Matthew.

Mama had died in her arms.

The doctor came that morning and told Papa there was nothing he could do—that it was in God's hands. Papa had left, probably to find another card game so he could forget the bad things. That's what he always said—that the games and the drinking made him forget.

If only he didn't spend all their money forgetting, there might have been food to put in Matthew's belly so he wouldn't cry at night.

Now it was all up to her. Her brother was her responsibility. She'd find a job, no matter what. She could clean or be a lady's maid. She could even read and write. Papa said Mama wasted her time teaching her and Matthew, saying that they needed to learn more practical skills. She'd insisted, even working with them when she'd been almost too sick to speak.

Grace could cook, too. The lady who owned the rooming house taught her. It was fun and the skill seemed to come so easily. She wiped away a tear that always came when she thought about how good things had once been.

Before Papa started gambling and drinking.

Before Mama got sick.

Matthew stuck his head inside the room. "You ready, Grace?"

She gave her reflection one last check, happy that she could still wear her Sunday dress. It was a little tight, especially across the bodice. She was embarrassed at the changes in her body, and without Mama to talk to, she didn't know if she should be worried. Mama had explained about her "woman's time," but Grace hated it. She hated the pains in her gut, and she worried her "woman's time" might be something more, something like what took Mama away from them.

"I'm ready." She went to the door to take his hand in hers. "You look very handsome."

"My britches have patches."

"That's because you enjoy wrestling with the other boys so much. I had to sew them on because you had holes in both knees."

The affection behind her words softened the rebuke. Her brother was all she truly had left in the world, and she loved him more than he could ever know. She'd promised Mama she'd watch over Matthew, and Grace always kept her word.

"Are we really getting to eat in a fancy place, Grace? A real meal? Steak and potatoes?"

"That's what Papa said."

Papa came in the door whistling. It had been a long time since he'd whistled. Maybe that meant his card game had gone well—that he'd won money for once. He'd stopped by about an hour ago to tell the children to get cleaned up because he had a special treat for them. They were going to the San Francisco Palace.

The Palace.

She could hardly believe it. Something kept niggling at her, telling her to look more closely at what was happening. Her father had mentioned a benefactor. Although she knew what the word meant, she had no idea how someone could win a *benefactor* at a card game.

Papa hired a hack to take them to the Palace. The carriage was old and smelled like people who didn't wash much, but it was the first time she'd ridden in one in almost as long as she could remember.

When the grand hotel appeared in the dirty window, her breath caught in her throat. It was so beautiful. So big. So rich.

If only Mama could have been there with them.

Papa took Matthew's hand and led his children through the front doors. She could only gawk at everything and everyone. She'd never seen so many wealthy people.

Their clothes were made of silk and fur. Many of the men carried walking sticks with silver and gold handles shaped like eagles and wolves and lions. The women smelled of strong perfume that made Matthew wrinkle his nose whenever a lady passed close by.

Leading up the winding staircase covered in red carpet, Papa had to tug Matthew to keep him moving. He seemed as enraptured with the wealth around him as she was. Then a lady walked by her, gave her a hard look, and frowned.

Grace bowed her head. Vanity hit her hard, making her want to disappear. How ugly she and her brother must be in their too small clothes with the mismatched patches when compared to the other children in their crisp, starched dresses and pants. Matthew's shirt seemed gray as a young boy in a winter white passed them.

Humiliated and sad, she wished they could leave. People turning their noses up at her stung. She didn't want a fancy dinner, even if it was steak and potatoes. Nor did she want to meet Papa's new benefactor. Her stomach hurt and she had to fight hard against the urge to turn and run.

Papa stopped at a door and knocked loudly. Then he turned to grin at his children. "Got something special planned for you, Grace."

"For me, too, Papa?" Matthew asked.

Papa said nothing as the door to the suite opened.

A young man in black suit smiled at Papa. "Back so soon?" He gave Matthew a quick glance before settling his gaze on Grace.

She'd never seen eyes so dark. A shiver of fear ran the length of her spine. She reached for Matthew's hand. His fingers squeezed hers, telling her that he was every bit as anxious as she was.

"You must be Grace." The man opened the door wide. "Come in. Come in."

The suite was opulent. A red velvet settee. Tables made of dark wood. Drapes of heavy gold cloth. Such a beautiful place. If only Mama could've seen it. Mama loved nice things—probably because she'd had so few in her life.

"Grace?" Her father's voice pulled her back from her sad reverie.

"Yes, Papa?"

His eyes met hers, but then he quickly glanced away. "This is Stephen Shay. You're gonna have dinner with him."

Matthew reacted first. "But Papa! You said I'd get to eat too! I'm hungry, Papa. I'm always hungry."

"You'll eat," Papa replied. "Just you and me, Matty-boy. Down in the dining room."

He wasn't making any sense. They were *all* eating down in the dining room.

Weren't they?

The dark man—Stephen—strode over to put a hand on her forearm. His smile wasn't genuine, and Grace would have jerked her arm away if it wasn't for Papa. This man had some kind of hold on him, making her afraid she'd offend the man if he knew exactly how much she wanted to get away.

Papa tugged at Matthew's arm. "It's time to go."

"Papa?" Grace asked, eyes wide. "Can't I go too?"

"You're having supper here with me, my sweet." Stephen's voice was deep and rumbling. His eyes raked her from head to toe, and he made her feel as though she were standing there without a stitch of clothing. "We need to get better...acquainted."

"Grace is coming too, isn't she?" Matthew asked, throwing a worried frown at her.

"She's staying here for a bit." Papa dragged Matthew toward the door.

The black-eyed man walked over to the settee and picked up a big white box. He came to stand in front of Grace, blocking her view of her family. "This is for you."

"For me?"

"For you."

Trembling hands took the box from him.

Stephen's fingers slid over her elbow as he guided her toward the settee. As she sat down, she put the box next to her. Just as she looked up, the door clicked shut, the sound reminding her of the one Mama's coffin made when it finally reached the ground as it was lowered into her grave.

"Look in the box." Stephen pulled off the lid and dropped it on the carpet behind the settee.

A red satin dress lay inside.

Grace reached out and ran her fingertips over the shiny cloth.

He bent down to lift the gown from its nest. A pair of red satin slippers remained. "The color is perfect for you."

She'd never seen such a stunning garment. Mama had never owned anything half as fine. Despite her misgivings, Grace wanted that dress and those shoes. She wanted to wear something that made the other girls jealous—especially the girls who teased her and Matthew so much about how poor they were.

Those girls would be pea green with envy of her red satin dress.

"Pick up the shoes," Stephen ordered. "You can go into the bedroom and try your new clothes on."

Reluctantly following, she peeked into the bedroom. An enormous bed dominated everything else. Deep forest-green bed curtains had been pulled back to reveal a spread of the same color.

He set the dress on the bed. "Get dressed so I can see you in my gift. Then we'll have a bite of supper." He left before she could reply, shutting the door behind him.

She picked up the dress and held it in front of her as she hurried to see her reflection in the looking glass. Oh, how she wanted to keep that dress! The color made the red highlights in her hair gleam. Pushing aside her qualms, she stripped out of her gown and wriggled into the gift.

Her camisole was in the way of the bodice, bunching up so it overflowed the top. Should she leave it on, she would look ridiculous. Teeth tugging on her bottom lip, she glanced back to the door. Surely the man wouldn't disturb her as she changed. And she wanted someone to see her in the dress.

But to be bare, nothing between her and the satin?

Scolding herself for being a nervous ninny, she made up her mind. The camisole quickly fell to the carpet.

The laces were in the front of the dress, and she tugged them as tight as she could. Dropping the slippers to the floor, she slid her feet into them before turning back to the mirror.

Grace gasped at her reflection.

A grown woman stared back. The bodice was tight enough to force her breasts to swell against the fabric. The capped shoulders revealed all of her collarbones. The cinches made her waist seem so small, her hips so round.

The prim braid didn't suit the new look. Snatching at the pink ribbon, she unplaited her hair and shook it loose. It hung in waves and curls, cascading around her shoulders and down her back.

How she wished Mama could see her—that she could see how much Grace looked like her in these grown-up clothes.

A soft knock sounded on the door. "Grace? May I come in now?"

"Yes." She turned to face Stephen Shay.

He opened the door and took a step inside. A smile curved his lips as he let his eyes take their fill, from the top of her head to her toes before returning to her bodice.

Her face flushed hot.

"So very beautiful. Oh, yes, my sweet. Just as I thought. You're lovely."

Awkward silence hung between them before he closed the distance separating them in fast steps. "I fear supper might have to wait. After seeing you in my gift, I think we should...get to know each other first."

Things happened in a blur. One minute she was standing in front of the mirror; the next he'd wrapped his arms around her and pressed his lips against hers.

She hated the way he held her and didn't want him so close she could smell him. Tobacco and liquor. He was hurting her, squeezing tightly as he ran his hand down her back to press against her backside. She tried to pull her mouth away to tell him to stop, but his tongue pushed past her lips.

Panic sizzled through Grace. Wriggling both hands up between their bodies, she was able to press her palms against his chest. She pushed with all her might and twisted against his restraining arms.

He wouldn't let her go. His open mouth kept moving over her skin on her face and her neck.

She summoned all her strength and shoved him away.

Stephen took a stumbling step back. Then he flashed her a chilling smile. "If you want it rough, I can oblige you."

He backhanded her across the face hard enough she fell to her knees, cradling her throbbing cheek in her hand.

His hands were suddenly in her hair as he dragged her toward the bed. She tried to crawl away, but he twisted her long hair around his fist.

"You don't understand, Grace. You *owe* me."

Tears streamed down her face, making her cheek sting. "I don't owe you anything! I don't even know you!"

"Ah, but you do, my sweet. Your father lost a great deal of money at our game. I was foolish enough to take you in payment. But you're going to make it worth my while. You belong to me now. I. Own. You."

A sharp tug on her hair forced a scream.

Mama had explained to her about what could happen between a man and a woman, but she told her the union came from love two people shared.

Why didn't Stephen know that? Why was he doing this to her?

Another vicious tug at her hair found Grace at the side of the bed.

Stephen bent down, wrapped his arms around her waist, and lifted her. Despite her pleas and struggles, he tossed her onto the bed. Shoving a hand inside her bodice, he ripped open the satin. Her breasts lay bare before him.

Clutching at the bedspread, she tried to hide herself.

He merely chuckled, stepped away from the bed, and walked to the door.

Thank God, he was leaving!

The click of the lock took away her last ounce of her hope.

He came to stand at the foot of the bed. With slow motions—as if he had all the time in the world—he unbuttoned his coat, folded it, and placed it over the bureau. He did the same with his vest.

She didn't know what to do. "If you touch me, I'll scream."

His chuckle was as cold as his hands. "Go ahead. I like it when a woman screams. Besides, do you really think anyone will come to your aid?" He shook his head as he whipped his tie from his neck. "I'm a Shay. No one questions what I do."

Grace took a deep breath and screamed her loudest as she tried to rush off the bed.

He moved fast as lightning and caught her. He silenced her screams by covering his mouth with hers. His tongue thrust into her mouth again.

She bit down, gagging at the taste of the blood that seeped onto her tongue as she pulled away.

His fist crashed into her jaw a moment later.

Everything went fuzzy as pain shot through her head. As her senses cleared, she realized she was on the bed again with what was left of the ripped dress tangled up around her hips. Rolling to her side, she tried to crawl away.

He hoisted the twisted material of the skirt up her body until he trapped her arms. Her legs were bared to him. *All* of her was bared to him—even her most personal and private place.

Helpless, all she could do was scream and cry as he settled his body between her thighs...

***

Stephen finished dressing as Grace huddled beneath the quilt, injured and silent.

"I'm going to see to our supper. You stay here. We'll eat in the room." Sliding his arms back into his jacket, he fixed those obsidian eyes on her again. "Wait for me in that bed. Don't bother getting dressed."

She had very little fight left in her, but he hadn't broken her spirit. Not yet. "I won't."

"Oh, but you *will*. I told you. You belong to me now."

The door closed, the sound of a key in the lock only making her feel more trapped.

Grace held her breath until she heard the close of the door to the suite. When she was sure he'd truly left, that breath escaped in a loud whoosh. She refused to let him hurt her again. Even if she had to throw herself out of the window, she would find a way to escape.

By the time she'd hurriedly dressed in her old clothes, tried to open the locked door, and searched every inch of the room, she realized she was trapped. If she really wanted to get away from this hell, she *would* have to jump—out the second story window.

The locking mechanism gave her no trouble, but the window was more stubborn. She had to wrestle and tug to get it open enough she could slip through. Thrusting her head outside, she stared down. Several pine shrubs were directly below. Perhaps they would break her fall.

Terrified that Stephen would return, Grace swallowed her fear of injury, wriggled her leg out the window, and said a quick prayer. With eyes closed, she let herself plummet to the ground.

The shrubs cushioned her enough that she was sure no bones were broken. Bruises, cuts, and scrapes would no doubt be riddled from head to toe, but they were of little concern. Her abused body almost refused to obey her wishes. Biting her lip to stifle a cry of pain, she got to her feet and limped away from the Palace as quickly as she could manage.

***

Matthew was alone by the time Grace made it back to their home.

He glanced up from where he played on the ground with his wooden horse and a smile lit his face. "Grace! I had a steak. And potatoes. And peaches. And—" His smile fell to a fierce frown as he scrambled to his feet. "What happened to you?"

The only sound came from the squeaky floor as she crossed the room.

Matthew followed her to her bedroom. Staring wide-eyed, he tried again. "How'd you get hurt?"

"I'm fine."

But she wasn't. The reflection in the mirror wasn't the old Grace Riley. Whatever vanity had existed had been burned away. Large, hollow eyes stared back at her.

Grace never wanted to stand out again. She never wanted anyone to take notice of her. She wanted anything tying her to that cursed vanity gone.

The scissors caught her gaze.

Trembling fingers slipped through the cool metal rings as she brought the blades to her hair. Grabbing long locks in her other hand, she hacked through the thick hair. Hunks of it fell to the floor.

Her brother bent to pick up several strands. "Why are you cuttin' all your hair off? You *love* your hair."

"I don't love it anymore." Anger flowed through her as she chopped and sliced until the tresses barely brushed her shoulders.

"You lose your senses, girl?"

The loud, deep voice startled her, but she simply raised her gaze in the reflection to see Papa standing in the doorway.

"You're making me angry," he said.

She didn't want him angry.

She wanted him *dead*.

She wanted Stephen Shay dead too.

Setting the scissors back on the bureau, she turned away from the mirror and vowed she'd never see her father again. "Go pack your clothes, Matthew. We're leaving."

Her father leaned a shoulder against the doorframe as he crossed his arms over his chest. "Leaving are you?"

As if she would even deign to nod at him. The man had sold her like some piece of meat. All for his gambling debts.

Leaving?

Oh, yes.

And she was taking Matthew with her before something bad happened to him as well.

Grabbing a burlap bag, Grace shoved the few clothes she owned inside.

"You need to go back to the Palace," Papa insisted. "Shay'll be looking for you."

She jammed the few pieces of Mama's jewelry that hadn't been worth enough to pawn or sell into the bag and closed it tight. Without a word, she pushed past the man she no longer considered her father.

"Grace, stop." He grabbed her arm.

She jerked it away and spat at his feet.

Matthew was waiting, holding a bag and his wooden horse. "Where are we goin', Grace?"

"On an adventure."

***

Grace labored to push the baby from her body.

The nuns weren't sure how to help. They wiped her sweaty brow. They offered words of encouragement. They even tried to ease her pain by rubbing her back and her swollen belly. Nothing helped.

Almost a whole day passed, and still the baby didn't come.

Convinced she would die, Grace worried more about Matthew than herself. Her brother needed her. They'd survived on what little she could make as a cook. What would he do if she left him all alone in the world?

Another pain hit, so hard she shouted a word that made all the nuns cross themselves.

That agony had no longer ebbed when another was on top of her.

Her body knew what to do as her knees pulled up, her lungs took a deep breath, and her muscles bore down hard.

A scream escaped her lips.

The baby came out crying.

"Is he okay?" she asked.

"He's wonderful," Sister Charity replied as she fussed over him, cleaning him and wrapping him in a blanket.

When he was finally placed in Grace's arms, she could only stare at him.

Her body ached from head to toe. She felt as if someone had beaten her, but she couldn't focus on that. All she could see was a tiny boy with dark curly hair and deep blue eyes. Ten perfect fingers and ten perfect toes.

Merciful God, how was she ever going to leave the beautiful boy behind?

The nuns cast furtive glances at each other as they helped clean her up and put the room back to right.

Sister Felicity brought Matthew in to see her a few hours later. He stood close to the bed, staring at his shoes and looking like he always did when he'd done something naughty.

"What's wrong, Matthew?" Grace asked when he didn't come close enough to see the baby.

He shrugged, refusing to let his gaze meet hers.

"Don't you want to see him?"

His teeth tugged on his bottom lip. "He's not coming with us?"

She answered with a quick shake of her head and sniffed back tears. Seemed as though she'd cried a river of tears from the moment she realized she was going to have a baby because of what Stephen Shay had done to her.

"He can't, Matthew. He needs a mama and a papa. He can't go on the cattle drive."

God bless Mother Superior. She knew of a Christian couple who'd been married for a dozen years and hadn't been blessed with a child of their own. The baby would live on a farm and have doting parents.

Grace couldn't offer her son a life. She could barely take care of herself and her brother. What could she offer this baby except starvation and misery?

Mother Superior had called in some favors and secured a job for Grace on a cattle drive. She would cook in return for the men teaching Matthew how to handle a horse and herd a cow. At least they could both eat regularly, get plenty of fresh air, and hopefully make themselves valuable to future employers.

They would leave in a month's time.

But the baby would leave *tonight*.

"Why are you crying, Grace?" Matthew hurried to her side and laid a comforting hand on her shoulder. "I hate it when you cry. Did birthing the baby make you cry?"

She blinked back more tears and kissed the baby's forehead, breathing in his scent and trying to brand it on her heart. "I'm just sad because I won't see him after tonight."

"Never again?"

"Never again."

"But you're his mama."

"I'm not his mama. Mrs. Curtis is gonna be his mama."

"And Mr. Curtis'll be his papa? Why can't you give him a papa? You could get married, Grace."

Matthew's curiosity and intelligence always made him attack anything he didn't understand in the way a dog assaulted a meaty bone. This time, she simply couldn't answer him in a way he'd understand. Hard to believe sometimes that he was only eight.

"I just can't." She nodded at the dresser. "Can you please fetch me Mama's gold pin?"

With a nod, he hurried to do as she asked. She took the heart-shaped pin from him with trembling fingers.

"This is for you." She pinned the heart onto her son's swaddling. "It's all I have to give you."

"Will he remember us?" Matthew's small finger stroked the baby's cheek.

The baby opened his mouth and turned toward the finger as if searching for something to eat.

The emotions swelling inside her choked off her air. She shook her head in answer and glanced up to where Mother Superior now stood in the doorway.

"It's time, Grace."

"Have they given him a name?"

Mother Superior nodded.

"Please tell me. I want to know what they'll call him."

"Grace..."

"*Please*," she pleaded.

"Jake. They'll call him Jake. They're here now."

Grace cuddled the baby a little closer. "Just a few more minutes. Please."

The kind woman sighed before she gave her a brusque nod. "Matthew," she said reaching her hand out for him, "come with me. Let your sister have a minute alone."

"She's not alone. She's got her baby with her."

"But she needs to say her farewells. Come. We'll get you a glass of milk."

"I like milk." He took Mother Superior's hand and let her lead him away. Right before he reached the doorway, he turned back. "Goodbye, Jake." He skipped out the door, humming a tune.

Mother Superior glanced back over her shoulder. "Just a few moments. Mr. and Mrs. Curtis are waiting."

Alone with her son, Grace tried to memorize every bit of him. His hair and eyes. The way his forehead wrinkled before he let out a bellow when he was hungry. How he stopped crying when he heard her voice. Those memories would have to last her a lifetime.

She pressed a gentle kiss to his lips. "I love you, Jake. I always will."

***

Through her tears, Grace clutched Adam's hand to her breast.

God, those memories still could rend her heart.

He stroked her hair. "Oh, Gracie…"

She hushed him with a shake of her head and finally said the words that needed to be said.

"Adam, Jake isn't my brother. He's my son."

Chapter Twenty-Four

"Aren't you going to say anything?" Grace asked when she couldn't bear the silence a moment longer.

She hadn't been sure how Adam would react. Would there be anger? Disappointment? Disgust?

He'd simply sat there, holding her hand.

"I've known for a while, Gracie."

"H–how could you know?"

He took a long breath that sounded too much like a disillusioned sigh.

Or was she being paranoid?

"Your nightmares. The way you reacted to Jake's cold shoulder. Little things you and Matthew—"

"Matthew told you?"

"I didn't say that, darlin'." He gave her hand a squeeze. "I put all the puzzle pieces together."

"You don't hate me?"

"Hate you? Dear God, Grace. Why would you think I would *hate* you?"

"I had a child out of wedlock."

"You were raped. You did right by that boy. Many another woman would have simply found a way to get rid of him—either before he was born or after." He leaned in and kissed her. "But not you. You gave him a home, a future."

"I ruined his life."

He pulled her against him, hugging her to his chest. "You couldn't have known what would happen to the Curtis family."

Leaning back, she swallowed hard. "But you rescued him. And Ty, too. Oh, Adam, thank you for that."

Adam enjoyed her praise, but he refused to let her believe he'd been some kind of hero. "It was the Christian thing to do."

Grace yawned, her eyes hazy with fatigue. The poor woman had been through an ordeal, not just in her past, but telling him the truth had to have been difficult.

"Rest, darlin'. Get some sleep. I've got some town business to do."

"You won't tell Jake, will you?" The fear in her voice pinched his heart.

"No, Gracie. I won't tell him."

When you're ready, you *will.*

She stretched out on the bed and fell asleep moments later.

He spread a quilt over her, marveling at the strength of his wife.

She'd been so young when her life had been thrown into a hurricane. For years, she'd tossed and turned in the storm. He leaned down to press a kiss to her temple, hoping his love could finally give her safe harbor.

God knew she deserved one.

Jake was waiting right outside the door. "How's she doin'?"

Adam wanted to go somewhere private and shout his anger and frustration. What Grace had gone through was nothing short of hell. He could picture her as a young woman, facing the rape and the pregnancy, and he ached to give Stephen Shay a gut wound and leave him tied to a tree to be attacked by wild animals.

"She's asleep." His words were clipped and harsh enough to draw a frown from Jake.

"You two fightin'?"

"No, we're not fighting."

"Then what's go you both so upset?"

"Can't tell you, Jake. Not ready to talk about it."

Jake furrowed his brow before he nodded. "Poor thing's probably exhausted. You know, she took right good care of Emily and Beth. I'm mighty grateful."

"I'm sure she'd like to hear that. I'm gonna let her sleep. Will and I have to find Reverend David for a quick town council meeting." With a nod to the door, he asked, "Keep an eye on her?"

"Of course."

Adam headed down the stairs and found Will working behind the bar.

He flashed Adam a worried frown. "Grace feelin' poorly? Is it the baby?"

They all wanted answers he couldn't give. "She's just tuckered out. Taking a nap she truly needs."

"Should we find David now?"

"Good as time as any. It's past time to get this resolved."

***

Victoria reined her mare to a stop in front of the barn.

The place appeared deserted except for the horses, and she hoped it would stay that way. After all the excitement of Beth's birth and Stephen's departure, she simply wasn't up to facing Matthew Riley.

He was still leaving. Then again, she couldn't blame him. It wasn't as if she'd given him a single reason to stay. She'd be bound for Denver just as soon as she could make the proper arrangements, knowing she needed to go soon because she couldn't stand watching him ride away. Better to be the first to leave than to know he'd left her behind.

The smell of smoke hit her as she closed the gate to Cleo's stall. Her heart leapt.

Fire.

A frantic look around told her the barn wasn't in danger. The horses remained too calm for the fire to be that close. A few might have caught the scent, but they did little more than whinny and snort in response.

She hurried outside, trying to find the source of the smoky haze that now permeated the air. She gave a silent prayer of thanks the ranch house appeared undisturbed. It wasn't until her gaze settled on the bunkhouse that she found the source of the smoke.

With a loud crash, flames shot out of the building's only window.

"Matthew? Ty?" She kept shouting their names as she hiked up her skirts and ran to make sure neither man was in the bunkhouse.

Pressing a palm against the door, she found it cool. Throwing the latch, she hurried inside the tack room. Thin lines of gray smoke snaked under the threshold to the bunk room. The door was warm, but not hot enough for fire to be directly behind.

She grabbed a kerchief from one of the shelves, held it over her mouth and nose, and carefully opened the door.

Matthew lay on the floor, holding his head and groaning as he tried to sit up.

There weren't any flames in the room yet, but thicker smoke billowed down from the ceiling, hovering over the bunkbeds like gathering storm clouds. The fire broke through a moment later, slapping at the ceiling and spreading down the wall.

She rushed to him, falling to her knees. Dropping the kerchief, she tugged on his elbow with both hands. "You've gotta get up. We have to get outta here. Where's Ty?"

As he pulled his hand away from his head, there were smears of blood on his fingers. There wasn't time to determine the extent of his injuries. She had to get him outside.

"C'mon, Matthew." She tugged hard at his elbow.

"Ty's gone. Went to check the fence line, then he's headed back to town." He tried to stand up as coughs began to spill from him.

She jerked him right back down. "Stay low. There's more air." The words cost her an inhale of the thickening smoke that forced hacking coughs.

Crawling on her hands and knees, Victoria headed back toward the tack room, checking over her shoulder to be sure he followed. Just as he reached the doorway, a large chunk of the burning ceiling crashed over several of the beds.

Not giving in to the panic searing through her, she tried to get him to his feet. It was akin to moving an uncooperative horse. She'd never get him out of the burning bunkhouse without his help, and she sure as hell wasn't leaving him behind. "We've gotta get outside!"

Her fear must have finally registered because he stumbled to his feet, grabbed her by the arm, and dragged her outside until they were a good distance away from the bunkhouse. He collapsed onto the grass, and they both coughed for a good long while, watching as the flames greedily licking at the structure.

Within a matter of minutes, the roof gave a groaning death rattle and caved in.

Victoria kept a wary eye on the barn and the house, but the bunkhouse was far enough away the fire wouldn't spread. Her father had always joked that he built it a good distance from the barn so the cowboys didn't have to smell the horses—and a good distance away from the house so his family didn't have to smell the cowboys.

Thank you, God.

Once she could draw a breath without a bout of coughing following, she turned her attention to Matthew. Kneeling next to him she ran her fingers through his hair. Although he tried to slap her hands away, she found the injury. It wasn't bleeding any longer, but he had a good sized knot forming on his crown.

"What happened?" she asked.

"Not sure." He slapped at her hands again. "Quit it. That hurts."

She couldn't help but smile. Had he been seriously injured he wouldn't have made such a bad patient. "Did you fall and hit your head?"

"Someone hit me. Coldcocked me from behind."

That made no sense. Who would want to hurt him?

Or was Matthew just in the way of someone who wanted to hurt her father?

Far as she knew, neither of them had any enemies.

"Gotta be Shay." He frowned. "Stop fussing over me.

As Victoria's heart slowed to a normal rhythm, the weight of what had happened settled on her, sending it right back to pounding a hard, fast cadence. Had she not ridden home from White Pines, he would be dead, buried beneath the burning rubble of what was left of the bunkhouse.

She threw herself at him, knocking them both to the grass.

Matthew held her tight, not entirely sure what had caused her to suddenly embrace him. Her lips rained kisses on his cheeks.

"What's wrong?" he asked.

"I could have lost you!"

Before he could respond, her mouth settled on his.

A new fire kindled, quickly burning out of control. She deepened the kiss before he could. The rub of her tongue and her lithe body pressed against his ignited all sorts of erotic thoughts.

He wanted to drown in her. She was everything beautiful in the world—everything that he'd ever wanted.

How on God's green earth could he ever have thought he could ride away?

There was no way he would ever leave her.

Victoria's tears made him pull away. "Sweetheart, please stop crying."

"I–I could've lost you." She laid her cheek against his shoulder and breathed a shuddering sigh. In a voice so hesitant it could have been the whispering wind, she said the magical words he thought he would never hear. "I–I love you."

He rolled, taking her with him until he had her pinned beneath him. As tenderly as he could with his calloused hands, he framed her face.

Her cheeks were covered in soot, and her tears had left streaks of clean, pink skin. She was the most beautiful woman he'd ever seen.

"Never," he said. "You'll *never* lose me."

Then he kissed her again. Long and deep and promising her all he could give. His heart and his soul rested in the palms of her hands.

Matthew stared into Victoria's blue eyes. "I love you too."

He hadn't meant to make her cry again. Only kissing her got her to stop.

Her tongue eased into his mouth. There was no shyness, no hesitation. No guile. She took her pleasure from him the same honest way he took his from her.

Her lips followed his as he pulled away. He kissed her again to show her how much he liked that hunger—the same hunger that gnawed at him. Once he was on his feet, he helped her up. Before she could ask the question in her eyes, he swept her into his arms and carried her toward the ranch house.

He stumbled through the kitchen and mounted the stairs, taking them two at a time. When he reached her bedroom, he nudged the door open and headed toward the bed, kicking the door shut behind him.

Their lips locked in another kiss as he released her legs and let her body slide down his. Before her feet touched the floor, he squeezed her tighter, kissing her all the while.

His conscience bellowed in his head. Victoria was a lady, the type of woman you married, not the kind you took for a lover. She deserved better. She deserved a man who had a future. She deserved a man who wasn't about to toss her on her bed and make love to her without the benefit of a preacher's blessing. Easing his hold, he let her put both feet on solid ground.

How he was going to be able to stop was beyond him, but he tried anyway. The choice would be hers. At the very least, he owed her that much.

"Victoria..." His hands reached for hers where they'd encircled his neck. With a gentle tug on both her wrists, he moved her arms away and took a step back.

She went with him, fisted her hands in his vest, and jerked him back until their bodies touched. "I *love* you." Her voice was harsh, belying the tenderness in her sparkling eyes.

"We shouldn't..."

"Oh, yes, we *should*." Rising on her toes, she kissed him, sliding her hands back around his neck.

He raised trembling hands to her bodice. His fingers felt too big, too awkward as he tried to undo each button on her white shirt. At least it had been white once upon a time. Now it was soot and grass stained and he wanted to rip it right off her.

Victoria took pity on him, helping undo the small buttons. She shrugged out of the shirt and wiggled out of her skirt. Her hands smoothed over his chest, sweeping the vest from his shoulders.

She traced the line of his arms, following the path of the vest, before she again pressed her hands to his chest. Button by button, she worked on removing his shirt.

With a growl, he grabbed the shirt and jerked it apart. Buttons flew through the air to clatter on the wooden floor like hailstones. Her smile shone bright against her cheeks darkened by soot.

Matthew pulled his shirt off and used it to wipe at her face. "You're quite a sight."

"I don't care." She snatched the shirt away from him and dropped it to the floor before reaching for the waistband of his pants.

He toed off his boots and replied to her efforts to strip him by tugging at the ribbon of her camisole. Both garments joined his shirt.

She was so beautiful, he couldn't stop staring. Her skin was unblemished, a bit aglow with a blush that spread from her face down her slender neck. Her breasts were peaked with rose-colored nipples that had hardened in invitation.

Her eyes stared at the ceiling, obviously having a hard time looking at his nudity. "It's going to be all right, sweetheart."

Her teeth nibbled on her bottom lip as her gaze made its way to his face, his chest, and lower. Just watching her as eyes took their fill of his body heated his blood. If he wasn't inside her soon...

She finally took a glance at his groin. With a gasp, she immediately stared back at the ceiling.

Matthew wrapped his arms around her, tugging her against him. His warmth and scent surrounded her, comforted her. "I won't hurt you," he whispered.

His hand pushed between them, grabbing at the ribbon holding up her drawers. The sound of tearing fabric filled the air. The fabric puddled around her ankles.

He knelt beside her. As he removed her shoes and helped her step out of her torn pantalets, she balanced herself against his shoulder. His hands brushed every inch of her legs as he peeled off her stockings. Every place he touched felt hot enough to burst into flame. He scooped her up in his arms and laid her on the bed, then he sprawled on top of her.

Victoria wanted to touch him everywhere. His body was so different than her own. Hard and masculine. The dusting of hair on his chest felt crispy. Her hand moved lower.

He grabbed her wrist and gently moved her hand away just before she had his erection in her grasp. "Wrong?" she asked, her voice a whisper.

"Not wrong. I just... Not now. I want you too much."

She rewarded him with a tongue-dueling kiss. He tore his lips away to kiss her neck, laving the sensitive skin with his tongue. Moans slipped from her, but she was too lost in what he made her feel to stop them.

His kisses moved lower until he set his mouth against her breast, drawing the nipple between his teeth. She arched into him so hard she feared she'd buck him right off.

He slid his hand over her flat belly, down the outside of her hip, and up the inside of her thigh until he was caressing the very core of her.

"Sweet Lord, you're perfection," he murmured.

Separating her thighs with his knee, he rose to gaze down at her face. "I want you." He choked out the words. A hard kiss followed. "Victoria?"

She answered him by cupping his neck and pulling him down for another kiss.

Matthew's erection pressed against her center, and she tried to drown in his kiss, fearing the pain. He eased inside her, filling her completely. The pain never came.

Relieved, she gave herself over to all he made her feel.

Wonderful.

It felt wonderful to have him so deep inside her. But he wasn't moving. She hadn't realized she'd squeezed her eyes shut until she forced them open to look at him.

He was staring down at her, his dark eyes searching for an answer.

"No pain. There's no pain."

"Thank God."

He pulled back, and she wrapped her legs around his hips, fearing he was leaving her. Then he thrust back inside. It felt so marvelous, she begged him to do it again. He kissed her hard and obliged her.

The rhythm of his hips meeting hers became more frantic, the kissing no longer teasing but deep and heartfelt, driving them toward fulfillment.

Panic griped her, the intensity of her feelings becoming overwhelming. Before she could give voice to her fear, he soothed her with three whispered words. "I love you."

Victoria surrendered, fracturing into a thousand rays of sunshine that raced from her core through her limbs.

He plunged into her, fast and hard until he shuddered.

She held him tight, keeping her legs around his hips and whispering her love in his ear.

Chapter Twenty-Five

Grace leaned against Adam, fighting the drowsiness that still held her captive. Her feelings were battered and bruised despite all her husband had done to calm her.

She'd awakened at the Four Aces in the throes of a nightmare where Stephen was trying to steal an infant—her new son—right from her arms.

She'd fought with the intensity of a mother bear trying to protect her cub and hold her tormentor at bay until Adam could find her. Arms had reached out to grab her, to keep her from fleeing. When she'd forced her eyes open after several insistent commands, it took long moments to realize her husband was the one holding her close. Releasing the ghosts that haunted her dreams hadn't been easy. Simply remembering the images now made her blood run cold.

They hadn't spoken about her confession, but she knew that reprieve wouldn't last.

Mercifully, no one had questioned them as they'd said their farewells, but all eyes had been on her. The curiosity reflected there told her the time would come where she might have to lay all her cards on the table.

Thank the sweet Lord, Stephen was gone. His presence would only make a volatile situation worse. Had he stayed, there was no doubt he or his people would sniff out the truth, and then there would be no way to protect Jake from the Shay family or herself from shame.

Her heartbeats sped to a frantic tempo at the thought of Stephen ever learning about the secret she'd held close for so very long. Fear that he'd come for his son had been one of the reasons she had given Jake up to the Curtis family—so that he would never know the facts of his conception or be dragged into the evil Shay dynasty.

With their money and power, they could've easily taken him away, and she almost sobbed aloud for the horrible future he would've had in their hands—how easily he could have become another of their ilk.

That notion made Grace even more sure that she could never tell anyone but Adam about Jake's parentage—no matter how much her new friends might push and prod her for the truth. No, she would keep her secret and protect her son. She trusted Adam to do the same.

The scent of smoke made her head pop up. "Do you smell that?"

Adam had already urged the horses to a faster pace. "Fire."

Tendrils of gray smoke rose above the trees lining the road leading to the Twin Springs.

Her heart jumped to her throat. "Matthew and Victoria are here.

Ty, too."

"Ty's back in town."

Reins slapped against the horses' rumps increased the speed, drawing the couple closer to the ranch.

The first sight of the collapsed bunkhouse drew a frightened squeal. "Matthew!"

"Easy. We don't know he's in there." Adam brought the wagon to a stop, jumped out, and lifted her to the ground. "Check the horses. Victoria and Matthew might be in the barn keeping them calm." He sprinted toward the bunkhouse.

She fisted her hands in her skirts and hiked them high so she could run to the barn. A quick look inside told her the horses were fine, but there was no sign of Matthew or Victoria. She met Adam at the door to the ranch house. Eyes wide with fright, she searched his gaze.

"No one's in there," he replied to her silent question.

"You're sure?"

"Very sure. The place is gutted."

"What happened?"

"Can't tell. When the mess cools, we'll sift around and see what we can find."

"Where are Matthew and Victoria?"

He glanced over his shoulder at the house. "Let's check inside."

His hand on the small of her back, he guided her to their home.

The kitchen stood empty. About to ask where they should check next, Grace heard the noise. Shuffling footsteps from the second floor ended her worry. But then a high-pitched squeal sent Adam hurrying to the stairs with her following right behind.

He'd stuck his head inside Victoria's bedroom when another squeal pulled them both toward the bathroom. Voices drifted through the closed door.

"Stop!" Victoria said with a giggle. "I told you. That's the *cold* water."

"As if I've ever used a bathtub before," Matthew replied.

Adam stopped just as he reached for the doorknob. Turning back to Grace, he flashed her a knowing smile. Then he put his index finger to his lips.

Her chuckle slipped out before she could stop it.

Victoria's responded with a gasp. "Is—is someone there?"

Grace's chuckle became a full-blown laugh, and heavens, she felt guilty for disturbing an obviously intimate interlude—one both Matthew and Victoria had been needing for quite some time.

"Grace?" Matthew called. "You out there?"

"We *both* are," Adam replied. The scolding and decidedly fatherly tone in his voice was in direct contrast to his beaming face.

For several drawn out moments, quiet reigned. Then there were frantic movements in the bathroom.

"Daddy's here too!" Victoria's words were filled with dread.

"Why don't you join me downstairs in five minutes? *Both* of you." Adam took Grace's elbow and guided her down the stairs.

As he sat down next to her on the couch, she felt the need to defend her brother, silly though her words might sound. "He wouldn't have…been with her if he didn't love her."

Her husband arched an eyebrow. "You know this because?"

"I know my brother. After every payday, most of the cowboys would go to town and spend their money on whiskey and…and…*whores*." She whispered the last word, still feeling awkward talking to him about anything so personal. After all they'd done together, her timidity was misplaced.

A blush heated her cheeks. Sure, the cowboys might have cursed openly, and she was used to *hearing* the word.

But saying it aloud?

"And *what?*" he coaxed, wiggling his eyebrows and clearly enjoying her embarrassment.

"You're a wicked man." She gave him a playful slap on the arm. "Matthew didn't visit those women. He'd buy a new shirt, some pants, and maybe a book."

"Your point being?"

"He loves Victoria. I've seen them together. He wouldn't dishonor her."

Adam was amused by how deeply Grace could blush whenever intimacies were mentioned. The woman became a wildcat when she was in his arms, but to discuss coupling in the light of day? She turned as prim and proper as any schoolmarm.

"We'll have to see what his intentions are," he said. "When they get some clothes on."

Victoria and Matthew came down the stairs, heads bowed like condemned prisoners approaching the gallows. If they walked any slower, autumn would set in before they made it to the couch. Both had wet hair. He was wearing some of Adam's clothes, and she'd missed fastening a few buttons on the bodice of her dress.

He held Victoria's hand, and she wouldn't let her eyes meet her father's as she nibbled on her bottom lip the way she had when she'd been a child and caught doing something naughty.

"Nice pants," Adam quipped.

"Sorry." Matthew stared at the pants. "Mine were filthy from the fire. The rest are gone now. Did you see the bunkhouse?"

Adam nodded, figuring he'd ease into the conversation about what the two of them were doing in that bathroom after he assuaged his curiosity over why his bunkhouse was a gutted pile of smoldering ash. "What happened to it?"

Matthew shrugged. "One minute, I was searching for my spurs—the next I'm waking up in an inferno."

"Someone hit him," Victoria added, reaching up to touch the crown of his head.

He winced in response.

"Hit him? Someone *hit* him?" Grace's voice rose in panic. She turned worried eyes on Adam as she wrung her hands in her lap. "Stephen Shay."

Victoria shook her head, but Adam was inclined to agree with his wife. He laid a comforting hand over his wife's and was pleased when she immediately stopped her nervous actions.

"But he left town," Victoria argued.

Matthew snorted. "As if *that* ever mattered."

A meaningful look passed between brother and sister and finally—at long last—Adam lost his patience. "We've got *a lot* to talk about. You both best sit down." He nodded at the chairs. "Why do you think it's Shay?"

"He's followed her from town to town, he or his detectives," Matt replied as took a seat.

Victoria set herself on the chair's arm and reached for Matthew's hand. He glanced up to smile at her before turning back to his sister.

Then his gaze grew stern. "Grace, you've got to tell him *everything*."

She started twisting her hands in her lap again. "I–I did."

"Clearly not everything, darlin'." Adam took her hand in his.

"He's been tracking her like an animal for most of her life," Matthew said. "Started not too long after our first cattle drive. Why do you think he turned up in White Pines?"

"Because of Ty." Victoria knit her brows. "He stopped those men from robbing Ty. I don't understand. Grace already knew Stephen, but only in passing. Right?"

Adam glanced at his wife, wondering if she was ready to tell Victoria all that she'd shared with him back at the Four Aces. He wouldn't spill her secrets unless he had her permission.

His wife didn't look up, but she gave him a brisk nod.

"Grace knew him when she was younger. He...well, he attacked her."

"Attacked her?"

"He raped me," Grace whispered.

"Oh, my God! And I brought him here? Oh, Grace. I'm so sorry!" Victoria's eyes brimmed with tears as she hurried to give Grace an embrace.

They clung for a few long moments, probably understanding each other in a way only women could before Victoria returned to Matthew's side.

She leaned closer to him. "You don't think he knew about Ty being in Den—"

"I damn well do," Matthew snapped. "He probably had Ty beaten as a way to get to Grace. Then he charmed you into bringing him back here so she didn't have any warning or a chance to run."

"Thank God, he's gone," Victoria said.

The heat in Matthew's eyes was intense enough to start another fire. "Who do you think hit me? Who do you think burned down the bunkhouse?"

"I'm inclined to agree," Adam replied.

Grace's voice was so soft, Adam almost missed her words. "He won't stop until he catches me."

"Catches you?" Damn, but it was hard to keep the anger out of his voice. He didn't want to frighten Grace, but the time had come for the whole truth to be told, even if her trembling made him feel a bit guilty.

She nodded while Matthew continued the story. "The man's obsessed with her, has been since she was fifteen. Sends his Pinkerton spies to follow her or shows up himself whenever we finish a cattle drive. We've ducked out of just about every railhead in the West to get away from that bastard. Shay's made her life miserable for years. If he catches her—"

"You kept me safe, Matthew," Grace said, her voice still low and fearful.

Adam squeezed her hand. "I'll protect you too, Gracie." Turning to Matthew, he added, "From this point on, Grace is never alone. Victoria, either."

His wife's worried brown eyes found his. "Who will protect you? Who will protect *all* of you? He'll hurt anyone who helps me."

Matthew jumped to his feet. "Grace, you're not thinking of—"

"He could've killed you!" Her voice quavered. "There's only one way to keep all of you safe."

Adam didn't appreciate the direction this conversation was taking one damned bit. "You'll let me handle this."

"But—"

"*No,* Grace. This isn't open for discussion. You'll let me handle this." He turned his gaze to Matthew. "I'll need the marshal's help to catch Shay."

Matthew snorted again. "Oh, for the love of... His help? You need *his* help? That man couldn't catch a cold."

"Sit down, son. We need to talk."

He sat, wrapping his fingers back around Victoria's hand, but he clearly didn't want to listen. "If you're trusting that man—"

"I meant the *new* marshal."

Victoria tilted her head. "New marshal? Did you and the town council finally get around to finding us a new marshal?"

Adam nodded. "Past time to act."

"Who is it?" she asked.

"You're sitting next to him."

Both of Matthew and Victoria gawked at Adam.

Grace didn't seem at all surprised. His wife, he'd quickly discovered, was a very intelligent woman.

"It's the perfect solution," Grace said, breaking the quiet tension.

Matthew still frowned. "I've never been a lawman. Why me?"

"You've got a good head on your shoulders," Adam replied. "You're young, strong and hardworking. Job comes with a salary and the small house on the other side of the jail." He looked at his daughter. "Perfect home for newlyweds, and I imagine the two of you will be newlyweds *real* soon."

His daughter's blush was bright as she met his gaze. "You can't force him to marry me."

"My shotgun says I can."

Matthew's grin told Adam things were going to work out fine. "No shotgun necessary. My intentions are honorable."

Adam scoffed. "I would say what we stumbled across in that bathroom wasn't entirely *honorable*."

"No, sir. I mean, yes, sir. I mean...I was gonna ask her and then talk to you. Just didn't have the chance." With a grin, he turned to Victoria. "Will you have me?"

His daughter had some mischief in her. "Not sure I want to be married to a lawman."

"Damn it, Victoria! You'll marry me."

"You have no right to order me around, Matthew Riley."

"I'm gonna be your husband. That gives me the right."

She pulled her hand away and crossed her arms over her breasts. "I haven't answered your proposal yet."

They were both far too stubborn for their own good. Before Adam could say anything, Grace intervened. "Do you love her, Matthew?"

Not even a moment of hesitation before his response. "You know I do."

"And do you love him, Victoria?"

She rolled her eyes before she nodded. "God knows why, but I do."

With a satisfied grin, Adam slapped his knee. "Then there's gonna be a wedding." Getting to his feet, he helped his wife up.

She hurried to her brother who stood up to take her into his arms. "I'm so happy for you."

He sighed as he hugged her. "Don't cry."

"I can't help it."

Victoria hugged her father.

He couldn't help but give one fatherly scold. "If you hadn't agreed, princess, I would've pointed the shotgun at *you*."

***

Grace scooted over on the bed to give Adam more room.

He slid beneath the linens as she snuggled up against his warm body. She'd finally gotten used to him sleeping naked but couldn't seem to share the same habit, even if her nightgown ultimately ended up on the floor most nights. She did, however, enjoy sharing his warmth. Her fear of Stephen made it more than a want—she *needed* it. Just as she needed Adam's strength.

"Are you going to rebuild the bunkhouse?" she asked.

"Not necessary. Don't plan on employing enough cowboys to need one. Gave Ty a piece of land he can build a house on, and Matthew will be living in town."

Her fingertips traced his collarbone. "Would you really have forced Matthew and Victoria if they hadn't wanted to marry?"

"Absolutely."

"Why?"

"Because despite their eternal obstinacy, they're perfect for each other."

She rubbed her cheek against his shoulder and teased the patch of hair on his chest with her fingertips. "Thank you for giving him the job."

"The council gave him the job. I simply suggested he might be a good candidate."

The man she married had a heart as big as the Montana sky. Just another of the reasons she loved him so very much.

"Besides," he added. "I'm a selfish man."

"Selfish?"

"If he stays close, it makes both my wife and my daughter happy." He kissed her forehead. "You've had quite enough excitement for a while. You didn't need to face watching your brother ride away when

God only knows how long he'd be gone."

"I want him to get to know our son after he's born." Then she chuckled. "I hadn't thought about it 'til now, but Matthew and Victoria marrying will make for some... unusual relationships."

"Meaning?"

"Our baby will be Victoria's brother—but also her nephew."

His laugh was always so warm. "He'll be Matthew's nephew *and* brother-in-law."

"I don't even want to think about if Victoria and Matthew have a baby."

"Why, Gracie. Are you vain enough to worry about being a granny?"

She playfully pinched his side. "I'm too young to be a granny." Then she froze, a bit amazed she hadn't thought of herself that way before.

A grandmother, yes.

But a granny?

"I already am."

"Beth."

"But no one can know that. No one can *ever* know that."

His sigh sounded more like a disgruntled grunt. "You should talk to Jake. Consider telling him the truth. Secrets have a way of slipping out. Usually at the worst possible moment."

As if she'd give that suggestion even a passing thought. "I won't do it. I don't ever want him to know."

Thankfully, Adam didn't push her, although she knew better than to think he'd dropped the topic forever. She didn't want to think about it—didn't even want to imagine what would happen should Jake find out he was conceived when his father raped his mother. The Curtis family had been good to him, and she wasn't about to destroy the few good memories he had from his childhood.

His fingers stroked her upper arm. "Since you're a granny, you should sit in a rocking chair all day and knit."

How like her husband to try to tease her out of her worries.

She tossed back a remark of her own. "Hard to do when I'll be busy nursing our baby."

A surprised squeak slipped out when Adam suddenly rolled to pin her to the bed. The hard length of his erection pressed against her stomach through the thin material of her sleeping gown.

"You're right, darlin'. You're far too young to be a granny."

His kiss was deep and damned thorough. He only stopped ravaging her mouth long enough to yank her gown over her head and banish it to the floor.

Kissing his way from her mouth to her ear, he ran his tongue around the shell, sending shivers racing over her skin. As he turned his attention to her sensitive neck, she let a little giggle escape, followed by a moan when he palmed her breast.

"Oh, Gracie," he murmured as he moved lower, kissing the valley between her breasts. "You're so soft."

Her back arched as he drew a nipple into his hot mouth.

All the times they'd made love, he'd been the aggressor, showering her with pleasure. Now, as he again took the lead, she wanted to show him how much she loved him—that he wasn't the only one to take charge in their lovemaking.

"Adam," she whispered as her fingers tickled down his side to his hip. She gently pinched his backside. "I want you to get off me."

Raising himself up on his elbows, he stared down at her. Confusion colored his features. "What's wrong?"

She pushed at his chest until he moved to her side. Then she lifted a leg to straddle his hips, trying to force him to his back.

He wasn't cooperating.

"Roll over," she ordered.

"Why?"

"Because it's my turn to make love to you. That's why."

Rolling to his back, he stacked his hands behind his head. "Well, then. By all means. Go right ahead."

As she straddled him, her teeth tugged on her bottom lip. "Perhaps I'll start...here." She kissed him. When he groaned in encouragement, she smiled against his lips and deepened the kiss, hesitantly pushing her tongue into his mouth. He caught it gently between his teeth.

Grace stroked his chest as she ended the kiss to touch her lips to his chin, tracing the line of his jaw with her tongue. She pressed her lips to his throat.

Her kisses moved to his chest, and she sighed as she ran her nose through the patch of hair. Her teeth grasped at his nipple before she moved lower, kissing his stomach as her hands stroked up the inside of his thigh. When her fingers finally wrapped around his erection, he hissed his approval.

He fisted his hands in the linens. His eyes were pressed tightly closed until the first touch of her lips against the crown of his cock. Then they flew open. "You don't have to—"

"I told you," she scolded. "It's my turn to make love to you."

She didn't know exactly what to do, but the moans and growls coming from her husband meant he enjoyed her attention. His approval gave her courage to take him into her mouth.

A guttural groan rose from him, and she decided she liked having that kind of power over Adam. His erection grew firmer and a little larger against her lips.

Another surprised squeak escaped when he grabbed her under her arms and dragged her up his body. Before she could ask what she'd done wrong, he rubbed himself against her core. "Take me inside you, Gracie. I need to be inside you."

The man loved her enough to always make her feel in control. Not used to the new position, she wriggled and shifted until he was at last able to thrust inside.

He held tight to her hips, setting a rhythm she quickly caught. He reached between them, finding her sensitive nub and rubbing until she threw her head back and cried out her pleasure.

She came first, Adam following a heartbeat later. She had just enough energy left to collapse against his chest, and she fell asleep before he left her body.

***

Breaking the intimacy of their embrace, Adam settled Grace at his side. He kissed the top of her head as she snuggled up against him like a content kitten.

Sated though he was, his thoughts grew troubled.

Matthew and Ty were both lucky to still be alive. Either or both could have been killed in that fire. He had no doubt whatsoever Stephen Shay was behind the attack. White Pines might no longer be graced with the man's presence, but men like that never did their own dirty work.

It was baffling to think of the lengths the man had gone to pursue Grace. Years of tracking her. Seeing up Ty's attack. Luring Victoria to Denver simply to escort her back.

Adam didn't even want to speculate on what could've happened to his daughter in that man's company, especially after the horror his wife had confessed of her rape. While Matthew might have hinted of the type of life Grace had led being constantly chased by Shay the way a wanted man was dogged by a bounty hunter, the real story had to be much worse.

Tomorrow, he, Grace, and Matthew were going to sit down and make some solid plans that would allow Adam to protect his wife and hopefully figure out Stephen Shay's next move.

Chapter Twenty-Six

Matthew sighed in resignation as he looked around his new home.

So much work needed to be done, he wasn't sure exactly where to start. The main room was badly illuminated by the sunlight peeping through the ratty curtains that framed the dirty window. Considering the mess of filthy dishes and petrified food littering the place, the lack of light actually served as a blessing.

Victoria wrinkled her nose. "This place is a pig sty."

She kicked aside one of many empty whiskey bottles resting on the floor until it rolled to stop against a pile of what appeared to be soiled, abandoned clothes.

She gave her head a shake. "How the man could live in this filth is beyond me."

His hopes for the future had been soaring as high as the Rocky Mountains. He was now the White Pines marshal—a job with enough pay and stability that he could provide a good home for Victoria when they married. The small pinch in his happiness was that it wasn't at all like the life she was used to. But remembering that a little house came with his new job made him at least feel as though he could be a good husband by offering her a place she could turn into their home.

Then he'd gotten a look at the inside of the house.

Victoria was right—the place *was* a pig sty.

How in the hell was she supposed to be happy about coming to live in this pit after she'd spent her life on the beautiful Twin Springs?

A small hand wrapped around his and squeezed. "It'll be nice, Matthew." Her smile made his heart skip a quick beat. "Just wait and see. Some cleaning. A few pieces of furniture. Some new curtains and bedding. We'll make this a nice home."

He gave her a smile in return, letting her comforting words and confidence wash over him.

A home.

This house would be their first home. "We've got less than a week before the wedding."

She plucked out an apron out of the bag she'd brought along. She shook it out, tied it around her waist, and rolled up the sleeves of her calico dress. "Then we might as well get right to work. I suppose the hardest chore will be deciding where to begin."

The morning passed by swiftly as they cleared out the mess the odious old marshal had left behind. Grace and Adam joined in the cleaning frenzy, and the men worked on either mending or getting rid of the broken furniture. They were able to salvage a bed and a small kitchen table. The rest was beyond repair and would be turned into firewood.

The sun was high in the afternoon sky by the time a list had been made of the things the couple would need to make the place livable. A dresser. Chairs. Kitchen utensils. Victoria's hope chest.

Grace wiped her dirty hands on her apron. "I think we should stop for a bite to eat. I packed a lunch."

Adam looked at his own hands. "I've got a layer of dirt on me. I should wash up, then I can help you." He opened the door for his wife. "After you, darlin'."

With a sweet smile, she led him outside.

While it warmed Matthew's heart to see his sister so happy, he sighed in relief. In the week since Stephen Shay's departure, no one had left her alone for anything longer than a trip to the privy. She'd borne it with her typical grace. Although there had been no sign of Stephen or one of his detectives or minions, no one held out any real hope that he'd leave them in peace for too long.

Yes, he was glad Grace remained safe. But Matthew was ready for her and Adam to leave his new home. He hadn't found a moment of privacy to be with Victoria since the bunkhouse burned down, and he ached to touch her. Both Adam and Grace had been helping clear away the debris, and while Matthew had been grateful for their help, his thoughts constantly returned to the passion he and Victoria had shared.

His gaze settled on his fiancée. She was bent over a large barrel full of dishes and kitchenware, her pretty backside wiggling as she practically climbed inside. Heavens, but she was a little bit of a thing.

Coming up behind her, he grabbed her hips and pressed his groin against her bottom. Her startled gasp was quickly replaced by a giggle. He dragged her out of the barrel, and she turned in his embrace.

"Why, Mr. Riley. I do believe you're trying to take advantage of me." Her eyelashes batted in coy invitation.

With a grin, he winked. "Of course I am. What I need to know is if I'm succeeding."

She answered him with a kiss, encircling his neck with her slender arms as he wrapped his own around her waist and lifted her. After only a few strokes of her tongue, she had him hard and throbbing. He growled when she playfully coaxed his tongue into her mouth.

The door opened, pulling a startled gasp from Victoria.

He put her on her feet and turned her to face Grace as she came back through the door, carrying a wicker basket. When Victoria tried to take a step away, he gripped her shoulders and pulled her back against him.

Leaning down, he whispered in her ear. "Stay put or you'll embarrass us both."

Her face flushed red all the way to her ears.

Adam followed his wife inside. He gave the couple a quick appraisal and chuckled before he pulled a blanket out from under his arm and spread it over a clean spot on the wooden floor.

Matthew regained control and finally let Victoria free to help Grace set up lunch. After a quiet meal, Grace packed away the remaining food and supplies and returned them to the wagon.

Then the work started again.

***

Matthew was astonished at how some hard work had transformed the house into a place he could bring his new wife.

"Amazing," he whispered.

Victoria came to his side. "A little bit of elbow grease goes a long way."

"My thoughts exactly."

Adam clapped him on the shoulder. "Got a few hours before sunset. Figured I'd take the wagon back to the Twin Springs and fetch a few of the things you'll need."

"I don't feel right taking furniture from you, Adam."

"Nonsense. With just Gracie and me living there, we won't be needing nearly as much."

Victoria smiled. "Until the baby comes."

Her father smiled back. "Even then, we've got plenty to spare. You two are trying to get on your feet. Least you can let your father do is help set up your first home."

Grace leaned against Adam's shoulder and yawned.

"You okay, Grace?" Matthew asked. It was hard to remember that his sister was expecting a baby. "Didn't want you to get too tuckered out."

She dismissed the notion with a wave of her hand. "I'm fine. I wanted to help."

The door opened, and Emily came inside followed by Jake, who held Beth cradled against his shoulder.

"Wow," Emily said as she looked around. "Cleaned up nice, didn't it?"

"A bit bare," Jake added. "But a nice place."

Grace hurried over to see Beth, feeling as if she could never see her often enough to feel satisfied. She might not be able to openly claim the beautiful little girl as her grandchild, but she could fuss over her anyway. They were still supposed to be kin, after all.

She rubbed the infant's back and cooed to her. "May I hold her?"

"Sure thing, Aunt Grace." Jake shifted his daughter and passed her to Grace's waiting arms.

Settling her precious bundle, she smiled down at Beth. Big, brown eyes stared back. "I can't believe how quickly she's changing. Why, her eyes aren't even blue anymore."

"Nope," Emily replied. "I told Jake that Beth's eyes look just like yours."

That notion brought tears to Grace's eyes.

Adam came to stand at her side, reaching up to let Beth grasp his pinkie.

She squeezed it in her tiny fingers.

"You alright, darlin'?" he asked.

Grace sniffed back a few happy tears. "Just a lot of dust in here. That's all."

"I'm supposed to bring you all back to the Four Aces," Emily said. "Daddy figured we could all catch up, and I think he's got a few things to give Victoria and Matthew for the house."

"I think he's hoping to bribe Grace into cooking supper," Jake added.

Grace leaned in and kissed Beth's forehead, loving the sweet smell only babies had. Her eyes filled with tears again as she remembered cradling Jake's tiny body in the same way. Before she could blink them back, a few spilled over onto her cheek.

"Why you cryin', Grace?" Jake asked.

"She's gonna have a baby," Emily replied, sparing her an explanation. "That's what women do when they're gonna be a mama."

"Lord knows you did enough of it." Jake took his daughter back and kissed her on the cheek.

He was always loving to his daughter. Despite the horrors of his childhood, the Curtis family had obviously treated him well, teaching him to be a giving person. Adam had finished his rearing and helped train him to be a good father. And, sweet Lord, she wondered if she would ever stop weeping when she saw Jake and Beth together.

Adam wrapped a reassuring arm around her shoulder. "Let's head over to see Will. Maybe you can sit down for a spell before he twists your arm to get you to cook."

She leaned into her husband. "That and a glass of lemonade sound heavenly."

Jake led them all back to the Four Aces, and Grace found herself settled at one of the big tables with a tall glass of lemonade Emily brought to her.

Grace's cheeks flushed warm. Would she ever get accustomed to people being so concerned about her?

Adam leaned down to brush a quick kiss on her lips. "I'm headin' back to the ranch to fetch some furniture. Matthew and Will are gonna stay here to keep an eye on you. Ty and Jake will help me bring things in, especially if they know one of your suppers will be waiting for them when the chore's done."

Will was just coming down the stairs. He stopped in his tracks and looked to Grace. "Grace is cooking supper?"

She smiled at him. "Grace is cooking supper."

He slapped the banister. "Hot diggedy damn!"

***

Grace picked up the skillet and flipped the thick slice of ham to warm the other side. Cooking always made her happy, and doing so for family and friends only made the task more enjoyable.

Victoria chuckled and shook her head as she stacked plates for the meal. "I have no idea how you do that. If I tried, it would hit the floor."

"Lots and lots of practice. Can you please hand me the eggs?"

Handing the bowl over to Grace, Victoria sighed. "Poor Matthew. He's used to your cooking. Now he'll have to get used to mine. It sure won't be a step up."

"Oh, I imagine he won't complain too loudly. Not after what your father and I stumbled in on that day the bunkhouse burned down." She threw her daughter-in-law a wink.

Victoria's cheeks flushed crimson. "I thought the way to a man's heart was through his stomach."

How wonderful it felt to be so lighthearted and open with another woman. She gave her stepdaughter a crooked smile. "I imagine sometimes it's a bit farther south."

"You'll have to give me some cooking lessons just to be sure."

Scuffling steps drifted into the kitchen from the main part of the saloon.

Grace glanced up at the clock, a bit surprised to hear so much noise when only Emily, Will, and Beth were still in the Four Aces. "Too early for customers. Adam, Jake, and Ty couldn't possibly be back with the furniture yet."

"Matthew might be back from his...*adventure*." Victoria's giggle was always so warm, and her love for Matthew rang clear in her voice. "I'm sure that rescuing a boy from a well wasn't quite the type of task he thought a marshal would be taking on."

Grace stirred the potatoes. "I suppose he had grand visions of capturing evil men to keep them from hurting anyone ever again."

"Where is she?"

The shouted words froze her to the spot, terror wrapping itself around her chest and squeezing until she feared she could never breathe again.

"Grace! I know you're here! Show yourself!"

Victoria turned to her, the fear as plain in her green eyes as it was in Grace's thoughts. "Stephen?"

She gave Victoria a brisk nod and swallowed the bile rising in the back of her throat. "Stay here. No matter what happens, *stay here.*" Dropping the wooden spoon, she took hesitant steps toward the door.

Victoria grabbed her elbow and jerked her back. "No! Don't you dare! Daddy will be back soon."

"Not soon enough." They'd been gone a good two hours, but there had been so much furniture to load into the wagon. The ride to the Twin Springs and back ate up quite a bit of time.

No, she had no choice.

"Grace! If you don't show your face, I'll kill the baby!"

She ran from the kitchen, throwing a harsh command back at Victoria to stay where she was.

The sight that greeted her made what little food she'd eaten at lunch fight to come back up. Stephen Shay stood in the middle of the room, arms folded over his chest as he looked utterly bored.

Grace knew better. The man was furious, which made him even more dangerous.

Will lay sprawled on the floor, a bloody gash on his forehead and the gun he kept holstered at his side lying several feet away. Thank the Lord, his chest rose and fell with his breaths.

Emily knelt on the floor next to her father, crying as she cradled Beth against her shoulder. Stephen's lapdog had a gun pointed at the back of Beth's head.

With a deep breath and a desperate prayer, Grace faced her tormentor. "I'm here, Stephen. Call off your man."

Stephen doffed his top hat and gave her a mocking bow. "Ah, my sweet. So you've deigned to...grace us all with your presence." He snorted a disgusting laugh. "If you shall excuse the pun."

"What do you want?"

As if she didn't already know the answer. The man's timing was incredibly lucky—or brilliant. For the first time in days, Adam, Jake, Ty, and Matthew were too far away to help, thinking Will was watching the women. Matthew was closest but might not return for quite a while. No, she was good and trapped. The best she could hope for was to keep Beth, Emily, Victoria, and Will safe, which meant she'd have to leave with a man she hoped would one day find his soul tormented in Hell.

Adam will find me.

But would that miracle happen before Stephen hurt her again?

Heart hammering in her chest, she refused to show him her fear. Her hand rose to touch her stomach before she quickly dropped it. She couldn't allow the man to figure out she was pregnant. He would surely know some unholy way to end the child's life, and there was no doubt that would be his plan should he discover the truth.

"We'll be leaving now, Grace. That's what I want. That's all I've ever wanted." He strode across the room and gripped her upper arm so tightly tears stung her eyes.

She blinked them back, refusing to let him see any weakness.

"You belong to me," he said as he narrowed his eyes in anger. "Now and forever."

"Get that gun away from that child," she ordered, pleased her voice held no quiver of the fright threatening to paralyze her. "Promise me you'll leave these good people alone. Then I'll go with you."

"You dare to demand?" He jerked her arm to force her a step closer. His chest pressed against hers as he stared down into her eyes. The black depths revealed no soul. "You'll go...whether I kill them all or not. And I'll start by killing *it*." He pointed at Beth.

A shot rang out.

Grace screamed and whirled to face Emily and Beth, terrified Stephen's lackey had followed through with Stephen's threat. Instead, she stared in amazement as the man sank to his knees. When he collapsed next to Will, blood seeped onto the sawdust covered floor from the wound on the back of his head.

Another shot quickly rang out, this time from Stephen. That's when Grace saw Matthew standing just inside the saloon doors, his gun still smoking from the shot that killed Stephen's man. She sobbed when her brother collapsed to his knees as a dark red stain spread over the wound to his right shoulder.

Stephen slipped his gun back in his coat pocket and marched toward the front doors, dragging her with him.

Grace dug in her heels, trying to stop to see her brother, to assure herself he would survive.

"Come with me, Grace," Stephen said as they stood next to Matthew's prostrate form. "Or I swear to you, I'll kill him right now. And then the others."

With a smothered cry, she gave him a nod and let him haul her to his waiting carriage.

Dear God, please let Matthew live.

And please help Adam find me.

Chapter Twenty-Seven

Adam knew something was very wrong the moment he walked into the Four Aces.

Emily was crying and holding Beth against her shoulder while Victoria fussed over Matthew and Will. Both men were slumped in chairs, looking pale and shaky.

Bloody rags rested on the table and what appeared to be a dead body had been draped with a sheet.

His heart pounded hard, increasing the speed even more when he realized there was one thing he *didn't* see.

His wife.

"What in the hell happened?" he demanded.

"Stephen," Victoria hissed. "He knocked out Will. Then he shot Matthew and took Grace."

Jake pushed past Adam to go to Emily.

She released a sob and let him enfold her and Beth in his arms.

"It's okay, now, Em," he said softly, rubbing her back.

In ragged, tearful snatches of words, she said, "H–he–took Grace. Sh–she left to save Beth."

Adam strode over, trying to make sense of what Emily was saying. "He threatened to kill Beth?"

"After he hit Daddy, h-he held a gun t–to Beth's head." She sobbed again and buried her face against Jake's shoulder.

Since the poor thing was too upset to give him any real answers, he turned to his daughter. "Tell me everything."

"He came here with his man." A nod to the body. "The guy knocked Will out with the butt of his pistol. Then he demanded Grace go with him—told his man to kill Beth if she didn't obey. He would've killed us all, Daddy."

"You took a bullet?" Adam asked Matthew. A ridiculous question considering Victoria was tending his wound.

Damn, but he was having trouble concentrating because of his fear for Grace. He wanted to run back outside, jump on his stallion, and ride.

But where?

Never in his life had he been tempted to kill another man. But at that moment, blood lust raced through every part of him—body and mind. Stephen Shay was going to die at his hand, and if Adam had any say in it, the death would be unmercifully slow and very, very painful.

"It's just my shoulder. Went straight through, so we don't have to dig the damn thing out," Matthew said. "As soon as Victoria patches me up, we'll track 'em."

Grabbing a fresh towel, Will held it to his forehead. "Stitch me up, Victoria. I'll ride with 'em too."

Already forming some plans, Adam watched how sweaty and shaky Matthew and Will were. His ideas couldn't include them. "Jake?"

"Ready to ride with you," Jake replied, taking his daughter from Emily's arms. Then he tucked his crying wife against his shoulder again. "What about Ty?"

"Didn't he come back with you?" Victoria asked.

"He's back at the Twin Springs, tendin' to the horses," Jake replied.

"He can stay there to take care of things while we're gone," Adam added. "Victoria can explain everything to him later. Get a few things together, Jake. We'll hit the trail now, while it's still fresh."

Matthew frowned up at Victoria. "Get this thing sewn shut. I need to go with them."

"Me first," Will insisted.

Victoria gave him a quick shake of her head.

"Not this time, Matthew. You, either, Wil,." Adam said.

He needed to ride hard, and wounded men could easily be laid low if those wounds weren't properly cared for.

Matthew brushed her hands away and jumped to his feet. "The hell I'm not... I'll be...fine..." His words slipped to a mere whisper as he sank back into the chair. What little color his face had held disappeared.

"You've lost too much blood." Victoria pressed a clean cloth against his wound. "Curse it... Now you've got it bleeding again."

"But... I've always protected Grace." With a heavy sigh, he hung his head. "I let her down. I let that bastard get her."

"You did no such thing." She smoothed her free hand down his cheek. "Stephen would've killed you if you even raised a hand. Grace knew that. She went to save you—to save all of us."

"I need you here, Matthew," Jake added. "You need to keep watch over Em and Beth. You need to stay too, Will. Watch over my family for me." Leaning down, he planted a kiss on his wife's lips and then kissed his daughter's forehead before handing her back to a calmer Emily. "Let me grab a few things, Adam. Then we'll get the wagon back to the ranch and grab some horses." He took the stairs two at a time.

"Princess?" Adam asked.

She glanced up.

"Could you please pack us some food? Jerky. Bread. Cheese. Just a few things to keep us going."

She nodded before checking Matthew's wound again. "I'll stitch that up soon as I get things ready. Will—you're next." Dropping the cloth on the table next to the rest of the bloody rags, she hurried to the kitchen.

"I should be going with you," Matthew insisted.

"I need you here. When Victoria gets you sewn up, get to the telegraph office. Send out a few messages to some of the railheads to see if—"

"Stephen probably took her to his Pullman car! Brilliant, Adam. You and Jake send messages back when you can so we can share any information."

Jake ran down the stairs, carrying a small satchel and wearing his Colt holstered against his hip. "Ready."

"Matthew?" Adam asked.

He quirked an eyebrow.

"I need your best guess where he'd take her."

He pondered it before he answered. "I wanted to say he'd haul her to New York City. His brothers are there. But now I'm not so sure…"

"Why?"

"Goes back to when I searched for her before she came here. Talked to a couple of people in Frisco just to be sure Shay hadn't snatched her right out from under my nose. Found out some of his family's not so happy with him because he's spent so much time and money chasing Grace over hell's half-acre all these years. The only one who still cares is the old man."

"You mean his father—the senator?"

"That's him. Hiram Shay."

That boded well. If the Shay family had tightened Stephen's purse strings, that would limit how far the man could travel and where he might be able to hide Grace. "What's your gut tell you now?"

"He'll head back to his father to beg for money."

"San Francisco?"

Matthew nodded. "That'd be my guess. He'll go by railroad. The guy enjoys traveling in style."

"Then San Francisco it is."

***

Grace curled up under the layers of her skirts, drawing her knees up to hug them where she sat on the settee. She was tired and hungry—not that she'd ever make a peep of complaint to Stephen Shay.

She'd sooner starve to death.

That notion brought her problems back full force. Much as she wanted to spite the man by refusing to eat, she had to think of her unborn child.

Adam's child.

No matter what happened, no matter what Stephen did to her, she had to protect her baby. She'd already let one of her children down—there was no way she'd allow something to hurt this one, too.

Her tired eyes searched the room. The wealth of the Shay family echoed from every corner. Velvet-covered chairs. An oaken bureau. Thick rugs covering the floor. The railroad car was nicer than any room at the fanciest of hotels.

Stephen had held his pistol to her side as he forced her into that damned Pullman car—the same one she'd seen waiting for her at the end of far too many cattle drives. He'd locked her in the sitting room and left. She was sure he'd gone because she'd tried to pick the lock with anything she could get her hands on to no avail.

An ornate letter opener she'd found was now tucked away in the folds of her skirt. Made of gold and accented with rubies, it was probably worth more than she'd earned in her lifetime. The size seemed more dagger than humble tool. She'd save it for the best possible moment—one that might earn her freedom—and do what she had to do to protect herself and her baby.

The door opened. Stephen stepped into the room, said something to someone on the other side of the door, then slammed it shut.

"Grace." He gave her a long look. "It appears we're going to be on our way any moment."

The train lurched into motion, the timing drawing a reptilian smile from his lips.

What did he expect her to say? Was the man wanting her to beg for her freedom?

She wouldn't give him that kind of satisfaction. Instead, she simply stared at him, hoping he would feel every ounce of the hatred flowing through her veins.

"Don't you wish to know where we're heading, my sweet?"

All she offered him was a silent glare.

"I've secured a...safe place for us."

Her fingers gently brushed against the soft folds of her skirt, caressing the hidden letter opener, reminding herself that if the man tried to attack her again, she had a weapon. While it might not have been as effective as a gun, the letter opener was better than the despair of helplessness.

Grace refused to be his victim.

He walked to the small bureau and retrieved a glass. Then he pulled a flask from his breast pocket. "Are you hungry?"

I'm starving, but you'll never know it.

Stephen took a long pull from the amber liquor he'd poured into the glass. "I have dinner being brought in shortly."

You'll be eating it alone.

"Once we're on our way, I'm afraid there will be one more…important stop. Some small hamlet outside of San Francisco. You see, Grace, there's a doctor there who has arranged to take care of your little…problem."

Her eyes widened, but she bit the inside of her cheek to keep from screaming.

The glass suddenly flew past her head, close enough she flinched. It shattered against the wall, surrounding her with the reek of whiskey.

"Did you think I didn't know?" he bellowed.

Her eyes rose to meet his, and she hoped he saw the challenge there. The Grace he'd tried to destroy was gone. She wasn't a scared child any longer. She was a woman who would do anything to protect her unborn child.

"You let him touch you! How could you? After all I've done for you? After what we meant to each other? How could you give yourself to another man? Especially to that.. that… *buffoon?*"

"He's more of a man than you could ever *dream* of being."

The taunt earned her a hard backhand across the face—hard enough her ears rang and she tasted blood. Although tears filled her eyes, she refused to give him the satisfaction of knowing he'd hurt her. Her gaze rose again to defiantly stare at her tormentor, the throbbing of her cheek keeping her grounded and determined.

Stomping over to the door, he jerked it open. "You may forget about dinner this evening. Sit alone with your hunger as punishment." His eyes narrowed. "Know this—you belong to me, Grace. You've always belonged to me, but I won't touch you until that…*abomination* is removed."

He slammed the door.

Thank the Lord, Stephen wasn't going to rape her again—at least not now. And if he thought the time would come that she'd calmly allow anyone to try and kill her child, he was sadly mistaken.

The letter opener would remain hidden while Grace prayed that when the right time came, she'd be able to use it.

Chapter Twenty-Eight

With a despondent cry, Grace gave up trying to get out through the window.

The train had stopped in some town just outside of San Francisco, where—after some maneuvering—the Pullman had been detached and left behind. As the remainder of the train pulled away, all she could do was watch with panic out the small window. Her hopes of gaining help or getting lost in the confusion of Union Station turned to ashes.

When Stephen left her alone, telling her he'd come back for her later, terror set in.

The door wouldn't budge, even when she'd tried to jimmy the lock with the letter opener. Trying to find some calm, her gaze again settled on the window. It was too high for her to kick out the glass, but could she smash it with something heavy?

Unfortunately, there were no statues or paperweights—nothing heavy enough to do the job. Everything in the car had been nailed down, probably to keep it from shifting during travel. That, or he'd planned well for her captivity.

Using the letter opener, she tried to pry the trim off so perhaps the window could be lifted away. Her struggle yielded nothing but more frustration and several shallow cuts to her fingers and palm.

She was out of options.

The door opened.

Grace sank back down into the chair, quickly tucking the letter opener back into the pocket of her skirts.

Stephen said something over his shoulder as he walked into the room. The door was left open, which meant he was taking her off the train.

She had to swallow the fear threatening to make her do something foolish—like make a mad dash past him. Stephen was smart. He'd have some of his goons waiting for that contingency.

"It's time to go, my sweet. I've secured a place for us to wait for the doctor."

"I won't go."

"You will."

He motioned for one of his men, a large, burly guy who looked so much like some of the cowboys she'd worked with through the years hope crept into her heart. Surely if she let this man know the disgusting crime Stephen planned, he'd help her find a way to get free.

Stephen frowned. "There's a carriage right outside the door. You *will* get inside and you *will* behave."

He pulled that damned pistol he'd pointed at Beth out of his coat pocket as he crossed the room. Grabbing her upper arm, he jerked her to her feet. With a push to her back, he sent her stumbling toward the door.

She let her eyes meet the new man's, pleading with him best she could to help her.

The gaze that met hers seemed colder than a Montana winter.

"Please help me," she whispered as she passed him.

He looked away.

"To the carriage." Stephen gave her another push.

He'd planned well. They were in the middle of nowhere. There was no one who would hear her should she shout. The driver of the carriage wouldn't even make eye contact, meaning he was another of Stephen's hirelings.

Grace was utterly alone as the few hopes she still grasped dwindled.

When Stephen gave her his hand to help her in the carriage, she dug in her heels, folded her arms over her breasts, and refused to budge. "I won't go with you."

His cool smile shouldn't have surprised her. Then he pressed the gun to her ribcage. "You will."

"Shoot me. I'd rather be dead than let you do what you're planning."

He motioned to the man who'd followed them out of the car.

The big man stepped up. "Mr. Shay?"

"I'm tired of dealing with this...nuisance. Take care of it."

"With pleasure."

The blow came quickly—a sharp hit by a meaty fist against her chin.

Stars shot through her mind, and then there was nothing but darkness.

***

Adam stepped off the train with Jake following right behind him. The latest message from Matthew had narrowed their search to the outskirts of San Francisco, so they'd stabled their horses in Idaho and taken a train the rest of the way. A bit surprising that Shay's family seemed anxious for Adam to find Grace. Perhaps year after year of dealing with the man's ever-increasing insanity had finally convinced the high profile members that Stephen needed to be stopped.

Yet they wouldn't offer any help but advice.

Now it was up to Adam and Jake.

"We're not even sure which way that damned house is." Jake's tone betrayed his loss of patience.

"We'll find it, but we've gotta have a plan," Adam insisted. "We can't go charging in there with guns blazing."

"Why the hell not? We hire a couple of horses, get our asses out there, and take back Grace."

It was hard enough to keep his own raging temper at bay. If Jake's was allowed to run rampant...

This couldn't end well.

Dear God, all Adam could do was worry about Grace—about their child.

No, he needed to keep himself reined in, and he needed Jake to maintain control. "Shay's family might have washed their hands of him, but I've no doubt he's still surrounded by hired guns. If we rush them, she could get hurt."

Jake fixed his mouth into a grim line. "Then what do you wanna do?"

"We go to the sheriff first. We get fresh horses and find the house. Then we can decide the best way to snatch her right out from under Shay's nose."

***

Adam had expected a rebuff. He'd even anticipated that he and Jake would be on their own when they went for Grace. But he sure hadn't expected the sheriff of the sleepy, little burg to threaten to arrest him when all he wanted was to get to his wife before that bastard Shay could hurt her again.

"You're damn well gonna tell me where Shay's house is," Adam demanded. "Or I'll—"

"Or you'll spend the night in a cell!" The sheriff pushed his chair back hard enough it toppled to the ground. "This is my town. *Mine!*"

"Bullshit. You're nothing more than Stephen Shay's hireling. Nothing but a damned lap dog."

Blinding anger finally pushed aside all the eternal patience everyone believed Adam possessed. They'd been wrong.

Even *he* had his breaking point.

Knowing every minute he wasted with the corrupt sheriff could mean more pain and suffering for Grace erased any threads of tolerance he had left.

Adam took a threatening step toward the smug sheriff, his hands fisted, ready to pound the man into the floor if that's what it took to get the information he needed.

Jake's hand settled on his shoulder.

It took all the tenuous self-control Adam had remaining not to shift his frustration to his adopted son.

"We need to go," Jake said in a low tone.

"Go?" Adam gritted his teeth. "Not until this son-of-a-bitch tells me where Shay's house is."

A tight squeeze on his shoulder stopped him from taking a step forward. "Trust me, Adam. Please," Jake whispered.

He glanced back and recognized the look on Jake's face—he knew something he didn't want to share with the sheriff and his deputies. Perhaps he'd gleaned some information from the deputy who'd remained outside for a smoke and talk to Jake as Adam went in the office to argue with the sheriff.

Adam nodded, threw one last scowl at the curs who refused to help him, and followed Jake outside.

They mounted their horses, and he let Jake take the lead. As soon as they were far enough away from the tiny town to speak freely, Jake reined his horse to a stop.

Adam pulled up beside him.

"The house is three miles north on this road."

"How did you find that out?"

"Deputy told me—also told me no one would stop us if we went after Shay."

Adam threw a glance back toward the town. "What about the sheriff?"

"He's in Stephen's pocket." A hesitant smile. "But the deputies belong to his brother—the oldest brother who wants him gone."

"Then what in the hell are we waiting for?"

Jake smiled, reined his horse north, and gave it a kick.

Adam followed close behind, riding hard for the house, and praying—again—for wife's safety.

***

"Damn it!" Grace kicked the door, letting her frustration find an outlet.

She wanted to pound on the thing with her fists—to scream, cry, and carry on like an angry child. None of that would help her, so she took a deep breath instead and tried to find some calm. Perhaps then she could come up with a plan for escape.

She'd awakened in a room lit only by a hurricane lamp. The place was empty except for the bed she'd been lying on and an oaken dresser.

A frantic search of the drawers yielded nothing more than linens and indecent garments that couldn't rightly be called nightclothes. She didn't even want to know why there were silk ropes or barbed whips. A shudder ripped through her, knowing that if she didn't get out of there, Stephen might find a way to put those things to use against her. Figuring she could wield at least one against him, she'd grabbed a leather whip.

She fumbled through her skirts to find the letter opener, and she offered a whispered prayer of thanks that it was still there. While she prayed, she also asked for the strength she'd need to keep Stephen from his despicable plan so she could protect her unborn child. And though she held little hope she'd win in a physical fight, in each hand she now brandished a weapon—she wouldn't give in without inflicting plenty of damage of her own.

"Oh, Adam. Please find me."

***

"I count three," Adam whispered to Jake as he stared at the tiny house.

The thing was smaller than the home Matthew and Victoria would share—probably nothing more than two rooms. Shay obviously used this place when he needed some privacy. A man of his wealth and stature sure as hell wouldn't deign to live in that shack.

A silent nod came in reply as Jake pointed at the man stationed right outside a small, high window and held up one finger. Then he pointed to the entrance before showing two fingers. "Third's at the other door 'round back."

"Where in the hell is Shay?" Damn, but Adam wanted to get his hands on that man and wring his neck like a chicken being prepared for Sunday supper.

Jake shrugged. "There's no carriage. No horses, either. Maybe he had someplace to be and will be back later."

"Then now's when we have to make our move."

"We're only getting one shot at this."

Adam flashed Jake an angry scowl. "You think I don't know that?"

"Easy there. Just want this to work."

Holding in his fear and anger was one of the hardest things he'd ever done. A slow count of ten didn't help much.

God, he needed to see Grace—desperately needed to know she was well.

He drew in a shuddering, deep breath. "I'll take the guy at the front door. You go 'round back."

"If we can be quiet, we can keep him—" Jake nodded at the man lighting up a cheroot under the window, "—out of the fight." He frowned, his features stern even in the fading light. "Don't like the notion of killin' any of them, but—"

"They wouldn't hesitate to kill you. Just remember that bastard pointing a gun at Beth."

Jake's frown became a glare.

Coming around the far side of the house, Adam plotted how to silence the goon watching the door. Just as he pulled his Colt, Stephen Shay's carriage ground to a halt close to the house. A glance back revealed the door was no longer guarded, but before Adam could figure out where the guard had gone, a sharp pain sliced through his head.

His world spun in a dizzying circle before it went black.

***

The door burst open, forcing a squeal from Grace's lips before the identity of the intruder settled in her thoughts. "Jake!"

Her heart was hammering so hard, she feared she'd faint. Jake had come for her. The whip hit the floor. "Where's Adam?"

"Taking out the guy guarding one of the doors."

Dear God, but she had to get him out of there. If Stephen came back, he wouldn't hesitate to shoot him.

She gathered her skirts in her hand and hurried toward the door. "We're getting outta here."

Suddenly his hand was on her elbow, hurrying her faster than she thought she could move. She stumbled alongside him, daring to hope that they could escape.

The hope vanished the moment he reached the doorway and came face to face with Stephen.

Jake tugged Grace's arm, took several steps back, and shoved her behind him.

She fought, trying to get around and put herself between the two men.

"Why, Grace." Stephen sounded almost bored as he entered the room and shut the door. The gun he had pointed at Jake said otherwise. "What a...surprise. We have a guest. How kind of your brother to join us."

"Let him go, Stephen," Grace begged, struggling against Jake's strong arms.

She had to get between them before Stephen could harm him.

Jake kept moving her back, making her feel as if she were a fish trying desperately to swim upstream.

Why couldn't he understand? Stephen was toying with him.

She hadn't protected him when he was a child—she was damn well going to protect him now.

"Ain't going nowhere, Grace." Jake leveled a menacing glare at Stephen. "I'm not afraid of him."

A sinister smile crossed Stephen's face. "Not afraid, eh?" He chuckled, the sound as grating as discordant music. "What do you think, my sweet? Should I dispatch him now? I know how distressed you would be should I let my men mess up the boy's handsome face. He is, after all, your brother." His black eyes considered Jake before shifting to Grace. "Perhaps you will bend to my will to save his life?" He pointed the gun at Jake's chest.

The surge of fear gave her strength. Jerking Jake's arm hard enough he took a stumbling step back, she slipped in front of him. "You'll have to kill me before I'll let you touch him."

He clucked his tongue. "So noble. So brave. Putting yourself between your brother and my gun."

Jake's hands encircled her waist, and he tried again to shove her behind him.

She changed tactics and whirled to face him. Wrapping both of her arms around his waist, she clung to him like a human suit of armor.

A growl rose from his chest as he tried unsuccessfully to pry her away from him. His pride might be dented, but she was keeping him alive. Stephen had taken too much from her already.

He couldn't have their son.

Jake's voice came low and angry in her ear. "Don't feed him your fear."

"What shall it be then?" Stephen asked. "Do I shoot him?"

"No!" Grace turned to confront her tormentor, snatching the letter opener from her waistband and standing with it at ready.

A muscular arm pulled her back, and before she could fight him, Jake had her tucked behind him again. "You best back away from that door. I'm taking Grace, and we're leavin'."

With a chilling smile, Stephen leveled the gun at Jake's chest again. "What you're going to do, my friend, is *die*."

"No!" The scream ripped from her throat as she found more strength than she ever thought she could possess.

She set herself between the two men. Facing Stephen, she had one choice left.

Taking a deep, gulping breath, she held the letter opener in front of her and narrowed her eyes. "You would kill your own son?"

Chapter Twenty-Nine

Jake's sharp intake of breath registered in Grace's mind, but she couldn't think about him right now. Saving his life was more important than keeping her secret.

"He's your son, Stephen. This boy is *your son.*"

"What are you talking about?" Stephen's eyes bored holes through her as the hand holding the gun trembled.

She held her ground. "Nine months after you attacked me, I gave birth to your son."

"You're...you're lying!" Stephen's face flushed red as his mouth opened and closed over and over. "How could you?" Obsidian eyes focused on Jake. "My...my...*son?*"

Her heart beat so hard, she thought she might be ill. "Your son. Your rape left me with child."

The confusion on his face morphed to anger. "How could you keep him from me? You had no right!"

"No right?" Hysteria tinted her voice. "You raped a fourteen-year-old girl! You think I'd let you or your despicable family anywhere near him?"

"He's *my son!*"

Before she could reply, the door slammed open hard enough it bounced off the wall. Adam's tall frame filled the space as he took a step into the room.

Stephen whirled to face him, pointing the gun at his head.

The scene slowed down in Grace's mind until seconds became minutes. The letter opener was gripped tightly her hand. As she hurried to protect her husband, she stumbled on her skirts. It didn't matter because she achieved her ultimate goal. The weapon slid into Stephen's back, and the feel and sound as it sliced through him would forever be etched in her mind.

Sickened with what she'd done, she jerked the letter opener free and dropped the blood-smeared blade to the floor, the clatter echoing with the intensity of a church bell. She collapsed to her knees, the world around her growing cloudy.

Stephen turned and aimed the gun at her again.

There was no fear. Her fate had been predestined from the moment Stephen raped her. With infinite sadness at the fate of her unborn child, Grace surrendered to that destiny, bowing her head and waiting for him to shoot.

A shot sounded, but instead of pain came the sting of hot drops spraying her face.

Adam's bullet had exited through Stephen's chest, leaving blood over her face and hands.

Still, Stephen kept his pistol fixed on her.

Another shot—Jake's shot—pushed Stephen backward, forcing him to flail as he collapsed back on the wooden floor with a sickening thud.

***

Adam kicked the gun Stephen dropped out of reach, although the man had to be dead.

He wasn't taking any chances.

Holstering his weapon, he crouched next to his trembling wife. Jerking a handkerchief from his vest pocket, he tried to gently wipe away the blood from her cheeks, not at all surprised his hand shook.

"Is it over?" Grace's voice was nothing but a whisper as she smeared some blood across her cheek with the back of her hand. Her wide eyes settled on his now stained handkerchief.

He dropped it to the floor. "It's over, darlin'. Are you well?"

Her hand went to her still flat stomach. "Will I have to go to jail now?"

His heart ached at her anguish—she didn't care about herself, only the child she carried. *His* child. "You didn't kill him. I did."

"No, *I* did." The strong voice behind him came as a reminder that there was still much to do before the curtain rang down on this drama.

"Doesn't rightly matter which of us ended his life. The man deserved killing," Adam replied, looking at his wife but speaking to Jake as well. "He kidnapped you, and he would've shot any one of us."

About to pick her up, Adam stopped when a soft, tormented cry rose from her chest. She held her right hand in front of her, gaping at the blood covering her palm and fingers.

He gathered his wife into his arms, wanting to carry her all the way back to Montana so he could keep her safe—so she could put all this trouble behind her and heal. "Hush now, Gracie. It's over."

"What about the warrant for attempted murder? Won't I go to jail?" She sniffed hard.

"What warrant?" he asked.

"Stephen has a warrant for my arrest from when I shot him in San Francisco. That's what he threatened me with to make me stay silent when he arrived. He said I'd have my baby in prison."

After suffering so much, she didn't deserve to be haunted by that bastard from his grave. "If there's any kind of warrant, Matthew will take care of it. I'll hire a lawyer if I have to. Our baby won't be born in jail."

Jake stepped forward to place his hand over hers. "You saved my life. You saved Adam's life."

Her eyes searched his, probably hoping to find forgiveness there. Not for having stabbed Stephen, but for keeping the truth from Jake his whole life.

Despite his fingers covering hers, there wasn't anything in his tone nor his expression that spoke absolution.

Things were far from solved.

With a shuddering sigh, Grace leaned her cheek against Adam's shirt. "I want to go home. Please take me home."

"Gladly, darlin'."

***

Grace stood next to Adam as they waited for Jake to board the train back to Montana. She'd tried to make some pleasant chit-chat, but her son remained stoic.

They'd spent very little time together as the sheriff investigated Stephen's death. Adam had kept her sequestered in a room at a small inn, and she'd slept most of her time away. Fearing she was too weak to make the trip back, Adam was sending Jake ahead so he could return to Emily and Beth. He'd demanded she rest up for a few days before they'd follow.

Her heart ached, and she wanted to throw herself into Jake's arms and beg his forgiveness. His cool aloofness felt like a slap across the face.

How was she ever going to make amends if he never let her have a chance to explain? Couldn't he at least *try* to see why she'd made that difficult and heart-rending choice so long ago?

Who was she trying to fool? How could Jake possibly forgive her for all the wrong she'd done him in his short life?

Adam wrapped a comforting arm around her shoulder just as the gray clouds began to leak a drizzling rain. "We need to get Jake on the train and get you out of this weather." He offered his right hand to Jake.

After the men said their farewells, Grace laid a gentle hand on Jake's arm and murmured a wish for a safe journey.

When he frowned and pulled away, his shun reached all the way to her soul.

Fighting the need to weep, she released a shuddering sigh and kept as much control over her tumbling emotions as she could. "Please tell Matthew and Victoria we'll be back soon. God be with you."

Jake nodded, grabbed his satchel, and boarded the train.

Watching Grace suffer such heartache was almost more than Adam could bear. While he wished he could make everything better for her and take away all her pain, he knew that to heal her heart, she would need time.

Jake would need time as well. Time to come to terms with what he learned about his lineage. Time to figure out just what his mother had done—how much she'd sacrificed to try to give him a good life.

He'd shared a short talk with Jake about the ramifications of being a Shay and of what that meant to him and Grace. Since the only people who knew the truth were family, Jake asked for time to consider whether he would do anything with the news. While he could find himself with money and connections he'd never dreamed of, he could also learn with money and connections came trouble. The choice would have to be his to make once he came to terms with what he'd learned.

Grace turned to walk away, still looking far too fragile. The woman had been through so much, and now she needed some peace and some rest, especially since she was expecting.

"I want to go home, Adam," she whispered.

"Just as soon as you're well enough to travel, Gracie."

Not that he would tell her the sheriff still hadn't given them permission to leave.

The Shay family had a dead son, and despite how Stephen had been ostracized for his obvious bouts of insanity, they still wanted someone to pay.

Adam had every intention of making sure that *someone* wasn't his wife.

"Soon, darlin'."

A promise. A vow. Stephen Shay was dead, and Grace's life was now her own.

He'd see to it that her future dawned bright as a rising sun.

Chapter Thirty

The cake had to be perfect—at least that was what Grace told herself to keep her troubled thoughts at bay.

Cooking occupied her nervous hands, and she threw herself into finishing Matthew and Victoria's wedding cake and preparing a nice meal for after the ceremony, which would be held at the Twin Springs.

Victoria was in town with Emily helping her finish the alterations to Grace's pink wedding dress. Flattered that her stepdaughter wanted to wear it, she promised to make sure the wedding guests had a feast.

She wished Emily had come here instead so she could see Beth, but traveling with an infant was difficult. Her heart ached to hold her granddaughter in her arms, and she tried to banish thoughts that Jake wanted to keep Beth from her. At least he would bring his family to the wedding, and she prayed some of the shock would have worn off and he would speak to her.

Setting the eggs aside, she blended the butter and sugar and let the incessant, scolding monologue in her head turn her feelings sour. Had it not been for the baby she carried, she'd probably do nothing more than sit in a chair and stare out the window. She couldn't concentrate on any of the books she tried to read. Food tasted like sawdust. Adam had to all but force her eat. She found herself alone far too often with her own troubling thoughts.

Why didn't I find the courage to keep Jake?

How could I just blurt out the truth?

Will he ever find it in his heart to forgive me?

Grace picked up the first egg and slammed it against the rim of the bowl with none of her usual finesse. Pieces of the shattered shell fell into the batter and sticky egg whites clung to the edge.

Disgusted with herself for her lack of control, she picked the shell out of the batter and grabbed the next egg. Just as she picked it up, the kitchen door opened, forcing a startle that made her drop the egg.

Adam looked at her, glanced down at the broken egg, and then grinned. "You missed the bowl, darlin'."

He'd been trying for days to coax her out of her melancholy. God love him, he gave her a safe harbor in the storm that had been her life. She wished she could chuckle at his teasing, but joy never came.

"It's broken," she said, fighting the strong emotions bubbling to the surface.

"It's just an egg."

"I can't fix it." Just like she couldn't fix anything else in her life. That egg sitting in a mess on the wooden floor became a symbol of all that was wrong. "I can't *ever* fix it."

"Gracie?"

The hurt rose to the surface.

Swiftly on its heels came anger.

With a scream, she picked up another egg, turned, and hurled it at the wall. But that didn't make her feel any better. So she picked the bowl of batter and flung it. The ceramic shattered against the hard wood, splattering the wall, window, and door with the yellow sticky mess.

"It's not fair!"

She'd done what she thought was right. She'd tried to give Jake a home—a real home instead of a life bouncing his childhood away in a bumpy, hot, and dirty wagon. She shouldn't have to pay such a steep price.

Closing her eyes, she reared her head back and let out a scream.

Suddenly, another egg was placed in her hand as Adam's fingers closed around hers. He eased away and nodded at the messy wall.

"It's not fair!" She launched the egg.

Just as soon as it was released, Adam put another in her hand. It joined the other the broken eggs, shattering against the wall.

"I did the best I could!" Instead of an egg, she found the cool surface of a plate against her palm. She gripped the plate with both hands, lifted it over her head, and then smashed it to the floor.

Adam calmly handed his wife another plate, relieved to finally see a crack in the wall of painful silence that had surrounded her since the kidnapping. Watching her struggle through the days had been agony, and unless she found a way to accept all that had happened, she would never put it behind her.

The scene at the Four Aces played in his mind, the time when Grace had understood Jake's pain from never forgiving himself for what he thought was his part in his parents' deaths. It was clear she'd never given herself any forgiveness for giving him up for adoption.

After the sixth plate, she regained some control. As he handed her another plate, she shook her head and collapsed onto the bench, breathing hard. A tear traced a wet path down her cheek.

He sat next to her and wrapped an arm around her shoulder.

She surrendered against him, laying her head against his chest.

He kissed the top of her head.

Her hands reached up to tuck her hair behind her ears. More of it was down than up, and he didn't think this was the proper time to tell her she had cake batter and egg on her face.

Adam grabbed the dish cloth, then he put a gentle finger under Grace's chin. As she looked up at him, he tenderly wiped her face clean. "He'll come 'round, Gracie."

"Never," she whispered. "He'll *never* change his mind about me."

He leaned in until their foreheads touched. "Take it one day at a time, darlin'. It's like planting a seed in the spring. If you stare at it all day and night, it'll never sprout. Stop watching for a change and just...live. Time has a way of healing all wounds—even those on the heart."

Grace's gaze wandered the kitchen. "Look at the mess I made. People will be here tomorrow for the wedding. I can't let them see this."

"I'll clean up."

"I still need to make a cake."

"I'll help with that, too." He smiled. "Got a surprise coming in for you on the morning stage."

"A surprise?" His announcement cleared the lingering sadness from her beautiful face. "For me?"

"You won't be alone here anymore."

"But I'm not alone—I have you."

"And right after the wedding, you'll have Daisy, too."

A smile spread across her lips. "Daisy's coming back?"

He nodded. "You've spent your whole life taking care of people. Now you're gonna let us take care of you and the baby."

Grace suddenly looked...hurt. "You don't want me to cook for you anymore?"

"Oh, darlin'. Of course, I want you to cook. As Matthew always says, you could make a feast out of shoe leather. What I want is for you to cook when you *want* to. You've earned the right to relax. To read if you'd like. To take a nap when you want to." His hand caressed her gently-rounding stomach. "With a child on the way, you'll need more rest. Daisy will be here to help any way she can."

Threading her hands around his neck, she kissed him. "I'm married to a very thoughtful man. Thank you, Adam."

"I've a notion to let my wife show me how grateful she is." He scooped her into his arms. "Cake later. Husband now."

***

It was a beautiful day for a wedding. The sun shone bright and clear. Summer flowers bloomed. An early morning rain had given the air a scrubbing, making everything fresh and clean.

Victoria smoothed her hands down her pink skirt and tried not to be nervous. Most new brides probably feared the wedding night. That certainly wasn't a problem, not since Matthew had introduced her to the joys found when a man and woman made love. Her nerves were on edge for her family.

Grace's sadness seemed to be lifting, but there was still much to resolve between her and Jake. A wedding was supposed to be a time of celebration, not to have family members stare at each other in sullen silence as she feared they might. Having Daisy arrive this morning had been a welcome surprise, and Victoria hoped the woman's eternally cheerful mood would bring some spark to the festivities.

A knock on her door drew her back to the present. "Who is it?"

"Grace."

She hurried to the door to let her in. "I thought Daddy might be coming up to get me for the ceremony."

"He's downstairs, talking to the reverend and keeping Matthew busy." Grace's smile was a ray of sunshine that Victoria was grateful to see. "My brother seemed intent upon wearing out the soles of his new shoes pacing around."

"He's nervous?"

A reassuring hand touched her shoulder. "Not about the marriage. I believe he muttered something about marrying you before you came to your senses." Grace turned Victoria so they were both reflected in the mirror. "You look lovely."

"Thank you." Victoria ran her fingertips along her crown of flowers.

Grace kissed her cheek. "I know your mother would be proud."

Closing her eyes, Victoria tried to picture Clara Morgan smiling down on her. Would her mother be shocked that she'd shared a bed with Matthew before they spoke vows?

Shared a bed?

More like tore each other's clothes off in their haste.

In her heart, Victoria believed that Clara might not have approved but would've understood the love she and Matthew shared.

Another knock sounded. "Princess?" Adam called. "You ready?"

Grace answered the door, whispered a few words to him, and left.

The proud look in her father's eyes as his gaze swept her from head to foot made tears sting Victoria's eyes. "You look so much like your mother."

All she could do was offer was a tight-lipped nod or else she'd start weeping.

He held his elbow out in invitation. "Time to take you to your groom."

As he led her downstairs, she took a deep breath to steady herself. Feelings flew through her, twinkling like fireflies in the night sky. The people she loved stood gathered in a semi-circle around Reverend

David and Matthew.

How handsome her groom was in his new clothes. She caught the quick roll of his healing shoulder. The wound had closed quickly and hadn't become infected, so the time had come to let that worry go. Matthew was hale and hearty.

And he would soon be hers.

Her father had offered to loan him some Sunday attire, but Matthew was gifted with his finery by Miss Alma and Miss Hila when he'd rescued the elderly ladies' cat from where it had perched itself in an exceptionally tall tree. They'd been so grateful, they insisted upon rewarding him with something, and since what they did best—besides gossip—was sew, they made his wedding clothes.

Adam laid his hand over Victoria's. He gave her a few affectionate pats. "You ready?"

She favored him with a nervous smile. "Will I make him happy, Daddy? I'm afraid I won't be a good wife..."

"Oh, Victoria. How could you think you'd ever fail at *anything?* Your heart's as big as this territory." He brushed a kiss on her cheek. "You'll make him happy."

She released the breath she'd been holding as she nodded her gratitude for his kind and reassuring words. "I'm ready now."

He escorted her to stand before the reverend as Matthew stepped up to her right side.

Reverend David gave them all a big grin and opened his well-worn book. "Dearly beloved..."

***

The ceremony seemed to pass in a blur for Matthew.

From the moment he'd seen Victoria coming down the stairs—dressed in Grace's pink wedding dress, her dark hair crowned in flowers—he'd felt like the luckiest man on the face of the earth.

He made all the right promises and said all the right words. The vows were important and he meant to hold himself to each and every one, but he couldn't concentrate on anything except the beautiful creature standing at his side—binding herself to him for the rest of their days.

Damn, but he was blessed.

He noticed everything about her. The teardrop pearls dangling from her earlobes. How slim and white her fingers looked when twined with his tanned and calloused ones. The light blush staining her cheeks. The smell of roses that seemed to be her very essence.

Oh, yes indeed, he was blessed.

Lost in his thoughts, it took a moment for him to focus on what the reverend was saying. "I'm sorry...I..."

Reverend David grinned. "You may kiss your bride."

As Victoria lifted her arms around his neck, Matthew wrapped his arms around her and settled his mouth on hers. So sweet, so soft, and full of promise of more to come.

He suddenly wished Grace hadn't gone to the trouble of making a meal for everyone.

All he wanted to do was take Victoria back to town, to their new home.

***

"Grace?"

She glanced up from cutting pieces of cake.

Jake stood by her side. Words stuck in her throat, wanting to spill out in a tangle of emotion that would probably make no sense to her son. She chose to nod and tried to paste a smile on her face.

"You feelin' better now? I..." Jake looked down at his daughter, then turned his eyes—the ones so much like her own—back to Grace. "I was...worried about you."

"You were?"

He nodded. "You're carrying, and things were so bad in San Francisco... Glad that business is over. Just wanted to make sure you're well." The man actually blushed. This clearly wasn't easy on him.

Jake taking the first important step lifted the heavy weight from her heart. "I'm very well. Adam takes very good care of me." A smile toward Daisy at a table, where she fussed over Victoria and Matthew. "Now that Daisy's back, I doubt he'll let me lift a finger around the ranch."

"I've been meaning to talk to you. 'Bout Stephen Shay."

Grace held her breath.

His mouth bowed to a frown. "You don't hate me 'cause of him, do you?"

The serving knife clattered when it fell to the floor. "Hate you? Why would I *hate* you?"

"Figured you see him every time you see me—that I'm a bad reminder."

"Oh, Jake. You're not a reminder of him. You're my *son*."

"Yeah, but—"

"I only see you, honey. Just *you*."

He scuffed the toe of his boot against the hardwood floor. "I–I wanted to thank you for all you did for me. For takin' care of me, even with you bein' so young and all. Took guts. 'Specially after what he did to you."

"You're *thanking* me?" Tears welled in her eyes as she stooped to retrieve the cake knife.

As she rose, his strong hand settled on her shoulders. "Of course I'm thanking you. If you hadn't done what you did, I'd have spent my life with that snake."

The Shays could never know about Jake. "You won't go to them, will you? I mean, all that money..."

"No, ma'am. Don't want nothin' from 'em." He glanced back at Emily, who ate another forkful of cake as she listened intently to whatever Miss Alma was saying. "Wouldn't dream of putting Em or Beth in harm's way."

Relief flooded through her.

"Figured you might wanna hold Beth—I mean, you might wanna hold your granddaughter."

The subject was clearly closed for now. Knowing how hard it must have been for a quiet man like Jake to say all he did, Grace didn't push him. She nodded, knowing that if she tried to say even one word, she would burst into happy tears. Trying to keep her hands busy, she wiped the knife clean on a towel.

Jake smiled down at her then turned to greet Adam as he came to join them, empty plate in hand. "Cake any good?"

"Of course. She doesn't know how to make anything that's not." Adam set his plate aside and stood at his wife's side. "Need any help, darlin'?"

The silver cake knife was set aside, and she reached for Beth. "What I need to do is to hold this little angel." She cradled the baby in her arms.

Jake picked up a plate, stuffed a forkful of cake in his mouth, and grinned. With a nod, he headed toward his wife.

She stared down at Beth and smiled.

The baby smiled back.

Grace's heart melted like butter in a hot pan. "You were right, Adam."

He arched an eyebrow. "About?"

"Time. All we need is *time*."

Chapter Thirty-One

Matthew kicked the door closed, letting contentment wash over him.

He was home.

His home.

With his new wife.

God was truly smiling on him this day.

They hadn't made love again—not since the fire—but he understood why Victoria had kept him at arms' length. They'd known a moment of passion after a frightening experience, sharing their fear and relief, but he'd promised himself he wouldn't take her to his bed again until he made her his wife. He loved and respected her too much. Yet even the lingering ache in his shoulder hadn't dampened his desire for her.

Now that she was his, he wanted to get her alone and show her his love.

Her hand brushed his cheek.

He turned his head to nip at her fingers. "You can put me down now."

"Why?"

"Because I'm too heavy for you to keep holding."

"You're light as a feather."

"Then take me to the bedroom and make love to me."

"Anything the lady wants."

Not that the bedroom was too far. The home only had two rooms—the larger serving as both a kitchen and parlor. But the house did have a nice private bedroom, and that was the only place he wanted to be this glorious night.

As he carried her to the bed, she let her breath out on a rush. "Look at all this."

In the dim moonlight spilling through the window, the room appeared to be a haven for lovers. Flower petals had been lightly scattered over the bed, which had the covers turned back to reveal fluffy pillows with embroidered pillowcases.

"Grace and Emily were here earlier today," Matthew said. "Looks as though they were busy."

Anxious to be skin to skin with Victoria, he let her slide down his body until they stood toe to toe. He wanted to rip the pretty pink dress off her, toss her on the bed, and join their bodies. The only thing holding him back was knowing this was the beginning of their married life. He wanted it to be filled not only with passion but with love.

She surprised him by reaching for his shirt before he could start unfastening the buttons on her bodice. Nimble fingers had his shirt unbuttoned faster than he could have managed, considering his hands trembled. He savored her cool palms slipping inside to stroke his chest and push the shirt off his shoulders.

Her dress put up more of a fight, but he somehow found the patience to get those impossibly tiny buttons undone. His hands brushed her shoulders and breasts before he pushed the dress down her body until it settled in a pink cloud at her feet. Pulling her close, he kissed her long and deep.

In the passion of their first coupling, he'd missed the seductive nature of undressing each other. That day, clothes that hadn't been easy to remove were simply torn away. While that had been an incredible experience, one Matthew would always remember, he enjoyed the teasing, the nibbling kisses, the torture of waiting for the pleasure to come.

Stepping back out of his embrace, she threw him an inviting smile as her fingers moved to the ribbons of her camisole, slowly dragging each open until the garment parted.

His new wife wanted to drive him mad. That was the only explanation for the tantalizing way she was disrobing. While he could see the swell of her breasts, only a shadow of the nipples showed through the thin material. Instead of ripping the camisole from her as he wanted to, he decided to play along with her seductive games, admitting to himself how much pleasure he took from knowing she wanted to enflame him. If she would only glance down, she'd surely notice that he was more than ready to consummate their marriage.

He covered her breast with his palms before sliding his fingers inside the garment to push it from her shoulders. When he leaned down to draw a nipple between his lips, her fingers dug into his shoulders and she arched forward. He fumbled with the drawstring on her petticoats until he could push them over her slim hips. As he shifted to feast on her other breast, he stripped her of her pantalets.

She quickly kicked off her shoes and stockings while he toed off his boots.

When she reached for the waistband of his pants, he gave thanks that the garment gave her little fight.

They reached for each other at the same time, coming together in a tongue-dueling kiss as hands stroked and petted and worshipped. He swept her into his arms and laid her on the crisp sheets before sprawling on top of her.

His knee parted her thighs, and he settled so his erection rubbed against her core. The dance of undressing had left him ready to bury himself deep inside her. "I want you so much."

Trim thighs wrapped around his hips. "I want you too."

Moist heat greeted him as he eased into her, making him groan in pleasure. A mewl rose from her throat as he slid deeper.

He braced himself on his elbows to frame her face with his hands. "You're mine, *wife*. Now and forever."

Victoria smiled up at him. "I've always been yours—from the first moment I saw you." She squeezed his hips with her thighs. "Make love to me, *husband*."

Withdrawing slowly and then sinking back into her welcoming body, Matthew watched pleasure wash over her features. The rhythm grew faster as she lifted her hips to meet his thrusts. He became more demanding as the tension grew.

With a cry of delight, her hips rose one last time as her back arched. His name spilled from her lips in a breathless moan.

The feel of her tight heat clenching around him sent him hurtling to his own climax. He joined her in paradise, pressing his face to her neck and whispering his love.

***

Adam closed the book since Grace had fallen asleep.

She'd stretched out on the sofa, asking him to read *Little Women* to her after she and Daisy had finished preparing Daisy's bedroom.

When he glanced down, he saw brown eyes staring back at him. "Thought you'd fallen asleep."

"Not yet. I'm just not ready for this day to end."

He stroked her hair, playing with a few of the soft tresses. "It was a right fine day."

"I know Matthew and Victoria will be happy together."

A nod in reply as he let his finger lazily trace the delicate lines of her ear.

"Thank you for bringing Daisy back."

"She's always been like family, and I sure don't want you to overdo."

Grace took his hand and led it to her gently rounding stomach. Then she grew still. As he started to caress her, she flattened his palm. "Wait."

He quirked an eyebrow and was about to ask what it was he should wait for when he felt the movement—weak as the flapping of a butterfly's wings, but there nonetheless.

His child was saying hello.

Dear Lord, but he was a content man.

A smile spread across her face. "You felt that?"

He gave her hand a squeeze. "Thank you, Gracie."

"For?"

"For bringing so much joy back into my life."

"Thank you, Adam."

"For?"

"For giving me the first home I've ever known. For giving me back my son." Her voice choked with emotion. "And for showing me what love truly is."

The End

ABOUT THE AUTHOR

Author Biography:
Sandy lives in a quiet suburb of Indianapolis, where she teaches psychology. Published through Grand Central Forever Yours, Carina Press, and indie-published, she has been an Amazon #1 Bestseller multiple times and has won numerous awards including two HOLT Medallions. Please visit her website at sandyjames.com for more information or find her on Twitter and Facebook. Represented by Danielle Egan-Miller of Browne & Miller Literary.

Other Books by Sandy James:

Damaged Heroes Series
Murphy's Law (Book 1)
Free Falling (Book 2)
All the Right Reasons (Book 3)
Faith of the Heart (Book 4)
Twist of Fate (Book 5)

Safe Havens Series
Saving Grace (Book 1)
Runaway (Book 2)
Redeemed (Book 3)
Hideaway (Book 4)
False Pretenses (book 5 ~ Coming soon!)

Ladies Who Lunch Series
The Bottom Line (Book 1)
Signed, Sealed, Delivered (Book 2)
Sealing the Deal (Book 3)
Fringe Benefits (Book 4)

Alliance of the Amazons
The Reluctant Amazon (Book 1)
The Impetuous Amazon (Book 2)
The Brazen Amazon (Book 3)
The Volatile Amazon (Book 4)

Single Titles
Turning Thirty-Twelve
Rules of the Game
The Seeker

Nashville Dreams Series
Can't Walk Away (Book 1)
Can't Let Her Go (Book 2)
Can't Fight the Feeling (Book 3)

www.ingramcontent.com/pod-product-compliance
Lightning Source LLC
Chambersburg PA
CBHW051453170626
46811CB00002B/466